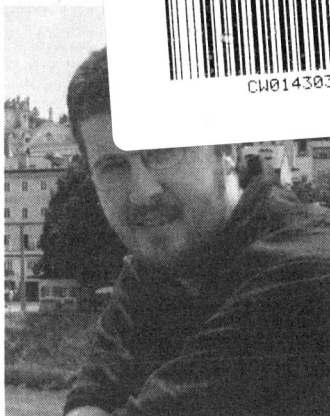

Stephen Reilly was born in Sydney in 1972. Having lived and worked in Singapore and London, he has returned to Sydney where he lives with his wife and his widescreen television.

Ninety East Ridge is his first novel.

NINETY EAST RIDGE

Stephen Reilly

PAN

Pan Macmillan Australia

This is a work of fiction. Characters,
corporations, institutions and organisations in
this novel are either the product of the author's
imagination or, if real, used fictitiously without
any intent to describe their actual conduct.

First published 2002 in Macmillan
by Pan Macmillan Australia Pty Limited
This Pan edition published 2004 by
Pan Macmillan Australia Pty Limited
St Martins Tower, 31 Market Street, Sydney

National Library of Australia
Cataloguing-in-Publication data:

Reilly, Stephen, 1972– .
Ninety East Ridge.

ISBN 0 330 36446 4.

1. Title.

A823.4

Typeset in 11.5 on 13.5 pt Palatino by Midland Typesetters
Printed in Australia by McPherson's Printing Group

Papers used by Pan Macmillan Australia Pty Ltd are natural,
recyclable products made from wood grown in sustainable
forests. The manufacturing processes conform to the
environmental regulations of the country of origin.

For Rebecca,
whom I love

ninetyeastridge

There is truth.
There is lie.
And then there is my memory.

The memories flash before me in a heartbeat. My feelings, my actions—others' actions: as they were or as I
wish they were; everything that happened skips through
my thoughts in a moment.

A kaleidoscope of instants in time whirls before me:
images of wrong weddings and glass walls, of refugees
and rubber band engines, of headless snakes and dances
with devils, of Crystal Towers and Tokyo sex tours, and
her . . . always her . . . on her the montage in my mind
seems to linger . . .

I try to shake it off. I get up, make my way to the
window. The memories blur into introspections of fate.
Was there anything else we could have done—I could
have done? Was there one moment more important
than all the others? Was there—is there—a moment of
truth, or lie, a cusp, a crossroads, upon which all
depended?

Even now, I'm torn between wanting a reason and
wanting none. Was it fate, or fellow man, that conspired
against us? Were we always destined to fail or were we

simply beaten by a better vision? Perhaps what happened was deliberately designed to shape our character, to prepare us for new challenges, or maybe it was just to discourage us from such folly in the future?

More than anything, I want to know, just want to know, that it was all beyond our control.

I stare at the stars and remember.

But my memory is biased and distorted—I do not deny it—a hallucination of truth and lies shaped by the chemical magic of desire, bitterness, pride and pure imagination. I remember events as I want to remember them, as a blended dream of how I saw them or see them now, as I believe or would like to believe them. I didn't even have to be there: for such moments, my mind forgets who I am and presumes the memories of others— Anna, her father, Laikali, Ford, anyone at all involved— interpolating time and circumstance, replacing gaps with hearsay, logic and self-deceit.

The memories flash before me in a heartbeat.

I blink and see people, places, destiny and tragedy— they all return to me in a way that twists and shrinks time to my mind's own design. For though nothing can change what happened, neither can history influence how I remember it.

Remember them.
Remember Anna.

There are lies.
There is truth.
But both are one within my memory.

a new world

[days 1 to 3]

It all began the day her father died—a senseless death,
    random and ridiculous.
And then all of a sudden, she was here.

day one

'A New World,' is what she called it, her words deliberately grand and aspirational.

'A hole in the ocean.' Words approved by Isaac as catchy and intriguing.

'One drop at a time.' Softer, image-rich; conveying both the magnitude of their ambition and their determination to achieve it.

Words designed to make their way into every paper in the world a day later.

Words she hadn't even said yet.

Clattering up the steel stairs, shuffling and sorting her speech, Anna Lucy Spires recited her key words and catchphrases over and over. 'Four hundred Hoover Dams'—'A clean slate'—her rote-murmurs rising, as if to hear her thoughts over the wild wind and rain which lashed against the windows—'Four point four trillion dollars'—'Engineering and architecture of an unprecedented scale' . . .

Between heavy breaths, she acted out pauses and facial poses. The heavy breathing was because of the stairs, not nerves, she told herself. 'This is it. This is it,' she huffed, psyching herself up. The eyes of the world were now just moments away. 'You can do this'—'Make or break'—'Stay calm'— 'Concentrate' . . .

She came to the landing exit. Her future, more frightening and unpredictable than ever, lay through that door. 'A New World,' she mouthed. 'One drop at a time.' Pausing to steel herself, she was distracted as the magnitude of her chosen future presented itself through the window beside her.

This far out to sea, there were no birds. The nearest land was over two thousand kilometres east. The nearest major metropolis almost twice that distance away on the west coast of Australia. The ocean hulked between her and the horizon, as if flexing, as if breathing, as if it were the belly of some enormous beast, and she, like some microscopic gnat, was standing on it, swaying as it rumbled and grumbled.

Initially, she had found the enormity perversely comforting—the logic being that she was too small to be noticed and too weak to pose a threat—but now, as the wind howled and the rain slammed in sheets against Platform Seven's windows, she wondered if the great beast had sensed her presence, and this was how it scratched and swatted: the rain its raking talons, the wind its swishing tail, herself a puny parasite.

'Come on, Grub,' she said softly, staring at the beast, staring at the future, and steeling herself to defy them both. 'No turning back now.'

She breathed deeply, her hand now reaching for the door.

This moment, for so long so far away.

And then all of a sudden, it was here . . .

Step forward my friends. One and all: say hello!
Then tell us how you're going to change the world.

high hopes ladies and gentlemen

At least we're back on dry land, thank God—well almost, Glory thought, preening her hair, paying scant attention to the introductory formalities.

She had high hopes for herself, Glory O'Shay, and sitting in a storeroom-turned-makeshift-pressroom on a spartan converted oil rig, reporting on some middle-of-the-ocean engineering project for an outdated medium like radio, was not what she had in mind. It didn't matter how rich Isaac Blackwell was.

She looked around the room. *The usual shit-job suspects.* That only confirmed that this was another nothing assignment; filler only likely to be used if there was not enough other newsworthy material.

Still . . . this was a lot of expense for what appeared to be a drilling platform. *Come to think of it,* Glory thought, they had not been given any detail at all—*perhaps it's not just some deep-sea research project, like I assumed.*

She would have considered it more, had the murmurs around her not stopped and the atmosphere in the room not changed at that instant. An official party was entering.

There he is. Glory sat a bit more upright, pulled her shoulders back, pushed her chest out and adopted a studious face of interested concentration. After all, if she had to be here, about as far away from civilisation as was possible, she might as well flirt with the world's most eligible bachelor.

'Ladies and gentlemen,' a woman said into the microphone, but Glory only had eyes for Isaac Blackwell, who had taken a position at the rear of the stage.

'Ladies and gentlemen,' the nobody said again, annoyingly gaining Glory's attention.

'Who's this?' Glory whispered to the hack beside her.

'Name's Anna Spires. Apparently she's the CEO.'

Really? thought Glory. *But the CEO of what?*

'Ladies and gentlemen,' Anna said for the last time, the din finally silencing. 'Let me present my vision for a New World.'

Looking back, even Glory herself would probably admit that she didn't get it that day, didn't understand—had no idea, in fact, about its importance, its ramifications, its consequences—or even that this remote press conference would be her first stop on the road to superstardom.

'. . . a hole in the ocean . . .'

It took some time, not just for her but for

everyone, for the true newsworthiness of this 'New World' to become clear.

'. . . a hole seven kilometres wide, over sixteen hundred metres deep . . .'

Like most of her media colleagues in that small, hastily converted conference room, initially Glory only latched onto the grandiosity of the plan . . .

'. . . imagine four hundred Hoover Dams, fifty-eight side by side in a circle, stacked seven high . . .'

. . . the scale of financing required . . .

'. . . four point four trillion dollars . . .'

. . . the magnitude of engineering, the logistics, the planning and the ambitious three-year time frame . . .

'. . . for a thousand days, the world's most creative architects, its finest structural engineers and an army of craftsmen will unite in the most ambitious building project of all time . . .'

When questions were allowed, a few of her colleagues asked unwittingly insightful questions about the legal issues and jurisdiction of the undertaking. If only they'd known how much Anna had rehearsed her answer to such questions. Delivered in a convincingly unconcerned tone, the response raised few 'sensation antennae' and barely made the newspaper, radio or TV reports the next day.

'This project,' Spires said, 'falls under the same legal jurisdiction as an oil rig or a deep-sea research station, so there are no issues to be concerned about.'

Glory, in fact, barely registered the response, so intent was she to ask the next question, her arm tautly poised to shoot into the air and grab Ms Spires' attention.

She fired it in: 'What is the involvement of Isaac Blackwell and the GJS Investment Group?'

Having asked the question in her most serious newsvoice, Glory remained standing with her head tilted in sincere, thoughtful interest. It's a reporter's right to hold the floor for both the asking and answering of a question, and her professional pose was as much for the benefit of the other newsmen and women in the room as it was for Ms Spires.

Ms Spires, for her part, could not help smiling at the question, secretly relieved that the legal line of interrogation had been cut off and would probably not be revisited.

'Mr Blackwell's involvement in this—'

'Mr Blackwell's involvement in this enterprise,' interjected the man himself, moving forward from his backstage position, 'is in a personal and purely advisory capacity. GJS has, at this stage, no official connection with the New World Project.' He closed the sentence like a father putting his foot down. There would be no more questions. He backed away from the lectern.

'Ah, Mr Blackwell,' voiced Glory. She was not going to let the most eligible multi-billionaire in the world off the hook, no matter how authoritative his tone. She was sure that she'd already impressed her peers by attracting him to the microphone. They'd be even more impressed by her take-no-prisoners boldness. Maybe Mr Blackwell himself would be impressed.

'Mr Blackwell, what exactly is your personal connection to the New World Project?'

But Isaac Blackwell had already resumed his position at the rear of the podium. He simply waved his hand as if swatting away her question. Glory's triumph was immediately forgotten as another hack seized the floor to ask a question about how much concrete would be required to complete the New World Project.

Who cares about fucking concrete? thought Glory O'Shay. She didn't even listen to the answer. She put her pen in her pocket and started to wonder if there might be a way to steal a *private* interview with Mr Blackwell after the press conference.

The sounds of the street pass by beneath the window.

It's hardly music to dance to.

If I lean my forehead against the glass, I hear it—and feel it. Feel the glass shake, reverberate, whisper the sounds of the world below: the inconstant hum of the traffic, the clinking clattering of the building site across the street, the muffled screeches and screams of televisions out open windows, even the distant rumble of the subway; the unknown lives of unknown ants far beneath my window working and living and loving and dying. And obliviously listening to the undanceable music all around them.

Maybe they hear it. Maybe they don't. Who am I to say? People feel music different ways. And how it's felt affects how it's heard. Through the feet, it can make you dance. Through the head, it can make you think. Through the hands, it can give you something—or someone—to hold on to. Through the heart, it can make you lose control of your feet, head and hands; it can make you fall in love.

I remember when I first heard her music. The sounds of the street pass by meaninglessly beneath my window, and all the while the siren song of Anna Spires rings in my heart and my memory. Reminding me of where I was, of where I've been.

But most of all, of where I'm not.

The first time he saw her, he loved her.
But then what do we ever know for sure?

the siren sound of an idea

From the first moment he saw her, he loved her.

'Ladies and gentlemen,' she said.

Like all of us, Matthew Turner was a different man then. Twenty-nine years old, old enough to know the power of the world but young enough to not yet be overwhelmed and disillusioned by it. He still believed in long life and beautiful dreams. He still believed that some people get to live those dreams. And he still believed—despite occasional all-engulfing fears that maybe he was wrong—that he might as well be one of those people.

From the first moment he saw Anna on television, announcing and defending the concept of Ninety East Ridge, he loved her.

Her eyes, he loved her eyes, eyes that were alight with conviction and determination. In her eyes, he saw her passion.

'Let me present my vision for a New World.'

It was as if he had always known her, as if he knew how she thought, why she chose the words she chose, and how important it was to her to get those words right. She spoke with certainty—

outlining her plans, critiquing the 'old' world, answering questions—but Matt also heard what she did not say, sensing, in the way she blinked or breathed, her true ambition, her hopes and her fears.

It's unclear, even now, how much of Anna's vision he paid attention to that day. Without doubt, it appealed to his frustrated idealism, his preference for grand gestures. Without question, Matthew Turner was one of the few who ever truly understood the potential of Anna's New World. But that first day, that first moment he saw her, it was not about the vision or its potential.

That first day, it was about the way she stood before the world but looked at and spoke to him alone through the camera lens; it was about her presence, which commanded respect and understanding; and it was about the knowledge— the hard, absolute, irrefutable knowledge—at least to him, that here was a woman who could, and probably would, change the world.

And from that first moment he saw her, he wanted to be there, beside her, when she did.

Laikali Rulé was introduced to Anna Spires in a sidebar of the *Washington Post* over breakfast the next day, an insignificant abbreviated Reuters extract highlighting the fact that the story was not America-centric enough to warrant greater coverage. It simply read:

Isaac Blackwell was present at a press conference to announce the start of a major Indian Ocean

*engineering project. Anna Spires, CEO and lead
engineer on the 'New World Project' described their
objective as being to build a city in a hole in the ocean.*

By nine, she had found more information on the
Western Australian newspaper's website:

BILLIONAIRE HIGHLIGHTS FREMANTLE FOR New
World PROJECT

**Concrete industry gets boost for jobs and
economy**

*Isaac Blackwell, one of the world's youngest (and most
eligible) billionaires, was present at a most extraordinary press conference which announced a potential
boom for the concrete industry of Western Australia.*

*Held on a converted oil platform some two
thousand kilometres off the north-west coast, the
announcement came during the launch of the New
World Project. Ms Anna Spires, Chief Executive for
the project, said that the NWP plans to build a city
on the floor of the Indian Ocean.*

*The project, one of the most expensive and
logistically challenging of its kind in history, will
involve erecting walls over sixteen hundred metres
tall and pumping out ocean water from an area
approximately the size of Manhattan and a height
almost four times taller than the Empire State
Building.*

*The project promises to be a bonanza for the WA
concrete industry and the Fremantle docks which are*

> *one of only three primary ports chosen to supply*
> *labour and building materials to the site. Ms Spires*
> *estimates that some $500 million worth of building*
> *materials will come through Fremantle. The other*
> *primary ports chosen were Singapore and Bombay.*

By ten, Laikali had put a call in to GJS, only to be rebuffed by an official statement that this was a personal matter of Mr Blackwell's and not related to the investment bank in any way.

By eleven, she had finally found some more useful information from a contact of hers in Sydney.

By lunchtime, she was on a plane and on her way to see her contact in person. She would then make her way as quickly as possible to Perth, and then out into the Indian Ocean.

She had her assistant call the US Secretary of State to cancel their afternoon meeting and reschedule it for the following month.

The man who did not exist spoke softly and evenly: 'It will end when I say it ends, it doesn't matter how beaten they are. The war will continue until one, we've made our point, and two, we've made our budget.'

The man, occasionally known as P. Jefferson Ford, sat in darkness, as was his wont, scotch in one hand, phone in the other. He listened as his peon at State asked panicked speculative questions—what if this? what if that? 'What if the White House don't do what you want?'

Ford let out a long frustrated breath, loud enough for his man to hear his disappointment and long enough for his man to realise he was deadly serious when he said, 'You still don't understand. The White House has no power here. The Pentagon has no power here. This issue is too important.'

But, but . . . more concerns.

One last sigh. Enough already. His ghostly precise voice brooking no more discussion, 'Listen carefully. Just do as I've asked and watch how affairs unfold. I think you'll be surprised how many of them come around to seeing things our way.'

The fading, rattling okays, thank yous and yes sirs were cut off as Ford hung up the phone and, for a moment, savoured the silence.

But as he sipped his scotch, his free hand was already reaching for the remote control, and soon his dark isolation was once again breached by the familiar tones of international radio. Despite the internet, despite twenty-four-hour news television, he still relied on radio as the most immediate source of on-the-spot information. He listened to the foreign broadcasts because their perspectives were generally wider, and more revealing.

Besides, he liked the different accents. They brought back memories of when he used to do most of his work in the field:

'. . . and in other news, it was announced today that a private enterprise advised by investment baron and oil heir Isaac Blackwell will undertake one of the most expensive and logistically challenging engineering projects of all time. Blackwell and company plan to excavate over 60 trillion litres of water from the middle of the Indian Ocean and build a new, open-air city* *suspended over a kilometre above the sea floor. Glory O'Shay reports from the Indian Ocean:'*

'I am reporting live from a converted oil rig in the middle of the Indian Ocean where Ms Anna Spires, hitherto unknown Chief Executive and lead engineer for the auspiciously titled New World Project, today announced plans to build a new city in what she described as "a hole in the ocean". At a cost of almost four and a half trillion dollars, the initiative must rate as the most expensive and logistically challenging engineering project of all time. Isaac Blackwell, one of the world's wealthiest investment bankers, is a "personal advisor" to the project. Other advisors include leading oceanographers and marine biologists, who state that every care has been and will be taken to ensure that there will be no harmful effects on the Indian Ocean's marine ecology.'

Intrigued, Ford turned his head towards the radio, as if hoping to entreat Glory to tell him more. But she had nothing more to say, except:

'This is Glory O'Shay, BBC World Service, reporting from the New World Project in the middle of the Indian Ocean.'

Byron Lybrand watched the television coverage first—as the Iceman's message on his answering machine had instructed him to—then checked the other major financial news media.

They all covered it, to varying degrees, skewing the story to the biases of the reporters or their audiences. To Byron's surprise, however, few led with the story. Despite the scale of the project, most chose to run it as a novelty piece on the strength of Isaac Blackwell's presence and because they currently had too few details to really run with. Even the dedicated business information services gave it low billing since the key business questions of engineering, energy and technology contracts had not been extensively addressed.

The Boss himself had told Byron that the story would not merit significant newspaper coverage until TV or the newsmagazines raised its profile. They would wait, for the time being, classifying the story as a remote engineering project without mainstream appeal. Newspapers, he had explained, are in the franchise business—there was no point in running this story until more details were available, or until they knew that network television, cable, radio, the internet and, most importantly, the other newspapers were likely to support their ongoing story.

Byron knew he should not have been surprised by how closely the wide but low-key coverage matched Isaac's predictions. The strategy—the remote location, the carefully rationed release of information, the focus on the unknown Spires, the teasing presence of the Iceman himself—had been designed merely to get the ball rolling, nothing more. The key concepts and catchphrases had all been reported. The idea was now out there.

And even though it was the middle of the night in New York, he called the Iceman to update him.

As instructed.

Dreaming is a human miracle, a universal art form that no one understands.
Dreammaking is a science, elite and where the money is.

quality and novelty

Isaac Blackwell.

The Iceman. The Legend. The Dreammaker.

Rich, good looking, with a square jaw, an athletic muscular body and perfect hair, he was the epitome of the privileged overachiever. He had literally flown through school—straight As in the semester, then off to far-flung vacations: maybe Aspen, Switzerland or the Maldives. No doubt, he had been the desire of every schoolgirl and the envy of every schoolboy. He was a sportsman, excelling in skiing, diving, tennis, even at football. He could speak four languages—how else could he travel? And with his parents being who they were, he was a socialite of the very highest order and, since the age of sixteen, one of the ten most eligible bachelors in America.

He was the ultimate All-American student who soon became the ultimate All-American businessman. The youngest ever partner of mega-investment bank Gill Johnson Shek—the word on the street was that GJS might soon become GJB—he was the master of raising capital for anything from an airport to an Olympic stadium, from an oil rig to a space station. They called him the 'Dream-maker' because he could make anything possible. It was said that he could take a kid selling lemonade in his driveway and get him the rights to be the official soft drink supplier to New Year's Eve in Times Square.

He was a hero to the hangers-on who milled around the Wall Street bars to rave about his latest feat of corporate daring. His legend grew on the back of his ability to stare down a crisis, and stories like his rescue of news empire MediaCorp, one of GJS's biggest clients. When they had looked like going under, the 'Iceman', as the Legend was referred to by some, was able to arrange new funding by overturning a court ruling, guaranteeing new supportive legislation and allowing bailout financing which he himself had arranged, and all just twenty-four hours before the company would have had to declare bankruptcy and dissolve. The legislators hated him that day, having spent millions trying to bring down MediaCorp, but they could hardly hold a grudge since he had saved their own skins less than a term ago when they had underbudgeted some tens of millions of dollars for government office refurbishments.

He was something of a god incarnate. Women worshipped him. Men wished they were him. He counted presidents, dictators and movie stars among his closest friends. His hobbies included yachting with other billionaires, cocktailing with Nobel prize winning scientists, coffeeing with

Booker prize winning authors and brunching with Blackwell prize winning painters.

He had it all, and then some. And now he was supporting this New World Project. *The* Isaac Blackwell. How, asked the people in the know, could it fail?

'Ladies and gentlemen,' she said again, 'let me present my vision for a New World.'

Isaac stood at the back of the room, mobile phone to one ear while the other ear and both eyes focused on the bank of TV screens. Anna and Xavier also watched intently, standing to one side to allow Isaac a clear view.

'Yeah . . . yeah . . . yeah, they're showing it now . . . yeah, I can see that.'

They had come straight from the press conference—or rather, as soon as they'd been able to shake a flock of flirtatious, billionaire-smitten reporters.

Xavier had met them at the door to the War Room with two glasses of champagne. He was already monitoring the international television coverage on a number of satellite-broadcast channels when they walked in. A bank of ten televisions, four computers and two newswire terminals pumped out a cacophony of light and sound and information.

'This is going great,' said Isaac, already dialling another number. 'There's some recognition of the engineering magnitude, but most of the networks are covering it as a novelty or personality piece—Cecilia, it's Isaac, any calls yet from Obermann or the other investors?' He retreated to his corner to talk to his North American secretary. He'd call his European secretary, Jennifer, in London next. Then Carrie in Hong Kong.

A novelty piece! Anna returned her gaze to the TV.

It had taken her a while, but she was now used to him flipping in and out of conversations with her and his mobile phone, much as they were now flipping between TV channels.

Out of habit, she pinched her earlobe between thumb and forefinger and tried to refocus. Looking at herself on the screen gave her a feeling of separation from her own body. She felt surprisingly calm and dispassionate watching herself, despite a vaguely anxious, not-quite-real awareness that the third and first persons were in fact the same.

Isaac had trained her well, taught her not to panic. But this was her first high-profile appearance—it was only natural to feel a little slighted by his satisfaction that the world had chosen to treat the story as novelty because she, not he, was the focal point.

'And look at you,' shouted Isaac to her, not even bothering to cover the mouthpiece of the phone still attached to his ear. 'You look great!'

She grinned a little. She couldn't help but be impressed by his ability to recover whenever he realised he might have offended her—and all the while maintain multiple phone calls and simultaneous media monitoring.

'Thanks, Carrie,' he said, flipping closed his cell

phone. He was one of those people who didn't say goodbye at the end of a call.

'No, I mean it,' he said, continuing his last comment as if he hadn't finished a phone call in between, 'you look sensational. For a first-time television CEO, you were great.'

'So you mean you could still tell I'm a first-time CEO?'

At that moment, his phone rang. It didn't happen often, because he was usually on it. It had to be Byron—only Byron would sit on the redial button for as long as it took to contact him.

'No, no, that's not what I said—though it *was* your first time—and you were great—I said you're a natural—who called first, Golum or White?'

She shook her head and grinned again. There was something about the way he back-pedalled, flattered and answered a cell phone at the same time that was almost endearing. Almost.

'Another champagne, Ms Spires?' asked Xavier, appearing at her shoulder.

Sometimes she thought they choreographed everything, the two of them. Champagne, phone calls, unexpected crises requiring his immediate attention—she had seen Xavier interject at awkward moments too often to consider it coincidental. She arched her eyes at him, but Xavier just smiled, surely knowing what she was thinking as she took another glass from his tray.

Of course it was Byron on the phone, telling him about how, as planned, Isaac's presence had ensured media coverage across the globe, while the leading role taken by the hitherto unknown

Ms Anna Spires had diminished critical press interest. It remained to be seen whether this would mute subsequent government inquiry.

She watched the televisions, trying to distil Isaac's strategic gossip in the corner from the press's efforts to make the story—and her—look or sound interesting.

'Ladies and gentlemen,' one TV showed her saying again, 'let me present my vision for a New World.'

She wondered how many people around the world would understand what they were doing? Would the investors? Would the governments? Would real everyday people?

Sometimes she asked herself if *she* really knew—lately she had often felt like she had woken up from a dream to find the dream coming true. At such times, she considered that perhaps she had only dreamed waking up.

Everything seemed so surreal: the setting, the voices, the words. Here she was, drinking champagne on a converted oil rig watching ten TVs showing her over and over while the most desired man in America talked shop on the phone behind her.

'Thanks, Byron . . .' she heard him say. 'Of course I know how hard you're working . . .' A rare moment of levity, yet always so smooth and professional. 'Sure I appreciate it . . .' He laughed, his confidence softening his sarcasm, 'But you know my motto: sleeping's overrated.'

Isaac Blackwell. The Iceman. The Legend. The Dreammaker.

Rich, good looking—and everybody loved him.

Except me.

Let me make my position clear from the start: I never liked that man.

The man was not real, he was a caricature of what people aspired to be. The man did not understand struggle or failure, primarily because he had experienced neither. Through good luck or good management, it doesn't matter—he had only ever overcome fortune, not misfortune, and so he was not worthy of respect. To that man, the rest of the world was an amusement, a game to be played, a newspaper crossword to be solved then thrown away, a television show to be watched, enjoyed, then forgotten.

Worst of all, the man was an arbitrageur, the lowest form of life—taking advantage of someone else's lack of understanding and, instead of educating them, profiting at their expense. That man—who he was, how he thought, what he did—I called Arb, for arbitrageur. And let me make my position clear: I didn't like him.

Arb Blackwell. The Iceman. The Legend. The Dreammaker.

Arb Blackwell was 'slick'—no other word for him.

She would say, 'It's unrealistic to aspire to perfection.'
He would say, 'And unacceptable to aspire to anything less.'

perfect world with a rubber band engine

Arb's success at raising funds had been phenomenal, especially considering that he was offering no pecuniary payback.

Donations were what he called them, what he asked for, although he did manage to get Anna to allow him to offer all investors a place (although what was a place: a home? a business? a factory?— he only ever offered them a place) in the New World.

Perhaps he implied there would be business opportunities. Perhaps he didn't.

Perhaps he insinuated that donations would provide new market advantages. Perhaps he didn't.

Certainly, the radical concepts around which their New World would ultimately be built never came up during the 'sell'. Despite all the rhetoric of 'clean slates' and 'new ways of life', no one thought to ask fundamental questions, like whether there would be money.

Perhaps he deceived them, misled them by omission. 'We still don't know what it will look like or how it will work,' was all the warning he gave. 'About the only thing I can guarantee is that it will not be the same as the world we now know.'

Perhaps he didn't.

'Cheap, cheating, deceiving bastards. And mark my words, Little Worm, nothing'll change if you don't complain.'

That's what her father used to say. It was his way of explaining heated words with a restaurant manager taking too long to serve the food, or a taxi driver who'd gone the wrong way, or a passionate letter to the editor. This day, it was about a faulty battery he'd bought for a music box he was building.

'Don't swear, Daddy,' Anna would scold in reply.

Watching her father complain was how Anna discovered that the world was not perfect. But also that there was nothing that couldn't be changed, nothing that wasn't possible . . .

'But you can't expect perfection,' her mother would say, much to her father's annoyance.

Watching her mother annoy her father was how Anna discovered that not everyone in the world wanted to change it.

Her father wanted to fix it, remake it, start it over if he had to. Her mother said to make the most of it, the best you could with it.

'The world, like you,' she would say, 'is changing all the time, growing, learning and improving all the time.'

'But not all change is positive,' her father would reply. 'Change needs to be managed, guided. Without intelligent application, improvement is just theory. And proper, intelligent application takes more time than our world has patience for.'

Sometimes, Anna realised, for someone who claimed such a passion for the world, her father could display a real disdain for it.

'The hell with it, they say. It's not my problem, they say. A previous administration, they say. Old management, they say. In the world today,' he would say, 'if there are no votes, no profits, no payback, then there's no progress.'

'You swore again,' she said, admonishing him with a little wagging finger.

'Do me a favour, Grub?' he said, cherishingly patting her on the head, not expecting his sad, casual words to stick in a young girl's mind, to attach themselves to her heart, to drive her to such a remarkable future. 'Do something original with your life. Create something new.'

Something new.

New meant different. New meant improved. New meant changed. And although the world knew nothing yet of just how new the New World Project would be—Arb had gently but firmly advised against revealing any detail during the money-raising stage—every thought Anna had, every breath, every moment, was obsessed with just how different, improved and changed life would become in her hole in the ocean.

Long before the Philo Group was formed, long before mid-ocean press conferences, long before there was even a site, the controversies had begun one-on-one with Arb:

New energy sources . . .

'People have tried to isolate the oil community before and they've always ended up the worse for it.'

'I'm sorry, Isaac, but if we are building something new, something better, then it's pretty clear that reliance on highly polluting, non-renewable fossil fuels has to be the first thing to go.'

New political structures . . .

'I don't understand why there's a question here, Anna. Liberal democracy is surely the only acceptable system of government. Monarchies, autocracies, communist states have all tried and failed. Political scientists everywhere agree: LD is the winner.'

'For business maybe. For the economy and expedience, yes. But not for healthcare or education or poverty. Don't you see, we've sacrificed the ideal for a brand name. Democracy, as you're proposing, is not of, for or by the people. Its priorities have been subverted. All I'm saying is that we either get it right, or we find a better way.'

And that was how the concepts had evolved. Anna telling Arb her vision. Arb standing with his mouth open for a few seconds, then trying unsuccessfully to talk her out of it. He had worked with inspired obsessives before, but no one like her. For every question, she had an answer. For every problem, she had a solution. The answers were by no means irrefutable. And the solutions were by no means foolproof. But for every issue, there was a response, there was the considered response of half a lifetime's thought, there was the response of a woman who had studied and dreamed about every facet of finding, founding and building a New World. It was no accident that she was one of the best engineers in the world, Arb was sure. Even if she had never thought her dream possible, then subconsciously she had driven her whole adult life towards making herself uniquely qualified, just in case such an opportunity came along.

So every time, at least for now, convinced or not, Arb would eventually concede, incorporating Anna's concepts into his sales pitch as inclusions— fantastic, potential opportunities!—or exclusions better left unsaid.

The music box he was making was just a carved wooden base. A lid, a drawer, a model ballerina and a small motor sans battery lay beside it on the bench.

Anna sat on the steps that led down from the doorway to his little workshop, watching him tinker and rant and rave.

'Commerce and government are experts in only one thing: compromise. And they're interested in only one thing: profit—measured by money or votes. They've got voters or shareholders to woo, and only a year, three or four maybe, before new elections or annual general meetings. If the payback is not in their term of office, what then? Let alone a benefit that may not exist in their lifetime! They can't do it. Can't even consider it. The closest we get is environmental planning, and that's only because they've figured out it's fashionable.'

He looked at her now, his eyes sad, his head tilted forward gravely, as it often was when he had an important point to make.

'But mark my words, Grub, as powerful as they are, commerce and government are as vulnerable as we are to the one great constant . . .'

He paused, his flair for the melodramatic the only thing that could slow down a full strength tirade.

'Time,' he said poignantly. 'Time.'

Most of the time, she wasn't sure what he was saying. But every now and then she latched on to something that made sense.

'One day, without them even realising it, time will bring along their successors, and there'll be nothing an election or IPO can do to stop it.'

New economies . . .

'No money? No *money*? You can't be serious.'

'Money makes the world go around. You've said it yourself. And money's priority is one thing: more money.'

'But that's impossible, Anna. You're talking about caveman days, not the future. How will people get paid? And if they don't get paid, why will they work? And how will we get anything done?'

'I don't know yet,' Anna said, 'but I know that you haven't done any of this for the money, and look how much you've done.'

The music box was for Anna's baby sister. Or so Anna hoped. She was seven, almost eight years old at the time, and it seemed like her mother had been pregnant for her whole life. Her father assured her that she would have a new playmate any day now.

More than anything, she didn't want it to be a boy. Because what can you do with boys? All they know how to do is run around and beat each other up. They can't talk. They don't like flowers or animals or good music or anything.

Her father had had to change the plans when he'd found out that the new battery was faulty. Having called the store to berate the helpless shop assistant for shoddiness and exploitation, he'd grumbled and mumbled something about showing these fancy electronics shops that he didn't need them.

He had then disassembled the small electric engine and reassembled it, adding a red rubber band to an extra gear, as well as attaching a short steel shaft affixed to a silver handle.

He smiled at her with self-satisfied anticipation as he turned the handle expectantly.

'Hell, with enough willpower and a big enough rubber band, you could turn the whole world if you wanted to,' he said proudly, as a glorious, tinny tune started to play.

'Don't swear, Daddy,' she scolded him again.

'Sorry, Grub,' he said, patting her proudly on the head.

They couldn't stay away.
And they weren't the only ones.

couldn't stay away

He'd left a note on the kitchen table. It said he would call if he could when he got there.

He'd packed all he needed into an oversized sports bag. He didn't really have that much anyway. With the bag thrown over his shoulder, he had caught a bus to the train station, then bought a ticket as far west as the money he had brought with him would allow. He should have brought more, he thought briefly, but then he had felt guilty enough already.

He'd spent the last three hours standing on the side of a deserted dusty highway with his thumb pointing due west.

This was not the sort of thing that Matt Turner had done before. Sure, he'd made rash decisions. Some odd choices at times in his life. But this—this!—throwing his life in a sports bag, spending his last cent on a train fare halfway across the country. It would be fair to say he'd never even conceived of such a trip, let alone contemplated how to do it properly.

He'd barely even thought about it before he'd found himself on that train staring out the window, watching the familiar red-brick and weatherboard civilisation of Sydney become the hazy greys and greens of the Blue Mountains. Soon the trees had begun to dwindle and the landscape had transformed into the starched sunburnt sparseness of inland farms. Hours later, there had been no more trees and the space between the train and the horizon had been filled with the scorched barren plains of the outback.

What was he doing?

The wind whipped dirt and dust across the road. He kept his eyes squinted, despite the partial protection of his out-of-fashion sunglasses. He clutched a dirty newspaper in his right hand, his non-hitchhiking hand, the ink now starting to smear across the front page and stain his skin.

He reshouldered his bag, lifting and bouncing his shoulder and the bag until they each found a relatively comfortable spot. It was getting heavy now. But he wouldn't put it down. There was something he couldn't place, something that told him he shouldn't stop, couldn't stop, couldn't hesitate, couldn't think; something that said just keep on going, keep on going . . .

. . . and he'd make it.

A semitrailer thundered towards him, chased by a wave of dust.

He couldn't stay away. Every sense propelled him onward. It was pure soulful instinct driven by the image of her on the podium, the siren sound of her certainty, the smell of history, a taste of the future—the need to touch it, feel it, be near it. The image of her on the podium, her presence so resolute, addressing the press . . . and yet, addressing him, looking right at him, her eyes peering inside him, spying on a secret part of him that no one else had ever seen. Her eyes—that was it, her eyes—had invaded him in some way, his sovereign skin incapable of repelling her; his thoughts, his dreams, his future unable to escape; his heart not wanting to, drawn as if by gravity towards her.

He threw his bag up into the cabin before he pulled himself up and in. He looked over to make friendly eye contact with the Samaritan, but his bearded, tattooed head had already turned back to the road as his foot hit the floor. There was no need for the driver to ask where he was going. It was either this way or that way.

Matt kept the inky, dusty newspaper page grasped in his hand in case he hesitated or stopped to think about just how crazy this was. Crumpled, creased and now smearing, it was her—her photo—and a caption, now fading away.

Anna Spires, Utopian Dreamer and New World Project CEO, the caption read.

Next to the photograph was a link to the newspaper's multimedia site, where Laikali was able to watch a video of the whole press conference.

There was something about it: the idea, the location, this Anna Spires, that had caught Laikali Rulé's attention. Intrigued her. Entranced her. This was important, or going to be, she was sure. Now, as Mrs Rulé disembarked the airliner in Sydney and stepped straight into the waiting chartered jet, she considered the difficulties faced by previous New Worlds.

All the 'New Worlds' of the past had, at one stage, been discovered, conquered and colonised. From Christopher Columbus to Captain Cook, founding New Worlds had always involved finding them first. And from the conquistadors to the East India Company, by sword or by trade, conquering had been required. By the time colonisation had begun—in the name of either lords or Our Lord—all the pious words and noble gestures had rarely not sought payback. Finding, founding, civilising and civicising New Worlds, is expensive. And payback, from gold to spices to land to oil to taxes, had always proved the priority.

But what payback does this Anna Spires want?, Laikali wondered. The press had not reported what Ms Spires was hoping to achieve with her New World Project, and so Laikali was left to speculate.

Other thoughts troubled her. Creating New Worlds had more often than not involved violent displacement and replacement—of worlds, lives, cultures, ecologies, histories . . . Fish this time—and very few fish, the marine biologist assured—were the only tenants about to be evicted. But who would come to take their place? Why would they come? And why couldn't the press ever ask insightful questions?

'There's something about her,' she said to her dead husband, 'something that tells me she will not fail.'

Still, she was left with no answers to her more important questions and she would have none until she knew more about this Anna Spires. Initially, Laikali had been more than a little concerned by the presence of Isaac Blackwell behind her, but having seen the video footage, having seen this Spires speak, she could tell quite clearly that this was *her* New World, not his.

'You can see it in her eyes,' she said to Augusto. She could hear him saying something about a girl's eyes *he'd* once seen. She blushed a little. 'This is not about me, Augusto, we are going to meet *her*.'

She had made her decision to come almost immediately upon reading the sidebar in the *Washington Post*. The subsequent information which she had sourced from the internet had only piqued her interest. This chartered jet would take her to Perth on the west coast where she would board a private motoryacht.

She looked out the window as the red heart of Australia opened up beneath her. She had not been here for a long time, not since her days as an idealistic Polynesian politician on the speakers' tour, so many years ago. She had seen the whole world that way, she mused, seen it for the first time—seen its wonders, its diversity, its enormity. In the years since, with advancements in technology and communications, and the seeming ubiquity of brands and commerce, it was easy to think of that Old World as getting smaller.

'But it's not so,' she told Augusto. 'The differences remain. The choices facing countries, cultures and individuals remain. And the wonders never cease. I thought I saw the whole world when

I was young—but there has always been some-where else to go since. There always is.'

Today, for example, she thought, she was going somewhere new. She looked at a map she had printed of the Indian Ocean. Latitude twenty-three degrees south, longitude ninety degrees east, the reports said.

'That would put it here,' she said, placing her finger on a prominent submarine mountain chain called Ninety East Ridge.

'Yes, I know it's a long way,' she replied to Augusto. 'But I have a hunch about that, too. I have a hunch it's a long way for a reason.'

Because roses attract both beautiful women and bees that
  sting.
Because songs of love to some can be bitter memories to others.
Because every story needs its bad guys.

cue the evil music

'Enter.'

Aldrich Ridder tentatively opened the door. He
was not a man accustomed to feeling nervous.

'It's a door,' said the voice, calmly and politely.
'You open it,' it said, without a hint of frustration,
'walk into the room and close it behind you.'

Hesitantly, Ridder made his way into the
darkened room. Across the room, behind a grand
mahogany desk, a figure sat motionless, his head
haloed, his face shrouded in the half-light that
crept through the half-closed venetian blinds
behind him.

'Mr Ford? My name is Rick Ridder.'

There was no response, only semi-dark silence.

'Rick Ridder, sir. Aldrich Ridder.'

'Yes, I heard you the first time. Now sit and
speak, Mr Ridder.'

It took a moment for the order to register, his
nerves only worsened by the lack of posturing the
voice carried, and the true level of power that
implied. As he was about to sit in the studded red

leather chair in front of Mr Ford's desk, it occurred to him that he should shake hands so he rose again to lean forward, hand extended—

'Speak!'

The chair almost swallowed Ridder as he fell back into it, hand pulling away as if to avoid being bitten by an animal. Ridder swallowed hard before he spoke. He tried to feign bravado.

'Mr Ford, it's a pleasure to finally meet—'

'Mr Ridder, do you know why you're here?'

'Well, sir, I understand that you have summoned me through the Secretary of State's office . . .' He let his voice trail off as Mr Ford's right hand waved away his answer like a fly or a bad smell.

'Well, sir,' he pushed on, 'although I did not receive a briefing, I might conjecture that . . .' Mr Ford's hands were now frustratedly rubbing his face. 'Well, sir—'

'Mr Ridder,' interrupted Mr Ford, laying his hands firmly on the desk, 'let me ask you one last time: do you know why you're here?'

'Not a clue, sir,' Ridder responded, surprising himself with his own lack of artfulness.

'Finally.' A hint of a smile may have flashed across his face, Ridder could not be sure. 'Learn fast, Mr Ridder. There is no time for political rhetoric in this office.'

Ridder did not know how to respond so, wisely, he remained silent.

'That's good, Mr Ridder,' said Mr Ford. 'Now, let me tell you why you are here.'

Ridder wrongly expected something about his skills or at least his department.

'I understand you went to school with Isaac Blackwell.'

Ridder tensed, his body stiffly trying to hide his sudden fear and anger. 'We were freshmen at Harvard together. And then I worked with him at GJS for almost ten years.'

'I also understand that Mr Blackwell had you fired from GJS and blackballed from ever working on Wall Street again.'

No reply. At that moment, it wasn't possible for Ridder to open his mouth without saying something he'd regret.

'And you were branded a liar, a cheat and an insider trader.'

There was no point debating it. The truth was clear to both of them. All Ridder would say was, 'Well, he would know.'

From his backlit position, P. Jefferson Ford was voyeur to his own face-to-face conversation. He watched Ridder stay silent out of fear—of him. He also watched as behind the fear, nerves and anger, he saw Ridder's eyes narrow and his body lean the slightest bit forward at the realisation that Blackwell might be the enemy here.

'Your job,' Ford said, 'is to destroy him.'

And with that, he had him.

The young climber could barely hide the sneer as he tried to laugh off the directive.

'I don't know what it is you think I do, Mr Ford. I'm simply a liaison officer for the Justice Department.' Now edging forward in his chair. 'Of course, I have been seconded from time to time to the State

Department . . .' He was trying to appear offhand, but Ford could see his excitement growing. '. . . the Federal Reserve, the National Security Agency . . .' Not to mention, Ford knew, the CIA, the Pentagon, the IRS, NASA, the National Rifle Association, and perhaps his most effective work at '. . . the Food and Drug Administration, but that was mostly communications management and public relations and general helping out.' Ford could not help but be impressed as Ridder humbly distanced himself from his successes.

'Isaac Blackwell,' Ford said, getting down to business, 'is in the process of raising more money than has ever been raised before for what will be the greatest infrastructure project that has ever been attempted in history.'

'Illegally?' asked Ridder hopefully.

'No, not yet anyway. Plus, he's doing so without promising profit or financial return of any kind.'

'He's mad,' concluded Ridder, hands out, palms up, as if it was obvious.

'Maybe,' said Ford, although he did not believe it for a second, 'but he may also be the first man in history to have the skills and the resources to be able to pull it off.'

It took a while for Ridder to get his head around the idea.

'A city? In a hole in the ocean?' He surprised Ford by rising from the chair, his mind clearly more at ease when he was standing up, pacing. His responses had also assumed a greater sharpness now that he was dealing with a specified target.

'Can we delay government approvals?'

'It's offshore, middle of the Indian Ocean. No country has jurisdiction.'

'No. Jurisdiction is unclear,' corrected Ridder, hesitating immediately as he realised what he'd done. He continued quickly, trying to obscure what might be seen as petulance, 'We could go after the investors? Impose tax penalties for investing in non-recognised sovereignties?'

'Maybe,' advised Ford, 'but tread carefully, Mr Ridder. Mr Blackwell's been in street fights before. We might hurt him but we won't beat him that way. That's his turf. He's the best at what he does for a reason.'

'Then the builders, suppliers, freight handlers . . .' said Ridder as he paced around the room, rubbing his hands. 'I'll get on it immediately.'

Ford smiled as he was again left alone in the semi-darkness.

His instincts had been right. There had been plenty of options, both within and without the administration, who had experience in propaganda and project manipulation. But the personal relationship had been the key. He could see the history, the resentment, the bitter jealousy of wealth and its accompanying self-justification of their respective levels of success. In addition, there was the barely hidden covetousness of Blackwell's public profile—and there was the lust for revenge that could only exist where personal feelings were involved.

Take a picture of your life today: your face, your friends,
your house, your street.
Then take a look at those pictures ten, twenty years,
sometimes days, from now,
And note the inevitability of what changes . . . and what
endures.

the world BA

Rain pounded on the roof, pounded on the window, pounded on the dust, exploding in a million bursts of red mud.

It hadn't rained here in three years, the waitress had told him, he must be good luck.

That was yesterday. Yesterday he had felt some feigned pride—he might as well take credit. Yes, yes, it's happened before, he'd said.

Stupid rain.

It wouldn't stop. It just kept pounding. There wouldn't be another ride until a day after the rain at the earliest. The road was likely flooded some forty kilometres back, the waitress had said, so the truckies would be detouring around the area.

His lift had dropped him here before turning south. Matt was still going west. He had about four hundred klicks to go. He'd get a ride all the way in, no problem, the driver had said. About ten minutes after he'd arrived at the truck stop, the rains had started.

Smudged, the caption now almost illegible, the crumpled newspaper with her picture on it remained folded in his pocket.

'Do you have any newspapers?' he asked the waitress behind the counter.

'In the corner,' she said. 'But they're three or four days old.' They were four, in fact.

Matt took a copy back to the natural light by the rain-smeared window and spread the broadsheet paper out on the table. As he flicked casually from page to page, he realised that four days ago, the world had had no idea who Anna Spires was.

The world BA: Before Anna, he pondered.

The front page spoke of a national health scandal implicating a secret ministerial agenda. A highlighted box listed similar embarrassments during the government's administration and the ministers involved. The opposition leader was quoted as saying the government should be ashamed for their continued deception of the Australian people. The Prime Minister's only statement was that the opposition had no right to complain, given their disgraceful misuse of taxpayers' money in their previous term in office. There would be a government inquiry into the alleged misdoings, the paper reported.

Smaller headlines on the front page covered a local police scandal and the results of a recent study which showed road safety levels were at an all-time low despite denials by the relevant ministers and automotive company public relations officers.

In BA world news, there was an economic summit in Tokyo. Representatives for the eight most powerful economies in the world (the G8) were meeting to discuss how to support the out-of-control growth in emerging markets. Pollution levels, they stated, although not dissimilar to the choking levels of the West's own industrial development, were unacceptably high and sanctions were being considered. Inexplicably, they could not agree on an environmental standard for themselves.

The continuing civil conflict in central Africa was not addressed by the summit, nor the Americans' latest sovereign incursion in the name of freedom. The former was clearly too far removed from the G8's political agendas, the latter too uncomfortably close. The paper covered each in neat half-page pieces, in both cases describing recent military ambushes and the plight of thousands of homeless refugees now making their way to the perceived safety of the border.

There was a passing reference to Gill Johnson Shek Investment Bank in the business news section, but no mention of their most famous frontman. There was no reference to the New World Project. And no mention of Anna Spires.

He soon put the paper aside. He'd read it before, he realised. All just a little bit of history repeating. The names might change, the value of a dollar, the skin colour of the ethnic group in global power. This paper could be four days, four months or four hundred years old—but the news would essentially remain the same.

Outside, the sun was beginning to break through.

'You never know your luck,' said the waitress excitedly. But her interests were different to his. 'The last time it rained like this, the road was closed for weeks.'

a world away

[days 4 to 6]

I turn from the stars and look into the red and yellow firelight that flickers and licks at the top of the hearth. It's alive, changing direction every moment. Each flame tapers to a sharp, dancing, fiery tip. The ring of flames forms a bright shining corona. Every day, I see reminders of what she achieved.

By the time the New World Project would truly finish, there would be a brave New World flowering from the seed she planted in the middle of the Indian Ocean. There would be new lifestyles, new values, new concepts of wealth, new ways to work, means of transport, methods of generating power. There would be a glorious crystal tower rising just above sea level, but outrageously high above the ground, rising, shining, guiding, inspiring with its gold and silver crown.

But then, even before it was visible, it was bold and brilliant, awe-inspiring like a baby's birth: a miracle to stare at, marvel at, wonder at—adjudged a dream come *true before anyone knew what it would look like or what it would grow up to be.*

And like every baby, it needed a name so that everyone could talk about it.

Ah, that we might know our place in history
So that we could properly relabel ourselves.

naming a rose

'Daddy, what would you have called me if I was a boy?'

He bent at the knees so that they were eye to eye and looked her hard in the face. 'If you'd been a boy,' he said dramatically, 'we'd have still called you Anna.'

'You would not,' Anna said, laughing and punching him in the arm.

Her father clutched at his arm and fell to the ground in mock pain. She jumped on him, demanding an answer.

But he ignored her, defiantly declaring, 'And that's why, regardless of whether you get a new baby sister or brother, its name will be . . .'

She stopped, suddenly excited—what were they going to call her new brother or sister?

'. . . Godzilla!'

Aaaggh! He was impossible! Her father was impossible! She crashed down on him, arms flaying, face laughing and her body safe and happy in his wide protective embrace.

'What was that, Anna?'

She looked up. It was Isaac.

'You said something. What did you say?'

'Godzilla,' she said. 'Why don't we call the place Godzilla?'

Arb laughed, as they all did—all except one. 'I don't think we should forget what a truly historic undertaking this is,' said Arts and Culture. 'The name should somehow reflect what is arguably the greatest achievement of the century.'

'Good, Mary, good. What did you have in mind?' asked Arb.

'I don't know—something from the classics, maybe—something like Shangri-La or Babylon.'

'Or New Camelot!' suggested Politics.

'Or New Troy, perhaps,' said Anna.

'No,' said Economics firmly. 'We can't be named after history's losers.'

'Everyone's a loser in history, eventually,' said Heritage.

The room paused for a moment, surprised by the anthropologist's atypical poignancy.

True to form, Arb was the first to shrug off the thought, 'Heavy, Tom, very heavy, but let's not weigh this down—come on! This is good, we're on a roll. Let's just keep bouncing these ideas off the walls and see what doesn't fly out the window. Mary, those ideas were good, keep going with that . . .'

'Okay . . .' she nodded, picking up on his momentum, 'perhaps after an author or a poet—'

'What about Byron Island?' said Byron Lybrand, who couldn't help laughing.

'Or Chaucerton?'

'Whitmania?'

'How about Huxleyville?' said Technology.

'Only if you think we want to be known as a brave new *repressive* world,' scathed Mary.

'Come on, people,' urged Arb. 'Less judging, more suggesting.'

Heritage Tom stood up, his usual levity now restored, and threw his arms extravagantly wide. 'How about Hugo?'

'Or Jules Vernia?' said Ecology, rising beside him and then holding her hands in front with her thumbs together like a film director framing a name, 'Or Cousteauville, as in Jacques Cousteau?'

'Clarke Town perhaps, as in Arthur C?' Tom again, clearly enjoying himself.

'What about Ulyssium?' proposed Engineering proudly, his classic idea belying his well-known preference for beer and a football game. 'Sorry, are we allowed character names?'

'Absolutely!' said Arb, taking the stage again. 'Anything goes here! But Mary's right: we are creating a name for history. I don't care where it comes from. It doesn't have to be original. It doesn't have to be profound. In fact, it doesn't have to be anything.'

'Yes, it does,' Anna interrupted.

She didn't counter Arb often, so the room turned to her now in serious attention.

'It must be beautiful.'

She was beautiful.

A little dumb-looking maybe, but she was beautiful. Her mother cradled her in her arms; the most fragile, pure, harmless creature.

'Anna,' said her father, 'meet your new little sister, Natasha.'

Natasha. *Natasha*. She tested the name again in her head. It was a nice name.

Her mother angled the baby's head towards Anna, who reached out and tentatively touched the baby's face.

'Hello, Tazza,' she said, unaware of her inability to pronounce her sister's name. 'I'm Anna and I'm going to be your big sister.'

She felt her father's hand come down and pat her on the head, ruffling her hair.

She couldn't help but smile at her sister, at her father, her mother. At her family.

'Hello, Anna! Are you with us? Hello, Anna!'

'Sorry, Zac,' she said, returning to the world in front of her. 'Yes?'

'What do you think? It is your baby after all!'

There was now a list of names filling the whiteboard. She looked them up and down, noting the ones she hadn't already seen.

Nobel, as in prize. Hmm, maybe.

Atlantis. No, you might as well call it Flooded.

Tuscan Waters. God, it sounded like a retirement home.

New Eden, Nova Gloria, Ocean Gloria—too religious, too pious, too corny.

'What about a completely new word, like Sony or Nintendo?' suggested Economics.

'No. No company names,' rejected Mary.

'No, they're examples. When they started Sony,

they deliberately invented a new word which had no direct associations. What they did was take the Latin word for sound, *sonus*, and play with it.'

'Okay, okay,' Arb facilitated. 'Any ideas— anyone?'

'How about . . .' mused Politics, thinking out loud, 'Adeesia. It doesn't mean anything that I'm aware of, but it sort of sounds like an ancient Greek paradise.'

'Write it on the board,' enthused Arb.

'Hey,' cried Byron excitedly. 'Go back a bit to Mary's comment.'

'What, no company names?'

Byron tapped his nose, nodding. He clearly believed he had the answer, the revelation was at hand:

'Why don't we auction off the name to the highest bidder? You know, why not sell, or better yet, lease the naming rights?' He was on his feet now, holding his hands wide to embrace their approval.

'Great idea, Byron,' enthused Tom. 'Maybe we could sell the national anthem separately!'

'And instead of a constitution, we could have a slogan!'

'Or a mission statement!'

'And the flag . . .'

The whole table was now lambasting Byron for all they were worth.

'Needs a fancy logo.'

'Bright colours,' said Economics knowingly, 'to catch the eye and make potential immigrants hungry.'

'Would you like fries with your bill of rights, sir?' asked Technology, barely able to keep a straight face.

'All right, all right,' deferred Byron, both hands patting down the air, hoping it would also suppress the laughter and wit which now assaulted him. 'But there's something to this idea. I know there is.'

'I suggest, people,' voiced Arb above the sardonic din that the room had become, 'that we wind up our meeting there. We've all got plenty to do, but I'd like everyone to keep thinking about this. This is branding at its most important level. Our decision will be critical in building the values and long-term credibility that we all want Star-bucks McUnderwater World to become.'

Still laughing and joking, the room began to clear. Arb leaned back in his chair, clearly happy with how things had gone.

Anna paused at the door and turned back to him with a mischievous look in her eye.

'Would a Blackwell by any other name smell as sweet?' she swooned.

'Don't look at me,' he said. 'I liked Godzilla!'

With a flourish, she screwed up her face, melodramatically disgusted and delighted, then trooped from the room to check on further dredging preparations. Arb watched her go, then stared out the window, his mind in cheerful thought.

'Excuse me, sir.'

It was Xavier, clearing drinks from around the table, his cultured, proper voice filling the otherwise empty room. 'May I suggest a more traditional approach?'

'Of course.'

'I suggest that you name the city after its founder. And call it: Spires.'

The world possible is beyond description,
Only conceivable in dreams,
And moments of genius or madness.

the philo group

'. . . he's calling it the Philo Group, as in philosophy group. They are, in fact, a sort of steering committee or advisory council making all the decisions about how the city will look, how it will function, everything from macroeconomics to waste management.'

'So what have you done?'

'Well, of course, I've tried to get some of my guys into the Group, but most of the members have been lined up for three to four months already. I'm guessing that it's probably a closed shop, unless they find an outstanding candidate. I thought that you might know someone we could "suggest" as an expert advisor to their worthy scheme.'

'Who's on the team already?'

'There's an economist, that's Saul Obermann, he's worked with Blackwell for years. A social scientist-slash-sociologist, Byron Lybrand: ditto. There's a futurist by the name of Miles Alia: he's a hack novelist and dot-com millionaire from Seattle. There's a real novelist: Sanjay Mathur, the Booker Prize winner from India. Two historians, a husband

and wife team: Thomas Mills and Mary Minken—'

'Mary Minken?'

'Yes. You must know her—they, Blackwell and her, were an item for years. But then, one day all of a sudden, she marries this politician's son called Mills.' He started to comb through his notes, 'That was . . .'

'Seven years ago—yes, I know his father.'

'You think there's something we can use there?'

'Nothing yet. Go on, who else makes up this politburo?'

'There's Jay Diaglio, Blackwell's usual political advisor, he's a doctor of politics from Yale.'

'Yes, I know about Jay.'

'There's Helen Rainey. She's the marine biologist and resident environmentalist who helped select the site. She was probably the only expert that they could convince to say publicly that the project would cause no lasting ecological damage.'

'Now, now.'

'And lastly, there's Harold Pont, an engineer who has made everything from skyscrapers to bridges to the longest deepest tunnels in the world. He's also Ms Spires' former mentor.'

The War Room was located directly beneath the helicopter pad at the top of Platform Seven. From here, Harry Pont could see the other six converted oil platforms and the dozens of cargo ships, fishing trawlers, construction barges and transport vessels scattered across the site. While three of the former oil platforms had been customised for pipewall construction, the other four, including Platform Seven, had been rigged not for building or drilling, but for living. These were to be the living and working quarters for all on-site contributors. Already they housed everyone from divers to doctors, from mechanical, electrical and civil engineers to marine biologists and meteorologists, from the administrative staff speaking over thirty languages, dealing with everything from food supplies to concrete deliveries, to the growing support crew of chefs, cleaners and odd-job indispensables; and, of course, their families.

Taking a deep breath, as if breathing in the scene might fortify him—already he could see his protégé's new community forming—Harry turned to rejoin the Group's proceedings.

'In medicine, communications, modes of air, land and sea transport,' Anna was saying, 'we have made more progress in the last century than in the rest of history combined. But no technology has probably advanced more than our skills in construction.'

The Philosophy Group had been meeting on and off for three days now. Most of these meetings had been spent getting to know each other, and discussing broadly their developing roles and responsibilities. They were each due to present introductory papers in their chosen fields in the coming week.

To start the ball rolling, Isaac had suggested that Anna detail the physical challenges and timetables facing the Project. Up to now, the Group had only received the same broad building plans that had been presented to the media. No one, except for himself, Anna and a small team of engineers, had seen the full plans which they were about to present. Harry grinned as he watched Anna set the scene, confident that the team's creative juices would be truly flowing by the end of this presentation.

'We've built skyscrapers over one hundred stories tall and tunnels ten miles long. We've learned how to build rockets to take us into space and submarines to take us to the bottom of the ocean. In fact, when you think about it, the pipewalls we are constructing don't appear that difficult if you compare them with man's major accomplishments over the last century.'

There were glances of disbelief all round.

On cue, Harry circled the room and joined Anna at the front.

'Put simply,' he said, 'we are just trying to build a wall around the city—a dam, nothing more. Now, as you know, and as the world is now reading in the papers, the catch is that this dam needs to be about a mile high and some twenty-two kilometres in circumference.' He let his face broaden into a knowing inclusive smile. 'But when it's all said and done, don't forget it's just a wall.'

'So how many in total?' asked Ford.

'They don't appear to have set a limit, but for now, if you include Blackwell and Spires themselves, that makes eleven. They're also talking to the leading bodies of four or five major religious groups. It's still unclear whether these people will sit on the Philo Group or whether Blackwell and Spires will consult with them separately. My information is that along with a number of philosophers and culturalists, they will be asked to be part of a separate panel.'

'So you're saying that the leading group, the so-called Philosophy Group, has no recognised, professional philosophers?'

'Hmm,' Ridder mused, sensing an opportunity, 'that's right. Credibility issue, maybe?'

'Not if they keep it that way,' said Ford.

'There are two key obstacles for us to overcome to make this successful,' said Anna as she flicked some of the audiovisual control switches. 'The first is making sure that the floor of the ocean will actually support such a wall. The second, and probably more obvious one, is ensuring that the wall is able to resist the weight of water pressing against it, as well as the changes in pressure which can arise from tidal movements, deep sea currents, rough seas and monsoons.'

The lights dimmed and a blueprint schematic appeared on the screen behind Anna and Harry Pont.

'The first wall, therefore, is really just a test.' As the words Stage One appeared on the screen, a series of straight lines descended from the wavy sea line at the top of the screen down to the uneven ocean floor below. The point of view then rose to view the wall at an angle, revealing its shape as cylindrical, as numbered dimensions flashed up.

Stage One

1600 metres

Ocean floor

80 metres

30 metres

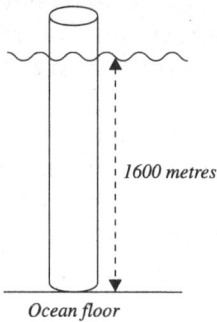

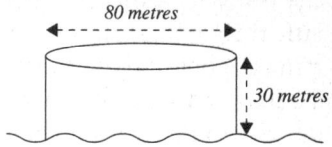

- First pipewall
- To be filled with concrete
- Will act as anchor

'It will be only eighty metres in diameter, but this will be sufficient for us to test the solidity of the ocean floor and the design of the wall itself. Once these tests have been conducted, we will fill the shaft with concrete to create a solid pillar, an anchor to stabilise the superstructure and a vertical base from which subsequent construction will take place—but I'll come back to that in a minute.'

'Question,' said Mary Minken, raising her hand like a schoolgirl. 'Why haven't we seen these plans before?'

'Well, even as we build,' answered Harry Pont, 'we have continued to conduct tests and simulations. The reason you haven't seen these plans before is that no one has seen them.'

Ridder laid out the blueprints with the care and enthusiasm that something so precious deserved. He had been beside himself when Ford asked what else he had uncovered.

'It's really quite brilliant,' he said grudgingly of the plans. 'Apparently, the technology does not currently exist that will allow them to build up from the ocean floor, so instead, they are having to build down from the water level using specially designed compressed air slings to support the weight. Because the walls are concrete reinforced by inserted steel lattice-work, they are too big to make and lower in one piece. So they are having to build interlocking columns.'

'Like a paling fence,' said Ford.

'So you see,' explained Harry, 'all we're doing is building an interlocking, watertight, reinforced concrete, paling fence.'

Anna pressed a key, and the title Stage Two appeared. In a moment, another series of descending lines formed a second cylinder much wider than and surrounding the first. Then a series of spokes seemed to grow out of the concrete shaft.

'In Stage Two, you can see how the first pipe-wall, once it has been filled with concrete, will become a vertical base for further construction. These horizontal branches protruding some five hundred metres below sea level—what my guys are calling the Foundation Spokes—are approximately fifty metres wide—that's about the width of a twenty-lane highway—and sixty metres in depth. These spokes will form "the Top Deck"—or what you might otherwise think of as the ground—on which the open air portion of our city will be built.'

'Why are they so thick?' asked Tom Mills.

500 metres

'Top Deck'

1 kilometre

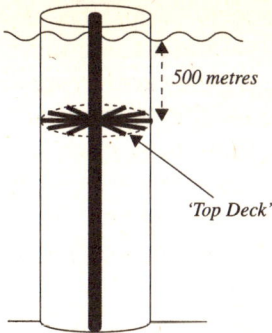

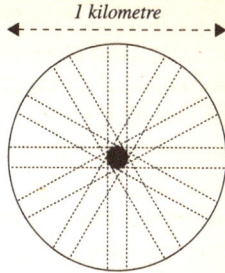

- *Second pipewall (diameter—1 km)*
- *Top Deck Foundation Spokes (width—50 m depth—60 m)*

Harry answered, 'They need to be if they're going to support the foundations of buildings as high as our Anna's ambitions.'

'Another thing to note here,' said Anna, 'is that the part of the second pipewall which rises above the Top Deck is only temporary. It will allow us to start building the centre of the city before we finish the third and final wall.'

The paper rolled back to reveal a third, even wider cylinder surrounding the first two.

'So,' assessed Ford. 'Stage Three.'

A horizontal dotted line extended from one side to the other. The diameter was shown as seven thousand metres.

'The third and final wall,' Ridder explained, 'will be seven kilometres across, and built in the same tubular shape as the first two. The Top Deck Foundation Spokes are to be extended, but only in the south-east quarter in this stage. My sources tell

Stage Three

7 kilometres

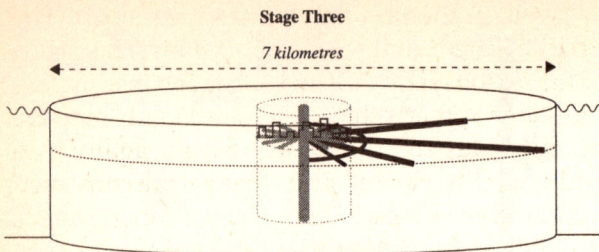

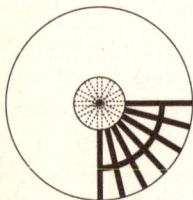

- *Third pipewall (diameter—7 km)*
- *Extended Top Deck (south-east corner only)*
- *Building construction commences (within second pipewall only)*

me once the third pipewall is completed, they initially only intend to drain it to the level of the Top Deck, to make sure no one falls to their death, presumably.'

'Just how strong is the pressure of the ocean?' asked Saul Obermann, trying to sound knowledgeably concerned. 'Bottom line, how do we know it will hold?'

'Very strong,' said Harry simply, 'is the answer to your first question. The pressure will fluctuate between three thousand and five thousand pounds per square inch. At a depth of fifteen hundred metres, or five thousand feet for you older folk, it will be as if three concrete-filled Empire State Buildings were leaning against us on all sides.'

'And the second question?'

'Well, in the first answer lies the second. The Empire State Buildings are on *all* sides. This is one of the reasons why the city is designed in a circle— the shape spreads the pressure because there are no flat sides for the ocean to lean against. In addition, the "paling" posts that we are constructing have been specially designed with an ingenious dodecahedral cross-section, created by our own Anna Spires.'

Anna ignored her former master's accolades, continuing, 'They are intended to channel the pressure of the ocean into the neighbouring pillar, thereby strengthening the entire pipewall.'

'You mentioned at the press launch,' said Mary, perhaps aggressively, 'that our army of architects, builders and craftsmen would be working hard for the next thousand days. I take it that was a mistake, or at least creative licence, given the extent of the task before us.'

Anna glanced over at Arb before she answered the question . . .

'Well that's about all to report,' said Ridder, rolling up the blueprints and closing the folders on the table before him.

'Thank you, Mr Ridder. Your research has obviously taken some effort. I applaud your resourcefulness, and openly hope that we shall continue to see more of the same.'

Ridder let a proud smile slip before quickly replacing it with a humbler mask of grateful enthusiasm. 'Just doing my job,' he said, as he reached for the door.

'I hope you don't mind,' said Ford—Ridder's hand freezing on the handle—'but I took the liberty of doing a little research of my own. And there's something here of which I think you should be aware before you go.'

'Let me make one thing clear,' Anna said. 'I don't believe in secrets. But for reasons which will be abundantly clear, what I'm about to tell you is not yet public knowledge. Apart from Isaac, Harry, myself and a very select band of engineers, no one outside this room is aware of what I'm about to tell you.'

*

Ford looked his lapdog in the eye.

'Blackwell and Spires began construction of their first so-called pipewall almost five years ago . . .'

'Construction on this site began almost five years ago,' said Anna.

Ford pulled from a drawer a number of enlarged photographs—satellite photographs, Ridder saw as he approached the desk—infrared satellite photographs obviously taken of latitude twenty-three degrees south, longitude ninety degrees east—infrared satellite photographs which clearly showed the seven platforms, the fleet of trawlers and barges, and there, larger than Ridder imagined, three concentric circles clearly visible just below the surface of the water.

'The pipewalls, all three pipewalls, have been built up to less than fifty metres from sea level,' said Anna. 'So even though there is still almost three years to go, to put it plainly . . .'

'They're almost finished, Mr Ridder.'

Keeping secrets is powerful,
Breaking them even more so.

one more thing

'But how? How did they build it without us knowing? Look at the size of it. You can't just build something this size without people knowing about it. There are people and equipment and materials—Jesus, they must have cornered half the world's concrete market.'

'Yes,' said Ford, waiting out Ridder's apoplexy.

'How did we not know? We must have known. Someone must have known.'

Ford shook his head.

'But—but—the CIA? The NSA? No one? No one knew?'

Satisfied that Ridder had talked himself out, Ford spoke plainly: 'Don't underestimate just how wide the world is. Our influence may extend further than any empire in history, our technology may allow us to monitor any part of the world at a moment's notice, but don't pretend that everything that goes on does so with our permission, or even our knowledge. Blackwell did his homework, Mr Ridder. The site is well away from the major shipping lanes. The equipment, if anybody had spotted it, looked for all the world like oil platforms and ocean-going barges. To a passing tanker they would have looked like they were drilling for gas or laying cables. As far as the workers are concerned, I'll wager that most of them probably didn't know what they were building either. They only knew what they needed to know.'

Ridder was still stunned. He couldn't believe it.

'Believe it, Mr Ridder. The fundraising. The concrete supply. All done in parts small enough not to draw undue attention but large enough to demand confidentiality agreements. Your old colleague, Mr Blackwell, for all his faults, knows how to pull the strings.'

'Don't I know it,' said Ridder, his anxiety increasing. 'We need to work fast then, faster than I thought.'

He was making a determined beeline for the door when again Ford stopped him.

'Oh, Mr Ridder, there's one more thing.'

Ridder turned at the door. This had been a revelatory meeting already. How much more could there be?

'You might want to pick up an early edition of tomorrow's newspapers. I would like to apologise for them in advance.'

'What for? What's in them?' Ridder asked, not sure whether to be concerned or excited.

'Oh, it's all good, Mr Ridder. I'd just like to apologise for stealing all the fun.'

Ford made a point of watching Ridder all but salivate.

'What have we got? What have we got?' he barked.

'It seems that Mr Isaac Blackwell has been keeping secrets. It appears that he may not be the man the world thinks he is.'

Arb Blackwell was slick—and I didn't like him—but some people will tell you that he changed after all this; after all the lies and the truths; some may even tell you that he's now a completely different man. But then, no man is the same now as he was when Anna's New World was born, a world no one denies that Arb Blackwell fathered. In a way, the question of whether Arb was affected for better or worse—by the triumph of its creation; or by the tears of the tragedy which followed— is immaterial.

I won't deceive you: my memory of everything that happened is biased against him—slick, smooth, rich, never-failed, arbitraging Arb. I don't hate him. Hate's such a strong word, a word for burning bridges, a word used by people stating that they will not be swayed by logic or fairness or humanity. A lot of time may have passed, but I still can't say that I like him.

Back then, though, despite what I thought of him,

there were some who loved him.
   Like his father. Like his mother.
   And like his wife . . .
   . . . Anna Spires.

Love.

the adventure of a lifetime

They had met at a wedding, as old wives would have young men believe is the surest way to meet future wives. But old wives might have trouble dealing with the fact that these two were actually supposed to be at different weddings. Then again, maybe not—they would probably immortalise it as exactly the sort of magical, predestined, unavoidable, undeniable, fate-entrusted meeting that they prescribe.

Anna was supposed to have been at the wedding reception one floor below. She had arrived at the hotel and simply gone to the wrong function room, unwittingly crossing the class barrier in the act. Before she had figured out that she knew absolutely no one in the room, he had grabbed her by the hand. He would never let her go.

'Excuse me . . .'

If there was one thing about Arb, he could spot true value from across a crowded room.

'. . . let me help you . . .'

And you could bet that he would always have a solution in mind before he started a problem.

'. . . find the person you're looking for.'

He had spotted her the second she entered the ballroom. She had simply wandered in, innocently passing both the reception table and the attendant security, looking expectantly around the room for a familiar face.

'How embarrassing,' she said. 'I can't see a single person I know.'

'Tell me about it,' he replied. 'And the worst thing is when someone that you don't know comes up to you and says, "Hey, how're ya doin'?"!'

She knew exactly what he meant, but she hadn't experienced that feeling tonight. She didn't know a soul, and no one had paid her any attention, except—

'I'm sorry, I haven't introduced myself. My name's Anna. Anna Spires. And you are?'

She doesn't recognise me? He looked her in the eyes, measuring what to say.

'Zac,' he said at last. 'Call me Zac.'

'Ah, look, there's a reception table. Is there a table list?'

'Well, yes. Yes, let's see if we can find your name.' He started to escort her back to the entranceway.

'No, no, I'm fine,' she said politely. 'I'm sure Liz has made sure that I'll know someone at my table. Perhaps we can have a dance later?'

At that moment, the microphoned voice of the Master of Ceremonies interrupted them: 'Excuse me, ladies and gentlemen. The wedding party has arrived. If you could please return to your places, we'll begin the night's festivities.'

Arb, who had turned to listen to the announcement, turned back to see Anna making her way back to the reception desk, when all of a sudden it hit him.

'Liz?'

The woman behind the desk was shaking her head, running her finger up and down the lists before glancing meaningfully at the burly men on either side of her.

'An-na Spires,' Anna repeated, enunciating clearly.

The tuxedoed security men were leaning in, taking an interest, when he arrived at her shoulder.

'Anna Spires, there you are!' he said, taking her by the shoulders. She turned to him, confused, and missed the reactions of security and the desklady who recognised him straight away. 'Your seat's right at the front with us, but seeing as the wedding party's waiting to come in, let's just stand here at the back so we, ah, don't get in the way.' He smiled again at the gatekeepers, who nodded back with fawning respect.

'I don't understand,' said Anna, clearly embarrassed as he smoothly guided her away. 'I'm sure I have my invitation here somewhere.' She began to rummage through her handbag.

'Ladies and gentlemen,' said the MC, 'please welcome the respective parents of the bride and groom.'

Anna listened as the applause started but didn't look up until people began to rise to give them a standing ovation—the parents!

Arb watched her closely as she peered between the heads in front of her, trying to work out what was going on.

The MC's voice rose again above the clapping, 'Please maintain your applause and remain standing for the bridesmaids and the groomsmen.' And he proceeded to introduce them in turn. Anna, meanwhile, was still trying to spy what was so interesting about the parents.

'Don't they all look beautiful,' the MC said. 'You too, girls!'

'That's funny, I don't recognise any of them,' she whispered.

'And now, ladies and gentlemen, if I could direct your attention towards the entranceway . . .'

The bride and groom appeared in the doorway.

Anna gasped. 'Hey, that's not Liz.'

'. . . it gives me great pleasure . . .'

'Ah, no it's not,' winced Arb, as if the realisation must have hurt.

'. . . to introduce . . .'

'But that's, that's, that's . . .'

'Mr and Mrs—'

'Oh my God!'

'Yes, yes, it is,' Arb assured her, watching her figure out that she didn't know the Governor's son, his new wife or the Governor for that matter.

'Come on,' he said, grabbing her by the hand and whisking her out the doorway.

'Oh my God! That was the state Governor in

there. Oh my God! How embarrassing, that was his son's wedding. So that security . . . thank you so much.'

'Come on, I suspect you were looking for a different wedding when you came in. Let's see if we can find it.'

'Oh, no, no, no. Please don't come on my account. I'll be fine. Please. You can't just leave the Governor's wedding.'

'It's not his wedding. It's his son's. And it's all right, I'm not from around here, so I didn't vote for his father anyway.'

In typical Isaac Blackwell style, their romance had been whirlwind.

And secret.

His romantic style was much like his business style—behind the glossy charm, he was blunt, businesslike and easily bored, all of which appealed to Anna because, most of all, he was honest. He didn't have time to lie, and his wealth and success meant he didn't have to. So he was honest about what he wanted to do, where he wanted to go or not go, what he liked and disliked, what he wanted to eat or drink or watch on TV, what he thought of politicians, sportsmen and other businessmen, and what he thought of her.

His thoughts about her were the most endearing feature of all, not just because he said what he thought, but because he didn't know what it meant. In fact, she knew before he did that he was falling in love with her.

He had, of course, been a little less than completely honest at their first meeting. He hadn't lied, but he also certainly had not volunteered what some may have considered important information. He had subsequently escorted Anna to her wedding downstairs—after all, she had offered him a dance later. It was only when Anna retired to the ladies' room for a few moments that she discovered who he was.

'How on earth,' said the woman touching up her make-up in the mirror beside her, 'did you ever land Isaac Blackwell?'

'Excuse me?'

'I said I can't believe I'm in the same room as Isaac Blackwell.' She prodded and patted her hair manically. 'Is he a family friend or something?'

'What? Who, Zac?' responded Anna automatically. And then it hit her. *Zac . . . Isaac . . . Oh my God! Isaac Blackwell? THE Isaac Blackwell! The multi-zillionaire!*

She noticed the woman hitching up her bra, undoing an extra button and puffing out her breasts. She certainly did not want to say that they'd only just met.

'No, no, no. Zac's an *old* friend,' she said, arching her eyes suggestively as she turned away from the mirror.

She wondered as she pulled open the door if anyone else had picked who he was. Any uncertainty was quickly resolved when she re-entered the room and noticed a largely female crowd gathered around her table. She could see him smiling and nodding courteously to the gaggle of women (and one man) as they flaunted themselves gracelessly. She suddenly felt self-conscious, unworthy, lost—she'd lost her chance. If only she'd known.

She was about to turn around and find a lonelier part of the room when he spotted her.

'Anna,' he called, clearly relieved when he saw her approaching. Ten pairs of jealous eyes turned as one. 'There you are,' he said, for the second time that evening.

All at once, her self-esteem returned, one hundredfold.

'Sorry, Zac. If your new friends will excuse you for a moment, I thought we'd go over and talk to the bride and groom.'

Elegantly but purposefully, and plainly without asking their permission, Arb rose and made his way past the parade of women around the table. He glanced Anna's way as he politely emerged from the scrum and somehow she knew to link her arm under his as he walked by. He swept her along without breaking his stride.

'Someone just pinched me,' he whispered as they approached the main table. 'But I think it was the guy.'

'Liz, Greg, congratulations—you look beautiful.'

'Anna,' said Liz demurely, 'you haven't introduced us to your date.'

Anna hesitated, looked at Greg, but Greg was also leaning forward eagerly.

'O-kay. Liz, Greg, this is Isaac Blackwell. Isaac, Liz and Greg.'

'Hello, pleased to meet you. Sorry to crash your party. You both look great.'

Liz virtually swooned. Greg's hand shot out across the table—and handed Arb a business card.

'Hi. Greg Berger. GiroBank. You—I mean your bank—I mean you and your bank acquired us last year.'

'It's a pleasure to meet you, Greg.'

'Liz, Greg,' interrupted Anna, 'we're sorry, but Isaac has another wedding that we've also got to pop into. Have a great honeymoon. Give me a call when you get back.'

'Yes, of course,' jumped Greg. 'Maybe you and Isaac would like to come over for dinner some time.'

'That'd be great,' said Arb. Greg nearly fainted. 'Congratulations again.'

They had started to move away when Greg desperately got out another sentence.

'I saw you speak at the global strategy conference last year in Madrid.'

'You know, I thought I recognised your face.'

This time, Greg did faint.

'Come on, Anna,' said Arb, grabbing her by the hand. 'We're late. We'd better get out of here.'

They almost ran out of the hotel and when they hit the street, burst into laughter.

'I didn't think you recognised me.'

'I didn't,' Anna replied, a little ashamed. 'One of your fans in the ladies' room informed me.'

'Well, thank you for saving me. I'm sorry to make you leave your wedding.'

'I should say the same thing. Please, why don't

you go back to your wedding and enjoy the rest of your night.'

'Not so fast. I believe you promised me a dance later?'

She looked at him, not knowing what to say or do.

Again, he took her by the hand and led her away, this time into the night.

He'd never let her go.

Outrage, shame, disgust—but would life be worth living
Without the awkward moments?

scandal

Arb Blackwell. The new Mr Spires. Alone. Until . . .
The door slammed.

'Five years?' Mary screamed, throwing the paper on the War Room table.

Arb did not even look up from what he was doing.

She leaned over his shoulder and, speaking softly, as if trying to control the rising storm inside her, made plain her grievance.

'How the hell could you do this to me?' she breathed.

'Mare,' Arb finally said, 'you've been married for seven years.'

She was about to rebut when footfalls on the stairs announced the arrival of her husband.

Tom didn't try to restrain his smile. 'You sly dog,' he said, holding up a newspaper photo of the New World Project press launch that showed Isaac leaning past Anna to speak into the microphone. The seemingly innocuous action shot, linked with Tom's leer and the banner headline 'Blackwell's Secret Merger', suddenly reeked of scandal. 'But how could you not tell anyone?'

'Isn't it obvious?'

Glory O'Shay was distraught. She felt betrayed. Slighted. Worse than that, scooped.

Here she was, stuck on a glorified rustbucket of an oversized buoy, a shag on a rock literally in the middle of nowhere, in constant flirting distance of maledom's greatest prize—and she has to read in pieces written thousands of miles away that the contest was now closed.

Reactions wrestled with contingency plans and heroic fantasies of making him realise the error of his ways. She should move back to civilisation, she thought. She should give this game away, maybe. She had an uncle in real estate . . .

Focus, she told herself. There was only one thing to do—that was clear.

A bitter, vindictive, totally ruthless exposé of Blackwell's evil deception of the world.

Vengeance is a dish best served in the public spotlight.

There she is, thought Harry Pont.

The new Mrs Isaac Blackwell.

Hands black with grease, hair matted from sweat and sea-spray, shouldering burly labourers out of her way to fix a broken winch herself. Harry didn't know why he hadn't seen it before: they were patently made for each other.

'Hiding out?' he yelled above the grinding gears as the crank-engine kicked in.

'Your boys keep forgetting the lubricant!'

Typical. Although Harry still wasn't sure if this

was the diligent, never-let-anything-get-in-the-way-of-a-job Anna Spires that he knew so well, or an embarrassed, uncertain Mrs Blackwell retreating to what she did best.

'Well, I don't think they'll bother you down here!'

'I need to check the slings,' she said, pushing past him.

'You need,' said Harry, catching her under the elbow, 'to talk to old Harry.'

He saw her almost break into tears then and there in the bowels of the construction barge, then saw her hold them back with a fierce, determined sniff. For a few moments she kept her head bowed. When she raised it, she looked him in the eye and Harry saw the Anna he knew, the I-won't-be-beaten-and-God-have-mercy-on-the-souls-of-those-who-try Anna that he was so proud of.

*

The newsmedia had pounced on it: file photos, timelines, hearsay, rumours and an avalanche of reasons why everyone should have noticed it before . . .

'Well, they got the easy parts right,' Anna noted—the registry office, the judge sworn to secrecy, even photos of the official marriage certificate.

'They usually do,' said Harry, pacing the barge deck beside her.

'But . . . but . . .' She couldn't find the words; she couldn't understand why the media so often fell into making assumptions based on the easy stuff and seemed to forget—or deliberately ignore—the fact that life is more often than not built on circumstances without structure, situations without explanations, and personalities and feelings too complex to box, package and predict. '. . . don't you think they're getting a little carried away?'

'Five years is a long time for the world's most eligible bachelor to take you for a ride.'

'I suppose,' Anna agreed. 'But some of the things they wrote . . .'

Harry could only shake his head in sorry understanding. The media was clearly baffled by her: she was an engineer, yet she wasn't butch; she wasn't rich, or at least she hadn't been, and she wasn't normal, because normal people don't move mountains—or rather oceans—to make their dreams come true. Too hard to describe as she was, therefore, the media, he believed, had decided what she must have been.

Calculating, to succeed in a man's job in a man's world.

Calculating and seductive, to have landed the one man who might be able to make her dreams possible.

Calculating, seductive and obsessed, to have then made the possible happen.

'You know,' said Harry, 'they weren't right. But they weren't so far off either.'

Yes, she could be calculating. She had planned for her success, mapped out every inch of her career path and professional accomplishments before she turned seventeen. She had identified key goals and milestones, pinpointed potential allies and probable barriers, considered multiple scenarios. With the one exception of Isaac Blackwell, she had worked out exactly what she needed to do, then done it, done it all, done it all for a reason, reasons she had calculated a long time ago.

Yes, she was seductive. People liked her. Because she smiled, because she was polite, because she did her homework and thought before she asked or answered questions. She was well read and had a wide range of interests: in the arts, sport and current affairs. Yes, she was seductive, but not the way the papers insinuated. People liked her. And yes, she wanted them to like her. But she had no interest in anyone who was primarily attracted by a skirt, a flirt or possible dirt.

And yes, she was obsessive. Bull-headed might have been a better term. But there's a difference between fixating on a future so much that you become deluded, foolish and unreasonable, and working your butt off because you believe in the beauty of your dreams.

'So you think I am ambitious? Opinionated? Calculating, seductive and obsessive?'

Harry grinned as he steered her onto the runabout which would take them back to Platform Seven, back to face the Philo Group.

'In your own sweet way,' he said.

Suffice to say, there were some in the Philo Group who did not take the news too well.

'What the hell?'

'Don't believe in secrets, eh?'

'What does this mean for the project?'

'What should we do?'

'We should put out a statement.'

'We should arrange publicity.'

'We must call every investor.'

Anna sat quietly at the end of the table, her expression implacable, as Arb beside her tried to manage the panic. Finally it subsided, but only when an unfamiliar voice stated calmly: 'You must do nothing.'

Anna lifted her head to see a large Polynesian woman standing in the open doorway, her imposing frame brooking no disagreement.

'The media is the ultimate predator,' she said gravely, 'a relentless hunter, an insatiable appetite. It never stops hunting, never stops eating. Your only hope if you want to escape—and not everyone does, I admit—is to do nothing, and give it every chance to find a new prey to chase, a new target to stalk, a new tastier meal to devour.'

The Group was dumbstruck. Arb almost fell over himself when he realised who she was. But even as he rushed around the room to her, she continued, addressing Anna directly as if there was no one else in the room. 'You must understand: it's not a condemnation of your idea per se. If anything, take it as a compliment. It's simply the status quo trying to defend itself.'

'Anna, Group,' said Arb, taking the newcomer's hand. 'This is—'

'Laikali Rulé,' finished Anna, herself now circling the table, hand outstretched.

The awesome forces of nature and civilisation are actually
delicately unbalanced.
The slightest touch, even the very tiniest idea,
Might be enough to tip the world in a new direction.

walk with purpose

That night, Anna lay on her bed staring at the
ceiling, her body beaten and exhausted, but her
mind absolutely buzzing. To her own surprise,
however, her thoughts were not of could've-this
or should've-that regrets, nor were they of tomorrow's witty, vengeful responses to the stress-
laden media revelations of today. Instead, her
thoughts were focused on a day long ago, when
she was much younger, when the future seemed
even more beyond her control, when she was still
at university, when she first met Laikali Rulé.

She remembered the lecture hall . . . her friends
. . . her clothes! So many years ago, she mused.
How young she had been! How innocent!
Watching this great Polywaffle of a woman—the
great woman's own words—telling those girls,
telling her, about their potential.

It's a shame, she reflected, how despite
spending so much time daydreaming and
fantasising and practising award acceptance
speeches, most kids don't give themselves an even

money chance of ever achieving what they dream about. And if there are exceptions, kids with the boldness and self-confidence to believe in their dreams, then there are mothers and teachers and bosses to overcome. It's impossible to make it alone, she reflected, as she shrank into the middle of her bed. She herself had had so much luck, so much help: her father, especially, and of course her husband.

And other little things, moments that she hadn't realised at the time were so influential; events like Laikali's lecture. She had not given it a thought for so many years and yet tonight she could almost remember her speech to the letter. At least she thought she could—it didn't really matter if it wasn't the same. It was probably better now, customised, tailored to what she needed, tailored for her alone.

'I can see that there's no point in me telling you about what I do day-to-day,' was how the ambassador had started. She was addressing a reasonably well-attended meeting of the Women's Action Movement—or WAMO—although, truth be told, most of the students were there for socialising rather than low-risk solidarity, and certainly not for Laikali, who was unknown at the time. 'I can see by your faces that you're bored enough already, and I haven't even started yet.' There was a slight laugh from those who were listening and it was enough to get the rest to raise their heads, if only for a moment. 'I can appreciate that some of you are a little distracted right now by the rest of your lives and may not be in the mood for a career talk by a big fuzzywuzzy woman from the Pacific.' Using self-deprecation to break the ice is easy, thought Anna analysing her memory; using it to gain respect is an art form. 'I may not look like I do, but I know how it is to get disheartened by the size of the world around you, to get discouraged by the three or four years of the course before you, and then the two or three years after that of some grad course that you need in order to have a chance of getting into one of the good firms who'll treat you like shit for yet three more years because they can and because they were treated like shit when they were in your position.'

She paused for effect. She was good, even then.

'I understand what you're feeling. How can this possibly be worthwhile, I hear you say. How can I possibly make a difference? How can I possibly do what I want to, when what I want to do is change the whole world?'

She was a gifted speaker, able to look everybody in the eye at once. And Anna remembered her looking at them then, looking at each and every one of them, hard.

*

She had looked at each and every member of the Philo Group the same way that day.

'You're trying to change the world here, my friends. Some very powerful people are not going to like it because, right or wrong, you put their power at risk.'

But that was later, that was after Isaac had

stumble-charged around the table to introduce the new arrival.

'We've met actually,' Anna had said.

'We have?' Laikali had replied. It was her job to remember people and she was clearly not often surprised like this.

'It was a long time ago and I was just a face in a crowd. I was a student, and you were a Polynesian cultural ambassador touring the universities.'

'You know, Augusto did say you looked familiar.'

'I'm sorry, I don't know Augusto,' Anna had said, a little uncertain.

'Doesn't surprise me. He's dead,' Laikali had replied cryptically, gesturing into the air, 'and a bit of a fibber. Especially where young women are concerned.'

She should have seemed odd, Anna felt, but she didn't. Instead, she radiated confidence and power. Anna tried to place it and after a moment concluded that behind her eccentric cheerfulness, there was a steel in her voice which resonated with conviction.

Ambassador Rulé paused as a group of devastated young university women looked yearningly for her to say it wasn't so—even then, she had carried a capacity for reassurance—to say that despite how they felt, it wasn't true; that it was just a story they tell to scare university kids into studying harder.

But she wouldn't.

'So what to do, I hear you ask. Good question.

Well, the way I see it, you have two choices. You can ignore it or embrace these realities. Interestingly, the people who ignore them will actually *not* be so affected by them. In fact, their lives will be easier, more practical and less depressing. But then again, they won't be as challenged or inspired by life either.

'You're not alone with these questions, let me remind you. At one stage or another, every great achiever in history has had to make this choice. Hell, *even greater* men and women have probably passed through history unnoticed, too unnerved by just these questions, choosing instead to sit at home watching TV, tapestries or cave drawings—always waiting for a better time—never just the right moment—so full of potential that to use it would be to risk wasting it.

'You know the feeling. Everybody's felt this way. Overwhelmed by the world around you. Self-confined to inaction and corner-cowering. Doubters of the power of our very own dreams. We lie in our beds a little tireder, sit on the couch a little longer, ask ourselves what's the point in trying, beaten as we are into the belief of the impossibility of our significance—not beaten by actual events or circumstances, but by the fearful influences of pragmatism and conservatism that surround us.'

Again she paused.

'Before you all go and kill yourselves, let me say this.'

Only the extremely depressed were scribbling or daydreaming now. The rest she had in the palm of her hand, Anna included.

'Consider the awesome forces of nature and civilisation, so delicately balanced, so delicate, in fact, that the universe is always in motion, always in a state of self-correction and re-alignment, always leaning towards equilibrium but never quite there. You might *more accurately* say that the awesome forces of nature and civilisation are actually delicately *unbalanced*, and the slightest touch, the smallest movement, even the very tiniest idea, might be enough to tip the world in a new direction.'

She paused as sophomoric revelation dawned on her audience. She left the podium and moved into the aisles of the auditorium to hammer home her big finish.

'Ladies, every move you make will affect the balance of the world. So tip it, turn it, create it how you want it—because it will never stop changing— you might as well have a say in it. With or without you, ladies, this world will keep changing. And whether you like it or not, you will change it, because you get up in the morning, because you say hello to your friends, because you . . .'—she reached down and showily absconded an innocent note or doodle, read it to herself, chuckled and continued—'. . . have a great idea for your boy-friend's birthday present. Imagine the influence of a great idea for a book or the decision to have a baby or developing a new medicine, creating a new law or even a new way of life.

'Don't let the world overwhelm you. Don't forget, wherever you stand, the world lies beneath you and wherever you walk next will tip the whole balance—or imbalance—of the world. So walk with purpose, ladies. Walk with purpose.'

Anna stared at the ceiling. She hadn't thought about that day for years.

Laikali, Isaac had told her, was now a permanent secretary at the United Nations, a power broker of the highest order. She would be invaluable, he had said. Straight after the Philo Group had disbanded—some still fuming about secrets and deceptions, but all now resolved not to be undone by the predatory media—he had asked her to join them permanently.

And although Laikali had refused, stating that she would only stay with them a short time, there was something about her presence that Anna found comforting.

It had been a hard day—broken winches, Philo Group uproar, global revelations about a five-year deception—and Anna was exhausted. But Laikali's arrival had reminded her that good things were still possible. It was important to remember that, she told herself; it was so important, her thoughts repeated as she drifted off to sleep; so important, urged her father in his desperate loving way, as her head sank into the pillow, her arm fell across the body of her husband, and dreaming took over; so important to remember that good things were still possible.

The best form of defence is sensible attack.

the best form of defence

Good things were still possible.

But today, she saw them only as abominations . . .

'Today, I have with me the new Mrs Isaac Blackwell.'

. . . one of the prime motivations of her quest for a New World. Another example, she felt, of a good idea gone bad.

'Thanks, Glory. As always, a pleasure.' She tried to smile. But this was the seventeenth interview she had given today—and the seventeenth time that her identity had been lost inside her husband's.

In between their unsubtle invasions of privacy, they would smile at her and wink an empathetic eye. They seemed to think she might regard this as endearing.

They were wrong.

'It must be such a relief not to have to hide your love for each other anymore.'

They could achieve so much for the betterment of so many aspects of life, but instead bettered only the wallets of the media barons. They had the power to feed people's minds, but instead fed only the hunger of the masses for meaningless gossip and destructive criticism. Every now and then, a well-intentioned philanthropist would begin a bold endeavour to bring integrity to journalism through an even-handed, competent coverage of events and public affairs which actually made a difference to readers' lives. But inevitably, profits would fall, shareholders would change and the purpose of this bold endeavour would morph from altruism back to capitalism. The rationalisation would always begin with cries of 'market forces' and 'giving the customers what they want', then degenerate into unnecessary, and untrue, criticism of the 'self-righteous egotists' who had never had any right to claim the moral high ground.

'Yes, of course it's a relief and yet . . . I can't tell you how strange it feels to hold my husband's hand in public.' They shared a laugh. For an instant, Anna thought Glory was faking it also.

Overnight, Anna Spires had changed. Overnight, she had become interesting to the world. Suddenly and simultaneously, she had become inspiring—and detestable—to every woman on the planet. This Anna Spires, they now realised, normal and unglamorous by all indications, unremarkable and uninteresting (except for that mid-ocean project thing) by any reasonable measure, now held the hand, now wore the ring, now slept in the bed of the most desirable male alive.

Laikali Rulé's original direction to do nothing had come with a twist. Translated from politico-speak, 'do nothing' actually meant 'accept it, embrace it, run with it without excuse, without apology, without acknowledging that there might be even the slightest reason to consider this as a setback or compromise for the largest engineering project of all time'. It had worked like a charm. Not scenting impropriety, the media defaulted to gossip and romance.

'One final question,' said Glory. 'You know I have to ask it: how on earth did you land Isaac Blackwell?'

Seventeen interviews, seventeen identical final questions. She tried to overcome her irritation by remembering Isaac's instructions to view the media as a tool, *her* tool to turn against the system. But the thought only distracted her, reminding her of fatherly rants about poisonous minions used by the powers-that-be to spread their agendas to the unsuspecting masses . . .

'Excuse me, Ms Spires?'

'I'm sorry,' Anna said, refocusing. 'It's been a long day and I have a lot on my mind.'

'It's okay. We can edit that out. Let's try again . . . One final question. You know I have to ask it: how on earth did you land Isaac Blackwell?'

It occurred to Anna that the very same question had been thrown at her before she had even known that she had landed Isaac Blackwell. And while the ladies' room at a five-star hotel was now the pressroom on a modified mid-ocean oil rig, and while the billionaire-smitten wedding guest was now a gossip-smitten news reporter, one thing remained the same: she had the upper hand.

'Who knows how love happens?' she said, not answering the question. She had spent the whole day telling of wrong weddings and mystery identities. She was now toying with Glory's need-to-know, happy, as old Harry might have said, to leave her wanting more. 'That's what makes love so wonderful. You never know where it's going to come from, or when it's going to strike.'

man of the world

[days 14 to 34]

Among presidents, prophets, CEOs and billionaires, she found nothing;
With him, she found a friend, a fan, a philosopher . . . and a lover.

a man called Matthew Turner

The small tin-iron dinghy rocked back and forth. Natasha Spires arched her back, a stretch both to relieve the stiffness in her spine and the heavy sense of frustration she was feeling. Her body bent itself towards the sky, vertebrae cracking and settling, and she let out a long half-yawn, half-sigh. The sun was hot here. She brushed beads of sweat from the back of her neck.

They liked to get away like this. The sea was calm here, flat for nine days of every ten, they told her, for eleven months of the year. And the sounds and stress of the site were left far behind. *The runabout*, as they called it, was a modified lifeboat with a small but powerful outboard motor designed to ferry people between platforms. Although no sports vessel, she had more than enough guts to rattle far enough away that the whine of the hydraulic cranes was lost behind the soft constant lapping of the sea against the small tin-iron hull.

They had motored for over an hour today, some ten nautical miles, her sister estimated. Enough that only the top of the tallest platforms were visible as thin faint shapes to the west. Enough that for three hundred and fifty-nine degrees, there was blue, and only blue, between them and the horizon. Crystal clear above and shimmering below. If she let herself stare into the sky or over the side, Natasha could imagine the blurred blues enshrouding them, cocooning them in a new azure dimension.

At first, she had felt so small and insignificant in a space like this, herself and her sister the only living things she could see, the only sign of mankind on this face of the earth. But now, Anna having assured her that the dinghy would not capsize or run out of petrol or be attacked by sharks or whales, it had become an oasis. For both of them.

She looked at her sister reclining against the bow, her face covered by a big sunhat. She hoped she was sleeping, and did not speak in case she was. Anna needed to clear her head—of the pressure, of the criticism, of anything to do with the thin faint shapes that stained the horizon some ten nautical miles to starboard.

The sun was hot here. Hot and constant. Almost too constant, like the tension back at the base.

'Tell whoever it is to fuck off! I don't want to speak to anyone,' Anna had said earlier that day, sick of the intrusions and completely unable to tolerate what she saw as continuing invasions of her privacy.

'I don't care if—'

'It's the President of the United States.'

'—it's the President of the United States.' Then more meekly, 'It's the President of the United States . . . of America?'

'Yes, Ms Spires. Would you like me to tell him to "fuck off"?'

Good ol' Xavier, Anna thought, staring at the warm glowing inside of her sunhat. Never had two words e'er been spoken with such decorum and professionalism.

Wow, she had thought to herself . . . and then, ah! 'Why not?But before you do, get him to leave a number, and tell him I'll call him back some time next week.'

For the first, and last, time, Anna thought she had seen Xavier hesitate, although she couldn't be sure. 'Yes, Ms Spires.'

Then he was gone. Her throat had felt a little tense. She had breathed a little heavily. She had felt a tingle in her fingers; a shiver had crept up her back; her feet had begun to tap hyperactively; then suddenly, her head had been abuzz and she had smiled uncontrollably—YES MS SPIRES!!! OH YEAH!! It's not every day you tell the President of the US of A to go his own sweet way!

And then Xavier was back. 'Next Thursday, Ms Spires?' he had said straight-faced. 'I said that would be fine, although it means shifting your appointment to spit in the French President's face.'

Good ol' Xavier.

She breathed deeply, thankful that Natasha had dragged her away from there. The last ten days had seen interest in her rise and rise, to a point where she felt she would explode if anyone else asked for a piece of her time.

It wasn't so much the leaders of state and industry, who had begun to form a queue for her attention, that bothered her. Her husband's advice, 'just ignore them,' she had originally discarded with a 'hmmph—easy for you to say'. But as usual, he had been right: it was not as hard to ignore them as she had imagined. After all, they couldn't force her to speak to them.

More annoying was the mosquito-like press whose presence had increased substantially since the marriage revelations and subsequent public interviews. Their ubiquitous buzzing around the facilities—like the wind echoing down every corridor—was impossible to avoid and made her feel like someone trying to sleep but unable to ignore their incessant sound and forced to just wait in the darkness for the circling drone to swoop and sink in its fangs or its stinger or proboscis or whatever the hell mosquitoes use to bite people.

But they, too, were not the issue really riling her up right now. In fact, Isaac said that their public relations counterattack was working very well. The media, she knew, was a necessary evil and, nuisance-factor aside, she could deal with them.

No, for what was pissing her off so much, she had only herself to blame.

She had brought her major aggravation to the New World herself. Handpicked them herself—

although Isaac had provided the shortlist, she tried to rationalise—but no, when it was all said and done, she had been the one who selected them.

It wasn't that they were incompetent or less specialised than she had expected—far from it, the Philo Group was perhaps the most impressive think-tank in the world. They were visionaries in their fields, the foremost thinkers in economics, sociology, engineering and technology; they were idealists, all having doctorates, dissertations or comprehensive theories about how to improve the prevailing systems of society, including governments, markets, industry and welfare; they were visionaries, idealists, scholars, experts, geniuses . . .

. . . and they were self-centred, narrow-minded arseholes.

Taz had arrived on the day of the initial press conference, a surprise arranged for Anna by Isaac. A flight to Singapore; a berth on the media boat bound for the middle of nowhere; small talk with cynical sensationalists who had no idea who she was; and finally, the proud awe when her sister's floating interim civilisation had appeared over the blue horizon. The vessel had arrived just in time for the show (or perhaps the show had been held over waiting for it to arrive), and she had squeezed into the back of the pressroom to sneak a few photos of her sister presenting her vision for a New World.

Later, there had been hugs and kisses, maybe a tear or two. But then Anna had had to go.

Reviewing news coverage or something. She had hardly seen her since. Even in the few hours they had spent at this mid-sea refuge, few words had been spoken. Taz could see the pressure showing on her sister's face, her eyes drawn and shaded, her voice tired and frustrated. Best to give her some respite, the sort only family can give: default solitude, but with an option for company and support should she ask for it.

The problem, as Natasha saw it, was a side effect of the marriage revelation. While Laikali Rulé's press strategy had more than appeased those outside the project, it had failed to deal with the reaction of those inside. Suddenly, her sister's merit was suspect, and Anna could feel the Philo Group's confidence in her slipping. She had begun to sense condescension and mistrust whenever she addressed them.

To win them over, to assert her qualifications, to prove her worth, Anna had taken on more and more responsibility. Taz could see that her sister was now carrying a lot of pressure, and carrying it alone, refusing to share or delegate it: there was the construction itself, for which Anna oversaw all the plans, all the progress, all the problems; there was the press, for whom Anna insisted on reading her own statements as well as placating the growing gossip reporters; and then of course there was organising the Philo Group itself . . .

For the first four or five days following the press launch, Anna reflected, the Philo Group meetings had gone well enough. For the most part, these

War Room gatherings had been getting-to-know-you sessions, broad technical briefings and light policy discussions. To begin with, these 'warm-ups', as Isaac called them, had been constructive and team building, including an excellent, if animated, discussion of potential New World names—but lately these preliminary talks had been 'heating up'.

Concurrent with these preliminary meetings, each member of the Group had also been preparing a presentation in his or her area of expertise, highlighting the key objectives that a New World, a state-of-the-art world able to start from scratch, without any preconditions or 'baggage', should aim for.

When determining the agenda she and Isaac had thought long and hard about whether to start or finish with Anna's ideas for what the world should look like, what its objectives and overriding philosophy should be and how it should want to be positioned vis-à-vis the rest of the world. In the end, however, they had decided that she speak last. This way, the experts could state their ideals before Anna set any parameters for their thinking.

This option was also better for team building, Isaac had said. It was crucial for team members to trust each other given the challenges that lay ahead. The best way to achieve this, he was sure, would be to let them see each other's skills, and realise that together they were a formidable team. A formidable team supported by the technology, finance and workforce to make their visions happen.

The delivery of these presentations had begun just a week ago. Anna, with high hopes and genuine excitement, had expected to marvel at their genius, to be amazed by their insights, to revere and gasp and nod repeatedly at their ideas.

Unfortunately, her expectations had quickly faded—instantly evaporated, in fact—the second the short-sighted cement-headed egotists had opened their mouths.

Arrogant self-important slime—Natasha didn't know how Anna could sit in the same room as them for hours and hours as had become the norm. Taz herself had joined them for dinner just once and that once, seated in Siberia between Saul Obermann and Byron Lybrand, had been more than enough for her. Supreme patronisation on one side and an ivory-tower statistician on the other, the former had spent the evening tolerating her, the latter trying to understand why he could not understand her.

And Anna had to deal with them every day, every day for the next thousand.

Poor girl, Taz thought, as she closed her eyes and let the warmth of the sun wash over her face and her body. *Don't worry*, she telepathised, as the heat enveloped her in a welcome heavy weight, making her sleepy. *They don't know who they're dealing with.*

Saul Obermann, the economist, had presented first.

A master of the market, one of the few leading practitioners who was also a respected academic, he'd written theses, advised Federal Reserve Chairmen and made a million from his own trading—you'd have thought he'd have had more vision.

'Our priority must be to develop trading relationships and an absolutely free market,' he had begun, getting straight to the bottom line. 'This is the key to creating a society that allocates resources efficiently and therefore can be self-sustaining and progressive.'

He speaks like he's reading a broker's report, Anna decided, looking at the pinholes of light peppering the inside of her sunhat but picturing the War Room one week ago.

'To do this, we must establish a production capacity equivalent to the best in the world. To do that, we require infrastructure and people.'

No—an academic report—that matter-of-fact, assertion-of-unquestionable-conclusions tone.

'Infrastructure, the engine of our enterprise, must be cutting edge yet flexible, scalable and upgradable. Plus, secondly, on top of that, we must attract the best and brightest human resources, the fuel of our endeavour, educated leaders, ambitious innovators and skilled labourers willing to work hard.'

It had been impressive to begin with—numbers and economic models and sensitivity scenarios and utopian market case studies—but it had soon become apparent to Anna as he droned on that this was nothing more than a résumé, hiding behind a cohesive yet unstirring theory about perfect capital markets. There had been only one question asked at the end of the lecture, and he had answered it exactly as Anna imagined he would.

'This is not my opinion, Ms Spires. This is the opinion of twenty-five years of research and experience.'

I'm sorry I asked, she had thought to herself.

Jay Diaglio's presentation, the following day, had at least been easier to listen to.

'Friends,' the political advisor had said, his arms outstretched, 'a beautiful day approaches. A day like no other.' He used no notes. 'A day when society can start anew without the unfortunate legacies that history has provided all our homelands.' Smoothly, naturally, he caught each spectator's eye, engaging them personally as he spoke. Then seriously he had changed his tone. 'But a shadow, a cloud,' *a mixed metaphor?* 'looms over what we do. India and Indonesia, both overcrowded and militarily capable, stand to our north and north-east. Africa, starving for economic and technological development, stands to our west . . .' *So?* '. . . while we—a New World without poverty, without castes, without a history of tribal conflict—stand alone between them all.' *I don't think I like where this is going.* 'The ultimate symbol and proud achievement of western ideology and technological advancement.' *Now hold on right there.* 'Surrounded by political unpredictability. Let us be clear that the establishment of political ties should be our first priority.'

'Now hold on right there.' This time she had said it out loud.

'Now, Anna, we said no interrup—'

'I know what we said, but I also know that we never said this was a symbol of western ideology. We also never said,' turning her gaze towards Obermann, 'that this would follow the "last model standing" after the Cold War, regardless of how long we've studied it.'

'This is ridiculous,' Obermann had burst out.

'Do you have any idea what you're talking about?' Diaglio had cried, dismissing her presence with a theatrical backhand.

'These people are experts,' Isaac had said, clearly becoming uncomfortable. But he must have known this would happen, thought Anna—happen later, he must have thought, or hoped—much later than the second presentation. She knew what he must have been thinking: that he wouldn't be able to protect her for long if she went on like this.

'Yes,' she had said to them, 'but these have been presentations by experts of exactly the systems which have ultimately led us to the desperate act of having to create a New World as far away as possible from their old ones.'

Silence followed.

Then again, Anna reflected, she had always been able to stand up for herself.

The warm sun had put both Taz and Anna to sleep, and neither noticed the old trawler crawling between the blue sea and sky towards them. They both just lay there contentedly: Anna, slumbering beneath the shade of her sunhat; Taz, unhatted, snoozing dreamily, the sun weaving crazy coloured contours through her closed eyelids.

Taz stretched out full length, her young supple frame feeling longer and stronger in the heat. Despite her current role as resident sun-bather on Platform Seven, she was daydreaming about lying on a beach when some sixth sense told her to open her eyes.

The trawler had pulled alongside. Taz didn't move. Flat on her back, she looked up to see its tatty flaky blue-white rusted steel hull hanging over her.

Her immediate response was fear—*could they be modern-day pirates or kidnappers? how far were they from the base? would anyone hear if she screamed?*—then concerns for her sister. A rustling beside her told her Anna was now also awake and aware of their new company. Out of the corner of her eye, Taz saw her sister's sunhat-covered face tilt back and look up with the same alarm.

Footsteps above, approaching the rail. Both sisters motionless, not sure what to do.

Then the footsteps stopped. And a head appeared over the side.

His hair was ragged and unkempt, not long but standing out eccentrically around his head—much like Einstein's, except brown-not-grey, young-not-old, standing out-and-down-not-out-and-up. And he was smiling. Fear faded away . . .

'Hello,' he said. 'My name's Matthew Turner. I'm looking for the New World Project and a woman named Anna Spires. Can you help me?'

The first boat person was escaping neither political nor
   economic persecution,
But a lack of ideas and inspiration.

the refugee

Their fear had quickly become fascination, then relief, then embarrassment. Anna was the first to recover.

'I'm afraid I've never met Anna Spires,' she said, hidden behind her hat and sunglasses.

Natasha, who had been about to speak herself, coughed and spluttered instead.

'She's a very busy, important person, you know,' continued Anna. 'Why do you need to see her?'

'I'm delivering a package—door-to-door, personal service, that sort of thing. It's imperative that I find her.'

'What's in the package?' asked Anna.

'I'm sorry, but that's classified information.'

'You don't exactly look like you're from UPS.'

'My truck broke down. I had to flag down this passing fishing trawler. Can you take me to her?'

Anna turned to her sister, as if asking what she thought. Taz did not need to fake her indecision.

'Yes,' Anna said finally. 'But only if you tell us what the package is.'

Taz watched the stranger, this man named Turner, as he feigned professional anguish. He was cute, she decided, in an average kind of way.

'Okay,' he said, melodramatically reluctant, pulling a sportsbag from out of sight and throwing it down to the dinghy. With a wave to his former escorts, he awkwardly climbed down after it.

'Well,' said Anna, when he was safely on board, 'what's this package that you so urgently need to deliver to Anna Spires?'

Having cautiously seated himself on the rocking boat, he looked up to answer her question, his expression somehow managing to look both ashamed and pleased with himself.

'It's me.'

Arb looked out towards the horizon.

She was out there somewhere, no doubt brooding, thinking, worried to death about the confrontation she had begun within the Philo Group.

She had been right, of course. They were proposing modifications instead of new models. Improvements instead of original ideas.

She had been right, of course, even though he hadn't said so.

They just didn't get it—simple as that—they just didn't get it. Thus Anna's desire to swear at presidents.

The upshot of the last meeting was that there would be no more presentations—there was no point listening to career-prepared theory and rhetoric—until after Anna had outlined exactly what the premise of the New World was *initially* supposed to be. Mary Minken had insisted on the qualification, stating that everything had to be up for debate and everyone was there to work together.

Anna would present her vision for the New World tomorrow—she would make them get it. Tomorrow morning, the floor was hers, the shield behind which Arb had kept her ideas safe and secret was about to be torn away. This was not the press. These people knew what they were talking about—that's why they were here: because they knew more than she did about a great many things.

His only comfort was they did not know more about the New World Project.

'They're converted drilling platforms,' she said— Josephine was her name, she'd said. 'Actually, they don't drill at all. They are purely living quarters and office space.'

At first, Matt couldn't tell what she was pointing at. The old trawler and its hardy samaritan crew had turned and motored away, while the three of them in the dinghy puttered the other way towards what he initially thought was an empty horizon. Looking again, his gaze had fallen on the faint small sticks poking out of the sea-level skyline. Soon they were shapes, black indefinable shapes, and then they started to come into focus. The closer they got, the clearer became the unmistakable skeletal outlines of oil rigs.

As they whirred and puttered closer, there were other shapes, smaller forms that crawled beneath the towers.

'You can't quite make them out yet, but those other shadows are barges and supply ships. We use the barges to insert the pipewalls.'

'The what?'

They were still a long way out from the oil platforms when Josephine pointed to a bending line of bright orange buoys.

'You see those markers? They form a circle about seven kilometres across. As we get in closer, you'll see another marked circle—we call them circles of construction or the three rings—anyway, the second circle is about a kilometre across. The third circle is right at the centre and it's only eighty metres across. The pipewalls are circular walls, kind of like pipes, that we are building into the ocean where those buoys are. Once we bail out the water, we'll build a city in the space inside.'

Matt looked on incredulously. This floating, fledgling civilisation stood before him like a flag in the sand—somehow the vast immeasurable ocean around him had been claimed. It was like a lost world, now found; a mythical place, no longer legend. Where for days there had only been endless blue, his destination now rose, as if from the depths, before his very eyes.

'It'll be dark by the time we get there,' Josephine said.

Matt was startled to see the sun beginning to set now, so entranced was he by the sight around him. He didn't know what he'd expected to find but the presence of order, of development, of so many people, surprised him. He felt small. Like a child in the city on his own for the first time. A little helpless. Overwhelmed.

Maybe this had been a bad idea.

'This is a bad idea, isn't it?' asked Arb of Laikali.

'This is leadership,' she replied. 'And this is only the beginning.'

'I'm just not sure what we'll achieve except division.'

'Are her ideas really so outlandish?'

Laikali watched as Arb briefly hesitated, his consummate mastery of appearances momentarily failing him.

'Good,' she said before he could answer.

'I'm just saying,' said Arb, back-pedalling, 'that the Philo Group are not likely to consider them as realistic.'

'What, like this hole in the ocean?'

'Touché,' acknowledged Arb, tipping his brow, 'but you and I both know that it might be best if she just gave them a broad outline of her ambitions and then stepped back, got out of the way, focused on the engineering, which is a very important job, and let them get on with what they do better than anyone.'

'Yes,' said Laikali, nodding gravely, 'if you were aiming to do something best, but you're not. You're—'

'Aiming to do something new,' said Anna.

'Exactly,' said Laikali as she and Arb turned to see Anna, clad in hat and sunglasses despite the set sun, in the doorway. She was flanked by her sister and a stranger.

Husband and wife locked stares, defying each other for a moment.

'Who's your friend?' asked Arb, flinching first and deftly changing the subject by pointing at the newcomer with his chin.

Natasha leapt dramatically back beside him before launching into a ringmaster's pose, 'Ladies and gentlemen! Boys and girls! The Spires School of Human Fishermen is proud to present—'

'Matthew Turner,' he said, cutting her off, stepping forward and shaking Arb's hand.

'Isaac Blackwell.'

'Matthew Turner,' he repeated, taking Laikali's hand.

'Laikali Rulé.'

Then he turned on his heel and faced his chief tour guide.

'Matthew Turner,' he said again, putting out his hand. 'I'm sorry, but I forget your name. It was . . .?'

'Spires. Anna Spires,' she replied smiling broadly. 'When did you know?'

'The Spires School of Fishermen gave it away,' he said, lying. He had recognised her the moment he saw her.

Anna turned to Natasha, hands on hips, 'That's the last time I fake my identity with you around.'

'We found him hitchhiking his way here on a fishing trawler!' said Natasha, excitedly diverting the stageplay.

'I hope you don't mind. I saw you on television,'

Matt said, looking eagerly back to Anna. 'I came to help, to offer my assistance in any way I can.'

Arb spoke up: 'Well, there is a human resources department under development—'

'Isaac!' cried Natasha. 'Later. Later we'll send them there. But this is our first refugee. He's the first man to give away everything he owns to come here. He saw Anna on television twelve days ago, at his home in Sydney, then he packed a bag, left his house and thumbed his way across the whole of Australia—then across the Indian Ocean!'

'I meant to ask,' said Anna. 'What was it I said that so caught your attention?'

Matt shook his head, 'You know, for almost two weeks I've thought a lot about this, in trains, trucks and that smelly old fishing boat. But truly, I can barely remember a word.'

He saw her exhale—and knew he had disappointed her.

'But I remember you said it like you meant it.' Anna's eyes glanced up. Matt saw it and his chest filled with resolve. 'I knew straight away that this was going to be something special and I wanted to be part of it.'

'So how do you propose to contribute to this special something of ours?' she asked.

'Ah, I'm not entirely sure. To tell you the truth, I've got no idea.'

'Well, what exactly do you do?' said Arb, stepping into his vision. 'You do work, don't you?'

'Of course, absolutely . . . well, sort of. I get paid for it if that's what you mean.'

'For what exactly?'

'I make games.'

'Games?' repeated Arb and Natasha simultaneously.

'What sort of games?' asked Laikali.

'Well, any sort really. I've made computer games, video games, board games, board room games, business games—training-type stuff. Any sort really.'

The conversation paused awkwardly.

'What's your favourite?' said Laikali finally.

Matt Turner shifted his weight from one foot to the other, seemingly a little uncomfortable with the question. 'You mean what's the favourite I've made, or what's my favourite game of all games?'

'Both.'

'Well . . .' he said, his gaze wandering around the room as if searching for his answer when he was suddenly captured by those eyes, Anna's eyes, filled with the idealistic intensity that had first so captivated him. He stuttered and stammered and then, like a mother having to break stride, reach back and pull her lagging child from a toy store window, he had to consciously drag his own eyes around to Laikali. 'Well, I've done a number of God games which I'm quite proud of.'

'God games?' Arb said, stepping forward.

'Sorry?' he said, remembering Arb was in the room.

'What are God games?'

'To use industry-speak, they're scenario simulations, where the player takes the role of a god or a president or an all-powerful leader of a historical or made-up society. It works best on a computer where you can simulate the colonisation of a planet or the reconstruction of Rome or the—'

'Building of a new city?'

Surprise and then excitement ran through him as he turned to Laikali and tried to sound as professional as possible, 'Yes. Yes, of course.'

'So, did you ever make a God game?' asked Taz.

'Yes, yes, I've made several.'

'Well, recommend me one,' she said. 'Which one are you proudest of?'

'Hmm.' He always had a tough time recommending this one, but he always loved doing it. 'Well, if you insist, then you might try to pick up a copy of the Future Turn series.'

'Future Turn!' Taz laughed out loud. Anna, however, did not react.

'What's it about?' Arb asked seriously.

'Well, they are a series of games all based around the premise of rebuilding a society after a great disaster—after the Future takes a Turn for the worse. So in the first game you get to rebuild Los Angeles after an earthquake. In other games, it's London if they lost World War II, or Kabul after the discovery of the world's richest oil vein. In the latest version, Future Turn: Salvation, you're in charge of this gigantic spaceship—it holds a million people— escaping the impending destruction of Earth and your mission is to colonise new planets throughout the galaxy.'

'So you have to manage two societies?' Laikali asked, intrigued. 'One on the planet you are colonising, and the society on the starship itself.'

'Well, yes, yes that's right.'

'And what's your favourite of all games?' asked Anna's sister.

'Yes, Mr Turner,' urged Laikali, watching him closely, 'what is the best game of all time?'

'Well, if I had to choose, I'd choose chess, although I'm not very good at it—too little luck involved. I need games of chance, with more room for gamesmanship and guile. But it's a silly question really, like choosing the best book or best song. Everything's a game of some sort, don't you think, Mr Blackwell?'

'Call me Isaac, please.'

'Don't you think . . . Isaac?'

'We don't play games here, Mr Turner,' Arb replied firmly.

Matt's response was automatic, trained, the result of years of reactive provocation. He said it and regretted it immediately: 'You might be surprised.'

He had no choice now but to stand his ground. They both held their stares a second longer than they needed to.

Natasha tilted her head interestedly between them, resorting once again to levity to get back to more interesting topics.

'So Mr Turner—Matt—God games are your favourite of what you've done, chess is your favourite for all time, but—'

'But what game do you do best?'

Even though his words were innocuous, Matt couldn't help but feel that Isaac Blackwell's question was assessing more than just his pastimes.

He chose an answer partly in jest but mostly to avoid a contest—Matt suspected that his new host did not back down from a challenge, or the opportunity to make one, very often.

'Drinking games, Isaac. I hold my own at drinking games.'

'Excellent!' cried Taz. 'Come, let me show you around and then you should join us this evening for dinner and then drinks at Jabba's Palace.'

'Yes,' said Arb impatiently, obviously wanting to get back to business, 'and then maybe tomorrow we'll be able to figure out something for you to do here, maybe some computer modelling or scenario envisioning or something.'

'We'll do nothing of the sort,' said Laikali magnanimously. 'The way I see it, Mr Turner, you're the first person I've seen here who actually has experience in building a New World from scratch. Now I've had to decline their offer to join them full-time, but if Ms Spires and Mr Blackwell don't mind, I'd like you to be my representative on the Philosophy Group which guides this ragtag ensemble.'

All eyes turned to Anna.

Matt watched as her mouth widened into an intrigued grin . . . but would she say yes?

'If that's the only way to keep you involved, Laikali,' she said finally, 'then it's fine with me.'

'Of course, you'd have to help out in other ways,' Laikali said to Matt. Then to Anna: 'Although I think you'll be surprised at just how useful Mr Turner might turn out to be.'

'Well then,' said Taz, pulling on the hook she

had around Matt's arm and wheeling him towards the door, 'I suppose if I plucked you out of the sea and found you a job, I really should give you a tour and find you a place to sleep. And remind me tomorrow to take a bigger boat—if I'm going into this recruiting business . . .'

'Mr Turner.'

It was Anna.

He stopped anxiously at the door, concerned she was about to change her mind.

'I apologise for my welcoming ruse.'

'Don't worry about it,' said Matt. 'Sometimes, I'd rather be someone else, myself.'

'It's just one of those days. Everyone seems to want a piece of me, and there's so much to do, and I have a lot on my mind. You understand?'

'You'll find a way.'

You'll find a way, he had said, the phrase flooding Anna's mind with thoughts and memories. A moment later, when she returned to the present, the forces arrayed against her suddenly seemed less overwhelming.

Matt watched as a smile washed over her face, and he felt it rush through his entire being.

'Welcome,' she said, 'to the only game in town.'

It's not a maze. There is no cheese.
There are no wrong turns and no dead ends.
Just don't stand still and you'll find your way.

finding her way

'If you simply want to know, then let me tell you,'
her father would say. 'But if you want to learn,
you'll just have to work hard and pay attention.'

In this way, their roles were defined. She would
put her head down to think harder, and he would
then deliver his next line, giving her the confidence
she so desperately pined for: 'You'll find a way,'
he'd say.

Considering her later life, it was probably not
surprising to anyone that as a child, Anna loved to
make things. Be it building or fixing, creating or
improving, she liked finding problems and designing solutions. Without meaning to, she came
to love any challenge and, especially with her
father watching over her shoulder, found that she
liked working hard for things.

'Do you remember the time when you wanted
to be able to turn your bedroom light off from your
bed?'

At home, she would make Christmas cards out
of brown paper and photos cut from magazines.
She liked to use her hands. She could sew a hem or

hammer a nail, repair a dress or a chair alike. If she wasn't to be found digging around her father's workshop or her mother's craft boxes, then chances were she was 'inventing' something of her own in her room. Initially, these ground-breaking inventions involved toppling a run of dominoes which tipped a rod that set a tennis ball rolling across and off a table into a net which pulled a pulley which . . . well, which didn't do anything except pull the pulley—which was okay, this was just the beginning. She had bigger plans. Much bigger plans. She just didn't know what they were . . . yet.

'Do you remember, Grubbergirl?' her father would say, dragging out his antagonistic exercise in daughter embarrassment.

Like most schoolgirls, her room was her retreat, her space, but it held nothing of the usual 'teen idol' posters or girly things one might have expected. In fact, a stranger thinking in stereotypes might have initially thought it a boy's room. If the stranger were a robber in the night, he'd have had to pick his way carefully over a veritable worksite of dominoes, Lego blocks or Meccano construction sets (depending on her age at the time), littered across the floor, to get to the only likely booty that lined the far side of the room in the form of hand-crafted Christmas cards, 3D jigsaws, painted model ships and airplanes. The booty, as in a museum, changed from season to season, age to age, to reflect popular trends—or at least the curator's interest in those trends.

'Your room was a great big mess, just like it is

today.' It didn't matter when he told the story. 'And you thought that you were getting too old to have parents tuck you in and turn off the light.'

There was no jewellery box to steal or plunder, only a couple of simple pendants or rope bracelets left carelessly on rare, spare corners of bench space. A computer huddled amidst papers, plans and boxes on a desk which itself stood in the far corner of the room, away from the door and out of the way of the always-in-progress construction—the worksite foreman's office, as it were. Indeed, a wise robber, on surveying the room, would have quickly changed his focus from theft to industrial espionage, taking the time to read the diaries and notepads that lay stacked in the overfilled desk drawers, or hacking into the computer instead of absconding with and fencing it, because he'd have realised that the most profitable booty in this room was the potential of the one who slept in it. Armed with this *inside information*, he should have then followed the course of her life, become a strategic stalker, following her until the moment came to invest in her and her inevitable success.

'But you needed us to tuck you in since it was impossible, as it remains today, to make your way safely from the door to your bed in the dark. I used to tease you every day about finding a way to solve the problem.'

The clues were there, if only the stranger-robber-industrial stalker knew what to look for, clues that in hindsight would have provided some illumination of Anna's future. A fishtank stood against one wall. It was deceptively large, the stranger fooled by the crammed nature of the space both without and within the glass walls. The aquarium was filled with a typical schoolgirl's fish—goldfish mostly—but not the usual piscine paraphernalia. In fact, instead of a castle or coloured rocks, the fish roamed in and out of a sunken doll's house. It was one of those houses that unfolded into two halves and had been left open to allow the owner to see inside, rearrange the furniture and so forth.

'And I remember you saying, almost daring me to disagree, "I'll find a way".'

It was hard to tell whether the fish regarded the house as a home. They simply acted as fish act, seeming not to notice anything, their only goals to swim, eat, swim and wait for the food to appear again. In this way, you could say they were happy living in the doll house in the fishtank in Anna's room—after all, she fed them well.

'And you did find a way, jerry-rigging some strings and levers across the ceiling so that you could turn the light out from your bed.' If he was telling the tale to an audience, he'd turn and proudly shrug his shoulders, lamenting, 'She was supposed to clean the place up!'

Unbeknown to the fish, Anna had built the house specifically for them. She'd done it because she just thought it would be nice for the fish to live in a house like everybody else did.

'You'll find a way,' her father would say when she was faced with a challenge. And even if he didn't tell it, she knew that he was thinking about the jerry-rigged light switch story.

Every night, having tucked herself in and pulled the cord that flipped the lever that tugged the string that flicked the switch, the room would be bathed in the soft glow of the aquarium lights. And every night, some time later, sometimes before she fell asleep, sometimes after, the door would creak and a shaft of white light would creep across the idea-strewn floor. Although she often feigned sleep, Anna took great comfort from the silhouette that silently appeared to check on her.

'Sweet dreams, Grub,' he would say. And she would smile—even, she believed, if she was sleeping.

Older now. Wiser now. But Anna knew that the words her father would have used if she had told him her tale of woe were exactly the same.

'You'll find a way,' he would have said.

She knew exactly what she would tell the Philo Group tomorrow. She had known for so long: known when she left home, known when she stopped speaking to her mother, known when she began studying engineering, known when she chose her first job and every subsequent career move. In fact . . .

. . . she had known since the day her father died.

They were the most brilliant minds of our time,
Plus one.

more siren suckers

They all had amazing résumés, extensive working histories, outstanding academic and industry backgrounds. And they all had well-rehearsed introductory speeches about how they'd ended up here.

They weren't all dining together tonight, Matt discovered; for some reason two of them had decided to eat in their quarters, Laikali Rulé had had some important phone calls to make, and Anna had retreated to her quarters to prepare a presentation for the following morning. But over dinner and a few bottles of wine, the rest all took a quick turn explaining how and why they them-selves had come to be here . . .

. . . there was Sanjay Mathur:

'Mr Blackwell literally chased me all over India. He was like a ghost of my childhood from whom I could not escape, or a bad case of the Bombay flu. I drove to Delhi for a book signing one day and there waiting for me, copy of my book in one hand, outrageous proposal for a New World in the other, was Mr Blackwell. A polite rejection, thank you but no thank you, and you'd think that would be all. But then I flew to Calcutta to watch a cricket match, and there he was again. I'm sorry, Mr Blackwell. I cannot, Mr Blackwell. Then on a train through Bengal: there he was! I deliberately, on the spur of the moment, changed all my plans and diverted to Rajastan: and there, among those ancient sandy castles, he appeared again. Finally, to escape my ghost, I had to embrace it—and here I am.'

*

. . . there was Harry Pont:
'Well, I'm happy to say that my ghost was much prettier than Sanjay's. Anna turned up at a railway tunnel I was building through the Rocky Mountains. She told me what she was doing, and I told her, interesting enough as it sounded, I was booked for, well, pretty well until the end of the decade.'

There were raised eyebrows but understanding head-bobs all around the table.

'Anyway, the next thing I know, she's booked a cabin on the mountainside and every day for the next month, first thing in the morning, she's there waiting for me with a thermos of hot coffee and, well, let's just say, ask anyone that knows me—I'm a sucker for a good cup of coffee.'

. . . there was Byron Lybrand:
'Actually, I've worked with Mr Blackwell for the last eleven years. I do a lot of things: I'm

his financial advisor, accountant sometimes, a professional mathematician by training, sociology researcher most of my career, until I met Mr Blackwell, of course, and, well, my role here is actually as social scientist and chief statistician.'

'Statistician?'

Arb explained, 'Byron knows, or is able to access, more quantitative research than any man on the planet. You want to know how many rabbits are living in Greenland, he'll tell you; you want to know the last time twelve people sat in a room and determined the fate of the planet, he'll tell you. Byron's our way of basing our decisions on real data and our defence against trying to achieve the impossible.'

. . . there were Thomas Mills and Mary Minken, the husband and wife historian team:

'I've known Isaac since the cradle,' said Mary, her red wine glass poised whilst she orated like East Coast royalty, as if she was choosing baser words than usual to match her audience. 'Our mothers used to play poker together. Even so, I only made it here because of my beloved Tom.'

Tom gave her a good-humoured nudge with his elbow as he took over storytelling duties: 'My speciality is ancient history—you know, Egypt, Mesopotamia, Mayans. Technically, my field's anthropology, you know, studying the development of mankind and all that by digging up old cultures with funny writing and dead languages. Mary here studies the modern stuff, more familiar languages and history that might still

142

be standing in some places—anything from the Renaissance to the Cold War. Zaccy boy here called us because—'

'Don't I know you?' said Matt. There was something about his face.

'I doubt we've ever met,' said Tom nodding, reluctantly it seemed. 'But you probably know my father . . .'

'That state Governor.'

Tom gave him an overacted congratulatory wink, 'So, after all that frilly stuff about my expertise and whatnot, now you know why I'm here.'

There was polite laughter around the table; Arb, too, grinned, shaking his head and wagging his finger.

. . . there was Helen Rainey:

'As a matter of fact, I helped Anna choose the very location we're sitting in today. She came to me one day—I didn't know her, had never met her—until this one day this woman who just wouldn't hear no walks in and says she has this idea for building a city on the ocean floor by sticking a straw seven kays wide on its end and sucking out the water and where, she asks, where would the best spot on the planet be to stick such a straw.

'Anyway, this is all just too much for someone to take in one go. I tell her to let me think about it, but she says no. "I'm obviously in the right place," she says, and she proceeds to keep questioning me about suitable ocean topography, weather patterns, tidal ocean currents, tectonic plates, and four hours later, *four hours* she hounded me, four hours later we have a site—not exactly here, but pretty close; they needed to do sonar tests and other experiments to check the ecology and also make sure the ground would be stable enough. Anyway, some years later, after I took my own turn at barging into *her* office, I received a very kind offer to join the Philo Group.'

. . . there was Miles Alia:

'I'm the geeky member of the team, the guy who likes the glow of his computer better than sunlight, the bug-eyed techno-nerd who does everything from ordering pizza to solving the world's problems with one suave stroke of his keyboard.'

'Miles Alia?' said Matt, as if sifting the name through his memory banks. 'Not the day-trading, dot-comming, most-successful-technopreneur-ever Miles Alia?'

Miles rose theatrically in his seat and bowed. 'The same,' he said, 'and let me say: everything you've read about me is true.'

. . . and there was Isaac Blackwell:

'All I'll say,' Arb said, in showman-mode, more for the benefit of the others at the table than for Matt, 'is that everything you've read about me is *not true.*'

The rest of the table laughed, on cue.

'Except, of course, that whole thing about Anna and me being secretly married for five years.'

Another chorus of laughs went up around the table.

Matt laughed too—at the absurd idea, he supposed. After all, he hadn't read a paper for almost two weeks.

. . . and now, there was Matthew Turner:

'So you just jumped on a boat and hitched a ride to . . .' Tom hesitated, suddenly aware he'd raised a point of keen interest to everyone. 'Where did you say you wanted to go?'

'Well, I didn't know where I was going. There I was, standing on the docks in Fremantle asking all and sundry how the hell to get to that New World in the middle of the Indian Ocean and being summarily told time and time again that it was not possible, it was too far off the usual shipping lanes, when this guy comes up to me and says, "You the guy who wants to go to the Ridge?" "The Ridge?" I say. "Ninety East Ridge," he says, "where they're building that hole in the ocean." He said he was piloting an empty fishing trawler bound for the Middle East at sunrise. He said he wasn't going exactly here, but that he'd pass pretty close by.' He tossed his hands in the air, 'Close enough, so it proved.'

'Did it ever occur to you that you might end up being turned away at the gates?' questioned Mary. 'That you might be acting somewhat naively?'

Matt nodded, 'Yes, Ms Minken, it certainly did. Time and time again. Every day in fact. But—'

'I don't think we can criticise ambitious thinking, Mare,' said Tom, looking around the table for support. 'After all, we are *all* here to change the world!'

'Tell us, Matthew Turner,' said Sanjay Mathur, 'how would *you* like to change the world?'

Matt shook his head humbly, 'To tell you the truth, I'm not sure . . . yet. But I do know this: that you can't complain about an election if you don't vote. There's an opportunity here that's never, ever existed before. This place will change the world, I know it, and when it does, I want to be able to say that I voted, that I was part of it, that I made some sort of contribution.'

'Indeed you already have, Mr Turner!' Tom lauded, laughing out loud. 'When you jumped on a boat and hitched a ride to the Ridge.'

'All roads lead to the Ridge, it appears,' said Matt, trying to play it down.

But Tom was already raising his glass to the table, then back to their new companion.

'A toast to Mattie Turner, our first Old World refugee, and anyone else with the guts to hitchhike, backpack, swim or do whatever it takes to find their way to our little town on Ninety East Ridge. To Mattie Turner!'

'Mattie Turner!' they all chorused.

Anything is possible with enough nights spent dreaming
And enough days spent doing.

fifteen down, nine-eight-five to go

Gotta make a good impression.

Everything was so clear.

Impress them with your scenario-building skills.

He was calm, serene, supremely confident.

Dazzle them with your experience in building brand-new cities.

They were going to love him. This was going to be great.

Just gotta be yourself. Gotta be calm. Gotta be good.

Shit! Gotta wake up!

Matt's head throbbed with last night's alcohol. When he moved, his brain pounded like a cracked lead bell. He padded his way from the bed to the bathroom and almost fell over when the light overwhelmed him like a tidal wave in the surf. He tried to look at himself in the mirror. He couldn't possibly look as bad as he felt.

Well, maybe he could.

He kept his eyes low, avoiding the daylight, as he made his way out and up the metal stairs which zigged and zagged their way up between metal floors. As he made his way up to the War Room, the Philo Group's regular meeting room directly beneath Jabba's Palace, he wondered if anyone else felt as hungover as he did. He hoped so.

He came to the top of the stairs, pausing at the door to stare out across the ocean. The sun, far too bright for this time of the morning, and the Indian Ocean were the only things in existence between himself and the horizon. All the construction, the cargo ships, the siphoning circles, the rigs, stood behind him to the west.

For a moment, he imagined the sun as a cop happily following his daily beat, whistling as he strolled past the Pacific, then Australia to his left, South-East Asia to his right, looking expectantly for the magical blue waters of the Indian Ocean to appear. Everything seems in order until he tops the horizon and sees a commotion where azure used to be. Ships and people and steel and smoke, and a man outside a door on the landing of a rig looking up at him just as perplexed, sharing a moment, then turning and opening the door.

'What I'm saying, or trying to say if you'd let me finish, is if people want to live here, then they should agree to live by a certain set of rules and law.'

'No, Jay, but that's not what you're trying to say. If it was, I think we'd all agree with you. What you and Saul are pushing for is a moral decree to be followed or else.'

'No, Harry. That's not what I'm trying to—'

'Excuse me, gentlemen,' interrupted Arb. 'Mr Turner, good morning. Nice of you to join us. Please take a seat. While we are waiting for Anna to set up, we were just discussing how we might establish a social balance. Perhaps you could enlighten us with some artificial intelligence solutions which might be helpful?'

Matt, still standing, looked around the table. They were all there, including Laikali Rulé. Isaac Blackwell presided from one end of the long oval table next to Anna, who was busily sorting or resorting her notes. There was a vacant seat halfway down the other side, between Tom Mills and Miles Alia.

As he sat down, they all seemed far away, the distance exaggerated by the bare space on the table in front of him. He noticed that the others had notebooks or PCs or voice recorders laid out in front of them. They seemed alive and alert, and they all looked at him, waiting for his response. Isaac, in particular, leaned forward, showily opening his eyes wide in eager attentiveness.

'Well,' Matt began, before coughing to clear the huskiness from his voice, 'less alcohol for starters.'

For a second that seemed like a year to Matthew Turner, nobody moved.

Then Tom Mills laughed out loud and slapped him on the back. 'Absolutely! I don't know about anyone else, but I feel like shit this morning, myself.'

A tension seemed to break around the table and the rest began to laugh and moan and complain of headaches and echoes. Serious and thoughtful postures around the table broke down. Byron Lybrand shook his head and nodded at the same time as he buried his tired face in his hands. Anna lifted her head and smiled in agreement. Even Isaac seemed to find it amusing.

Matt Turner, for his part, although relieved and deeply grateful for his support, was still feeling Tom's slap on the back reverberate through his head.

Soon Anna stood up and moods were serious again. She didn't say good morning. She didn't smile. Her eyes were all determination and focus. There would be no interruptions, that was clear. Until she was finished, they would all have to keep their thoughts to themselves.

'A thousand days. A thousand dawns. A thousand sunsets. Less than three years. That's all the time we have. We've got a lot to do, and little time to waste. Now I realise that we've had a couple of not-so-pleasant conversations over the last few days, talking about what our New World should look like, what it should be called, how it should run, how it should position itself with respect to the rest of the world, and so on. With this in mind, I am now going to lay out the timeline before us and the vision for the New World as it was conceived some years ago, and how it has evolved up to today.'

Mary Minken, Modern Historian and Cultural

Connoisseur: Oh, I get it. This was YOUR idea, therefore the rest of us bow and pay homage. This is so like Isaac. Well, you are out of your depth little Ms Spires, let me tell you.

'The timeline first. Harry assures me that we will have a fully functioning city infrastructure within a thousand days. In the tradition of what-the-media-didn't-know-didn't-happen, we will ignore some five years of submarine construction and consider Day One to be the press launch date of two weeks ago. Today, therefore, is Day Fifteen. The first pipewall will be complete within a month, fully dredged by Day One Hundred, and concrete-filled by Day Two Hundred.

'The second pipewall will be built by Day One Hundred and Fifty and dredged by Day Three Hundred. A city plan, with room for change and growth in the future must be finalised by this day, to allow Harry and his team to start the multi-level foundations which will branch out from the first pipewall.

'This city plan must give us homes, offices, factories, markets, parks, hospitals, waste disposal systems, sporting stadiums, roads, public trans-port, telecommunications infrastructure, airports—*or not*. Let me stress—because this is the major challenge before us—there are no certainties here, there are no givens, there are no assumptions just because that's the way it is elsewhere.'

Sanjay Mathur, Novelist: Your mind is so struc-tured, little Anna, and yet how could an inhibited mind aspire to such as this?

'To decide this infrastructure, we will first need

to agree on the founding principles of this society—its economy, its government, its social boundaries.

'It may be easier if I attempt to explain what the vision is by describing what it is not. This is not a case of taking an existing system and reconstructing it. In particular, let me stress that this is not a case of taking the western model and tweaking it with some selective modifications here and there. We can do better.'

Saul Obermann, Economist: You do not seem to understand that the United States has created a system which accumulates, allocates and distributes capital more efficiently than any model in history.

'The very reason that this project exists is because the Old World as it stands is failing us—failing us with deplorable levels of poverty and intolerable levels of violence, to name just two, and, perhaps most importantly, unacceptable levels of unhappiness.'

Mary Minken, PhD and Rich as well: Your desire to improve on the results of thousands of years of civil evolution only reveals your naivety.

'Now the argument will be raised—has been raised—that the trials of history have been conducted according to Darwinian laws, and that only the fittest, most efficient, best systems of society have survived. Assuming this is true, then it's lucky we did not create our New World in the Middle Ages when feudal systems prevailed, or in the 1930s when racist, dictatorial societies were naturally selected.'

Thomas Mills, Ancient Historian and Anthropologist: Cute theory. I like it.

'This, of course, begs the question: looking forward instead of backwards, how will our increasingly globalised society evolve and change in the future? More questions: what is the ultimate end state? Is there one? And another big question: seeing which way the world is going, do we really want to go that way too? Or is there another path?'

Jay Diaglio, Political Expert: Rhetorical nonsense. It doesn't matter. You've got to live in the real world. Right now!

'Does it matter?, I'm sure you're thinking. After all, we've got to live in the real world as it exists right now. But that is a separate issue: about international relationships and isolationism— essentially about what other people think.'

Arb, Slick: If there's one thing about you that I like, you've always said 'Who cares what other people think?'

'Well, who cares what other people think? We have to make our own decisions about who we are and who we want to be. With all due respect to social evolution, the Darwinian trials of history will never reach a final judgement, and that being the case, we are going to ignore the jurisdiction of that theoretical court . . .'

Miles Alia, Futurist: Yes, yes, it is so cool when you get all metaphorical!

'. . . in favour of a practical one.'

Mary Minken, Tom's wife, Arb's old girlfriend: Like what, little girl?

'Like what?, I hear you thinking. Well, I don't know yet. That's why you are here. Don't think this century. Or this millennium even! Think about life as you'd like it to be in the year four thousand!'

Miles Alia, never-worn-never-will-wear-a-tie-in-his-life: With ya, baby! Ooh yeah, am I with ya! Talk about an idea laboratory!

'I'm not saying that we will be able to build all of it, but we are sure as hell going to give it a shot.'

Harry Pont, Engineer: We'll build it, girl, don't you worry about that! You just stay strong. Some of these shaking heads are too full of themselves and their ivory tower theories to understand. I can't say I get it myself, of course, but I'm just a dumb builder. Take no notice of 'em—you're doing it, girl. You're doing it!

'This group is responsible for creating the blueprint of our New World—a blueprint that starts right now as a blank page. A thousand days. Fifteen down, nine-eight-five blank pages left for us to fill—'

Tom: You're all guts, Anna. I'll say that for you.

'Without the restrictions of legacy infra-structure . . .'

Saul: That's about the first sensible thing you've said today.

'. . . or legacy thinking.'

Arb: I wonder just how pissed off Saul and Jay are going to be.

'Without government driven by expedience or graft.'

Jay: Was that about me? Was that about me?

'Without pollution.'

Helen Rainey, Marine Biologist: Finally, something I understand.

'Without social, economic or political inequality.'

Byron Lybrand, Social Scientist/Statistician: World experience would suggest that that's not possible.

'Without poverty.'

Laikali Rulé: Noble sentiments, child. But are they too idealistic?

'Without prejudice.'

Augusto Rulé, Laikali's dead husband: Remember when you were this idealistic?

'Without crime.'

Mary: You're dreaming, little girl.

'Without violence.'

Harry: Grand plans, girl.

'Without illiteracy.'

Sanjay: Ah, if only that came true . . .

'Without disease, without traffic jams.'

Miles: Awesome . . . I wonder if they're going to serve those crabsticks again today.

'The real challenge will be to make it real. Because whatever we build, no matter how futuristic, no matter how fancy, no matter how slick and efficient, we're going to have to live in it. So when I say think Y4K, I don't mean jetpacks and food pills, I mean think how a society that's really got its shit together would live.'

Sanjay: Well put.

'Bear in mind, we are starting from scratch. We get to choose the advantages that we will draw from the rest of the world. And by our choices, we will also be selecting constraints.'

Laikali: An important point.

'This group will be making those choices, and there are a lot to make, let me assure you. So we want to get this group moving. The next nine hundred and eighty-five days will involve a lot of concepts, a lot of debate, and finally a lot of detail. That said, we need to recognise that, no matter what we do, some things will develop beyond our control. For example, the very name of this enterprise.

Arb: What's she doing?

'It has come to my attention that we require something more than the generic New World Project.'

Laikali: Got to admire someone who lights her own fire and then jumps straight into it.

'It has also come to my attention that the maritime community and sea trade have already given us such a name. Therefore, first and foremost, I would like to announce the working title of our little hole in the ocean as . . .

Matt: As what?

'Ninety East Ridge.'

*

Heads turned from side to side. Not all, but certainly a few.

—Huh? What the . . .

—Where the hell did that come from? How dare she!

No one said it out loud. But you could see it in their indignant pouts and screaming wide eyes.

—Did we even suggest this the other day?

—Did anyone agree to this?

—That's not a city name, surely!

—Sounds like an address!

Then there were looks of blame and recrimination.

—Sieg heil, mein Fuhrer!

—We might as well not be here!

And looks of disbelief when they realised that not everyone was displeased.

—Whatever, it's as good a name as any.

—Ninety East Ridge . . . cool, it's so Retro-Incongruous-Chic!

—Interesting, named after the geography, like Alice Springs, South Africa, Salt Lake City.

—At least it's not Ninety East Ridge City.

And then there was Arb's expression, one eyebrow raised, his shoulders shrugged, his message clear.

—Like it or lump it, boys and girls. You heard what she said.

When it was clear that she had finished, an awkward silence permeated the room. Matt was about to clap when the debate erupted.

'This is ridiculous, hopeless, pie-in-the-sky claptrap!' Jay.

'Don't you think people have tried to address poverty and prejudice before? Let me tell you, it's not as easy as you might think.' Saul.

'And what's with the name?' Mary.

'It sounds suspiciously like an isolationist policy to me.' Jay again.

'Of course you'd think something like this. You've got no experience in the real world.' Saul, hands flapping.

'Now hold it right there, Theory Boy. At least her experience is made of more than just talk.' Harry the great defender.

'Oh, here we go: the intelligentsia wish to support their own!' Jay with a backhand.

'Now there's a surprise: a politician saying what he means!' Harry returning with interest.

'Is this how it's going to be? We debate, she decides!' Mary, loud and direct.

'Take it easy, Mary.' Arb, his voice unraised.

'O-hoh! So everything's open to debate except what Mrs Blackwell says.' Mary with a low blow.

Silence.

Harry outraged. Helen and Byron stunned, open-mouthed. Sanjay shaking his head with disbelief. Tom staring, appalled by his wife. Jay and Saul, their faces still dark and resolute, now silently distancing themselves. Miles irked and wowed and simultaneously still wondering about crabsticks. Laikali leaning forward, more interested than ever. Anna, head bowed, inscrutable. Mary unrepentant, chin out, challenging. Arb a shade of red away from losing control for the first time in his life.

And Matt, dumbfounded, too astonished to speak: Mrs Blackwell?

It was Anna herself who finally broke the tension, lifting her head and continuing in a voice so matter-of-fact that her reaction to Mary's comment remained a mystery.

'So what do we do now?' She smiled as she answered her own question, easing the mood considerably: 'We get down to business. Everyone will be responsible for planning, presenting and reporting on the progress of a portfolio. All actions to be taken must be presented to and approved by the Philo Group before they can commence. This approval, to address Mary's question, will usually take the form of a vote—*however*—and it's a big however, Isaac and I both retain separate prerogatives to veto any proposal. That's the deal. Any questions?'

Her voice had firmed as she laid down the law, almost daring debate when she asked for questions.

Matt: You're married! It's true? To Isaac Blackwell?

Too stunned to stay silent, Matt spoke up with a wavering voice, 'Our portfolios?'

She shuffled through the deck of papers in front of her. 'Most of you know your own areas but, for the record, let me read out the complete list. Initially, there will be eleven portfolios. These will each include a series of sub-portfolios and specific projects that each portfolio Chief will be responsible for. The portfolios and their Chiefs are as follows: Finance and Economics—that's you Saul; Governance and Political Affairs—Jay; Environment and Marine Ecology—that's Helen, of course; Technology, Communications and Lifestyle Affairs will be headed by Miles; Mary, you're in charge of the Arts and Culture portfolio; Tom will lead our Heritage Creation and Preservation portfolio; Byron will specifically be responsible for Social Sciences and Civil Services Provision; Sanjay will lead our Education portfolio; Superstructure and Infrastructure—Harry, that's your game; Isaac will continue leading necessary fundraising whilst overseeing presentation deadlines and requirements; and I'll be covering Urban Development, Transport and Architecture— ah, Mr Turner, in addition to liaising with Laikali, I'd like you to assist in my department where your design skills might provide a new perspective.'

'And as always,' Arb interjected, 'there is a spot just waiting for Mrs Rulé herself, should she care to grace us with a direct commitment.'

Instead, she graced him with a courteous smile and a firm shake of her head.

'One last point,' said Anna. 'This Philo Group will be meeting at least twice a week each week for the next thousand days—the people in this room will get to know each other better than their own brothers and sisters by the time this is done. Any personal issues, any problems, any doubts that anyone might have should be aired openly and without reservation—in short, exactly as they have been in this meeting.

'This went better than I expected,' she then said seriously—*amazingly*, thought Matt. 'Thanks very much for your attention. I'll catch up with each of you individually later today to discuss your portfolios further. We've certainly got a lot to talk about,' looking at Jay and Saul, then at Harry, her old mentor and friend, 'and a lot to do.'

The meeting wrapped up soon after.

I catch a glimpse of my reflection staring at the stars, listening to the memory of her siren sound, and snap out of my reverie. There's a bottle of red wine on the coffee table. I pour myself a glass.

Timing is everything, my mind determines, unable to rid Anna Spires from my thoughts. If she had thought of her idea even five years earlier, she may have been considered only a visionary; she might have been spared the trials which followed; and I, too.

Only a visionary, I repeat the thought back to myself. I can't help but feel sad. I return to contemplate my reflection in the window. I'm like that, I know. Only a visionary. Barely even that, perhaps. Always full of great ideas and the best intentions, but I've never been like Anna—making something from nothing. It's more my nature to question, question, question, to fiddle with and tinker, to gild the lily as opposed to growing it. There was a time once, before fate conspired against me, when

I thought I may be significant, but that moment now has passed.

I suddenly feel sorry for the reflection in the window—how easily he forgets how exciting those days were: the New World now had a name, the Philo members now had tasks and a thousand days seemed to race by like a sunny afternoon.

We are defined by moments of truth,
By our actions and what we choose not to do.

secrets, ears and understanding

'Pleased to meet you, Anna,' said Arb's mother, Nancy, with a firm handshake.

'I'll say,' boomed Ben Blackwell in his hearty tenor voice. 'You are clearly the most interesting girl that Isaac's brought home in ages.'

After all, it was not every day that you met your son's wife . . . of five years.

'Who was the last interesting one?' Arb asked his father.

'Hmm, now let me think. Ah yes. I remember.' He grinned devilishly at the memory. 'Volleyball player. Legs up to here! Now she was *very* interesting.'

Embarrassment washed over Arb's face while his father winked fondly at Anna.

'I'll take that as a compliment,' she said graciously.

Ben Blackwell's laughter shook the chandelier. It was deep and loud and genuine.

'I can see I'm going to like you,' he said.

'Some people will like you. And some won't,' her mother would say. 'There's not much you can do about it.'

At the time, Anna was going through a phase where she was shy about meeting people. Not surprisingly, this coincided with the period when she was just beginning to be conscious of her appearance. Leaving the house became an exercise requiring extreme care; the slightest thing—a hair out of place, a stain on a shirt sleeve—could send her scurrying back to her bedroom for hours.

One summer, as part of some non-debatable fashion master plan, she changed the way she did her hair, the way she dressed, even the way she spoke. There was only one problem, a challenge not even Anna could solve: she hated her ears.

'Yes, I see,' her dad would say, not even trying to make her feel better. 'Of course, you got those ears from your mother,' he'd carry on, shaking his head, simultaneously commiserating and denying responsibility. 'I honestly don't know how you can go out in public. Small, round, so tight against your head that your silhouette looks like you've just got a bump on your shoulders.'

The humorous approach. Sometimes it worked, sometimes it didn't.

In any case, it worked better than her mother's weak solace that there was nothing she could do about it, so why worry. 'Just be yourself,' she'd then add unhelpfully. 'There's no point being anyone else.'

'That's right,' agreed her father. 'Better be

yourself, otherwise we won't recognise you when you come home.'

Arb's parents were Benjamin Blackwell and Nancy Saunders: what else was there to say?

Books, newspapers, magazines had thrived for decades on their lives—how-to-succeed-in-business books, how-to-succeed-in-life books, what they ate for breakfast, what they wore to the gala opening of this or that, what they talked about at the White House, their views on everything from politics to petroleum, from the kitchen sink to the Panama Canal, from football to city hall—anyone who had ever read their fair share of print media any time in the last thirty years probably knew more about them than they'd ever need to.

Anna had worn her hair out, covering her ears, to meet them.

'You are who you are, Anna,' her mother said.

'Yes, yes you are, but, but . . .' Her father struggled for the words, agreeing while clearly disagreeing. '. . . but even so, we are defined by moments of truth, moments which measure our character, outline our beliefs, state our values to the world around us. At these moments, we are defined by our actions and what we choose *not* to do.'

'Not to do?'

'That's right. When you choose not to lie, not to steal, not to cheat, not to take advantage, not to be unfair. When you choose not to eat the last biscuit, not to take the last seat on the bus when there's somebody standing, not to fart out loud in a crowded restaurant.'

Anna giggled, she couldn't help it.

Quickly he looked one way, then the other, then conspiratorially put his hand over his mouth: 'Soft ones are okay.'

'I call it plumbing, although my marketing people call it "fluids engineering". They'd probably call my liver a liquid alcohol processor.'

Arb's father was a self-made millionaire who had married a billionaire's daughter.

Plumbing was his business, always had been— 'a simple business', he called it—one that had started with fixing the kitchen sink, moved to fitting the pipes that run from the house to the street, and then ultimately progressed to installing custom-made watering and irrigation systems for farms from Idaho to Indonesia, golf courses and resorts from California to the Kalahari, even watering the grass and flowers of New York's Central Park.

Anna liked Ben Blackwell. Her dad would have liked him too. Ben was a straightforward man with simple beliefs, clear opinions and unhidden emotions. He was uninterested in impressions and too busy to filibuster. Anna surmised that he was perfect for someone as allergic to bullshit as his wife Nancy.

Her business was oil; the family business for four generations. She ran it with sheer willpower, 'just like her daddy did'.

What Anna particularly liked about Nancy

Saunders was that it had never occurred to her that the oil business wasn't geared for women, what with its sheikhs and Texans. Here was a woman who worked hard, bargained hard and never found the world before her too hard. All that mattered to Nancy, be it business or happiness, was that she got things done. And with her son, her business and of course her husband, it was clear to Anna that she usually did just that.

Watching Ben and Nancy talk was a treat—they 'clicked like two cogs made for each other', as Ben might say. Although understanding them required some getting used to. It was like listening to a conversation between two sides of the one brain. They didn't need to talk—maybe they did it just to keep in practice or as part of some ancient continuous courting ritual—but when they did, it involved skipping sentences, making a point with a raised eyebrow or raising a chortle by reciting only the punch line of a well-worn joke.

Anna struggled to remember how her own mother and father interacted. It annoyed her a little that she couldn't picture it more clearly in her mind.

It had always been a happy house, rarely disrupted by anger or shouting. In what she knew was deliberate revisionist hindsight, her inadequate memory interpreted that lack of domestic rage as a lack of passion.

They were so different. In interests. In temperament. Even in ambition for their daughter.

Her father, always encouraging her without restraint, without limits: 'One day, you know, you're going to have to fly on your own. And when you do, Little Grub, reach for the stars.'

Her mother, so unlike him, such as when she thought Anna could not hear her: 'If you make her aim so high, won't she forever be disappointed?'

The reply, ever-positive: 'There's always the moon, Jo.'

'The moon doesn't shine like a star, you know,' ever-too-cautious.

Her mother just didn't understand.

*

'Of course, I understand,' said Nancy. 'Keeping it a secret was essential to raising the money you needed.'

Ben Blackwell was less forgiving. 'You'd think he could trust his parents to keep a secret.'

Telling him that only three people on the entire planet knew did little to placate him, especially when one of those people was Xavier, their old butler, who had acted as best man. The other two were Natasha Spires as maid of honour, and the judge.

'Oh, give it a rest, Ben. You'd have done the same—well, no, you wouldn't. But you know that I would have done the same thing.'

'So?'

'So live with it.'

'I do, every day, dear.'

Even at his own joke—or perhaps just sheer joy in his marriage, Anna thought—his laughter shook the chandelier.

She wondered if her own mother would resent not being told. Probably not, given the overall scheme of things.

'You know we'll love you, no matter what,' she used to say. But that was simply her way of saying failure was inevitable. She just didn't understand. And biased though she knew they were, Anna's memories of her family consistently regressed to a father-daughter crusade against maternal conservatism:

'Why don't you start with something smaller?' her mother might say.

'Why?'

'Well, what if you run out of something before you're finished?'

'She won't run out,' her father would interject. 'And even if she does, she'll make do—manufacture some solution. You'll find a way, won't you?'

'Honey, you'll put too much pressure on her,' her mother would say.

'Pressure?' her father would repeat, genuinely surprised, immediately turning back to his Anna to hold her by the hand and pat her gently on the head. 'Don't you see? There's no need to feel any pressure. Ever. 'Cause we'll always love you, Anna. No matter what.'

And then, she would remember the warmth of his arms enveloping her.

'You know that, don't you?' he'd say.

pontifications

When the door opened and the sun streamed in like an Egyptian plague, Matt was neither inspired nor prepared for Arb Blackwell's wake-up call:

'Come on, Mattie Turner. Time to earn your keep.'

'What's the time?' he managed.

'It's six-seventeen. Sun's up, so should you be. You've got a busy day ahead.'

Packing his bag had not taken long. He didn't have that much to take.

Arb's parting words had been, 'H-pad in ten minutes. You'll need some clothes and your passport.'

Before that, there had been a conversation that was still fuzzy in Matt's morning memory.

'I thought you were in Dallas,' he remembered saying.

'Was. Back now. Work to do,' Arb had replied, grabbing Matt's sports bag and throwing it at him.

'Anna too?'

'Yep.'

'How'd it go?'

'You can ask her on the Osprey. She's coming

170

with you.' Happy that Matt was up—staggering but up—he had headed for the door.

'Coming with me? Where are we going?'

'Mumbai, for starters.' He was in the hallway now, yelling back over his shoulder. 'H-pad in ten minutes. You'll need some clothes and your passport.'

*

Anna and Arb had left what was now to be called 'Ninety East Ridge' almost immediately following Anna's policy speech. But not before she had conducted one-on-one sessions with each of the Portfolio Chiefs.

Subsequently, the debate that had been left to simmer at the end of the Philo Group meeting had flared again that night in Jabba's Palace, fuelled by individual meetings with Anna. With brand-new, less-informed audiences to hear their grievances, their complaints had quickly become more theatrical, more cant.

'She wants me to consider economic models without money or personal wealth,' said Saul Obermann with exaggerated disbelief.

'She specifically told me to check if democracy was a requirement of the United Nations' Declaration of Human Rights and US Bill of Rights,' related Byron Lybrand incredulously.

'She asked me to form a plan about what we might do if the United Nations and its member countries failed to recognise us,' moaned Jay Diaglio shaking his head. 'I ask you, what is she planning to do?'

The helicopter pad sat at the top of the platform, an oversized stencilled verandah outside Jabba's Palace. Parked on the pad was the strangest chopper Matt had ever seen.

It looked more like a small plane with wings, a fuselage and a tail. The only apparent heli-feature were two enormous propellers that faced up, not from top and tail as usual, but from the wing-tips.

'Isn't it a beauty?' said a delighted Indian voice beside him.

'I didn't realise you were a warhead, Sanjay.'

'I'm not. I am an airhead. And this,' indicating the aircraft, 'is a modified Osprey V-22. I've got to hand it to Isaac—not even the American Navy, who paid for its development, have one in service yet.'

'I didn't realise a helicopter could fly this far out to sea.'

'And therein lies the beauty of the Osprey. This baby has tiltrotors, which means it takes off and lands like a helicopter but, once airborne, its propeller engines rotate, making the aircraft into a turboprop aeroplane capable of long-range, high-speed, high-altitude flight.'

Matt couldn't help but be impressed. 'Sanjay, you *are* an airhead.'

Moments ago, the horizontal blades had begun to turn. They were now starting to blur.

'Come on,' yelled Anna, appearing from Jabba's Palace, Laikali Rulé in tow behind her. 'Time to go.'

Over the past fifteen days, Matt had watched with increasing fascination as his Philo Group colleagues wrestled with Anna's ideas, and the responses of those they complained to.

'What? A communist model?' a receptionist asked Obermann.

'Well no, that's not what she said. But what are the alternatives? Is it possible to have a free market without money?'

'Undemocratic, my God!' a concerned deckhand demanded of Byron Lybrand. 'What do you think—maybe she's planning a military dictatorship!'

'Actually,' tempered Byron, 'I don't think that's her plan—but who knows?'

'What does that mean?' asked a troubled accountant of Diaglio. 'Can this place survive on its own?'

'Well probably, but that's not the point, is it?'

They weren't exactly campaigners for Anna's radical ideas. Not yet. But they were no longer trying to tear them apart either. In fact, by a word here, a qualification there, Matt had begun to suspect that they were slowly coming to terms with the possibilities before them.

'I didn't know how much to pack,' said Matt to Anna as they bundled themselves into the aircraft.

'Here, hand these out,' she yelled above the rotors.

A one-page report, so Matt saw, written by Harry Pont:

- The first pipewall has broken the surface!
- Construction will continue until height rises one hundred feet above sea level.
- Water extraction due to begin, as per schedule, on Day 45.

With a lurch, more in his stomach than by the Osprey, Matt felt the aircraft rise into the air.

'Once we're high enough,' Sanjay explained excitedly, 'they will tilt the rotors and we'll be away.'

'Not yet, Sanjay,' Anna interrupted. 'There's something we need to see first.'

Staying in helicopter mode, the aircraft swooped away from Platform Seven and down towards sea level. Trawlers, barges and supply ships seemed to slide across the ocean beneath them.

Across the cabin, Anna was reaching into a bag, then pulling out a camera. Matt tried to look ahead to see what was coming. He turned to ask Laikali what they were looking for, when she suddenly lifted in her seat, her eyes fixed out the window.

Matt turned, and there it was . . .

Six or seven construction barges gave the game away. Although they were spread, they were shaped around a circle, a circle that on closer inspection Matt found he could see rising quite clearly above the waterline.

It was a ring of concrete rising no higher than a single step above the surface. But this was the middle of the ocean; this was thousands of kilometres from dry land; this was not an atoll, not a reef. This was the first pipewall, man-made, eighty metres in diameter and stretching over fifteen hundred metres straight down to the ocean floor.

Flying by the barges, Anna clicking proudly away, Matt could make out the faces of the workers looking up from the decks, cheering, whooping and waving joyfully.

Amid the buzz and excitement, Matt remembered he had a question and leaned over towards Anna. 'I was saying, I didn't know how much to pack—how long are we going to be away?'

'More than a day, less than a year,' Anna replied without concern. 'Like birds building a nest, Mr Turner, we'll be flitting in and out of here for the next three years.'

People think in different ways, people eat in different ways,
People work, play and wipe their bums in different ways.

pay attention

The first thing that assaulted Matt Turner when he arrived in Mumbai, formerly Bombay, the commercial capital of the massive subcontinent, was the smell.

'It's the same for us when we go to London,' Sanjay said.

The second thing was the congestion. Tides of people swept past one way, currents of crowds pushed the other, spinning him round. Sometimes he felt as if the small steel taxi was riding down the dusty streets on an endless wave of arms and legs and heads.

The third thing was the poverty. Dirty, grubby hands pawed at the cab window leading spirited, desperate, well-practised pleas for alms. Matt felt every bit the uncomfortable first-timer as he checked the door locks and edged towards the centre of the car.

And there was something else—something he found difficult to place, something he hadn't expected.

'It's the happiness,' said Laikali, as if reading his thoughts—and she was right.

Suddenly he saw it everywhere. Wide, happy smiles, row after row of yellowing teeth with bits of red beetlenut behind thin upturned lips. Taxi drivers. Shopkeepers. Babies, children, adults, old grey-haired brown-skinned skeletons sitting on chairs watching the world go by. Even the beggars were grinning.

When Matt made this observation to him, Sanjay explained why he thought this was so.

'Less discontent. It always starts with dis-content.'

'What? What starts?'

'Anything, everything. Change, progress, revolution, it doesn't matter what it is. The grander efforts usually start because of some sort of perceived imbalance, injustice or inequality. But big or small, whatever it is always starts with someone no longer content to refrain from intervening.' Sanjay nodded towards Anna. 'When people ask what made her want to do this, I know the answer.'

'But how does that relate to Mumbai?'

'A theoretical physicist not satisfied with explanations of the beginning of time or the theory of relativity is thus inspired to change it, or improve it. A crusader unhappy with Saracens holding the Holy City will invade it. A business-man discontent with his wealth will work hard to increase it.'

Matt shrugged, genuinely bewildered.

'This is just my way of explaining why I believe Indian people are so happy despite their apparent discomfort. They haven't been trained in the art of discontent the way people in the West have—not by their politicians, nor by their media.'

'Are you sure they're not just putting fluoride in the water?' said Laikali wryly.

Sanjay laughed. 'Perhaps. This is just my theory. Others will tell you that the prevailing Hindu faith would have us believe that life—life with all its dirt and poverty and hunger and uncertainty—is a relatively minor concern compared to our spiritual existence.'

'Pay attention,' Laikali said to Matt, pulling him aside as Sanjay led them on a tour of the town. 'The world has more shapes and more colours than we can possibly imagine. People think in different ways, people eat in different ways, people work, play and wipe their bums in different ways.'

The roadshow's goals, as Anna had described them, were threefold: to research their assigned portfolios, to foster political and corporate relationships and to continue raising money from carefully selected targets. Matt's only concern, as told to him by Anna, was the first goal, in his case specifically formulating a transport system for the New World. Matt's other role however, as liaison for Laikali Rulé, was still a mystery to him.

She seemed to have taken him under her wing, as if she had some secret intention for him. He assumed that she would be clearer about what she required when she left the Project in a few days. In the meantime, though, when she gave him instructions, she felt more like a mentor than a superior.

'It's important that you look beyond transport. This is an unparalleled opportunity for you to look at social structures, political systems, infrastructure and architecture of countries all over the world. Don't waste it, and don't let anybody convince you completely.'

'I'll try to learn as much as I can,' he said honestly.

But she shook her head. 'I don't want you to learn. I want you to *unlearn*, to open up your mind. I simply want you to realise that there is always more than one way to do something.'

He nodded, that made sense. 'So that I can choose the best one for Ninety East Ridge.'

'No. So that you can do anything.'

He was grateful for the advice to look beyond transport. Mumbai, with its clogged dusty streets, was hardly a mecca for urban planning. While the others dealt with their own responsibilities, he spent most of his days at town planning offices or crisscrossing the city via cab, foot or bicycle.

On the fourth day, Anna asked him if they might spend the afternoon together.

'After all, I am responsible for you,' she said. 'But you need to understand that I am going to be pretty busy with other things as well. You are going to be on your own a lot. For feedback, you should stay in close contact with the team of architects, engineers and town planners back at the Ridge—and don't let them give you any shit. I told them that your ideas are supposed to surprise them.'

'But I don't have any ideas.'

'Not yet,' she said.

'Why here?' he asked as they sped across town in a suicide cab.

'I wanted you to come here,' Anna told him, 'to see the endgame. Or a possible endgame. Who knows how many people we'll end up with, in three years, in thirty years? Here there are thirteen million people trying to get from one side to the other, and there are no tubes, no trams, no monorails. I didn't want to start with pre-conceptions.'

'Funny, that's just what Laikali said.'

'She's a wonder,' said Anna, shaking her head admiringly. 'Sometimes I think she knows what I'm looking for better than I do.'

She certainly worked hard, Matt discovered.

Until well after dark, they analysed maps and rode various routes. She had reams of statistics supplied to her by Byron about comparative costs, traffic flows and what-not. She never stopped speculating—'What about this?' 'What about that?'—and she never stopped trying to provoke ideas: 'Did you know that the French want to make central Paris a car-free pedestrian zone? I'd say the odds are stacked against them, given that *their* city has already been built.'

And questions, questions, so many incessant questions that it took Matt a moment to realise that they weren't talking shop when she asked, 'Are you hungry?'

Anna's favourite restaurant in the whole wide world—Trishna's—was in Mumbai, located down a seedy back alley lined with mouldy warehouses and garages that would have been declared derelict in the West. If they hadn't come by cab, Matt doubted they ever would have found it. Outside, the street smelt of sewerage, garbage and cats. Inside, it smelled like heaven.

'So, you've been with us—what? Almost three weeks? First impressions?'

'Overwhelmed.'

'Impressed?'

'Yes.'

'Surprised?'

'Definitely.'

'What surprised you most?'

He wasn't sure he should say so, but he did anyway. 'You being Mrs Blackwell.'

'You were supposed to say the size or the scale,' she laughed, unaffected.

'I was on the road, I think, when you announced it.'

Over the most sublime garlic butter lobster, Anna told Matt an abridged version of her fairytale meeting with Isaac, and how she had told him of her dream, how they had planned and married in secret, and how her life had changed since work began on the Ridge and their marriage had become public knowledge.

'He's a very lucky man,' Matt said when the story, randomly interspersed with her views on the world in general, finally ended. 'But didn't you ever worry that you were doing the wrong thing?'

He was glad when she chose to assume he was talking about the Project.

'No,' she said.

No matter what they say: choices cannot be taken back
And reality has a proud unconquered history.

Josephine Spires

Choices are right or wrong, never both, no matter what they tell you. *They* are just trying to make you feel better. Trying to stop you from blaming yourself. But it was your fault, and it's likely that they know that too.

Choices cannot be taken back. Yes, you can make amends. Later. Through other choices. Balancing acts. Corrections. Supersessions. But you cannot erase the fact that at a moment in time, a choice was made. You can't change that. Ever.

'We are not defined by the choices we make,' he used to say. 'We are defined by those choices we do not make. Not to make war, not to speak out, not to protest, not to steal, not to lie . . .'

If only that were true.

He wasn't perfect. And it wasn't true. He was playing with words. Mystical nuances and unnecessary distinctions. A mistake, noble and well-intentioned, but wrong nonetheless. Another beautiful sentiment. He was nothing if not sentimental.

He was the most beautiful man. An idealist who adored her. He kissed her and held her and protected her as if she were a precious jewel. He called her a gift, a goddess, his raindrop. He said that when he met her, it was as if he had been caught in the rain one day and somehow she, a raindrop, her, had sought him out and landed on the tip of his finger. He'd never noticed before that raindrops, like snowflakes, were unique, but somehow, when he saw her, when she landed on his finger, he knew she was exquisite, one of a kind, and he would treasure her forever. He cherished her. He worshipped her.

The fool.

Willing fool. Knowing dreamer. His weakness: his discomfort with reality. His weakness, his most endearing feature. And his fervent hope was that someday he could change it all. For all of us. Change reality, that is.

Long ago, Josephine Spires had stopped blaming Fate. Fate is passive, preordained, incapable of life's ironies and karma. It is therefore immune to censure and retribution, unlike Reality.

Reality, she had resolved, is a living force, an essence that surrounds the human condition. But it's also a lying force that pretends to be changeable by the power of will, that fakes its susceptibility to mankind's actions and achievements. It has its own will, Jo was sure, and a proud unconquered history, no matter what anybody says.

Effortlessly, Reality had drawn her husband into believing in impossible dreams. It had tempted him with visions of paradise, of a New World free of the old one's tyrannies and compromises. With the gift of a disciple, it had crept inside his once solid defences of cynicism and self-awareness.

And then Reality had taken his life.

And left behind his disciple.

Left behind his daughter.

Their daughter.

Their Anna.

Young, idealistic, inexperienced . . .
Her inspiration.

impressions

Back aboard the Osprey, bound for the United Arab Emirates sans Sanjay, who had remained in Mumbai, Matt listened in as Anna recalled to Laikali their first contact. To Matt's surprise, the imposing Polynesian woman blushed with embarrassment.

'A fresh, no doubt naive politician eager to rise beyond the confines of small Palwali's borders,' the older wiser Laikali mused, dismissing her young style as 'too cutesy, too formulaic and rhetorical, the style of a typically unrealistic idealist on the speakers' tour'.

'Time that probably would have been better spent elsewhere,' she then pondered out loud.

Anna was about to reply when Laikali spoke again, as if interrupting herself: 'However, if one of those speeches can claim even remote responsibility for touching the mind of a young Anna Spires, then maybe the naive idealistic preaching of my youth was not such a waste of time after all.'

This time, it was Anna who blushed. To divert the attention from herself, she turned to Matt.

'What you need to understand, Mr Turner,' she said, 'is that here is a woman from a South Pacific paradise where the sun is always shining, the beaches always golden, the sea always blue. Here is a woman from a healthy economy, based on tourism and coconuts, who married a rich foreign businessman, was respected by the community, and had more than most Palwalians would have ever dreamed.'

Then she raised her index finger as if to point to the rub.

'And here is a woman who left all that behind.'

Anna went on to detail how, as a young turk determined to influence the world beyond Palwali's beaches, Laikali Rulé had assumed the position of Minister for Foreign Affairs and Trade and made it her own, starting with speaking tours to promote awareness of Palwali and good relations with its South Pacific neighbours. Some years later, after her beloved Augusto had died, she had expanded her horizons even further and taken up the post of Palwali's representative to the United Nations.

True to her rhetoric, Anna acclaimed, Laikali had always walked with purpose. With undisguised admiration, Anna related how Laikali had quickly established herself on committees overseeing aid work in Africa, children's education in Central Asia and economic reform in South America, amongst other things. Analysing as she narrated, Anna noted that in a very short time, her network had widened, her skills had broadened and her understanding of how decision-making at the highest levels really works had become more and more complete.

'Some years ago,' Anna said, now completely absorbed in her subject, 'she resigned her post as Palwali ambassador, only to stay on in perhaps a more powerful role as a permanent secretary to the General Assembly.'

What exactly this meant, Matt didn't know, but it was clear that Laikali was now recognised as a principal behind-the-scenes decision-maker. Based in Washington, close to New York, willing to travel at a moment's notice, Matt also reflected that she was also always willing to follow her instincts just as she had some five weeks ago, when she'd read a sidebar about a young idealist trying to build a paradise in the middle of the ocean.

'Wow,' said Matt, as they landed in Dubai where they would go their separate ways. 'I'm impressed.'

'What do you think of your new assistant?' asked Laikali.

'Your liaison?'

'Yes, what do you think of our Matthew Turner?'

They had left him in Dubai, now on their way together to Europe where Anna would meet up with her husband and from where Laikali would carry on back to Washington.

'He's young, idealistic, inexperienced. Why?'

'I think he's likely to be the single most influential figure in Ninety East Ridge's future.'

Anna blanched in surprise. 'I don't understand,'

she said. 'I'm not saying he's stupid. But he could be called naive. It's clear that he has no concept of the financing or engineering challenges we have overcome. He seems to have zero awareness of the political context and little expertise in any of our fundamental areas. On top of all that, he has apparently never travelled before either.'

'You mean before he thumbed a ride across the ocean?'

Anna eyed her inspirational friend, trying to divine her message.

'You're saying he's untainted.'

'More important than that,' said Laikali, 'I'm saying that he's your everyman.'

The thought started to weave itself into Anna's mind. *An everyman*, she considered.

'What you said before is right also, of course,' continued Laikali. 'He *is* young, idealistic, in-experienced in the wiles of the world. You won't get any doublespeak or hidden agendas from him. All you'll get—or rather all you've got—is someone who hangs off your every word and genuinely wants to change the world. Harness that devotion, because it's powerful stuff.'

world(s) in motion

[days 42 to 172]

Power is control over another person's choices.
We all have power; who we are is how we wield it,
And how we don't.

lessons in power

'Let me tell you what power really is, Mr Ridder.'

Spray splattered across the rocking scene . . . the line between sea and sky blurring in the motion, perspective only possible when the oil rigs, barges and other ships came into view . . . then a woman, her face as determined as her fist was rigid, clutched around a bulbous microphone . . .

'This is Glory O'Shay reporting live from the middle of the Indian Ocean . . .'

'Power is control over another man's choices.'

'. . . on board one of two Greenpeace protest vessels . . .'

'It does not require pain or submission—or even knowledge that one is being controlled.'

'. . . which today seized control of a construction barge building the so-called hole in the ocean for Anna Spires' New World.'

Harry Pont and Helen Rainey watched the Eco-Warriors walking the decks of the barge from a balcony on Platform Seven.

A knock at the window behind them brought

them back inside the War Room where the faces of the travelling Philo Group members watched them enter from monitors arranged on the wall.

'They were not armed and remain not armed,' Harry summarised. 'A number of our younger workers resisted them at first but only so that the team leader had time to secure all of the barge controls. Then all my men disembarked the barge and returned to their platform quarters.'

'So you're telling me,' said Arb from Singapore, 'that the barge they've taken over is effectively dead in the water?'

'That's correct.'

'So there's no real physical danger, just a political positioning?' said Jay from Washington.

Helen Rainey spoke up: 'Maybe for now, Jay. But let me tell you, I went to Stanford with the captain, lived in a deep-sea research vessel for three months with the protest coordinator, and I think I've been arrested with half the rest of the crew at least once before. These guys are here for the long term. And Goodie, in particular, won't leave until he's had a victory of one sort or another.'

Glory adopted a studied gritty pose as a swarthy gritty man appeared beside her on the screen.

'Captain Goodsell is the man at the helm of putting a spanner in the works of the New World Project.'

She stuck the microphone under his chin.

'Glory, the New World Project plans to rape the final natural frontier still untouched and unspoiled by so-called progress. I'm here to say that there are people left on the planet who are not going to let that happen.'

'I spoke to him today,' said Helen, 'and he said that if they can't stop the barges building the pipewalls, then they intend to station one of their boats on the other side of the pipewall with their own bilge pump pumping water directly from the ocean back into the first circle.'

'Harry, how many other barges do we have in operation?' asked Anna, sitting beside her husband in Singapore.

'We've got five running now, and another twelve due to arrive on Tuesday to work on the second pipewall.'

'So this is not a real problem, is it?'

'Only politically,' said Jay. 'I don't think we should let these people be a front row peanut gallery, not with the TV access that they have.'

'Can we buy them?' asked Arb. 'Surely they'd be more comfortable on one of the platforms. We can give them updates about what we're doing and access to all our ecological research, as well as warm dry beds.'

Helen shook her head. 'The crews on these ships tend to repeat themselves for a reason. After all, you need to be keen when you consider that most field protests and campaigns involve camping in a cold, wet, windy forest in front of an approaching freeway; canoeing near the bows of oil tankers and nuclear warships; chaining yourself to a tree; being handcuffed and thrown in the back of a police van; or living off canned foods for months on a cold, wet, windy, rustbucket of a boat in the middle of the Indian Ocean.

'Besides,' Helen continued, 'Goodie told me that

they have more food and fuel than they've ever had. It seems that they have a very generous anonymous benefactor supporting this campaign.'

'Then Laikali was right,' said Anna. 'This is more than just Greenpeace protesting. Well, at least we know that our opponents are prepared to invest in what they believe in.'

'Then I see only one course of action,' said Arb.

'You may be interested to know that Greenpeace shares our concern for the New World Project,' said Ridder proudly.

'Well it's not as if the fish can speak for themselves,' agreed Ford, pretending to enjoy clumsy sarcasm. 'I'm sure they would appreciate some assistance. Deep-sea demonstrations can be quite costly, you know.'

'So I've discovered,' said Ridder mock-earnestly. 'Luckily, I was able to arrange supplies of fuel and food and an onboard news crew.'

'And what of our own initiatives?'

'Supply ships with parts and labour are steaming in and out of the site every day. We have a number of plants on board. I expect the New World Project to experience a number of labour strikes and supply shortages quite soon, although I've instructed our contacts to wait at least a month so that the project will be well and truly started, therefore ensuring maximum disruption.'

Let the climber enjoy his little games, Ford thought. *Maybe the little shit will get lucky*. It didn't concern him greatly.

He was reflecting that these were still early days

when an underling knocked on the door, entered, and tentatively handed him a note.

She didn't know whether to feel proud of herself, or just lucky. Everything had happened so fast.

Glory O'Shay looked at her new accommodations: a bed, formica table, two chairs and a bathroom, on what she was told was called the Low Road, the bottom floor on Platform Seven.

'I'm sure,' she had watched Helen Rainey say to Captain Goodsell, 'that Greenpeace, and you especially, would appreciate the opportunity for more amenable lodgings. Of course, you would have access to all . . .'

When Rainey's voice had trailed off, Glory had turned to see Goodsell just shaking his head.

'I didn't think so,' Rainey had conceded.

Then she had turned to Glory.

Everything had then happened so fast.

Yesterday, she was a frustrated radio reporter.

This morning, she had become a specialist TV reporter—what she had always wanted to be—covering a Greenpeace action which was supposed to last for up to six months.

Tonight however, the protest continued, but sans reporter, sans cameraman. While Goodsell and his Greenies accrued gold stars from Mother Nature for spending cold wet nights sleeping on cold wet floors in cold wet construction barges, Glory had a new contract.

When Rainey had turned to her, offered her double the pay and said, 'I know for a fact that Isaac Blackwell himself would like to see you on board,' it had taken exactly ten seconds for Glory to gather her things.

She wondered what the neighbourhood was like down here. Apparently, the guy next door had hitchhiked here.

Resident News Correspondent for the New World Project, would be her title. Exclusive access, they had promised her, exclusive interviews, inside information—an unparalleled position, they had assured her, for covering the biggest, most ambitious human undertaking in history.

She didn't know whether to feel proud of herself, or just lucky.

Proud, she decided. Who needs luck, when you're successful?

The note told of the correspondent's defection.

'Fear not, Mr Ridder,' Ford soothed his disappointed young attack dog. 'These things happen. You should not try to win a war in an afternoon. Besides, I think you can safely say that you drew first blood.'

'How so?' asked Ridder quizzically.

Ford answered his question with a question of his own.

'What was your reading of the effect of exposing Blackwell's marital status?'

Ridder shook his head with disbelief. 'It didn't appear to slow them down at all. He turned it against us. Even then, I thought it would have eliminated some of their investors, but that doesn't appear to have happened.'

'Don't worry about that, Mr Ridder. It's too late

to affect his funds for their New World Project, but let me assure you it had exactly the effect we desired.'

'It did?'

Ford paused, allowing himself to watch Ridder's anxious salivating grin unfurl with rabid envy.

'It made him human, Mr Ridder. Isaac Blackwell was infallible before everyone found out he was taking donations for his wife's pet project. Now there's a seed of doubt about Blackwell's judgement in the mind of every investor, every politician and every reporter on the planet.' A knowing smile crossed Ford's own face. 'Now we've painted him into a corner. Now he lives and dies on its success. If the New World Project fails, so does he.'

All civilisations grow this way.

like snake with no head

There were times when it didn't seem real, when his brain started to doubt his own eyes. It was akin to looking out the window and not being sure whether the train or the station had just started moving.

They had said to look beyond the abras, camels, rickshaws, trishaws, samlors and tuk-tuks. His opportunity, they had told him, involved more than riding el-trains, trams and cable cars. But now, after some four months, it felt to Matt as if he—or the world outside the window—was always moving, and he had to turn his head at speed to see life outside in focus.

Pontifications

DAY 54—THERE'S A HOLE IN THE OCEAN, DEAR LIZA, DEAR LIZA!

- Water extraction continues slightly behind schedule, due to Greenpeace occupation of one barge and delay of new barges from Singapore (due to administration mix-up).
- Progress update: 200 metres below sea level.

He ended up spending half his time looking over his shoulder or reading the steadily growing file of Pontifications reports to see what he'd missed.

While Harry focused on the pipewall construction, the rest of the Portfolio Chiefs had been scattered across the globe hard at work making preparations for a New World, envisioning and testing scenarios in their respective fields.

Saul Obermann's itinerary, for example, as he tried to imagine what a world without money would look like, had included meetings with share traders on Wall Street and barter traders in Timbuktu, kibbutzim in Israel and international volunteer organisations based in London.

Jay Diaglio had bounced from the political powerhouses of the first world to the Ridge's less developed neighbours in East Africa and South Asia, comparing systems of government whilst also calculating how to ensure that Ninety East Ridge did not allow itself to become a political football for new cold wars or a strategic target for regional empire building.

Matt Turner, for his part, had been instructed by Anna to look at the respective merits of the world's great internal transport systems, including road, rail, pedestrian and other. Hong Kong was the fourth stop on his fourth trip so far.

His first tour of duty had included Mumbai, Dubai, Cairo, Mombasa—and a long boat trip back to 'the nest'.

The second, although further from home,

had been much more familiar as far as Matt's experiences were concerned: Perth, Melbourne, San Francisco, Chicago, Washington DC.

Trip three had taken him to Paris, Berlin, Rome and Florence.

This fourth expedition had already taken him to Singapore, Kuala Lumpur and Bangkok. Following two more weeks in Hong Kong, there were only two more quick visits scheduled for Shanghai and Tokyo before he next returned 'home' to Ninety East Ridge.

Pontifications

DAY 69—HERE COMES THE CAVALRY!

- Finally! Twelve more barges arrived today from Singapore.
- Pace of first wall extraction and second wall construction expected to increase considerably.
- Greenpeace continue to occupy lonely barge—we wave to them from time to time.

To Matt, still conscious of being of value, still anxious to prove his worth, Hong Kong had provided both inspiration and desperation. An unholy mess at first glance, effective chaos on closer inspection. Its transport, an example that showed the simplicity of the concept of moving people and cargo from A to B. And a showcase of the awesome complexity behind making that concept a reality.

By way of comparison, he had already seen the much more pristine, although relatively small, mass rapid transit system in Singapore; he had been impressed by the more comprehensive, soft-tyred Métro of Paris; less so by the soft-earth-driven ideas of raised light railways in Bangkok and Kuala Lumpur; and least so by the car-dominated transport grids of all but a few American cities.

Now, to add to his list, was the super-efficient, hose-downable mass rapid transport system in Hong Kong. Underground, underwater, under mountains, the line had been built without regard for obstacles. Eight million passengers a day proved its usefulness. Here was a system which reflected the very nature of Hong Kong: fast, reliable, seemingly impossible to build—but here it was!

From concept to reality, Matt realised, would be the key to his success. There were so many complicated, changeable factors to consider. The transport system had to move workers, shoppers, students, goods and cargo. It therefore had to consider where people lived—would live, would work, shop, study, and what sort of products and supplies needed to be transported. And then there were sewers, communication lines, water and gas pipes, not to mention all those factors that hadn't even been invented yet, to complicate the issue further.

He had suddenly felt overwhelmed. And inadequate. Clearly, he was out of his depth—had anyone else noticed this yet? It would only be a matter of time, surely.

While each member of the Group pursued their own extensive travel plans, they crissed and crossed each other regularly. Today, Arb, Anna, Tom and Byron were also in Hong Kong. As was Laikali Rulé. Although she insisted she was in no way officially connected with their enterprise, Matt was pleased that *coincidence* found Mrs Rulé in the same place as an important Philo Group meeting. He had spoken to her regularly over the past four months, but only over the phone. Some of the time he reported on the Project, but usually she ended up briefing him before he arrived in a new city.

'Space is the highest currency here,' she had said to him of Hong Kong. 'Don't look for grandeur or extravagance. They haven't the land, or the time, for it.'

When the city had first come into view, Matt had understood what Laikali had meant. There it was, hemmed in between the harbour and sheer rocky green Mount Victoria, the most crowded assembly of skyscrapers he could have imagined.

It had disappeared as their limo did into the sub-harbour tunnel, and when they emerged out the other side, they were right in the middle of it.

Byways brushed against buildings. Third-storey windows watched traffic race one way while fourth-storey windows watched it rush another.

Cars in motion everywhere zoomed through tunnels into underpasses, over bridges and round and around overlapping slip roads.

Tall buildings towered on all sides, a random mix of soaring shiny glass and steel, and teetering older soot-covered edifices. A labyrinthine maze of dirty side streets and litter-strewn thoroughfares darting and weaving between skyscrapers which grew like weeds in every available space.

Pontifications

DAY 111—ALL SYSTEMS GO!

- Resistance and pressure tests: all clear.
- Ocean floor solidity: stable.
- Suitability of Ridge surface as foundation for planned city expected to weigh some four million tonnes: All Systems Go!

'Did they plan Hong Kong?' Matt had asked Laikali.

'Plan? To use their words,' Laikali had said, 'Hong Kong grow like snake with no head. Who know which way will go next?'

Matt had turned to her, stunned by just how poor a Polynesian's impression of a Chinaman could be, but Laikali mistook his dismay and had waved it aside.

'Don't be so surprised,' she had said. 'All civilisations grow this way.'

Waiting for a number.
Win Lose Victory Tragedy Glory Failure.

out of our hands

DAY 145—HONG KONG

Matt and Laikali . . .

On the edge of their seats . . .

Bated breath . . .

What will happen . . .

What will be . . .

This is the moment . . .

Everything that's gone before counts for nought . . .

'Go! Go! Go!'

'C'mon Star Lad! Go Star Lad!'

The crowd roaring as they turn for home, the thunder of hooves rising even louder.

In its yellow silks and the red cap, Star Lad moves to the outside.

'Here it comes . . .' she cries. 'Here it comes . . .'

Raw Prawn in the lead. But Star Lad charging, gaining.

A furlong to go . . .

'Go. Go!'

A length . . .

Half a length . . .

'. . . Star Lad . . .'

'. . . Raw Prawn . . .'

Neck and neck . . .

Nothing in it . . .

'Come on!!!'

A bob. A dip.

A pause, then a roar.

Cries of joy. Tickets in the air. Tickets on the ground. Jumping up and down. Shouts. Sighs. Hopeful tickets in clutched, anxious fists. The inside? The outside? The race is over but the rush goes on. Anticipation never ending. What next? Who won?

The silence—a split second of collective concentration—was as they crossed the line.

But now, a silent frenzy. Adrenaline exhausted. Blood rushing to take its place. The moment extended. Longer and longer. Unbearable.

Eyes on the scoreboard. Fingers crossed. Her hopeful, expectant whispering, 'Star Lad Star Lad Star Lad Star Lad . . .'

Waiting for a number. Win Lose Victory Tragedy Glory Failure.

Number two . . .

'Shit!'

Defeat.

Laikali's face immediately turned to the heavens, 'You expect me to believe you had nothing to do with this?'

Her head shaking in disbelief at Augusto's reply.

'What good are you then?' she moaned theatrically. 'You might as well still be alive!'

Matthew Turner was still jumping up and down.

'Go the Raw Prawn!' he yelled in glory, his ticket held high, triumphant.

It took Byron Lybrand's insistent shoulder tapping to turn Matt's attention back to work.

'We're starting in three minutes,' Byron yelled above the still-buzzing crowd.

Following Byron, who raced ahead at his usual hurried pace, Matt and Laikali made their way up through the grandstand to the corporate conference room that would serve as today's Mobile War Room.

The soundproof doors sucked shut behind him, as if vacuum-sealing them inside. Five video screens lined a wall—one for each location: Ninety East Ridge, Washington, London, Helsinki and one that showed themselves in Hong Kong. Anna, Arb, Tom and Byron were already seated as Laikali and Matt took their places before the Hong Kong camera.

'Okay,' said Anna, taking charge of the meeting. 'The agenda for today has been changed. Now I realise that Jay and Saul were supposed to report on their progress in DC and the UK respectively, Miles was to tell us what our Scandinavian friends can do for communications, and Byron and I were to report on some more fundraising here in Hong Kong. But we'll delay all that to the next meeting.

'You should all have a copy of today's Pontifications report,' she then said to the camera. 'Today, Harry has the floor.'

'What do you mean, they won't work? Why?' blurted Arb, almost losing control for one rare moment.

Pontifications

DAY 145—WHAT THE HELL IS GOING ON?

- Latest supplies from Perth and Singapore delayed for maybe a month.
- Barge workers call for industrial action.

'I'm sorry, Isaac, but they said that because the equipment has never been used before, they should be paid danger money in case of unforeseen accidents.'

'As opposed to foreseen accidents?' scoffed Arb, not hiding his sarcasm or his contempt. 'This is not supposed to happen, Harry.'

'I know,' Harry conceded from his video screen.

'You tell that union rep that when he agreed to do this job, he agreed to do it for a set fee by a set deadline. I don't care what he says, but you tell him if the job's not done according to our schedule, then he can kiss his reference from the greatest building project of all time goodbye.'

'I appreciate the sentiment behind your words, Isaac,' said Harry drily, shaking his head, 'but there's more to this than contracts. I think we have professional agitators in our ranks.'

A pause . . . then panicked words of wisdom rushed from the different screens. Industrial relations advice, negotiation tips, seemingly simple solutions were shouted and echoed from five fishbowl worlds.

Harry's voice finally managed to rise above them.

'Wait, there's more. There's more,' he said. 'In addition to our internal concerns and our supply bottlenecks, something else happened this morning which did not make my report.'

The four other screens were now silent. What else could possibly have happened?

'Greenpeace today commandeered two more barges.'

Children view the world with fresh eyes, fresh imagination. They do not start a thought with compromise.

ghosts and pandemonium

DAY 160—SHANGHAI

Culture, commerce, construction.

Luxury cars weaving between ringing rivers of bicycles.

The roads, the Bund, the buildings, even the sky, tinged with a red-orange dust of new foundations, of collapsing derelictions, of petrol-heavy pollution.

Everywhere, the future. New roads, tunnels, bridges in every direction. Cranes and skyscrapers in every sight-line. Ships, trains, planes trading with every corner of the globe.

Everywhere, the past. Chinese communism was born here. British, French, American and Japanese colonial architecture was left here. Galleries and theatres and dark smoky jazz clubs lurk in every alleyway. Fine and popular art mix without distinction, a reminder that Shanghai has been the centre of art and culture in China for centuries.

Everywhere, the present. Banks and billboards competing for prime space along the mighty Yangtze. Wealth and poverty, young and old, old and new, culture, commerce, construction, all riding their bicycles side by side. Twenty million people in perpetual pursuit of progress.

Shanghai: the leading edge of the most populous country in the world.

In history.

But to the Philo Group it all became irrelevant, reduced to a vague hum of horns and bells outside as tempers flared and voices rose again inside today's Mobile War Room.

Two weeks had gone by since the Hong Kong PGM where Harry had first voiced his suspicion that there were traitors in the ranks. Greenpeace still occupied three barges. Until now, Ninety East Ridge had offered no resistance, no defences.

There had been a moment of stunned silence when Anna told the video conference what Ninety East Ridge's response to the new developments would be.

Then pandemonium.

'Nothing?'

'What the . . .! Why not?'

'Can't you see we have enemies?'

'This is crazy!'

'How naive can you be?'

But Anna stood firm. 'We have been able to deal with everything that's been thrown at us. We've been able to do that because we have been well prepared and clear about our position.'

Jay Diaglio protested loudest from Moscow: 'Yes, but at least with an intelligence group of some sort—'

'We've beaten all efforts so far with hard work and planning. I do not see a reason why we should resort to questionable international ethics now.'

'It's not like an army, Anna,' Diaglio counselled. 'It's for defence only, not attack.'

'It's spies and lies and everything else associated with intelligence.'

'How many barges do they have to take before you understand?' said Mary from Paris.

Two items had arisen so far: first, Harry had informed the Group that Greenpeace had pulled the three occupied barges together to make a large, three-pontoon base; second, Anna had resolutely determined that Ninety East Ridge would not be creating security or defence forces of any sort.

'You have over four trillion dollars worth of investment in the Ridge—surely you want to protect that,' Saul Obermann implored from London. 'Every day we are breaking new ground, so to speak. Surely, there are or at least will be national secrets that you want to protect?'

'That's an outside axiom, Saul. Tell me, what secrets would you like to keep?'

'Well, our research, for example.'

'Let's share it.'

'But it would be worth millions.'

'It would be worth more if we shared it.'

Another moment's silence. Someone mumbled that it was like arguing with a child. Matt thought it was Paris.

'We need to think like children,' said Anna, still standing her ground. 'Children view the world with fresh eyes, fresh imaginations. They do not start a thought with compromise. Neither must we.'

'Well, maybe that's true,' said Arb, his soft voice underlining the seriousness of the precedent he was creating by disagreeing with his wife. 'But there's a lot more to it . . .'

Captain Goodsell was keeping watch that night.

The sky was clear and, though the ocean was placid, the moon lit the crests of the hulking muscular waves, reminding the captain just how small he really was.

Also outlined in the moonlight were the sleeping ships and platforms that surrounded him. Their silence and darkness—only the warning beacons which marked their edges were visible— were in stark contrast to the bustling industry which overtook them during the day.

He had to admit—although he would only ever admit it to himself—there was something about the New World Project which could not fail to impress. The scale of imagination, of enterprise, even of the construction work so far—not one hundred yards from him was the hole in the ocean that Anna Spires had promised.

Like a black hole in space, it was incongruous. Anti-matter where matter should be, open air where ocean should be. And like a black hole, it had a pulling power. There was mystery in its bottomless darkness, there was possibility in its impossible presence. It was easier to despise it in the daytime, Goodsell thought, when mankind racked the oceanscape with unnatural noise and industry.

But as the captain gazed into the darkness—of the hole, of the ocean, of the night sky—on the other side of the ship, a black hand reached out of the black waters and silently pulled its owner aboard.

'. . . the economy, for example,' Arb was saying. 'If our enemies know how much money is in the coffers, then they can try to bankrupt us. Or take intellectual property: corporate espionage could steal all of our advancements; in tidal energy, in communications, in deep-sea research, et cetera, et cetera.'

Anna took a deep breath, as if to fortify herself, before replying, 'Let's figure out how we want to deal with intellectual property before we start to nationalise it, okay? Byron's covering that ground, and we're exploring amongst other things whether intellectual property laws need to exist at all.'

'What?' 'Huh?' 'No IP?'

'Look. No! If we are honest about our work, open and transparent in our processes—and especially if we have no money—then we will have no need for intellectual property. And we will certainly have nothing to fear from foreign spies.'

'We all have secrets, Anna,' Arb said, a little strangely. 'And this place, Ninety East Ridge, will, I guarantee, have enemies.'

Clad in black from head to toe, the figure ghosted silently into the sleeping quarters.

Outside, Goodsell was trying to shake his growing sense of admiration by thinking about how many more barges they might be able to commandeer before the NWP would be provoked into some sinister-looking action.

Two of the crew were sleeping on the bridge of one of the barges. Over the constant lapping of the ocean on the hull, one of them thought he heard a dripping sound. He was half-awake, half-dreaming, and not sure which conscious state saw the shadow looming over him.

Maybe they should try to take a platform, Goodsell wondered. It was clear that the NWP had adopted a policy of non-confrontation and non-violence. If they could exploit it just a little more, then maybe they could create public support for their 'heroic' deeds.

The shadow eased in and out of each barge before returning to the command vessel. He slid in and out of the shadows until he was just metres away from the last remaining passenger.

Goodsell chastised himself for losing their media rep. He made a mental note to recommend to the Executive Committee that all future campaigns have dedicated journalists aboard. They were great for PR and gave the organisation at least some form of creative control over footage. And, if this one had been any guide, they also provided a nice pair of legs to distract a man settling in for a long, long protest.

The pleasant mental image of Glory O'Shay was the last thing Captain Goodsell saw before a firm hand and an ether-soaked rag covered his face, muffled his shouts and then gently lowered him to the deck.

Anna made one last frustrated appeal.

'I realise I'm being naive here. I realise I'm being simplistic. But sometimes simple acts are all that is required to raise people's standards. Let's raise the bar, shall we? Let's forget current standards and start our own. Start a completely new game with different rules. Let's evolve beyond petty one-upmanship and competition-through-sabotage. Let's be different and lead.'

There was silent acceptance in each location. Heads down, still some frowns and shaking faces, but there was agreement with Anna's ideal. This was a New World, and the easiest trap for all of them in each of their portfolios was making axioms of the world outside.

'It's always been done this way' was no excuse.

'There's a reason it's always been done this way' was no better.

The basic premise of Ninety East Ridge was that despite all of history's advancements, the evolution of society had produced a compromised, unacceptably substandard world.

They all agreed with the premise.

But none agreed with Anna's pleas.

Against her wishes, the Group voted to form a defence intelligence service and an internal security service. Not to defend what they were creating would have been senseless.

Anna vetoed it.

A senseless death, random and ridiculous.
No one was at fault. No one was to blame.

senseless

A senseless death, random and ridiculous.

The police report called it an accident.

No one, it said, was at fault. No one, it said, was to blame.

'She's so smart,' he was saying, gazing at the window, unable to take his eyes off her.

'Yes, she is,' Jo replied. There's nothing wrong with parental pride.

'Smarter than I'll ever be,' he said wistfully.

The driver, the report said, could not have seen him. Mr Spires, apparently, had been crossing the road just below the top of a rise.

The driver had tried to stop, as evidenced by the long skidmarks on the road; had tried to swerve, also evidenced by the weaving black trail.

'Do you think she's noticed?' he asked his wife.

'Noticed what?' Jo replied.

But he didn't answer, lost in a private

melancholic thought process that even though it spoke, did not require interaction.

'She will,' he said again, enigmatically.

There was nothing the driver could have done.

'He's really quite torn up about it,' the officer said.

'Killing someone is not an easy thing to live with,' Jo replied, meaning it sympathetically.

Noticed what?

But she knew him too well. He didn't need to answer. She knew his self-doubts better than he did.

That I'm a fake, I'm all talk, I'm just theories and nonsense, that I've never done anything.

She'd heard them all before.

Unrealised idealism is not a failure, she wanted to tell him. It's as common as a cold. But the way he battled on defiantly—even if only in words, not deeds—was not common at all.

He just never seemed to comprehend that it was exactly this dreamy nonsensical refusal to compromise that made him so attractive to their daughter.

And to her.

It was a senseless death, the officer said, random and ridiculous.

'There's nothing more I can teach her,' were his last words.

No one was at fault. No one was to blame.

But Jo knew there was fault. There was blame.
  She should have seen it coming.

One man's enemy, one man's shield, another's opportunity;
Yet for all of us, time is short.

personal timezones

DAY 161—HONG QIAO INTERNATIONAL AIRPORT, SHANGHAI

Anna, Isaac, Matt and Tom sat in a huddle before a bank of blank monitors in a specially arranged conference room at Shanghai airport, right next to their departure gate. The PGM had just finished and the four of them were trying to decipher what Greenpeace was trying to achieve by this.

They had, Harry had reported, untied and abandoned the barges, and restationed their own vessels a kilometre away from the main construction areas. No contact had been made, no messages left. Harry would not let any of his men reboard the barges until they got some bomb experts to check for sabotage.

Construction, meanwhile, despite all the setbacks, was continuing. The second pipewall was forming under the sea like a magic trick under a hat, and concrete had now almost half-filled the central pipewall.

Matt's mind wandered from the Group's debate. He tried to imagine looking down into a one mile shaft, eighty metres wide. He guessed, rightly, that you would not be able to see the bottom—like a hole to the centre of the earth, he thought.

The airline announcement interrupted his thoughts:

'Ladies and gentlemen, Flight JL868 to Tokyo is now ready for boarding. Would all passengers please proceed to gate 15 for immediate boarding. Please have your boarding passes ready.'

'That's us,' said Tom unnecessarily as he rose resolutely to his feet. Matt, as if attached by a piece of string, began to rise beside him.

'Hold on! Hold on!' said Arb impatiently, his hand dragging Matt's coat, Matt, the piece of string and Tom back into their seats. 'We've got ages yet. We really need to sort this out.'

Tom snuck a glance out an interior window which showed that the queue had instantaneously stretched fifty places.

Matt snuck a glance at Tom, then Anna, who showed no sign of urgency, and then Arb, who was ekeing out every last vital second he could before they got on the plane.

As he watched him, Matt began to suspect that there was more to Arb's motivation than the desire for productivity. It was more like something personal, almost as if he was driven by a personal vendetta. Against waste. Against inefficiency. Against God's most hapless invention.

Time.

In earth time, Mercury takes about eighty-eight Earth days to circle the sun. Yet it takes almost fifty-nine Earth days to rotate on its axis. Jupiter, on the other hand, has a year that lasts almost twelve Earth years. Ironically, or at least surprisingly, it spins so fast that the days are shorter than our own, taking about ten Earth hours.

Do the maths and you find that there are approximately one and a half Mercurian days, and almost ten and a half thousand Jovian days, in their respective solar years. If the average lifespan on Earth is seventy-five years, on Mercury it's three hundred and eleven, and on Jupiter barely six.

In his mind, Arb was most definitely a son of Jupiter. It was as if he had just six years to live— which meant every day had to count, had to count, had to count.

To achieve this, however, his bodyclock was set to Mercurian time, as evidenced by the hours he worked. Twenty-four hours in a day was clearly not enough for him; the fourteen hundred hour Mercurian day was—but only barely.

More than fame, more than power, perhaps even more than money, Arb's most precious commodity was always time.

Time. Vital to work in, a bonus to play in. It was crucial that time spent awake not be wasted. To make deals with brokers. To ask question after question, receive answer after answer. To read the news, the sport, the weather. To understand the investment implications, to make bar-room repartee, to have sex with his wife, to take profits on wheat or coffee beans or semiconductors. Time was money. Time was influence. Time was achievement.

'My life is defined by time,' he had told Anna once.

And time was short. Always.

There were times, Matt was certain, when Anna must have wondered how he could prioritise her ahead of all his other commitments. But he did. Constantly. She was, he had often said, 'his most important client'. It helped that he seemingly did not need to sleep, constantly shifting his schedule to meet her—it also helped that everyone else would change their schedule to meet him—to meet her for dinner, for coffee, for a meeting. For sex. Mercurian days (often for days on end) and Jovian nights. And he kept on discussing the Greenpeace security issue until the queue outside had dwindled to nothing.

Tom must have counted every one of the last thirty people to board the plane. He knew that it was near-impossible for them to miss the plane from here. Even so, he couldn't help but worry. Tom was, and would always be, Matt realised, a man much more comfortable dealing with time in the past than in the present.

History was his life—more than a job and more than a pastime. It was also his shield against the present, against life, against reality. To Tom, fossilised Pompeians and precivilised Africans were more easily understood than the present and the day-to-day. To Tom, the evidence that we routinely assume is reality was an unfathomable dangerous enigma. Subject to variation, unlike history. Subject to certainty, unlike history.

Subject to consequences, unlike history.

*

Time was still on Matt's mind some hours later as they disembarked at Narita International Airport, Japan.

Arb had met some potential investors on the plane and instructed Anna, Matt and Tom to make their way back to the hotel without him.

'He never stops, does he?' Matt said to all and no one as they slumped exhausted into the limo for the one-hour ride into Tokyo.

'Isaac? No. Not as long as I've known him,' Tom agreed.

'What drives a man to live his life that way, do you think?'

Tom deflected the question. 'Don't ask me. I have enough trouble making time for breakfast every morning. But I suspect *you* might know,' he said, directing the allegation at Anna.

Anna's eyes were focused on the world rushing by her window, but she knew he was talking to her. 'He was like that a long time before he met me.'

'Do you miss him?' Matt asked. 'I mean, when he throws himself into his work like this.'

'Miss him? Sort of. I think I quite admire it,' she said inscrutably, her gaze remaining fixed on the world outside.

Her answer, like many of her answers, was both philosophical and resolute. Matt and Tom had no further questions to match her depth, and the car became silent.

For a moment.

'It makes him happy. Makes him whole, I think,' she said. 'We all need a purpose, I suppose . . . and a pastime.'

'So which is which?' pressed Matt, realising almost immediately that he may have over-stepped—so he had to go further. 'I mean, what's his purpose, do you think? And what are his pastimes?'

Anna turned her eyes from the window, but she was neither offended nor defensive. Instead, she smiled mischievously, dipped her eyes and replied, 'What are yours, Mr Turner? Your purpose? Your pastime?'

'Good question,' he laughed. 'I'll tell you if I ever figure it out.'

'You can't tell me now?'

'Not unless you have a bottle of red wine in that handbag of yours.'

'Here, here,' supported Tom.

Several hours, courses and bottles of red wine later, Matthew Turner tried to summarise his purpose and pastimes.

'You haf to undershtand . . . my profess-shon iz pashtimes . . . it'sh a fery difficult queshtion.'

'You're drunk, M-mattie Tuuurner,' admonished Tom, his head rising for a moment from its place of rest on the table, then thumping back down.

'Drunk! Drunk? Do you think I'm drunk Mizz Shpires?'

'I think . . . drinking's . . . the least of your worries . . . Mr Turner. A bigger . . . concern . . . is how you're going . . . to get your two . . . semi-conscious drinking companions . . . back to their rooms.'

'Back to your rooms! Now,' he wavily raised his wrist-watch at her, 'hold on, you haven't told uss . . . your purpossse yet.'

'Same as Tom's, Mr Turner,' she said, her voice getting softer and softer until she whispered, 'Sleeping.' Her head then gently fell into her arms which lay crooked invitingly, a pillow in waiting, on the table.

Matt looked at Anna's delicate head rested on her forearms. He looked at Tom, his forehead more directly attached to the wooden table. He went to speak but realised no one would hear. She was right: clichés would have to wait.

'Come on,' he said, immediately forgetting no one could hear, as he tossed Tom's left arm over one shoulder then Anna's right over his other. Thankfully, perhaps driven by some childlike somnambulistic senses, they were able to support some, though not all, of their weight. His own senses reeling, Matt somehow directed the teetering, three-headed, six-legged monster out of the hotel restaurant and towards the elevators. The lift seemed to sway as they entered it. For a moment, Matt wondered if it was safe inside this tilting, swaying, was-it-spinning-also elevator. Then he realised that the only alternative was the stairs, and that this was for sure the fastest way to the bathroom, so he pressed the top floor where all their rooms were.

Tom's room was right next to the elevators.

Carefully leaning Anna against the wall, Matt tried to coax the walking Tom-zombie to find his keys. Failing, he began reaching into his pockets until he found them himself. An amazingly small slot later and Matt literally threw Tom onto his bed.

By the time he staggered back to the corridor, Anna had slid helplessly down the wall until she sat crumpled in a heap on the floor.

'Come on,' Matt said again, for himself as much as her, as he reached down to help her up. He tried pulling her hands but that didn't work, so he tried putting his arms under her and—suddenly she flung her arms around his neck. He almost fell, but somehow managed to right himself, her head now falling over his shoulder, her legs lifted off the ground.

So the monster, now two-headed and two-legged, began to navigate its way to Anna's room at the end of the corridor. Realising that a direct route would discount the advantages of being able to lean against the walls from time to time, it took an age for Matt to carry her the remaining twenty metres.

At the door, again he asked if his drunken companion might find her keys. Again, the drunken companion could not. But this time, searching her pants pockets, then her coat pockets was much more difficult, awkward, distracting. He was about to search those pants again when he noticed her handbag. Aaaah. Matt knew he was not thinking straight at all, but as he turned the key in the very, very small slot, he couldn't help but think that he should carry her inside and—

He almost fell through the door as Arb opened it for him.

'Matt! Anna!'

Damn, Matt thought, *I knew I should have taken her back to my place.*

Arb surveyed the scene with what seemed no small amount of amusement. 'Oh my, I leave you alone for just a few hours and look what happens. I'm sure Tom is no better. You've dropped him off already then? Or is he still in the bar?'

Matt could only nod automatically as Arb took the delicate, soft weight of Anna from his arms. He almost fell over again, teetering back until he leaned against the wall behind him.

Arb's voice came from deep inside the suite, 'Are you going to be able to get back to your room, Matt?'

Again, Matt could only nod and he managed a step down the hall before he did fall over. Through hazy dreamy vision, Matt saw Arb appear in the horizontal doorway, his feet walking on the carpeted wall. Moments, minutes or was it days later, he felt the world sway, then stop, then a feeling, a hand against his thigh, in his pocket, then removed, the sway again, then weightlessness, his body flying, soaring, then crashing into the divine soft cushion of his bed.

When he awoke at noon the next day, Matt found a note slid under his door saying Arb had been called to New York and Anna back to the Ridge. It also said that Laikali had arranged a tour for Tom and himself around Tokyo—something about 'important cultural research'—and that they should take it before also returning to Ninety East Ridge.

Remember—we're all the same,
We're all from alien cultures.

Osishiwa's Tokyo sex tour

DAY 162—TOKYO

Matt made his way down to meet Tom for lunch/breakfast. As he walked into the café, he saw a Japanese woman sitting at the table with Tom, who was laughing uncontrollably.

'Matt! Matt! Listen to this. Osi, tell Matt what you are.'

'I am Osishiwa. I am gift from Rulé-san. I am to show you good time tonight.'

Matt hedged his smile, expecting something more.

'Tell him where you are going to take us tonight, Osi.'

The woman looked a little dismayed at Tom's eagnerness to have her repeat their plans. Hiding her frustration as best she could, she faced Matt and said plainly, 'Tonight I take you on Tokyo Sex Tour.'

Needless to say, Matt had had no idea how to respond to such a gift from Laikali. At the time, he had just nodded, said thank you and exchanged looks of disbelief and confusion with Tom.

It was now early evening. Osishiwa was to pick them up in a few minutes.

Sans Osi, they had spent the afternoon seeing the sights: the splendid Meiji Shrine, the resplendent Sensoji Temple, the bustling surrounding markets, the more modern Ginza fashion shops and the electronics bazaars in Akasaka. Once again—it had been the recurring theme of his travels—Matt was struck by just how different the world could be.

And people, people, people—his lasting impression from the daytime excursion. Firstly, they had joined the crush trying to squeeze into the train. When as many bodies as was humanly possible had finally crammed their way in, stationhands then packed them in further, so that half a dozen more bodies could be inserted onto the carriage.

This was hardly the three-week study he had originally planned for getting to know Japan's renowned rail system, but it certainly qualified as a crash course. At Shibuya station, they had been spewed from the train into a current of blue suits that carried them off the platform and out onto the street.

People, people, people, wherever they went. And even looking out from the tallest Tokyo skyscrapers, civilisation, filled with yet more people, stretched to every horizon.

'Here she is,' said Tom, snapping Matt out of his reverie.

'Trust LR to set up something like this,' laughed Tom, shaking his head, as Osi led them up a creaking black metal fire escape that looked down on a pitch dark alley below. Tokyo, Matt had discovered, despite being the most phosphorescent place on the planet after sunset—bright neon signage and advertisements more than adequately replacing daylight in the entertainment parts of town— also has a netherworld cast in shadow, sunk in an endless maze of black back-alleys and behind doors without signs or welcome mats.

They reached the top of the stairs, where Osi was already in animated discussion with the apparently displeased maitre d'.

'What's going on?' Matt asked Tom.

'This kind of bar doesn't usually let gaijins like us in.'

'Gaijins? That's the word for foreigners, isn't it?'

Tom nodded. 'But don't worry. I'm sure our "gift" has it under control.'

And so it proved when, a few moments later, the door opened and Osi, Tom and Matt filed past the previously stern host who now stared impassively into the black alley behind them, his fingers idly massaging his suddenly fatter wallet.

The room was a blue shade of dark, lit only by shaded neon tubes scattered around the otherwise black room. Blue-black leather lounges. Blue-black tables. A blue-black bar save for some flashy gold railings and edges. Black curtains protected the room from any light which might find its way in from the night alley outside.

Matt was expecting to see a stage or a platform

where the 'show'—whatever it was—would be performed. But there was none. In fact, as he looked around, he could see no focal point for the room— the lounges were spread and angled in different directions—except perhaps for a surreal-looking fishtank which was set into the far blue-black wall.

Osi was now following a waitress in a black shirt through the room to the table. Only as he sat down did Matt realise that the waitress was not wearing a skirt or trousers.

It took a moment for him to rip his stare away from the only patch of black beneath her waist.

Tom leaned in close to him. 'Shabu! Shabu!' he said into Matt's ear.

'Surprise? Surprise?' Matt guessed.

'Actually, I think it means "pants down" but we've checked with the judges and have agreed, under the circumstances, to accept your answer too.'

The waitress apparently spoke no English and so Osi translated her request for drink orders.

'My head says sake,' said Tom, by way of un-necessary explanation, 'but my heart says beer.'

'Two beers,' supported Matt, happy to have something familiar in this strange, strange place.

As the orders made their way back to the bar, Matt only now noticed the other semi-clad wait-resses serving customers in the bruised shadows around the room. Some of the customers, too, had decided that parts of their usual attire were unnecessary or superfluous. He turned back to Tom, looking perhaps for a second opinion so that he might trust his own eyes again.

'If the stories I hear are true,' Tom began, 'then this is Normal, Illinois, compared to what we're going to see later.'

They tried to act normal while the world around them gradually changed into something they'd never imagined.

In front of them, a waitress (now down to a bra, still no pants) and a customer (underpants and a tie—and a bright red face) played a game of cards. One card each, higher number wins, lower number removes an article of clothing.

'So Mattie,' Tom said, eyes wide, staring at the scene in front of him, 'you're still a mystery man. Any women in that mysterious past of yours?'

The players flipped the cards simultaneously. An uproarious clamour from the customer's similarly red-faced drinking buddies. The card-combatant laughed also, drunkenly jubilant about his loss. The tie, surely—No! Apparently, he doesn't get to choose. The waitress leaned over and delicately helped him remove his briefs . . . over Matt's first— and only—sighting of an erect Japanese cock.

'The only thing that's a mystery about my past,' said Matt, also failing to look at Tom as he spoke, 'is the women.'

The tie or the bra?

Somehow, the beer perhaps, Matt's language skills were now able to understand the chorus of Japanese exhortations surrounding the contest before them: Tie! Bra! Tie! Bra! One card to him. One card to her. Tie! Bra! Tie! Bra!

'You have to tell me, Tom—you're the one who

married a beautiful billionaire—what I am doing wrong—because I must be doing it all wrong—the tie!'

Another roar from the crowd—and the happily defeated customer—as the waitress leaned over to, then against, then up and down the customer and teasingly removed his tie.

'I've gotta tell ya, Mattie,' forced Tom, unnecessarily maintaining the façade of not being absolutely captivated by what was going on. 'I've got no idea. One day, we were just friends—we studied together in France—and the next, she's all over me, we go out for a month, and then she tells me she loves me. I don't believe it! They're still playing!'

The bra or the . . . what? Matt's Japanese skills returned to their former non-existent state. The crowd was still chanting. Card for him. Card for her. A momentary, expectant silence. He flipped— she faked! A king for him! Now all eyes turned to her. She played the crowd, tantalising them as she peeked under the still-hidden card.

'They must be playing on until she's also naked,' said Matt, speaking to ease their tense confusion.

An ace! A roar! The customer, now only wearing his red face, covered it in mock-humiliation and despair. He leaned back. She leaned forward. And she pulled out . . .

. . . a lighter?

'We'll talk more later,' said Matt.

'Yeah, later,' said Tom.

Much later, because a second later they were

speechless for the rest of the night as the waitress set alight the lucky loser's pubic hair, and the Japanese crowd drank and chanted in uninhibited delirium.

How to lead a horse to water
And make it do whatever you want it to.

a whip in one hand . . .

Ridder's grin grew wide and vengeful as Ford finished briefing him.

'Finally, vengeance is mine.'

'Now, now, Mr Ridder. Who are we to claim the vicissitudes of fate?'

'We're the fucking power, that's who!'

He was enjoying this too much, Ford thought. Personal motivation was one thing, but losing perspective was another.

'Don't forget: it's only a minor victory in the scheme of things.'

'Oh no,' said Ridder, rubbing his hands with glee, 'it's gonna hurt big time!'

This was a forest-for-the-trees situation, Ford decided. Perhaps a change of approach was required.

'Well, you're welcome,' he said.

It worked. Ford could almost see the light bulb going on over Ridder's head.

'You know, I've been meaning to ask you about that,' said Ridder. 'About how you manage things like this. About how you're able to exert such control over people.'

Not quite what Ford had intended, but better than the spiteful parasite of a moment ago.

'I mean, how do you get a job like this? Do they advertise? Are there interviews? How do you qualify to sit in a room making phone calls that control the fate of the world? I mean, tell me, did you just wake up one morning and realise that this was the life for you?'

'Why does any man do what he does? How does anybody decide? To become a hairdresser, a taxi driver, a public servant? Luck, character, circumstances, forces even I can't control conspiring to lead us down our paths.'

'No. I mean, how do you maintain leverage over them?'

Ford stared at his attack dog and hid his disappointment. The little shit just wanted *how-to* tips. No doubt he was already dwelling on what it would take to push aside this all-but-blind old man. *Just let him try*, thought Ford with scorn.

'It's all about experience,' he said, hoping Ridder would get the hint. 'I'm like an old stable hand, the only one at the ranch who knows how to ride the wild horse they call the World.'

'What's the trick?' asked Ridder. 'You must have some whip.'

'It's not just the whip,' said Ford, happy to reveal more, satisfied that Ridder just wasn't up to it. 'It's the feed, it's the training, it's the cubes of sugar I keep in my pocket, it's knowing when to rein the beast in and knowing when to let it have its head.'

'So you admit that it's not completely under your control.'

'Do you know how big the horse we're talking about is?'

Ridder nodded, but Ford knew he didn't have a clue.

'So you admit that if Spires and Blackwell lead this horse to the water, you can't stop it from drinking?'

'Let's just say I'm profoundly confident of my influence.'

'Ha!' laughed Ridder, ignoring Ford's answer. He rose to his feet and leaned forward across Ford's desk. 'Your influence? With due respect, you're an old man sitting in a dark room . . .' His voice trailed off, the threat left hanging in the air. 'I promise I'd still make your phone calls.'

This time, it was Ford's turn to laugh. 'You're asking who'd miss me?'

'You tell me: who'd miss you?'

'I think Fabian would miss me.'

'Fabian?'

'Fabian.'

Ridder's head snapped around as a man now moved from a corner of the room. A burly man. A bodyguard? He must have been there the whole time! He didn't say a word as he walked past a bewildered Ridder now looking around the room again for more hidden man-giants. With soft gentle steps that defied his broad heavy width, Fabian approached the desk and stood towering over Ridder's shoulder.

'I'm sorry,' said Ford, the menace now in *his* voice. 'I thought you'd met. He has, after all, attended each and every one of our meetings for almost six months now.'

Ridder glanced over his shoulder as the big man nodded. He quickly shifted into recovery mode. 'Anyway, I've got a lot of work to do.' He headed for the door. 'Good news about tomorrow. I'll watch with interest.' He opened the door and shook his head. 'All I was saying is that it's nothing but a glorified dry dock. A concrete trough. I don't see why we don't just put a boot through the side and be on our way.' And then he was on his.

Ford let out the deep breath that had been containing his growing anger for the past few minutes.

'Why not flay the whip? Why not just drive them where we want them to go? Why not just put anyone that goes there down?'

Fabian said nothing.

'How do we stop them if they lead the horse to water? How do we stop it drinking?'

Again nothing. That wasn't his job.

'We teach the horse that the water is poisoned, that's what. Or that it's filled with piranhas. Or that Poseidon himself will reach out, drag you under and drown you if you get too close. That's how.'

Right place, right time—
Depends on your point of view.

shock and comfort

DAY 170—THE WAR ROOM, NINETY EAST RIDGE

With the exception of Arb, who was still dealing with some business opportunities in New York, everyone had returned to the Ridge. In addition to the Philo Group, Anna had asked for a contingent of senior admin and support staff to join her for a special announcement in the War Room.

'I have some bad news to announce,' Anna said to get their attention. 'It saddens me to have to announce the resignation of our good friend and Philo Group member, Sanjay Mathur.' A buzz of whispers and head-turning. Anna beckoned the mild-mannered Indian man to stand up. 'Before anyone gets the wrong idea, Sanjay's decision is his own, no one else's. For family reasons—and, so I'm told, the upcoming cricket tour of India by Australia—Sanjay has decided to return with his wife Anita to his beloved Mumbai. He has already contributed greatly to the inclusive, global basis of our New World, and it's a shame to see him go. His eloquence, imagination and fuzzy Indian logic will be sorely missed in the trying times ahead. We wish him well.'

There was sad but genuine applause around the room, and the little Indian man's cheeks grew red around a humble bashful smile.

'There will be a farewell—and, Sanjay, I really do mean "fare well"—gathering tomorrow night at Jabba's Palace. And given that Sanjay doesn't drink, I expect that the rest of you will do your ample amber best to make up for it, and give him a rousing send-off!'

'Shhhhh!' yelled Byron Lybrand, waving frantically at everyone to quieten down as he barged through to the front of the clapping crowd.

'Anna, you are going to want to hear this,' he said as he reached up to turn on the television behind her head.

Then the packed War Room watched in stunned silence, their faces shocked and solemn, as if they had just learned of the death of a family member.

'*To repeat,*' said Glory O'Shay oh-so-seriously, standing in front of a Wall Street street sign. '*Wall Street is abuzz with rumours that Isaac Blackwell has been fired by the investment bank Gill Johnson Shek, and may be facing charges of insider trading and embezzlement. Back to you, Jonathon.*'

No one knew what to say.

Anna was unmoved. Perhaps she'd been forewarned of the announcement. Certainly, no one else in the room had been.

Fear, anxiety and panic are all related contagious diseases. Matt felt the symptoms of all three spreading through the room. Distress, shortness of breath and watery eyes spread like a fever.

A hot hubbub of panicked people immediately engulfed Anna, who stood unflinching in the centre of demands ('Did you know about this?' 'If Glory is there, you must have known.'), questions ('Why weren't we told about this?' 'What does this mean?') and concerns ('The investment will dry up now, that's for sure!' 'They must be distancing themselves from us for a reason: are we bankrupt?').

She nodded calmly at this, shook her head at that, and then raised her voice above the pandemonium: 'If you'd just—If you'd just calm down—Calm down, people. This—This is not unexpected.' Finally, the anxious clamour died down enough for her to be heard. 'This is not unexpected. For obvious reasons, relating to confidentiality and changing circumstances, we could not alert you to this before certain actions were taken. We will explain these actions in more detail in the regular weekly meetings, forums and newsletters.'

Matt watched her—her eyes again, so fixed and determined—as she tried to control the maelstrom around her. That strength, that resolve. Why he'd come here.

He looked at the frenzied crowd encircling her, and as much as he liked to be near her, he didn't need to be here—she had enough people vying for her attention.

He dragged himself away, slipped out the side door leading to the balcony.

Glory felt the chills of excitement that she had been waiting for her whole career run up and down her spine. The intrigue, the secret instructions to come to New York, the direct reporting for network news—all forgotten now.

There was something about the camera, the visuals, the excitement of live on the spot reporting with a landmark in the background. It was so different from radio, something about the different stories they presented, something about how differently they presented the same stories. It was more real, more raw, trashier.

'I love television,' she said to herself.

'No, I'm not going into this now or on a one-to-one level with anyone. We will explain this via the channels we have created for just such an event as this. Please do not panic.'

A new wave of questions assaulted Anna as she paused for breath. She waved them away.

'And please, tell those around you not to panic. Let me assure you that Isaac—I mean we—that we have this matter completely under control. In fact, it is a deliberate and crucial part of our strategy.'

Her eyes scanned the room. There he was, ready as always to meet her every need. With barely a nod, Xavier moved assuredly towards her, placed a protective hand on her shoulder, then shepherded her back through the room and out through the side door, closing it behind her. Then, in his affable, gentlemanly, no-nonsense way, he took up a position in front of the door, ensuring the crowd could not follow her out.

As the door shut behind her, Anna collapsed against the railing, her strength gone, her determined eyes in tears. Her mind racing, despairing. *What the hell is going on? Why didn't he call?* It was so hard. Too hard.

But she was not alone. Matt stood back in a corner of the balcony, not knowing what to say or do. He wanted to go to her, lift up her head, hold her hand. He wanted to be with her. But he did not want to make a mistake.

He must have known—Glory was in New York! Why didn't I notice? Why didn't he tell me? Why hasn't he called? Through misty eyes, between sobs and heavy breaths, she took in the world in motion around her. The dredging stations, the other platforms, supply ships sliding through the sea. So much. So hard. So alone.

'Anna,' Matt whispered.

She jumped. Spun around. *Not alone.* Wiped her eyes. Checked her sobs. Tried to breathe. Pushed off the rail. *Not alone.* Matthew Turner.

'I—I'm fine,' she said, catching her breath.

Matt nodded. *What to say?*

'I'm sure everything is fine.'

She nodded. *Not alone.*

He took a step. Stopped. *What to do?*

Don't stop. Not alone. She wanted to run across the balcony and throw herself sobbing into his arms.

He wanted to hold her, comfort her. But he said and did nothing.

They stood there for a moment, a minute, an hour—he couldn't tell. He watched her face him uneasily, humiliated by his presence yet thankful for his comfort—and his silence. She needed to be alone, to think, to weep, to try to understand. But she needed support. Needed a friend. And he would stand there as long as she needed him to.

On television, so imposing and resolute. In person, her strong will matching her determined presence. A nobody, just a matter of months ago. A visionary now, a real-life Jules Verne. But all along—he cursed himself for not noticing, not realising what he realised now—she was still just a person. With feelings. Frailties. And self-doubt.

In her anguish, however, Matthew also felt a guilty rush of ecstasy. As they stood there, apart, their relationship had changed. He was now her confidant-in-adversity. He was now more than a refugee, a recruit or a colleague. Perhaps, he was even more than a friend . . .

Knock! Knock!

Instinctively, and even though two or three yards lay between them, Anna pulled away, straightening, breathing deeply. Matt, too, stepped back as she wiped her eyes and faced the door. A moment later, Xavier appeared.

If he was surprised to see that Anna was not alone, he didn't show it. He nodded to Turner, his gesture seeking excuse for his interruption.

'Ms Spires,' he said formally. 'Mr Blackwell is on the phone. He asks for a moment.'

'Yes, of course, Xavier. I'll be right there.' Xavier turned and left.

Anna stepped toward the door, then stopped. She looked at Matt, her composure almost completely regained. She gave the slightest nod.

He smiled at her, gave a nod of his own and a smile: *you're welcome*.

She drew herself up straight, as if about to step on stage. He watched her change, her posture and appearance, almost supernaturally. The puffiness had all but vanished, her nose no longer sniffling, a deep deep breath the only sign of the pressure she felt. When she re-entered that room, everyone would see confidence and surety, control and reassurance.

But for Matt Turner, whenever he would see her again, he would see something more . . . he would see that she needed him.

Let's just say that events which I described as self-inflicted
May have been less strategic than we are taking credit for.

good news, bad news

The next day. The War Room.

The Philo Group minus Arb, seated around the table, tense and uncertain.

Anna, standing before them.

'I have good news and bad news,' she said, not easing the tension. 'The bad news first: that Isaac was in fact fired from Gill Johnson Shek.'

Dismay.

'You see, as will be released to the press today, Isaac yesterday informed Messrs Gill, Johnson and Shek that he was about to resign to start his own investment bank.'

A-hah.

'As you can probably tell, they didn't take this too kindly. And GJS, well, as Isaac is all too aware, GJS likes to play hardball. This was not completely unexpected.'

Then why the wall of secrecy?

'The only way to break his relationship with GJS cleanly was to do it in person. While we trust in absolutely everyone associated with the Project, we obviously could not take the chance of premature leaks or rumours . . .'

There was some further discussion about whether this was a market signal that the coffers were actually empty ('No, for the last time, we are not bankrupt! In fact, we have raised more money than we need to build the superstructure—we are already planning how best to make use of the surplus.'), whether this affected the security of finance ('On the contrary, this act has been deliberately designed to ensure the security of all invested and/or pledged funds.') and finally, whether this affected the credibility of the New World's intentions ('Again, once the facts have been set straight, I think you'll find that Ninety East Ridge will benefit from an impression of increased independence and autonomy.').

'So what's the good news?' asked Mary.

'The events in question have absolutely no effect on the staging of Sanjay's farewell party tonight!'

'I'm going to take a wild guess and say that it wasn't quite as planned as that, was it?' Matt said to her, having waited until they were the last ones left in the room.

She looked up at him from her notes that she had been sorting and re-sorting until they were alone.

'No, not quite,' she said softly.

'Can I ask what really happened?' *She can only say no*, Matt thought.

'No.'

Hmm, serves you right, bright spark! he thought in reply, while his mouth said, 'Okay.'

She was looking at him again, appraising him maybe. Gauging perhaps how much to tell him, or how much not to. He was about to leave the room when she spoke again.

'Let's just say,' she said, 'that yesterday's events which I described today as self-inflicted and deliberate may have been less strategic than we are taking credit for. And our actions, now described as always part of the plan, may or may not have been more of a contingency.'

He smiled at her, aware of the trust it took to say that to him.

The party for Sanjay was loud and boisterous. An Indian band with sit-down string instruments, flutes and throaty voices had Jabba's Palace a-rocking, Bombay-style. The mood was upbeat, hedonistic in a mild-mannered Indian-kind-of-way, the concerns of the previous day forgotten. Even Sanjay, without a drop of liquor passing his lips, looked intoxicated, his whole face now blushing red from the attention and goodwill around him.

A few hours into the evening, Jabba called off the music to turn on all the televisions. A hush of dread silenced the room as Glory O'Shay appeared again in front of the Wall Street street sign.

'Well, a soap opera of events on Wall Street today. Prominent investment banker, Isaac Blackwell, whose surprise firing yesterday sent shockwaves through Wall Street, struck back today when he told a press conference that his firing was in fact, and I quote, "a technicality". Mr Blackwell was, he claims, in the Gill Johnson Shek offices to hand in his resignation, which the bank refused

*to accept. In fact, Mr Blackwell claims that he only found
out about his dismissal a couple of hours later when he
saw this reporter breaking the news on live television.
Mr Blackwell joins me now . . .'*

A huge roar shook the Palace as Arb appeared
on screen.

The man was all style—slick, no other word for
him. He stood comfortably alongside O'Shay,
looking confident, almost indifferent to the fawning investigative reporter seriously thrusting the
microphone between them. He wore no tie, his
shirt open—a look no doubt designed to signal his
voluntary decision to break with the system—and
his game-face wore a casual, brooding, intelligent
expression.

*'Mr Blackwell, after so many years of success with
GJS, why do you think they have chosen such a public
execution for you?'*

Here was the American dream, with the model
good looks, athletic, intelligent and, most
importantly, successful. GJS was done for before he
even opened his mouth.

'Glory, it's simple,' he said, pinning her with
a look which would have none of the typical, self-
emphasising, newshound interruptions. *'I had a
meeting yesterday with the Chairman, Mr Gill, where I
informed him of my intention to leave the firm and set
up my own investment bank. Needless to say, he didn't
take it too well and the rest, well, the rest you know.'*

*'Can you tell us anything about your new venture?
Does it have anything to do with the New World Project
in the Indian Ocean?'*

Another roar from the dance floor.

Arb smiled enigmatically, this time not at Glory but at the camera. *'Obviously I can't say too much about the new venture at this time. However, let me say this: as I'm sure you and your viewers are aware, Glory, the New World that we are building is setting out to be a better one—with better living conditions, better values, an altogether better way of doing things. Everything. And it wouldn't surprise me if that includes investment banking.'*

More cheering and applause, drowning out the sound of the televisions as the camera zoomed back to Glory for her self-important wrap-up and cross back to the studio.

The sitars and pipes started up again, with an extra zing in both the singing and dancing for the rest of the night. And Sanjay was farewelled in style.

'Thanks for the scoop,' Glory said, tossing the mike aside and catching up with Arb before he got away. He half-turned to nod in acknowledgement.

She took a deep breath, took a chance.

'Can I take you to . . . to lunch, maybe?' she said, her boldness losing its nerve towards the end of the sentence.

His face was a mask—an All-American, world's-sexiest-male mask. Finally, his perfect teeth cracked through.

'Sure.'

He was always so angry, as if the world owed him more
Than just a wife and two beautiful daughters.

the power of discontent

He was always so angry . . .

. . . so angry at the world.

Somehow, he felt personally betrayed by life's little inconsistencies, as if the world owed him more than just a wife, two beautiful daughters, a nice house and a good job. Actually, she often thought that maybe he would have preferred less from the world—the house and the job were superfluous, like too much ice in good scotch.

Too much ice, diluting his life somehow, watering down the flavours that should be so pure: like the soft familiar taste of his wife, so similar to the slightly sweeter, lighter aroma of their Taz, so different to the stronger, prouder sensation of their Anna.

If only he'd known . . .

. . . how wrong he'd been.

He'd tried so hard, wanted so much to create a beautiful world for his children, a world without limits, a world without pessimism. He'd tried so hard to show them the world possible . . . with just a little common sense and dedication. He'd wanted so much for them to imagine a perfect world.

He'd wanted it too much.

He was so scared.

He was so scared of how they would react when they realised that the world wasn't perfect. Couldn't be. Not even with all the common sense and dedication in the universe.

'Don't start with compromise,' he often said.

And he meant it . . . when the girls were younger, when he was infallible, when there were no mysteries of the cosmos that he could not solve for them.

'Why worry? You can't change them anyway,' she used to say to her.

She knew how much Anna hated her saying that, about her ears ('Your mother's ears,' he'd say unhelpfully), about boys, about grades, about anything that happened yesterday. She knew how much he hated it also.

But it was the truth.

It was not compromise.

And there was nothing Anna or her father could do to change that.

With some sadness, Jo watched her husband come to terms with his imminent fallibility.

'There is nothing more perplexing than perfection,' he said, trying to lecture her the way he lectured his daughters. 'It is at once mysterious and unattainable, and yet we see it all around us. We see it in the sky, the rain, the rivers, the ocean. We see it in the trees, the earth, the animals, our babies. We see it in the stars.'

This was the man she had fallen in love with. His sweet voice. His passion. Even his home-grown metaphysics.

'But the more I think about it,' he said, his voice cracking, his passion fading, 'the more I realise that the only perfection you can expect from your own life . . . is death.'

How could he have been so wrong? Why hadn't she made him see that?

'Every religion in the world recognises the mightiest power in the universe as being the one that can conquer death. Now I've never seen a resurrection or reincarnation or heaven or nirvana, so my fullest perception of perfection, until I do, is death itself.'

He tried to get on a roll, but she could hear the defeat in his voice, 'Death is relentless. It can be stalled, delayed, avoided for some time, but it'll get you in the end—it always does.'

Why hadn't she stopped him?

'And death is final. Yes, you can be clinically dead and then revived, but give death a day and it'll take forever.'

Why didn't she tell him that love, even imperfect love, is so much greater than perfection? Why didn't she convince him, true or not—did it matter if it wasn't true?—that life, with all its imperfections, with all its hopes and frustrated fantasies, with all its petty bitterness and selective memory, kicks death's arse every day of its existence?

'It has such power,' he would muse.

'It resonates like no other force on earth.'
'There is no greater sacrifice.'
'Lest we forget? Lest we could!'

It was a senseless death, random and ridiculous.
The police report called it an accident.

'There's nothing more I can teach her.' His last words.

He was always so angry at the world, as if the world owed him more than just a wife and two beautiful daughters.
If only he'd known how wrong he'd been.
If only she'd made him see that.

It was a senseless death, random and ridiculous.
The police report called it an accident.
No one was at fault. No one was to blame.

Five years later, almost to the day, Anna had left home, vowing never to return.
That was fifteen years ago. They hadn't spoken since.

worlds torn asunder
[days 300 to 325]

The games we play . . .
   And always so serious at the time.
   On the field, where we run and leap and hit and sweat. In the office, where we meet and tally and trade and sign. In the bedroom, where the thrills and tension are perhaps greatest of all.
   The games we play . . . Arb, with his numbers and networking. Anna, with her giant-sized building blocks. Ford, with his pawns and henchmen. As the distance between life now and life then grows, I see all their games, independent yet the same. From here at my window, I see more than I saw before, see the players for who they really were, see tactics and motives I never noticed at the time. I see the rules—the very game itself—being changed without warning.
   A straight flush beats four of a kind, which beats a full house, then a flush, a straight, three of a kind and so on. So said the naive young games expert when asked

what beat what. What he didn't mention was that five of a kind beats all—what he didn't know was that the devil was playing, and with a wildcard up his sleeve.

Hatred is a devil's trait, cursed to deal in absolutes.
But more dangerous is the devil that smiles and deals in
nuance.

dance with the devil on your birthday

DAY 300—NEW YORK

'Good evening, I'm Glory O'Shay, and behind me is the world-famous Empire State Building. Tonight, I am one of the lucky two hundred people in New York to hold one of these . . .' She held up a large white card with embossed gold writing. *'An invitation to the gala event of the season. The birthday bash of Mrs Isaac Blackwell.*

'Only the most A-list of movie stars, pop stars, recluse authors and politicians will be making their way to the observation deck of New York's most famous landmark, to celebrate a year which even Anna Spires could never have dreamed possible twelve months ago.'

The glitz and glamour of the occasion was a sight to behold, and they hadn't even arrived yet. The Philo Group filed out from their hotel, two by two, men in black tie, women in their finest gowns, into the limousines which escorted them the half-dozen blocks to a red carpet which led to the express elevator.

Matt was escorting Mrs Rulé. 'Augusto thinks you're a wimp, but I think you're all right,' she said to him in confidence.

Harry Pont and Helen Rainey filed into the limo before theirs, whilst Natasha Spires and her latest beau, a wedge-shaped riveter from Platform Five, waited for the one following. Behind them, lost in a crowd of well-wishers and hotel staff, were Tom and Mary, and Isaac and Anna.

'So how have you found the trip so far?' Laikali asked Matt as the chauffeur shut the limo door and the buzz of the world outside disappeared. 'Seen anything you like?'

He looked at her.

'Transportation systems, I mean, of course.'

Matt couldn't help but feel that transportation systems were not what she meant at all. Perhaps Augusto could read minds up there.

An attendant opened the door for them and they stepped out onto the red carpet. Onlookers lined the sidewalk, craning for glimpses of celebrities. Paparazzi, not allowed upstairs, assaulted them with clicks and flashes as they made their way inside and to the lifts.

Tom and Mary entered the elevator with them. 'It must have cost him a fortune to rent the whole deck for the night,' Tom commented to his wife. She stood attached to his elbow, but also detached, with her usual air of class superiority that she must have spent years practising. No doubt, she had also spent years practising how to walk in her four-inch heels and a designer dress that clung close to her hips but hung loose at the bust and low down her back.

'He has a few fortunes to spare, I can assure you,' she answered, somewhat dismissively.

Matt's ears popped as the cabin rose some fifteen hundred feet into the air.

Then, the doors opened and they stepped out into . . .

Heaven.

Chandeliers dominated the foyer ('They're not usually here, I can assure you,' Mary motioned pompously), the walls were draped with Chinese silk and exotic flowers coloured the corners. Outside, they looked down on life as Zeus might once have done. An awesome sight: a grand canyon of steel mesas and neon gorges.

Assumed gods mingled, toasting each other's star-spangled smiles, speaking of whims and destinies. The haughty satisfaction they took from the function's exclusivity reflected their divinity. Diamonds, pearls and tiaras reflected their wealth and power. A host of servants saw to keeping them entertained.

White-gloved eunuchs served ambrosia and vol-au-vents, hostess nymphs made sure that gods were amused with tittering conversation, roving Narcissi acted as barmen and eye candy for the goddesses.

Beautiful people basked in their own reflection

in every direction, all so certain that they belonged here on Olympus.

Matt was overwhelmed in this company. A movie star brushed his shoulder. A supermodel squeezed past him through the door. He knew each and every one of these people—and yet he knew none of them. Tom and Mary were nodding seriously at something this year's Pulitzer Prize winner was saying. Natasha seemed to have traded in her riveter for a pop star's bad-boy basketball boyfriend. Laikali Rulé was chatting with the Vice President.

Unable to approach these famous strangers, he found himself idly appreciating the captivating beauty of a potted tree in the corner, when the music stopped and the lights went out.

A spotlight focused everyone's now-silent attention towards the foyer.

A silky voice on a microphone grandstanded the moment, 'Ladies and gentlemen, please welcome the star of the evening, the mind behind the New World, accompanied by her famously unemployed husband, the birthday girl herself, Ms Anna Spires!'

Around the corner stepped Arb, resplendent and suave, as if he had been born in a dinner suit. And on his elbow, following him into the light, floated the most beautiful woman Matt had ever seen.

She wore a gown of white silk with gold lace brocade. The flowing skirt pulled in at the waist and out again, the bust line paralleling the ends of the long white velvet gloves that rose above her elbows. Her shoulders were bare. Her neck was adorned with a string of pearls and diamonds. Her hair was worn up, except for a curl that wove down past her little ears to her exhilarated smile. And her eyes . . .

When the lights and music returned, Matt immediately started forward. But in an instant, a crowd of the nearest onlookers engulfed her. He stopped, peering from a distance between the circling well-wishers. There, a glimpse of her smiling face. There, a laugh, her head tilting back in joy. And there, her shining eyes—so delighted tonight, the weight of her responsibilities lifted, if just for one night.

Anna found herself fumbling through handshakes and niceties. Greetings from familiar faces that she couldn't put a name to, familiar greetings as if they knew her. She tried to place who—or what—they were.

A gaunt, tanned waif wearing a towel as a dress said she could relate to having to fight for credibility in a man's world. She then asked a passing eunuch for another fluffy bunny cocktail and one of those little bread thingies with the creamy stuff on top. Model, Anna thought.

A hungry, gregarious man bounced her hand up and down, congratulating her on her achievements to date. Politician, no doubt—confirmed when he asked how she felt about professional government.

'Pity about GJS.' Rival investment banker.

'You're not as tall as I thought you'd be.' Movie star.

'It's so exciting to meet you. Yours is such a wonderful story.' Movie producer.

'You're a shining example to all women.' Non-working socialite wife.

Compliments about her vision and determination. Understanding solace about the pressures of the spotlight. Smiles. Handshakes. Polite laughs and one-liners.

And then an older man, silver haired, knowing smile, reached out to shake her hand. He stood stiff-backed and upright, but his handshake was casual and friendly—his smile, his face, and . . . she wasn't sure: was he blind?

'I'm sure your parents are very proud,' he said.

Some hours later, Anna found herself in another group of people she didn't know. But for the moment, the accolades had been replaced by more challenging comments.

'Are you concerned that you may be taking mankind where it's not supposed to go?' said a curly haired man with a prominent aquiline nose.

'What do you mean?' Anna checked.

'Do you feel like you're playing God when you're not supposed to?' the man pursued, a touch aggressively. 'You know, building a Tower of Babel in the ocean?'

'I'm hardly a god, Mister . . .?'

'Ridder,' he said. 'Rick Ridder.'

'I'm hardly a god, Mr Ridder. I don't pretend to be, or even want to be, a god.'

'Ms Spires, you are responsible for replacing some one hundred and thirty trillion megalitres of water with man-made construction. Did it ever occur to you that man was not supposed to live beneath sea level?'

'Did it ever occur to you, Mr Ridder, that we were not supposed to fly or walk in space or communicate across continents?'

He grunted a reluctant laugh. 'I'm just questioning, Ms Spires, what right you have, what authority or endorsement you have been granted by the people of the world to create such a thing.'

'We all create, Mr Ridder,' said an articulate voice. Heads turned to the tall silver-haired man whose tone now became more commanding. 'The true nature of a god, to address your earlier concern, is not, and cannot be, his or her role as a creator. For I create, you create, even a two-year-old child with brightly coloured building blocks creates.' Anna recognised him as the blind man—was he blind? She still couldn't quite tell. 'I'm sorry, Mr Ridder, I find your interrogation of Ms Spires as argument for argument's sake.'

'Well excuse me,' retorted Ridder sarcastically, 'Mister . . . I'm sorry, I missed your name.'

'Paul,' said the man, bowing his head slightly, although his eyes focused nowhere—Anna was now certain he was blind. 'Just Paul.'

Ridder breathed deeply, his exasperation unhidden. 'And if oil companies or mining companies sought to destroy the rest of the ocean in this way? Surely there must be some control. Surely, Ms Spires, you must have received support from some representative body?'

'I doubt very much,' Paul refuted, on Anna's

behalf, in his cultured unhurried speech, 'whether she has lodged an application requesting permission from all the governments of the world—a torturous death by committee, I'm sure, dragged out over a thousand years. Imagine if all the great ideas had required such agreement.'

At this point Ridder threw back his head, shook it in disgust, stepped back and made to leave. 'Happy birthday, Ms Spires,' he said through clenched teeth. 'May this coming year present you with everything that you deserve.' Then he turned and departed.

The surrounding spectators just stood in silence, taken aback by the sudden lack of cordiality. Anna herself broke the silence.

'Why, thank you,' she said, moving past a few people to shake Paul's hand again. His hand raised to meet hers—maybe he wasn't blind?

'Not at all,' he replied. 'My pleasure.'

He smiled a delightful refined smile. She couldn't quite place his age—sixty, maybe seventy, maybe more. He was resplendently dressed, immaculately well-groomed and his manner overflowed with style and presence.

'If you don't mind me asking again, who are you?'

'Paul's not enough, eh?' he said jovially, then he leaned a little closer to her. 'I'll let you in on a secret—I'm a superhero. This is what I do when I'm not being a mild-mannered public servant.'

She laughed. He smiled at her response.

'I'm sorry,' she said. 'Next time I celebrate my birthday—which will be in about a thousand years!—I'll be sure to invite people that I know.'

'God no!' Paul replied, shocked. 'Then how would infatuated admirers like myself get a chance to meet you?'

She smiled again shyly.

'Please,' he said, taking her hand again, 'if you'd indulge an old man's fantasies. Dance with me?'

Before she could answer, he surefootedly charged through the crowd, leading her by the hand. Lights and eyes flashed by her—but you're blind, she thought. Then, all of a sudden, he effortlessly drew her close as they glided onto the open expanse of the dance floor. His experienced hand, placed without self-consciousness on the small of her back, led her into a whirl of twirls and pivots.

There was a light polite round of applause.

'But you're blind,' she said, marvelling.

'A wonderful excuse if we hit anybody,' he replied, spinning and collecting her. He was smooth and he was good. He was so good. If he was thirty years younger and if she was single . . . she thought.

'One of the benefits of age,' he said, reading her thoughts, 'is a classical training that young men cannot compete with.'

'So you still compete with young men, then?'

She could have sworn that his eyes were focused on her as he twirled her again. 'Oh yes. Constantly. But I've learned to choose my games very carefully . . .' A dip. Her head hung back. '. . . as I see, have you.'

With no effort at all, he lifted her upright and

spun her out, extending his own arm out behind him. 'I don't think I've ever seen so many trillion dollars raised with so little explanation of its usage.'

More polite clapping.

'That's my husband's specialty, not mine, Mr Paul,' Anna said as he drew her in and under his arm.

'Rubbish,' he said softly, waving one arm naturally at the festivities around them. 'This whole party, this music, my dancing, are here because of your still somewhat disguised vision of the future.'

'As we've already established, Mr Paul—'

'Just Paul, please,' he corrected, pulling her close.

'Sorry—Paul—but as you yourself pointed out, I'm not a god. I can't predict the future.'

He nodded, impressed, his seemingly futile eyes shining with delight. They danced a minute more before he spoke again.

'Indulge an old man again, please, Ms Spires. I'm always intrigued by the motivations of successful young people. I'd like to know, what do you remember of your childhood?'

'Happy things mostly,' Anna replied, not sure where he was going. 'My sister and I playing. At the beach. At barbecues. At home in the yard. At school. Friends at school—'

'Fine, fine,' Paul said, cutting her off, gliding towards the middle of the floor. 'Now tell me about the unhappy things you remember.'

Anna hesitated, made to stop, but his hand

continued to lead her. Did he know what he was looking for—she was suddenly mistrustful—because if he did, then he'd also know that she would never tell him.

'There's not much, really. Nothing I can really remember.'

'Nothing?' he said, still smiling, all style, all charm. 'I only ask because I have a theory that negative motivators are the most powerful kind.'

'Not for me,' she said, trying not to sound defensive.

'Come, come, Ms Spires. We all remember the bad things.'

She made to break away, but suddenly the hand on her back felt like a lock and the edge of the dance floor, so far away.

'Not me,' she said with as much calm as she could muster.

'My, my, you must either be blessed with a wonderful life or a terrible memory.'

'Well, sure there are some moments,' she said quickly, looking around the room, 'like everyone else. But nothing I'd define as *bad*. Little things, you know.'

'No, no I'm not sure what you mean. Please tell me.' His voice was insisting, suddenly devoid of charm.

She answered carefully now, aware that he was enticing her towards a trap—perhaps she was already in the trap—but something made her determined not to be the first to turn away. 'Specific incidents, I guess. Arguments with Mum over going out, or make-up, or boys. Or with Natasha—'

'Your sister?'

'Yes, you know, fights over sister stuff, her breaking my toys, wearing my clothes—sister stuff, like I said. Break-ups with boyfriends, girlfriends—'

'Lies.' It was not a question.

He did know—suddenly she wanted desperately to escape, but everyone was still watching them dance, their faces enchanted. 'Yes, of course, I remember the lies.'

'What lies?'

Anna stopped, stopped dancing, stopped right in the middle of the floor.

He just stepped back and flowed into an exquisite gentleman's bow. Instinctively, she curtsied back, speaking hesitatingly, evasively, 'I don't know—'

'Yes, you do.'

He stared at her through his useless eyes. Instinctively again, she looked back at him. From the side, it must have looked like two dancers in a solemn respectful gaze. His head then moved awkwardly forward, tilting slightly, not quite balanced—those watching saw the old man's determination not to let his disability get in the way—leaning for a kiss, thanking her for the dance.

As they came together, he whispered in her ear. 'Who lied to you about your father?'

How could he? How could he know? How could he be so cold? But she wouldn't leave, she would not run. Resolved to stand and fight, she lifted her head back and forward again to kiss the other cheek. For a moment, she glimpsed his deceitfully innocent quizzical sightless eyes.

270

She tried not to cry. His cheek brushed hers again. He said nothing. She could feel his breath on her skin, and he hers. It was clear to both of them that he had struck a nerve. A raw, raw nerve.

She moved her lips closer to his cheek and whispered her reply: 'None of your goddamned business.'

Gravity. Time. Paul Jefferson Ford.
Real power does not need to be seen. ·

the most powerful man in the world

They deserted the dance floor in opposite directions, epitomes of grace and posture. Even before Anna's feet left the parquet, her eyes began to search frantically around the room for her husband. For what seemed like ages, but took less than a minute, she whisked around the rooftop, the anxiety, tears and pain building inside her. Her composure was threatening to leave her when finally she spotted Arb lecturing Matt Turner in a corner.

'It's as simple as that,' he was saying. 'A motto for life. Get the idea. Get the money. Get it done.'

'The man—' she interrupted, struggling to maintain her composure. 'The man I was dancing with . . . Did you see the man I was dancing with? Who is he?'

'Can this wait, Anna?' Arb said.

She grabbed him by the collar, leaning her face close to his, swallowing back sobs, tears baulking in her eyes as if afraid to roll down her face.

'What? What is it?' Arb said, suddenly seeing the yearning contorting her face.

She held his collar more tightly, trying to speak, trying not to cry. 'Who is he?' she forced out.

'I didn't see a man. I didn't see you dancing, baby,' said Arb, talking very quickly, trying to calm her down, his eyes scanning the room (was he looking for the man, or to see who could see Anna crying?). 'What did he look like? Where did he go?'

Her tight grip looked about to rip his collar off. The first tear fell, then the floodgates opened—she could not control herself any longer. Arb was panicking too, instinctively trying to shield her face from the main body of people nearby.

She pushed his arm away, her wet eyes staring at his through rivers of mascara.

'He knew,' she stammered between sobs. 'He knew about my father.'

Before he knew it, Matt, who had been stricken silent by Anna's state, was leading her quickly but discreetly to the tower elevator.

Arb had responded like a bullet to Anna's final words, grabbing Matt and ordering him to get her out of here.

'Back to the hotel?' Matt had said.

'Yes—no, there'll be cameras downstairs. The tower. Take her to the tower, and don't let anybody else up.'

He had successfully shielded Anna almost all the way to the elevator, when a group of socialites noticed them and began to rush over.

What to do? he started thinking furiously. *An*

excuse! Ahh, she's unwell—no, they might assume she was drunk. They were getting closer, swooping like busy-body owls. *She'd just received a phone call with terrible news—no, too much follow up.* The lead owl was waving her hand, trying to gain their attention. He pretended not to notice. *Just keep going. Ignore them. Maybe they'll stop. We're almost there . . .* But out of the corner of his eye, he saw the lead owl reaching out to tap him on the shoulder . . .

'Ladies!' someone said, all the owls turning as one. Matt almost broke himself and Anna into a run for the final few yards. As he supported her into the elevator, slamming the Close Door button, he glimpsed the owls flapping and fluttering around Laikali Rulé.

Anna leaned heavily against him, blinded by her tears and seemingly robbed of her strength by the stress of her recent encounter. The door slid open, and he led her out onto the small deck that circled the tower.

The cool night wind whipped by. Some two hundred feet below, the party was still in full swing, the indefinable buzz of music and people reaching up through the wind to their ears. Matt looked down, but the angle of the tower obstructed all but a corona of light.

He looked further down, to the city that never sleeps—headlights, streetlights, random office lights, apartment lights, boat and ship lights in the harbour, more cars, streets, homes and factories across the water.

He felt Anna's body holding tightly onto his,

her head against his chest.

'Did you know,' he said softly, 'that if you spit over the sides from this height, that your spittle would never hit the ground—because of wind currents and updrafts and stuff?'

He could feel her tears through his shirt, against his chest.

'And did you know,' he said again, his hand hesitatingly beginning to stroke her on the head, 'that this isn't even a quarter as tall as Ninety East Ridge?'

For a moment, the heavy rise and fall of her body stopped. A response!

'So you see where I'm going with this. Better not tell anyone because if people at the Ridge find out, no one will be able to resist testing the theory, and there'll be spit flying everywhere never touching the ground . . .' He felt her body shake, but it was muffled laughter not tears. '. . . spit rain! Spit rain flying up and down and sideways! You'd have to drive everywhere with the windshield wipers on. And that windshield spray would have to be a special chemical compound to break up the spit . . .'

He could feel her fighting for self-control, wanting to laugh, wanting to cry, unable to do either.

He could feel her soft beautiful hair.

'Did you know . . .' he started once more—

And she reached up and hit him on the shoulder. 'You're disgusting,' she croaked through her swallowed sobs and choked back laughter.

'. . . that you're the only reason I came to Ninety East Ridge?'

He said it softly, but well within her hearing. Even so, he couldn't be sure that she'd heard it; she was sniffling, her breathing still sharp and spasmodic, and she still had her head buried in his chest.

Matt was wondering what he should say next when he heard the elevator doors open.

'Thanks for the diversion down there,' Matt said.

Laikali smiled that wide, motherly, Polynesian smile of hers. 'Is she all right?' she said, as always getting to the point.

He was nodding, about to answer when Anna's head suddenly rose and she spoke for herself.

'I'm fine,' she breathed unsteadily. She closed her eyes, concentrating hard to retain her composure.

'You don't have to be strong around me, girl,' Laikali said plainly. 'What happened?'

Anna swallowed, still choking back tears, random details tumbling from her lips, 'He knew everything about me. We were dancing. He was kind, helpful earlier. Supported me. Us. Supported us. Said he was a public servant. He was blind—'

'He was blind?' said Laikali suddenly.

'Or almost blind, I couldn't tell,' Anna replied, shaking her head.

The sound of the elevator doors. Arb racing around the corner. Easing her from Matt's embrace into his own.

'We couldn't find him. He must have left straight away. But don't worry, we can check the security cameras—'

'Don't bother,' said Laikali. 'I know who he was.'

'Who?' Matt burst out, speaking for all of them.

'Anna Spires, you've just had the pleasure of the company of Paul Jefferson Ford.'

They waited for the guests to disperse before coming down. Anna, the guests had been told, had been called away urgently for an emergency conference call with some suppliers in Australia.

As they made their way to the main liftwell, Arb eased Anna back into Matt's arms.

'You three go back to the hotel,' he said. 'I'll be right behind you. I want to get a copy of the security tapes, so I can meet this mysterious Mr Ford.'

The doors slid closed.

'He won't find them,' Laikali said softly.

Matt didn't quite take her meaning. 'Who is Paul Jefferson Ford?'

'Some say he's a ghost,' Laikali said. 'That he haunts the halls of congress—he's usually referred to as P. Jefferson Ford, or just Jefferson Ford. Consider yourself very privileged, Anna Spires, to be on a first name basis with the most powerful man in the world.'

Matt still didn't get it. 'What? So he's a politician then? What do you mean, some say he's a ghost?'

'He doesn't exist, Matthew Turner. People claim to see him from time to time. Claim he ruined their career. Claim he destroyed their lives. But they can never prove it. They can never even find him.'

'Huh? What?' said Matt flustered, still

supporting Anna, who was now looking up at Laikali with fascinated, if red-rimmed, eyes. 'I don't understand.'

'How . . .' Anna's weak voice said, 'do you know . . . it was him?'

'I danced with him too,' Laikali said wistfully, 'once.'

'Oh, and could he dance!' she recalled as they sat themselves in the waiting limo, to herself as much as to Anna and Matt. Anna was nodding— apparently he could dance—whilst Matt was open-mouth, flabbergasted.

'He could see then,' she continued, lost in the memory. 'Augusto was alive—wow, remember my love—do you remember me dancing with Jefferson Ford?'

The roof of the car and Laikali stared at each other for a moment.

She shook her head, smiling at some private wistful humour, 'He claims not to remember. But he does. He wasn't very pleased either, that I could be swept off my feet by a complete stranger.'

Anna's expression suddenly softened in understanding.

'Yes, you see, I too didn't know who he was when he spun me around that Paris ballroom. He just appeared, much as I expect he did tonight, enchanted me with some eloquent rhetoric about the arrogant, selfish, Big Brother policies of the French. Then he asked me to indulge him in a waltz.'

'Did he . . . did he . . .' Anna tried to ask.

'Did he then rip my soul out with his bare hands?' finished Laikali for her.

Anna looked at her hopefully.

'Yes, he did, child. He pulled me close, showing me his watch and whispering in my ear: did I realise that these self-important French fucks regarded me as nothing more than a Gauguin sideshow to be distracted? And did I know that the first nuclear tests were being detonated at that very minute?'

They pulled into the hotel, but paused for a few minutes before getting out of the car.

'I almost gave up politics that very night,' Laikali said gravely. 'He devastated me. On the spot, he devastated me, let alone the next day when the newspapers showed me dancing—not with him, I'm afraid—as part of my homeland burnt in radiation.'

'And you think he planned it?' Matt asked.

'I know he planned it, right down to media coverage in Palwali itself.' She shook her head, the memory bitter and sad. 'The worst thing was the disappointment in me back home. When I returned, I had done more than fail so badly—there was a feeling of betrayal, of never being able to trust me again.

'There was nothing I could say,' she continued. 'It wouldn't have made sense to anyone. Here was my country, my friends, the international media all vilifying—rightfully vilifying—the French as shameful colonial hypocrites, and here was I, the only one who knew that the real enemy was not the French at all, dancing that fateful night away. They were being teased and deceived just like the rest of us.'

'You mean the US was controlling it?'

'No, I mean Ford was controlling it.'

'I still don't get it,' Matt said, shaking his head.

Laikali nodded her own head in understanding. 'At the time, I didn't understand it completely either. All I knew that day was that he had controlled me. I have had decades of international politics since to see his hand in every policy, in every budget, in every cross-border aggression and the protection and/or sale of US state secrets. He's not a numbers man or a lobbyist or a patron or political whip—but he's a kingmaker just the same. In fact, he is *the* kingmaker. He controls the events that force the numbers or the issues or the dollars or the debate.' She looked at Anna, sympathetic but angry. 'He is the architect of this Old World that you're so boldly seeking to improve upon, and its guardian. And as you saw tonight, he'll defend it any way he can.'

There was contemplative silence for a moment, then Laikali made to get out of the car.

'Why didn't you quit?' Anna asked softly. 'That night, when he ripped your soul out, what made you stay?'

Laikali laughed, at herself apparently. 'Anna Spires, I'd like to tell you that my passion was too great to be quelled like that, or that Augusto talked me around by reminding me why I had got into this business. I'd like to be able to say something gracious and inspiring and profound, but I can't.

The fact is, when I realised what he'd done, I became the meanest, most vengeful bitch on the planet, and I've held that title ever since, spending each and every day planning and preparing and just waiting for payback.'

'It's a shame Laikali didn't see him dancing with me,' Anna joked semi-sarcastically after she had left them in the elevator. 'He might have got to see the Empire State Building's view up close.'

They tried to laugh, but it just wasn't coming.

They walked out and stopped at her door.

'Well, good night,' Matt said. 'Try to get some sleep.'

She nodded in agreement and he turned to walk up the hall to his room.

'Thank you,' she said, her voice stopping him some paces away. He turned back to her. 'I mean it,' she said. 'Thank you for being there for me— not just tonight, but also back at the Ridge when Isaac got fired.'

Matt nodded, but he avoided her grateful eyes, selfconsciously focusing on his shuffling feet.

There was a kiss on the cheek and an appreciative smile as she went to close her hotel room door. And then she was gone. He was alone in the hallway, unaware of exactly what had happened— he could still feel the press of her hand in his, the light touch of her lips on his cheek, the trust of her words embracing his heart. Anna was now behind the door in the room she shared with her husband while Matt, alone, ouside, was sure more than ever that he loved her.

History. Tradition. Dirt.
London.

ebbs and foes

Laikali saw them off at the airport a few days after Anna's birthday.

'Once more, we must say goodbye,' said Laikali, her wide white smile distracting the stranger from the regret and sadness in her eyes. But she had again refused all of Arb's entreaties; she had no doubt that her value to Ninety East Ridge lay at the United Nations.

'How did things become so complicated?' Anna asked as she hugged her farewell.

'Girl, aside from a kazillion-litre hole in the ocean, your life's no different to anyone else's.'

There had been no security tapes. An unusually happy guard—'no doubt with a fatter wallet', said Arb—guessed that the earlier shift must have forgotten to reload the recording machines.

Arb had then disappeared the next day—'following leads', he said of some of his investment banking and government contacts. He was already certain that the rash of labour and supply difficulties that they had experienced at the Ridge had been coordinated by Ford. Now, he was trying to establish how.

'How do you fight an invisible foe?' he said.

By the time they boarded the plane, he still could not connect Ford to their troubles, but he had another name that meant something to both himself and to Anna.

That name?

Aldrich Ridder.

'We went to the same college, joined GJS together. I suppose you could say we were close once. He was ambitious, and I liked that. But it turned out he was too ambitious, and I had him fired for insider trading. He disappeared into government after that and I reasoned that his ambition would fade. I admit, I may have underestimated him.'

'He was at the party,' Anna said, when he told her. 'I thought he was a pompous superior prick. In fact, Ford . . .'—she felt stupid, only now putting the pieces together—'Ford argued with him—for my benefit, I can only assume.'

'Apparently he now holds an official position as Liaison Officer for the Justice Department.'

'What does that mean?' Anna asked.

'It means that he's an official gun for hire, available for "secondments" to any department that requires his services.'

'And what services exactly does he provide?'

'Aldrich Ridder is a political mercenary and a public relations assassin.'

DAY 324—LONDON

The last three weeks had gone well, thought Anna, excusing herself as they passed under Tower Bridge.

The presence of the entire Philo Group in one place for Anna's birthday had meant a larger than usual team for this leg of the roadshow. Herself, Isaac, Tom and Mary, Harry Pont, Miles Alia and Matt had taken full advantage of London's wealth of financial, cultural and educational institutions.

Isaac and Anna had been granted a special audience at Number Ten, Downing Street, as well as with other members of parliament. Tom and Mary had visited Oxford and then Cambridge, meeting with a number of experts to discuss the latest academic thinking about how great societies have been formed. Harry Pont had met with the engineers responsible for building and stabilising the enormous oil rigs that operated in the deep North Sea. Miles, as the portfolio chief for Technology, Communications and Lifestyle, had simply bought himself a mobile phone, then proceeded to spend his time going to musicals, pubs, movies, shops, tourist attractions and sporting events. As his portfolio was both dependent and influential on the nature of the city that was to be built, he also spent much of his time with Matt either riding the Tube or sitting in on his meetings with London's city planners.

Today, the last day of their stay in London, had gone well, Anna thought. Isaac, Tom, Mary and herself were the honoured guests of the Committee for the Royal Historical Society, an august body of prominent citizens, including the Prime Minister's husband, the Chairman of the Bank of England, the Head of the English Football Association, a number of Lords and Ladies, and their patron, the Crown Prince himself—as they cruised down the River Thames. Though they had seen all the sights before, the tour had provided some insights into the mix of planning, luck and stubbornness that create a heritage.

As Anna now made her way through to the back cabins of the river cruiser, the bombastic monotone of the RHS tour guide, absorbed in his own happiness at showing off the wealth and history of the greatest city in his great Britain, was lost wherever sound becomes lost behind her.

'On your left, you can see the Houses of Parliament, designed of course by Sir Charles Barry in eighteen thiry- . . .'

While not particularly large, the cruiser was effectively divided into two sections: a forward section with a wide dance floor-turned-auditorium just below the bridge, and a rear section where a zig-zagging corridor ran between small sleeping berths, a couple of meeting rooms and a few cupboard-sized WCs.

Anna was weaving aft to ask Isaac when the Prince might be able to get a tour of the Ridge. Isaac had been very clear about the potential strategic benefit of displaying their progress—she did not want to commit any errors now, inviting the wrong guest at the wrong time or in the wrong order.

Besides, if she had to say no, she needed time to figure out a politically correct excuse before she returned.

She was about to push in the door that had become Isaac's de facto office for the day—the place to which he retreated to make his never-ending phone calls—when she paused, distracted by his voice. And another's. Mary's. She hovered at the door a moment longer, not intending to be devious, but interested to hear what they were talking about.

Mary was speaking, that imploring self-important lecture tone in her voice: 'If we've learned anything from history, it shows us that iconoclasts and revolutionaries without a rigorous academic background do not have what it takes to achieve the profound. If you think of Hitler, Napoleon, Pol Pot—all self-taught or idealistically naive—you think of flawed, short-lived empires, thousand-year Reichs that last barely a decade, naive failed rebellions or disastrous revolutions.'

'Get to the point, Mare.'

Yeah, the point? thought Anna, sure she wouldn't like it.

'You know what I'm getting at. If she wants to do something that works, something meaningful, something that changes life on earth as we know it, then she has to withdraw.'

I what?

'That's out of the question,' Isaac said.

You tell her! thought Anna, nodding her head in angry, silent agreement.

'You saw her out there,' Mary persisted. 'Her

comments. Her questions. A fish out of water, to say the very least.'

Fish out of water? Anna thought, suddenly unsure of herself.

'She's trying to learn from them, Mare. That's why we are here.'

Yeah, hopeful.

But Mary persisted: 'That's why the Philo Group is here. We're experts, Izzy.' *Izzy?* 'You know that. We're the connoisseurs of what we do, the supreme authorities in our fields. Hell, Izzy, there're probably six bona fide geniuses in the Philo Group and four others that are too smart to be geniuses.'

'Yeah, well genius or not, none of you would be here without her.'

Damn right.

'You mean, none of us would be here,' suddenly the bite in her voice slackened and softened and seemed to stroke Isaac when she said, 'without you.'

All of a sudden Anna wished she could see. Suddenly, all her fears were real. She wanted to scream—or scratch—as Mary's svelte seduction continued.

'Let's face it,' she beseeched smoothly, 'it never would have happened without you, without the money, without Xavier.'

What's Xavier got to do with anything?

'We all think of changing the world every day. So this one idea happens to be hers—she never could have done it without you.'

Say something, Isaac! Say something!

'That's enough,' Isaac said softly. 'Now, who else have you discussed this with?'

'They all think it: Saul, Miles, Jay—even Byron.'

'They said so?'

'They didn't need to.' There was that svelte tone again.

Slut.

'Sometimes you don't need to say what you're thinking out loud.'

'What about Tom?' asked Isaac.

'Tom?' Anna could see the temptress smiling mischievously just by the way she said it.

'I mean, you have spoken to him about Anna, haven't you?'

That's it, Isaac. Hang in there.

'Tom, Tom, Tom,' she mimicked languorously. 'Anyone would think he's my husband or something.'

He is, you bitch.

'Well, you know how I feel about husbands.'

What? What are they talking about?

There was silence. No one spoke for a few seconds. Then a minute.

What to do? What were they doing?

Two, maybe three minutes. She was about to bang on the door, interrupt with some ridiculous excuse about why she was bursting in when—

Footsteps in the corridor.

What to do?

A door behind her.

She flew through it without looking, closing it swiftly, silently behind her, just as someone came around the corner.

A knock at the door, a quick rattle and squeak as it opened.

'Excuse me, Isaac, did Anna find you?'

Tom?

'She was coming back here to ask you about the Prince visiting.' It *was* Tom.

'No,' *his voice sounds rattled . . . what did you do, Isaac?* 'I've been here for the last half-hour and haven't seen her. She must have got sidetracked on the way back.'

'What're you up to?'

Yeah answer that, why don't you!

'Just phone calls, and some staring out the window, I admit.'

'Not a bad standard to aim for,' Tom agreed, watching the aged jumbled buildings that crowded the riverbank float by. 'A bit old, but all class.'

'Designed with an eye for still looking good in a thousand years.'

There was a moment's silence before Tom spoke again: 'Anyway, I better get back up front. Hey, you haven't seen Mary, have you?'

'No.'

No? What do you mean no? Where is she? She must be hiding.

A fumbled laugh. 'Perhaps they both got bored and dived overboard to go get a coffee.'

Anger wrestled with bewilderment in the dark. *I'll throw you overboard!* anger thought.

A laugh. 'No fair if they did. See you back up front.'

'Hold on, I'll join you.'

The door closing. Then Isaac's and Tom's

289

footfalls disappearing forward.

For a few minutes there was silence save for the repetitive slapping of water against the boat's sides.

Anna contemplated confrontation. *What to say? What to do?* She wanted to hit—*childish, thoughtless, foolish*, she knew—but . . .

Then the click and squeak of the door again, *Too late!* and the fading footsteps as Mary made her way up the corridor.

Then nothing. No movement. No sound. Anna waited a full five minutes to be sure no one was left behind or nothing forgotten was remembered and returned for. Then she slipped out of the cupboard, with no idea what to do.

She just sat on the settee in the alcove.
He just sat on the bed, watching over her.

(don't) tell me what to do

Nothing—nothing!—could possibly depress him today.

Nothing, Matt thought, as the doors began to part on his floor and he exited the elevator, could shake the overwhelming surety and satisfaction that had accompanied today's revelation.

Nothing, not even the infamous London Underground, which had just stolen two hours of his life—for a trip that would have taken fifteen minutes to walk—could mar this day, this day when his vision for the Ridge's transport system had become clear, during a chance visit to one of Miles Alia's internet providers.

No, nothing could get to him today.

Nothing!

Nothing that is, except the sight of a sombre, tearful Anna, sitting with her knees drawn up under her arms, waiting outside his door.

She just sat on the settee in the alcove.

He just sat on the bed, watching over her.

Random sentences. Words non sequitur.

'I didn't see them. It's possible I misunderstood.'

'Can I get you a drink?'

'Am I a fish out of water?' A whisper.

'Do you want me to leave you alone?'

'Idealistically naive? Hitler? Napoleon? Spires, maybe?' She wasn't making sense.

Matt said nothing.

'And then, nothing for ages.' She looked at him—Matt—her eyes longing, in pain. 'I don't know what they were doing.'

'Who?'

She just shook her head. 'They are experts, aren't they?'

'Who?' Matt asked again.

'I can't do this,' she whispered.

'What?'

But then she said nothing. She sat slumped in the settee, as if all her strength had been drained from her. Her eyes, those eyes that Matt had followed across a continent and half an ocean, were red with tears. And helplessness.

He had seen her despair before, only to then regather herself and hold court. He had seen her crippled with heartache in New York, only to rejoin the battle with even fiercer determination. But he had never seen her like this—beaten to the point of submission, ready to concede defeat.

'I'm sorry,' she said softly, although Matt wasn't sure if she was talking to him or herself. Or someone else.

They sat across from each other for hours. Eventually she fell asleep where she was, her body slowly collapsing against the cushions. Rather than move her, Matt simply covered her with a blanket.

He didn't know why he spoke—or even if she could hear him—or why he said what he did.

'It was always your idea, Anna,' he said tenderly. 'And it always will be.'

It just felt right.

Arb knocked on the door just after seven the following morning.

'Turner,' he said casually as Matt opened the door a crack, 'you haven't seen Anna have you? She didn't come home last—'

Matt opened the door fully to reveal Anna still sleeping on the settee.

Arb made to enter, but Matt's forearm planted itself against his chest.

'I don't know what you did, you corporate slut,' Matt snapped softly, surprising himself with his own aggression—the geekish no-hope hitchhiker threatening his All-American benefactor, 'but let me remind you how special she is.'

Arb swatted Matt's hand and advice away, entered the room, then stopped. Matt could see Arb's mind racing through scenarios he'd never envisioned before. He stepped forward again, then hesitated once more. When he turned back to Matt, his face had lost its invincible lustre. 'What did she tell you?'

'Only that she's underappreciated,' Matt said obscurely, guessing it to be true but wanting Arb to think he knew more than he did.

'Don't play games with—' Arb began to snap, his anger rising above the low volume of his voice.

Then suddenly, he looked back at Anna, still asleep. Then back at Matt. 'Don't tell her I was here,' he ordered quietly as he pushed past Matt and rushed back into the hallway.

'Don't tell me what to do,' said Matt back, unsure whether Arb had heard as he strode anxiously away.

Does it matter why we do things?
It must. Or else we are nothing.

why

'I wonder sometimes if I'm doing this for the right reasons.'

'Okay, I'll bite—why are you doing this?'

She was lucid now, her manner suggesting nothing out of the ordinary had taken place the night before. But she wanted to stay and talk for a few minutes, she said. Of course, Matt obliged.

'Well, usually I'd respond to that question with a series of statements about how the idea just came to me one day and I saw an opportunity for us to do something that had never been done before, an opportunity to start again, to do it better.'

'Sounds good to me,' said Matt, pretending to mull it over, but wanting her to go on.

'Of course it *sounds* good. It's an answer that has been carefully manufactured, preened and polished to sound good. It's supposed to sound good.' Matt was nodding in obvious agreement when he realised suddenly that she had stopped speaking. He turned to find she was looking right at him. 'The problem is: it's not the truth.'

Matt didn't say anything. He didn't know what to say. But as he looked at her, he could tell that she wanted him to reply, wanted him to ask her the question again.

'Okay, why are you doing this?'

'Because I love you.'

Arb pushed her away.

'I've always loved you,' she implored, tears in her eyes. 'Can't you see that? Can't you see?'

He asked himself why he'd come here, why he hadn't stayed to comfort his wife when she awoke.

'Mare! All I see is a former girlfriend now married to one of my best friends! What about Tom?'

'Izzy, you idiot! I only got engaged to him because I thought that would make you do something.'

Arb looked at her with disgust.

'Oh, come on!' Mary demanded, her tears now intolerant. 'You made me marry him! By continuing to not respond, not do anything, I had to go through with it! And don't tell me you didn't feel anything—it's no surprise that you rebounded into her arms on the very night we got married.'

'You're incredible,' he said, appalled by the gall of the suggestion.

'You know it's true,' she said. Even now, she was provocatively shifting her hips with an air of seduction.

'I don't know what to say,' Laikali replied into the receiver. 'I'm sure you can understand that I wasn't expecting your call.'

'You don't know how hard it was for me not to

ask *you* to dance,' his cultured voice said. 'Do you remember Paris as fondly as I do?'

Laikali felt her blood pressure rising. It took every ounce of concentration to resist his taunt. She told herself she had waited too long for this moment—she told herself not to waste it.

'You made a fool of me that day,' she said calmly, although she was sure he could hear her heart beating down the phoneline.

'And you made me look like I could dance,' he said wistfully. 'I haven't danced with someone as delightful and determined as you since.' He paused before getting to the point. 'Until her, if truth be told.'

'You can't beat her, Paul Jefferson Ford,' she said, now gaining in confidence. 'I won't let you.'

'Mrs Rulé, I'm very impressed by your boldness. I always have been. Tell me: how long have you been waiting for such a chance to be so bold to me?'

'Since my father died,' Anna said, breathing deeply, determined to share this with Matt, 'since he died—he was hit by a car when I was sixteen— since he died, I've known I had to do this.'

Matt tilted his head questioningly, trying to link her father's death to a four-mile-wide hole in the ocean.

Anna huffed a half-laugh. 'I mean, I've known that I wanted to build a New World so that a death like his couldn't happen again.'

'How so?' Again Matt was missing something.

'It's not—I know it doesn't sound logical,' she

struggled, 'but . . . that's where it came from.'

Matt shook his head, still uncertain what she meant.

'My father,' Anna said, choking up on the memory, 'you need to understand, was an idealist. He spent his whole life waging a one-man war against the world—in his head! He never really did anything about it, except talk about it to me.'

'So,' ventured Matt, 'you're trying to build a world that your father would be proud of.'

Anna smiled humbly, but shook her head. 'Yes, I *am* trying to do that—but that's not *why* I'm doing it.'

'Okay,' said Matt nodding, then shaking *his* head. 'Let me ask again then, why are you doing this?'

'Because someone lied to me.'

'You know it's true,' Mary repeated, edging closer to Arb who had turned his head away.

'Don't tell me what I know and don't know,' he murmured angrily, scaring her with the attention his soft bitter voice demanded. 'You don't know—have never known—anything about me.'

She regathered herself quickly. 'Izzy, how can you say that? We're the same, you and I. I know everything about you.'

'All you know is what you want.'

'That's right,' she said, demurely fingering her lower lip. Then she pointed, reached out with her wet finger and touched Arb on his lips. 'And I want you.'

'Anna Spires said you were blind,' Laikali said, controlling the urge to tell him anything about how she felt. 'Is that true?'

'Almost,' she could hear his amused smile down the phoneline, 'but not yet. I can still see when an idea poses a clear and present danger to our way of life.'

'Is that what you think? Do you really think that an unbuilt city in the Indian Ocean represents a threat to you?'

'Don't you?'

She knew that he knew she did. She couldn't let herself be sucked into playing his games. Stalling as she thought what to do, she repeated her earlier claim, 'I won't let you.'

'I heard you the first time, Mrs Rulé. You know I've watched you blossom and grow as a states-person since we last met—I wonder sometimes if you'd be where you are today if it were not for me.'

'You're so scared of her, aren't you?'

'Sometimes I think you'd be back on a beach in Palwali if it wasn't for me.'

'She's really got you on the run, hasn't she?'

'Tell me: is Augusto still your most trusted advisor?'

His flippancy, realised Laikali, meant that this was serious. She would not engage his slighting comments because suddenly, she realised, that she had the advantage.

'You shouldn't have called me,' she said.

'And why not?' Ford replied, blinking first in the face-off of separate conversations.

'You called because you're desperate. Because you're losing. Because—'

'I called because I wished to apologise for not dancing with you in New York. And because I was wondering if you'd be so kind as to save me a space on your dance card for the next United Nations Ball.'

'What do you mean, someone lied to you?'

*

'You're fired, Mary.'

'Goodbye, Paul Jefferson Ford.'

'She lied to me.'

'I'm what?'

'You want to know why I let them test their bombs in your ocean, don't you, Mrs Rulé?'

'She? Who? Who's she?'

'You heard me,' Arb said, showing her the door. 'Now go stick that finger someplace else.'

'You know I do,' Laikali said. 'But not today!' And she slammed the phone down.

Anna wouldn't answer. She just closed her eyes, closing off Matt's access to how she was feeling. When she spoke again, her eyes were still shut, as if remembering her father's death—or perhaps, trying not to remember.

'I wanted to create a world where commerce doesn't dictate medical and scientific research. I wanted to create a world where political rhetoric wasn't required to govern. I wanted a world where people try to improve everyone's way of life, not just their own.'

Matt reached out for her, his hand, for the second time, touching and caressing her soft hair.

'I wanted to create a world without compromise.'

In her voice was the usual passion, that unflinching conviction that Matt had spied from so far away so long ago. But there was also something else—something about the betrayal of the world and industry and governments and the people— no, it was something more, Matt realised. Something personal.

'Anna,' he said gently, his hand now holding hers, 'who lied to you?'

Words that cut her to pieces, made her so angry . . .
Because they were true.

home truths

It had been such a stupid argument. Something about her choice of friends or men or the freedom a twenty-one year old should have from fascist maternal dictatorships—Jo didn't even remember.

It had then become more personal, 'this is so typical of you' or the sort—again she did not remember—but they were hardly barbs that hadn't been traded before.

Then—and this she did remember—were words that cut her to pieces.

'Dad would be so disappointed in you.'

Cut her to pieces.

Made her so angry.

At first, her voice had been soft in its response: 'Don't say that.'

'Why not?' had been the incensed twenty-one year old's reply. Youth, like animals, can sense weakness, sense blood—and when they do, they press their advantage. 'Look at you! No ambition. No life. Nothing to show for anything since he died.'

'Anna, don't—'

'He would be so ashamed!'

'Be careful,' she had warned her daughter, her own passion rising.

'You know, sometimes I think it's lucky he died, so he didn't have to see you become so insipid.'

'That's enough, Anna. You don't know what you're talking about.'

'The truth is you never understood him.'

'Shut up.' She could feel herself losing control.

Weakness. 'The truth is I've always known him better than you.'

'Shut up.'

Blood. 'The truth is he always loved me more than you.'

'Yes! Yes! That's true! That's true! That's true!'

Anna had frozen, surprised that she'd just delivered a death blow.

'But you don't know everything,' mother had then said to daughter.

With a pity that only the powerful possess, Anna had let her speak.

For fifteen years, Jo had wished that she hadn't. There had been nothing but vengeance and hatred in her mind. There was no excuse. Even if it was true, she should never have said it.

'You don't know that he did it on purpose, do you?'

the world at stake

[days 555 to 649, plus
day 1365 (Year 1)
day 3000 (Year 6)
day 4652 (Year 10)
day 10000 (Year 25)]

I see her everywhere around me—in the stars, in the fire, in my reflection in the window—yet without her, I often ask myself if she ever existed at all.

There's a dictionary on a shelf in the corner. Her name's in it—proof that she existed—proof that Ninety East Ridge existed too. And other things like pipewalls, Crystal Towers, and Freekanomics. I flip the pages . . .

Freekanomics */fri:ke'nommiks / adj. colloq. of or relating to Moneyless Economic Principles relying on voluntary action rather than financial motivation or compulsion. First used to describe the moneyless market economy designed by Saul Obermann for the experimental city-state Ninety East Ridge (also referred to as Trade Free Economics or Modern Voluntarism).*

There it is, in black and white, tangible evidence of

307

her existence, and yet it's not enough: as helpful as the definition of 'freedom' just a few words above as 'a state of liberty'.

There's more to it, of course. So much more that can't be 'defined'. There's the ideal. There's the struggle. There's not just what is, but also what was and might have been.

What is . . . is truth. What was . . . is memory. And what might have been . . . is a lie.

A lie I cherish like a masochistic fool.

Ding!

let the real game begin

DAY 555—UNITED NATIONS

Laikali Rulé could feel the buzz around the entire assembly, but try as she might, she could not find out what it was about. Ambassadors flicked secretive glances back at her after they passed. Aides scurried by her deliberately avoiding eye contact. Even the orderlies and security guards seemed to have picked up on something that she had not.

It was like a smell that she could not quite place. A shadow she recognised but still could not identify.

She was in their sights, this much was clear. Ford's sights, probably. Her, or one of her causes.

'Harry, I'm sorry, I'm going to have to cancel our meeting tomorrow. Can we make it later in the week, or better yet, next week?'

'No, Anna. You know I'd never go against you without good reason—'

'What do you mean, go against me?'

'I think you will want to be there tomorrow, that's all.'

'Sorry, Harry.'

'World out to get ya again?' Harry asked, his grizzled voice suddenly softer.

'Yeah,' she sighed.

'Well tell 'em to fuck off! You're busy!'

'Thanks, Harry,' she said, feeling better. 'I'll see you tomorrow.'

*

The past eight months had not been easy for Arb either. Ever since the day that they returned to the Ridge from London and Anna had asked him about Xavier.

A thousand thoughts had rushed through his mind in an instant. *How does she know? Perhaps she heard me on the phone to him?* No, he had been too careful for that. *There was nothing with his name on it for her to find accidentally. Xavier had done most of his work at the Ridge itself, so there had been no need for covert communications. Maybe she had suspected for longer, checked Xavier out, had him followed when he took his recent 'holiday' . . . No, she wouldn't.* No, no, that just wasn't Anna.

'Who is Xavier really?' she had repeated.

How else could she have found out? Who else knows?

Surely no one would have told her. Only my parents know about him, and of course Byron, but they don't know what I'm using him for here. And then it hit him. *Mary. Mary knows. She said so on the Thames but I didn't notice—I was distracted by her tirade against Anna. Oh my God! Did she . . .? Could she have overheard?*

The realisation had made him step back, his thoughts nervously exploring possible consequences. *Truth or dare?* he had thought to himself.

Truth, he had decided.

The hall of the General Assembly. A massive cavern of ornate carved wood and endless tiers of leather-clad, tabled pews disappearing into shadows at the rear of the hall.

Members of the Assembly, flanked by fussing industrious entourages, were taking their places, showily shuffling decks of paper on the desks that grew from the backs of the seats in front of them. A soft bell was ringing, hurrying the throng that now filled the aisles to disperse amongst the vast red leather classroom.

Hundreds of urgent-looking messengers scurried between the thousands of important-looking delegates. There was a ubiquitous sense of dire seriousness, even in the pouring of a glass of water.

The cavern was vast and high enough to support a number of smaller galleries set into the walls, throwbacks to opera house boxes, with ornate rounded balconies. They were also furnished in leather, but shadowed by red velvet curtains.

Laikali often gazed up there—from the floor when she had been Palwali's chief ambassador, and now, from her official place at the front of the upper deck as Chairperson of a number of UN initiatives—and wondered if he could see her looking for him. Or did he have another vantage point? If he was now blind, perhaps he just took the audio feed in any one of a number of rooms throughout the building.

Wherever he was, she was sure he was following today's proceedings.

She just wished she knew why.

She should be happy with how things were going, Anna knew.

The third pipewall, though covered in construction netting and scaffolding, was structurally complete, and the draining of the third circle, the final circle, had progressed to sea level minus five hundred metres.

The Foundation Building was finished and waiting for furnishings, the first business and residential tower blocks were almost operational and the interior top deck foundations, the fifty-metre wide spokes that extended between the cement-filled first pipewall and the stable second pipewall, were lined with construction material just waiting for her okay to become a dozen more buildings.

On top of all that, they had begun the task of tearing down the upper third of the second pipewall, thus creating the first real glimpse of the seven-kilometre wide bowl in which Ninety East Ridge would found itself.

She should be happy, she knew. She had achieved more than anyone—scientists, engineers, politicians, environmentalists, everyone—could possibly have foreseen. To date, she had overcome all the subversion, ridden over all Philo Group dissension, always moved forward, every day, in some way or another. She never wasted a day.

No one doubted Anna Spires any more. No longer did anyone write her off as a lightweight idealist who would drift away in the current of reality. Agree or not, often not, no one doubted her resolve, no one doubted her skills, no one doubted that her vision of a New World would come to pass.

No, no one doubted her any more—except for Anna Spires herself.

'He's a spy,' was all he'd said.

He hadn't asked if she'd overheard Mary's plotting. Hadn't asked if she had realised that he had fired Mary for it. Hadn't asked if she had thought . . . thought that Mary and him were . . . thought that there was something else going on.

'He's the best there is,' he had added, uncomfortably feeling the need to justify himself.

She had turned away, staring at the vast ocean. They had stayed that way, as if stuck in a fresco pose, for some time, a long time for Arb who couldn't see her eyes, couldn't see what she was thinking.

'Ridder,' she had said finally, softly, almost to the window instead of him. 'Xavier is how you found out about Ridder, isn't he?'

'Yes.'

'He's also how you removed Goodsell and his greenies from the barges, isn't he? And the labour strikes, that's how you knew, isn't it? That's how you beat them all, isn't it?'

He had bowed his head, answering softly, sombrely, 'More or less.'

Her own head also looked at the floor, being shaken disappointedly, a sigh of disgust perhaps under her breath. He had been about to go to her, put his arms on her shoulders . . .

'And the money we've raised from investors . . .' Her whisper, barely audible, cold and serious, 'the games we've played with politicians. Tell me, honestly, tell me: did he spy on them too? Did *we* spy on them? Did we blackmail them, any of them, into giving us money?'

'No. No, that's all different. Any bargaining power we had with anyone had nothing to do with Xavier. No, that's different. I, or Byron or my team, did all of the research and bargaining strategies for the investors.'

She had said nothing.

He had felt compelled to go on: 'There was no blackmail. No extortion. Except, of course, for the carrot, the opportunity, of being able to invest in a once-in-a-lifetime deal.'

'Deal?'

He had grimaced, then clenched his fist, in anger as much as frustration. He had held his tongue. She knew what was going on. She had always known. What's more, he had always felt that, if she had found out about Xavier, he would have been able to convince her to admit that she had always known he had someone like Xavier in his employ.

'You know what I mean,' he had finally mumbled, as she stared gravely out the window.

The days since had been awkward. Days had become months. A distance had grown between them as Anna silently figured things out for herself.

Laikali refocused her attention on the agenda for the day. Military standoff in the Middle East. Civil violence in a number of neighbouring central African countries. Review of economic sanctions on some North African and Balkan states. The usual, really. Pre-prepared public statements, pre-prepared questions and answers, pre-prepared debate and conflict in the official recorded forum to maintain the masquerade of open transparent decision-making.

It was not really a secret. The public accepted the scripted process because it was more expeditious, more efficient, less prone to creating the uncertainties which stock markets and major manufacturers fear the most. The semblance of reality was maintained in much the same way as a professional wrestling match: every sense and instinct told spectators that what they got to see wasn't real, but there were just too many good enough reasons to believe that maybe—just maybe—it was. There was so much money at stake, so much fame, so many good reasons not to follow the script, even just once—a stray punch, an inch to the left, an apparent accident, may create one day a champion, instead of fall guy; a new viewpoint, an uncensored censure, a surprise breaking of political ties may score political points, if only for a day. Perhaps it was that chance of uncertainty which kept people interested, like sports fans at a car race who are really just hoping to see a spectacular pile-up.

The agenda was nothing unusual. Maybe she wasn't in trouble today after all.

Then the speaker rose to his mahogany lectern, the sea of heads hushed.

'Good morning, everyone. As a number of you are aware, there has been another item added to today's agenda. First item after the morning break will be a discussion of the legality and international status of the substantial construction currently taking place in the Indian Ocean, known as Ninety East Ridge.'

Self-doubt has a more unpredictable influence on the intelligent than on the unintelligent. It tends only to incapacitate the small-minded, while it can either motivate or demoralise a more thinking individual.

With some interest, therefore, Anna had watched the highly trained minds around her react to the obstacles that continued to rise before their quest. They were all relatively self-confident individuals, but the further the dream had proceeded, the more impassioned, the more opinionated and the more determined they had all become. They had needed to. They all knew that if any one of them broke down now, the others would have to leave them behind.

So they had each developed personal defence mechanisms. Disparaging the Group's development was common: Mary had labelled the group the politburo since her departure, Harry would refer to it as the Bridge Club, Matt and Tom agreed it was like the Jedi Council fighting to resist the Dark Side, while Jay and Saul would remark that any Group conclusion that did not match their own was exactly what to expect from an unelected dictatorial clique.

It made for an increasingly tense and serious Philo Group and the conclusion of arguments often became personal. Anna, in particular, was implicated by rejected geniuses as incompetent or naive: never directly, no one would dare with Isaac around, but by repeated references to doctoral studies which suggested diametrically opposing conclusions to Anna's preferences.

But these were their own self-doubts, she felt. They didn't worry her too much.

She had her own self-doubts plaguing her. And at stake was more than just the fate of their little New World.

A storm of self-doubt and anxiety now also swirled in Arb's head. Suddenly, success was not assured. Suddenly, his confidence suffered from a suspicion of presumptuousness. Suddenly, he didn't trust his judgement—that sense of purpose and certainty that had never, ever failed him before.

Initially, his misgivings had all been professional. Since the appearance of Jefferson Ford, he had begun to wonder, for the first time in his life, if there may have been other forces responsible for his success. Beyond the advantages of his parents' wealth and the networks he had grown up with, he wondered if he was just another pawn, like many senators he knew, like the reporters he himself often manipulated. A year ago, he had been sacked by GJS—and he hadn't had a clue. It had not struck him until Ford turned up at Anna's party that Gill Johnson Shek might not have acted on their own. The thought began to haunt him. He began to wonder how much else he didn't know.

Since their return, however, the professional selfconsciousness that had plagued him since New York had extended beyond work, beyond the markets and his peers, beyond that world that for his whole life had seemed so important, to touch his most precious possession.

It had touched her.

He had tried to mask his fears by busying himself with even more work. Phone calls in the middle of the night. Endless planning, strategising. Calculations and recalculations of their finances. But something was missing.

The spark, it seemed, that once unleashed torrents of abuse for even the smallest error was now slow to lose patience. His usual contempt for ineptitude, his drive for perfection—the Isaac Blackwell people expected—had become muted.

But it was Anna's own lack of anger that troubled him more. She had buried whatever she was feeling about him behind an inscrutable façade of nonchalance. He began to wonder if Ford was somehow plotting to steal her too. Or someone else, perhaps.

Matt clattered down the steel gantry stairs, running, tripping, rushing to where Anna stood on a corner of Platform Seven.

'Anna! Anna!' he called urgently when he saw her.

'What is it?'

Matt reached her, then while catching his breath stammered out, 'Laikali called . . . UN to discuss . . . Ninety East Ridge . . . today.'

'Oh my God!' She raced for the War Room.

Isaac was already on the phone to Laikali when she got there, Matt panting five paces behind her.

'A-huh . . . a-huh . . .' he was affirming into the receiver. Anna stood expectantly next to him. He extended one hand and patted her on the forearm. The rest of the Philo Group also gathered around.

With one ear still listening to Laikali, Isaac relayed what was going on: 'The United States ambassadors to the United Nations . . . are presenting a proposal declaring the construction project known as Ninety East Ridge . . . as an illegal acquisition of universal ocean territory . . . and as a crime against the global ecology. They will be proposing that the United Nations . . . condemn the project as such . . . and recommend . . . that an international body appointed by the UN . . .

take control of all further construction, development, settlement if deemed appropriate, and
administration.'

When he hung up a few moments later, the
room was deathly silent. Several of the Group
looked physically ill. Isaac himself seemed
uncertain what to say. Anna just stared at the
phone, so shocked, so stunned that her face
contorted quizzically, almost smiling but not quite,
her eyes wide with ironic disbelief.

'They can't do anything, Anna,' Matt said firmly
for all the room to hear. 'If they could they would
have done it already.'

The room didn't respond, wanting to believe,
looking at Isaac for his assurance.

Isaac swallowed, but then backed Matt up:
'It's a stunt. We checked all the legal claims before
we started. We took all possible environmental
precautions.'

But his audience wasn't convinced. Isaac had
hardly been strident in his defence. It must be really
bad if he didn't at least feign confidence. He sensed
their doubts and tried to make amends.

'All it means is that we have to fight for what
we've established. In the courts, maybe, or at the
UN. It's just another Ford tactic to delay us, to
worry us—get us to make a deal or something.'

'It's all falling apart,' said a sad voice from the
back of the room.

'You know, fired generally means not welcome
in the workplace any more,' Isaac said solemnly.

'My husband still works here, and as his spouse,
I still reside here,' said Mary, ever-defiant.

'You don't know shit, Mary. The last thing that's happening is that it's falling apart!'

This was the stridency that they wanted to hear. The ruthlessness back in his voice. The fire glaring from his eyes. No prisoners. No retreat. No surrender.

'Listen to me, all of you. Ninety East Ridge will be completed. They know it. And they know they can't stop it. This move is meant to discourage us, to make us lose confidence that it will be ours when we finish this, to make us give up—well don't let it! And as far as money is concerned,' he said, eyeing Mary with contempt, 'I know that some of you, who have absolutely no fucking idea how our finances are structured, have concerns about what our investors will think of our policies, and now maybe our UN troubles. Well, to those concerns let me say: if every investor took back their money tomorrow, and if every other investor fell off the face of the earth, there would still be more than enough. Give me some credit! You don't do to Wall Street what we're doing without a plan. Nothing can stop us from completing Ninety East Ridge. No one except ourselves.'

They were not exactly brimming with renewed vigour, but it was close enough. They had come too far to back out now, especially if there was a chance they would not lose. And Isaac knew exactly what they were thinking.

'We are going to win,' he said.

And he meant it.

To overcome barriers, opposition or obstacles of any sort,
    look beyond them—
Through them!—and understand the vision on the other
    side.

glass walls

She was in her office on Platform Seven when Harry called.

'Just a reminder,' he said, his voice bubbling without a hint of the previous day's anxiety, 'about our meeting in half an hour. We've got something special to show you.'

'Yes, Harry. Okay, Harry. I'll be there, Harry,' she said playing the reluctant slacker.

'Thatta girl, Anna!'

Ten minutes later, there was a knock at the door.

Matt was already talking before he had the door completely open, 'So are you ready? Come on? Harry sent me to make sure you were on time. Come on! There's a boat waiting for us downstairs.'

Matt virtually pushed Anna into the little runabout which would ferry them across from Platform Seven.

They had been spending more and more time together, coordinating their respective Urban

Development and Transport responsibilities, in her efforts to avoid her husband. She had begun to confide in Matt the way she had once done with Isaac. And she did so again now.

'What happens if we do win?' she asked. Their relationship now permitted random questions without explanation.

'Well,' cried Matt, clapping his hands, sensing an opportunity to rev up her spirits, 'we create a New World, a better world, a world without the compromises and inadequacies of this sad vindictive old one.'

'Aren't we just going to invent brand-new compromises and inadequacies?'

'Probably,' he said, giving her a wry grin. 'But that's no reason to stop, is it?'

Anna struggled to find the same amusement in it as Matt did. 'Well, let's say we do succeed and— best case scenario—we create the perfect world, what then?'

'Well, for a start, we make our immigration policy a priority, because everyone will want to move here.'

'And what then? What about when we run out of room?'

'Well, if it's that good, then I guess other places will start to model themselves after us and people will move there instead.'

'And what then, Mr Turner? What would the world be like if they all did what we did?'

'Well for a start, they all couldn't just go on building holes all over the ocean.'

'No, I mean what if they all adopted our values

and the lifestyle that we create here, what then?'

'But that's the point, isn't it? That's *exactly* what we want. This is what you've always wanted.'

'I think I am only just beginning to realise the responsibility that comes with changing the world.'

'This UN thing is just making you a little nervous, that's all. A little cold feet about defending it.' He held up her chin and stroked her cheek. 'We'll be fine,' he said. 'We're going to win.'

'I appreciate the confidence, but you're not exactly taking off the pressure.'

Matt just shook his head.

'Do you have any idea how much confidence we have in you?' he said, as they pulled up to the makeshift jetty linked to the mighty third pipewall. 'Your ability to see through the barriers before you, to see what you're looking for on the other side, to see what other people say you can't have—let me just say, you have to see this.'

The site—and the sight—was now a glorious one, extending right and left in a wide arc and then tracing back together in the distance. And in between, the bowl, sloping in down the third pipewall scaffolding, across the Foundation Spokes, past the descending second pipewall and the towering first pipewall to a mirror image on the other side.

'It looks like an enormous leaky satellite dish,' Matt said proudly, following her stare. 'Come on! They're waiting.'

As he dragged and hurried her down the ramps and steps which wound down the scaffolding,

Anna could see a crowd gathered on one of the Foundation Spokes.

'Is that where we're meeting?' she yelled at Matt ahead of her. 'What's going on?'

'I'm afraid I can't tell you. Top secret. You'll just have to wait like everyone else.'

Everyone else was waiting there too, Anna discovered. The entire Philo Group had been harassed and cajoled to ensure they turned up on time.

'I only want to do this once,' Harry said in his no-nonsense way. 'We have a little unveiling for you today.'

Anna looked at Isaac for some enlightenment, but he just shrugged his shoulders to signal that he too had no idea what was going on.

'Now this is about as profound as I get,' Harry went on, 'but we've all had to deal with some pretty mean accusations and name-calling in the last twenty-four hours. Well, this reminds me of a saying, "People in glass houses shouldn't throw stones".'

There was a small comradely cheer.

'Well, I'm afraid to say that we won't be able to throw any stones in return from now on.'

He waited for them all to react, which they did: confused, intrigued, defensive.

'But I don't think any of us will mind. Boys!'

At his signal, a giant section of the tarpaulin that was covering the third pipewall dropped away to reveal . . . the ocean.

'Ladies and gentlemen, let me present to you the Great Glass Wall!'

The third pipewall was transparent!

Not perfectly, but see-through nonetheless. Harry was talking, explaining it, but no one was listening, no one was breathing, so stunned were they all at the sight of the transparent pipewall.

'Of course, it's not actually glass. It's a transparent plexi-cement that we designed especially for this. There is some distortion, which myself and the team would like to apologise for, but on the whole it's not so bad.'

'It's fantastic!' yelled Matt.

'It's magnificent!' cried Tom.

Adulation came from everywhere and everyone—cheers, roars of triumph, high-fives, backslaps, hugs and kisses, more cheering—everyone, that is, except Anna, who just stared at the structure, tears sliding from the corners of her eyes. She knew what she wanted to say, but somehow the words just weren't flowing. Suddenly, all her self-doubt had evaporated. Suddenly, for better or worse, the world would have to deal with her contribution of Ninety East Ridge. Suddenly, it was all real, unstoppable. Everything was possible, including the chance that it might just be for the best after all.

Then she found the words. She said them softly, and only Matt, who was standing beside her, could hear them.

'It's beautiful.'

The famous Crystal Tower was made of concrete and steel,
*   not crystal.*
Except for its supernatural crown, which sat just above the
*   surface of the ocean,*
It was plain and practical.

what might have been . . . the crystal tower

DAY 1365—'FIRST BIRTHDAY' CELEBRATIONS, SINGAPORE

'No part of the famous Crystal Tower was ever actually made of crystal,' Harry Pont pointed out to the interviewer who sat across the stage. 'It was mostly prefabricated concrete and aluminium and polyfibres and plexiglass. Except for its supernatural crown, which sat just above the surface of the ocean, it was above all plain and practical.'

'A perfect symbol for Ninety East Ridge,' said the interviewer, Chee Wen Hao.

Quite a crowd had turned up, mostly students and lecturers, to listen to Harry Pont speak about the design and creation of the Ridge. The interviewer, a little too obsequious for Harry's taste— always trying to endear himself to Harry or the university crowd—was now asking about the Crystal Tower.

'Tell us please, Harry—I understand the design changed considerably over the course of the Tower's conception.'

'When they first presented the plans to the Philo Group, it was to be built into—or out of, depending on whether you are an architect or an engineer—the very first pipewall. Remember: the first pipewall was the centre of the city, eighty metres in diameter and extending down the full depth of the ocean, almost a mile. The bottom thousand metres of the pipewall—below what we referred to as the Top Deck—was filled with concrete to act as a vertical foundation for the foundation spokes, the horizontal foundations which extended out from the centre and on which we built other structures. Above the Top Deck, however, the weight of the pipewall was of only minor structural significance.'

'So,' interjected Chee, perhaps feeling that the content was getting too slow and technical for his audience—or perhaps him—to keep up, 'Donovan and the rest of the architects immediately seized on the opportunity to transform the upper five hundred metres of the concrete cylinder into a functional centre of the city, a cheating tallest building ever built, a symbol of the city—the way the Opera House symbolises Sydney, the way Big Ben is associated with London, the Eiffel Tower with Paris.'

'The first time I saw the plans,' chuckled Harry—he didn't mind being told to dumb it down; it had happened before—'I thought it was the Sydney Opera House stuck on top of the Sears Tower. Later it became a Pyramid on the Colosseum. By the last draft, it was—'

'Of course,' broke in the moderator turning to the audience, 'you can see how all these plans morphed in the exhibition in the hall next door.'

Drifting through the blueprints and models laid out next door was Miles Alia, who had not thought about Ninety East Ridge for over a year.

He had been in Singapore promoting his latest advancement in Remote Government Comm-unications Software—the Singapore government, always at the vanguard of technology imp-lementation, were likely to buy it—when he had seen an article in the newspaper about Harry's exhibition. Against his better judgement, he had felt compelled to visit, if at least just to say hello to Harry.

They had only spoken briefly before a busy organiser had stolen Harry away for a Question and Answer session about to take place.

'Well, if it's not the Pont Guard himself, the Pontiff, the Pontoon, the man himself!' he had said.

'Good to see you, Miles,' Harry had replied in his plain-speaking manner. 'What are you doing these days?'

'Back in the software business, I'm afraid—my superhero days are over, I guess,' Miles had said, starting upbeat but feeling sadder as his words trailed away.

He looked at the older man, as if for advice.

'I know how you feel,' Harry had said, before being dragged off to his lecture.

'The winning design looked like Superman's Fortress on top of an Art Deco Multicultural Tower of Pisa,' Harry said to Chee. 'Without the lean, of course.' That always drew a light laugh.

'What did you think of the design?'

'I'm an engineer,' snorted Harry. 'I just build what they tell me. But as I said, the original objective was to design a distinctive shape, one casting a silhouette unlike any seen on the planet. This objective never changed. I will say, however, that as the body of the building took shape, it was clear that something more outrageous was required.'

For once, Chee Wen Hao chose not to interject.

'The end design settled, as you can see in the display next door, on a crown of ninety crystal shards—one for each degree we were east of the prime meridian, I guess—and one central soaring larger shard representing Ninety East Ridge itself. This crown stood atop the two-hundred storey "building" that rose from the Top Deck, with changing stylised stonework motifs of classic arches and modern window frames, of dark flowing Gothic and stark angled Thai. The architects spent a lot of time softening the transition between styles, or at least so they told me,' he let his voice drift into the dreamy childlike voice that he often used to mimic architects, 'so that the building remained one coherent structure whilst the varied motifs allowed there to be a sense of distinction and therefore identity for those residing or working within the structure.'

'Do you think that the story of Ninety East Ridge is perhaps best summed up by the story of the Crystal Tower?'

The interviewer was already nodding in understanding, even before he finished his own question.

But Harry shook his head, his voice touched with a wistful sadness.

'Personally I preferred the Foundation Building. In fact, I have here,' he picked up a framed notice from under his chair, 'an update which I carry with me, which I think tells the story better.'

Pontifications

Day 575—THE FOUNDATION BUILDING

I am pleased to announce the completion of the first 'land-based' structure, appropriately to be known as the Foundation Building.

Please find included below an excerpt from the original brief given to the architects by Anna about what this building must aim for. I think it says a lot about this whole enterprise.

'I imagine a relatively small building made of bricks and mortar—"the old-fashioned way". It should be built to serve as a home—although it hasn't been decided yet who should live there—a simple home to remind everyone looking at this city of intrepid vision and

---

extraordinary engineering, of its more simple goal: to be a place where people live, laugh, work and, if they ever go away, look forward to coming back to. Coming home to.'

Negative motivators are the most powerful kind,
For better, impossible to forget, and for worse.

pride, lies and a letter

DAY 569—NINETY EAST RIDGE

'I think it's great,' she said, and Matt was overjoyed.

He could hear the pride in Anna's voice, even though she had been involved throughout the transportation project. It was an acknowledgement that this was his doing, his triumph—but what pleased him most was that her congratulations also contained an element of personal satisfaction.

'Do you think the rest of the Group will agree?'

'You should know by now not to judge yourself by what anybody else thinks.'

He liked it when she chastised him, tilting her head as if it might change *his* perspective.

'I should know, but it's easier said than done when you're about to present what you've spent the last year and a half of your life working on.'

'Tell me about it.' They shared a laugh.

They had been laughing a lot lately. Matt felt like a protégé of sorts who had become his mentor's most trusted colleague. Amid the pressure and constant lobbying that surrounded her, he had come to believe that he could see Anna's body relax and her stress lessen when he entered her office.

'It's funny, you know, I talk about eighteen months work, but it was really just six. For twelve months, I wandered the world looking for inspiration, then—bang!—one day it just comes to me. And it had absolutely nothing to do with the thirty-four countries I'd visited looking for the answer.'

Anna shook her head condescendingly. 'Of course it did. That research gave you the confidence to know what *not* to do.'

'I guess,' Matt conceded, nodding, when a knocking behind him made him turn to face the door.

'Come in,' said Anna, but no one did. Instead, after a few seconds, an envelope slipped under the door and across the floor.

Matt flew from his chair and flung open the door, but the anteroom outside was deserted. After abandoning the thought of racing out the door looking for who-knew-who, Matt returned to pick up the envelope. It was addressed simply to 'Anna Spires' and then underlined said 'Urgent and Confidential'.

He passed it to Anna, who opened it without concern. Secret entreaties for her to embrace people's great ideas were arriving often now.

'It's probably another appeal for the Ridge to adopt ancient Mayan values in forming its constitution. The ones without a logo or return address, like this one, tend to be the more extreme.'

She flipped open the note inside. Matt watched from across the desk as her eyes soon narrowed in angry concentration.

Seconds later, the note was in pieces, ripped and torn, and scattered in one of Arb's designer trash containers under the desk. Anna's face—tight, contorted—was a determined angry mystery.

Moments later, before Matt could ask what was wrong, what had happened, Natasha rushed in behind him, an identical letter held out desperately in front of her.

'Did you receive this yet?' she said.

'No,' Anna replied, lying.

'It's a lie,' Taz exclaimed without explaining. 'It's not true. It's not true.'

'Slow down,' said Anna. 'What's wrong? What does it say?'

Taz looked at Matt, wordlessly asking him to leave them alone. She looked as if she was about to cry. He began to rise.

'No, Matt, you stay here and keep working on your presentation. Come on, Taz,' said Anna, moving around the desk and taking her sister by the arm. 'Let's go outside and get some air.'

Initially, Matt did as he was told, checking his notes and blueprints.

But after a few minutes alone, he couldn't help himself. He reached under the desk and pulled Anna's bin towards him. Taking a quick glance over his shoulder and seeing no one, he emptied the contents onto the floor at his feet. It didn't take long to piece the paper jigsaw puzzle together.

Dear Ms Spires

I'm sorry to inform you that your mother Josephine has suffered a mild heart attack. Fortunately, she was able to call an ambulance. She is now in a stable condition at the hospital. Your sister has also been informed.

Regards

Elizabeth Patrick, Melprice Hospital

'So you're saying it's not true,' said Anna, as she finished reading the note for what she made out to be the first time.

'It's a lie. It's a cruel vicious prank,' said Taz distraughtly. 'I called the hospital straight away. She wasn't there. So I called Mr Maclean, the next-door neighbour, and he said he'd seen Mum just this morning. So I called home. And there she was. It wasn't true. She's just fine.'

'I'm glad,' said Anna impassively, lying again.

Behind the optimism, behind his enormous capacity to love,
There was always in him the fear that maybe he would not
amount to much.

the power of discontent

He was always so angry . . .
. . . at himself, she thought. Although he often vented it at the whole world.

He was so clever.

She knew it. And he knew it too.

But for whatever reason, for whatever it is that makes our mind so harshly judge our own strengths and actions, there was always in him that fear that maybe he would not amount to much.

The fear of what might be only compounded an unreasonable frustration about what he had achieved so far. Perhaps he was missing something. Perhaps he had always been missing some rare random element of character or biology which made some people special. Special . . . that was it. He so wanted to be special.

If only he'd known how special he was.

The way he cared for her, protected her—when he held her, nothing could harm her. His wit. His imagination—the scale of his imagination: so vast, so original, so far beyond the bounds of ordinary expectations—his ideas, like him, were one of a kind.

In a way, she understood his frustrations, his anger at a world which was placing restrictions of time and physics before him; his anger at a world which childishly, stubbornly, lazily, deliberately retained its preference for only moderate change.

One day—in his lifetime, she wished—science, time, the world's imagination might catch up to his vision, a vision now exiled to the world of make-believe, to coexist with works of fiction and games of no consequence. Once, his work may have been considered metaphysical. Once, his vision may have been lauded as prophetic. But now, in an enlightened world of modern economics and expedient politics, he was classed as entertainment.

It was an exile made all the more unbearable by the legitimacy that society afforded it.

She understood why he had to go.

A hole in the ocean. A New World. This was his chance.

Selfishly, she knew, she resented the note left for her on the kitchen table.

There were times when she wished that he had just disappeared. For the note, like his professional legitimacy, only served to authenticate her failure.

That was over eighteen months ago now. She hoped Matthew Turner was okay.

It was bold and beautiful, misjudged and misunderstood—
It had all the hallmarks of a great idea.

what might have been . . .
the grid

DAY 587—NINETY EAST RIDGE

Once again, leaders of state and industry had begun to form a queue for her attention.

'Just ignore them,' Isaac had said, once again. *Easy for him*, thought Anna.

The unveiling of the Great Glass Wall, as the press now also called it, had confirmed Ninety East Ridge as reality and everyone wanted a part of it. Lobbyists for free markets, the environment and cigarettes, to name just a few, sounded their trumpets through the press when Anna refused to let them in the front door. Politicians from the surrounding nation-states—Australia, Indonesia, Sri Lanka, India, the Maldives, Mauritius, Madagascar, the Seychelles, Tanzania and South Africa—played the part of friendly neighbours offering to lend cups of sugar, or their lawnmower, or any aspect of labour, trade, power generation or manufacturing in exchange for a friendly chat over a cup of tea. China, Russia, the UK and, of course, the US all sent emissaries of goodwill to 'commence a dialogue' with the New World. Isaac, to Anna's surprise, rebuffed them all, forcing those that arrived to remain on their ships or seaplanes or return to their five-star hotels in Perth, Mumbai or Singapore.

'The game has now changed,' Isaac continued. 'We hold the cards now and, more specifically, the most valuable political football and piece of real estate in the world.'

'Won't this make the UN even more likely to want to control it—and take it away from us?'

'We've got 'em beat, baby,' Isaac said super-confidently, holding up a piece of paper. 'We've got 'em beat. Laikali's on the case for us. She was so right to have stayed where she was. She's been making the calls and running the numbers, and she says that we're almost certain to beat it in the Assembly, which means not even having to go to court.'

Anna whooped for joy, before a double-take caught her: '*Almost* certain?'

'Look, nothing's certain in politics. Views can change. Votes can change. But since the Great Glass Wall was revealed to the world, public opinion is all behind us. People are comparing you to the pharaohs who built the pyramids. The Colossus of Rhodes, Hoover Dam, the Great Wall of China, the Panama Canal, have all been forgotten as footnotes of history. Papers aren't just calling this the eighth wonder of the world, they're calling it *the* wonder of the world. No one's going to vote against this, unless the walls cave in or you start making jokes about genocide.'

The unveiling had given a shot in the arm to everyone associated with the project. Builders now worked harder and faster, proud that they were part of something so special. The third pipewall was almost fully drained. The Foundation Spokes were fully extended to the outer wall. Construction of the city itself was progressing at a breakneck pace—in fact, the Philo Group were all planning to move their offices from Platform Seven into Building One—a tall, still mostly skeletal structure next to the Foundation Building, and the first building in Ninety East Ridge to have power and pipes in place and operational.

The next step was for Matt and the urban planning team to present their final plans for what Ninety East Ridge would look like—the landscape, the cityscape, the art and architecture—and how it would work, including power and energy, waste disposal and, of course, Matt's transportation system.

*

'We call it "the Grid".'

The War Room was dark, save for the bright image on the white screen and its reflected light on Matt's face.

'The Grid?' said a voice from the darkness.

The room was more tightly packed than usual. In addition to the Philo Group, Matt's transport planning team and the entire architects team stood around the walls.

'Yes, the Grid. We considered a number of other naming options, like the Tube, which is taken, or the Chute System, and some of us still call it the STM, which stands for Synchronised Transport Matrix, but we figured we needed something stronger, more marketable. It's not that important, of course. In the end, people will just come up with their own names for it anyway.'

He couldn't see their faces. Couldn't tell if that was polite silence or stunned surprise.

'We call them "motes", short for *remote* controlled cars, or re*mot*or cars, as in remote/motor cars.'

Arb groaned, as Matt knew he would, a fraction too loudly. Anna groaned also, but he could tell that she liked it. Hearing her, he zoomed confidently into his rehearsed spiel.

'The proposed press release you all have in front of you describes the Grid as a comprehensive, multilayer tubular transport system. The motes are driverless and fully computer-controlled with programs designed to ensure the most efficient distribution of commuters and traffic flows. It works like the internet: finding the fast way between two points anywhere in the world.'

'It looks like those old hermetically sealed suction mail chutes. You know, one of those pneumatic tubes.' Tom's voice. Approving, excited.

'It looks like a plumber's nightmare.' Arb's voice. Less convinced.

'That's not so far off, Tom. You simply flag down a mote and mail yourself where you want to go.'

'So you're saying that there will be no private car ownership?'

'No, I didn't say that. Yet. But we are recommending that the majority of motes in the system should be communal. Like automatic taxi cabs. People can still own their own mote if they want to. But remember, they won't be able to drive it themselves.'

'Won't be able to drive it themselves?' repeated Arb. Matt could virtually hear him shaking his head in disbelief. 'You do realise that we are trying to attract people who are used to owning fleets of cars.'

Matt caught himself before his anger replied. *You just made a mistake, Slick*. He let Arb's words hang in the room. *Didn't you?*

'No, I didn't realise that.'

'It doesn't matter who they are.' Arb's voice, frazzled and frustrated. 'You are restricting a fundamental liberty.'

'It's hardly a liberty. Think of it as an improvement. You get where you want to go in the quickest safest method possible. The computer not only calculates your route, but everyone else's route who is on the grid at the same time. People, in comparison, are inefficient, prone to making wrong turns or driving at dangerous speeds or road rage or getting drunk or stoned, all behind the wheel of a car.'

'People like to drive their own cars, Mr Turner.'

'People are used to driving their own cars. But this is a New World, Isaac, and we've come to the conclusion that time, space and safety are priorities above changing your own gears.'

'This is crazy,' hissed Arb softly to himself, although everyone could hear.

'—which brings us to the contractors.'

'Yes, I saw some of the lead designers for Mercedes and Toyota wandering through the halls some time ago, and a friend of mine at BMW said he was going to see you, last week some time I think.'

'Yes, yes—he mentioned that he knew you.'

'So, who is going to build the plumbing for these roadworks, or should I say waterworks, of yours?'

'Funny you should say that. Well, the car manufacturers have still expressed an interest in designing, manufacturing and selling communal and private motes, but as for the construction of the Grid itself, we recommend granting the contract to a consortium made up of HammerPipe Ducting Company and Playco.'

'Playco? They're a toy company! And Hammer-Pipe! You can't use my father's company—it reeks of nepotism. Why wasn't I told about this?'

'We're telling you now.'

'Have you announced this to the bidders yet?'

'No. We are supposed to check with you first before any public announcements.'

'Yes. Yes. And this is exactly why you have to check with me. This is a potential debacle.'

'They were the best proposal.'

'The best proposal! Of course, they were the best proposal; Playco must have designed millions of transport systems in their time—for wooden cars powered by four year olds!'

Matt struggled to maintain a calm, persuasive tone.

'They demonstrated an understanding of the concept which, quite frankly, none of the other tenders came close to.'

'Well of course not. They were probably expecting to deal with a solution for adults, not children! Hey, didn't you once work for Playco?'

'What's that supposed to mean?'

'This is a disaster! I knew from the beginning this was a mistake.' He turned to the architects. 'You were aware of this Grid idea? Surely you have some other solutions that you developed, some other options?'

'Isaac, this was clearly the best solution for our requireme—'

'I don't believe this—and how the hell did Playco partner with HammerPipe?'

'I—ah—I introduced Playco's president to your father.'

'My father? You went directly through my father! Oh great, come one, come all, to a brand New World, where we hope to overcome all the inequities and inefficiencies of the Old World through a concentrated program of favouritism and corruption!'

The ranting continued for a few minutes. Matt went from feeling scared to perturbed to disbelieving to frustrated to bored to outright disrespectful, rolling his eyes at each new burst of outrage.

When Arb finally finished, Matt just ignored him and continued: 'There will be other benefits also, such as the automation of most aspects of the transport industry. Cargoes, once unbundled at the dock upstairs, could then be distributed automatically to any shop, office or residence in the city. Similarly, specially modified motes could be used for automatic transport of refuse and other waste products, direct from homes, factories or community centres back to the docks or to appropriate processing plants.'

The shadowed heads were still a mystery when he finished his final slide, about how the transport system had been designed in conjunction with the city architects and engineers, for example, by locating most 'roads'—tubular transport veins— under pedestrian promenades, which minimised visual pollution and eliminated the possibility of pedestrians being hit by 'cars'.

There was awkward tentative clapping, but Matt wasn't sure if that was because of the presentation, or because of Arb.

Arb was expected to say something and introduce the next speaker. When he said nothing, Anna's voice interrupted the darkness.

'Thank you, Mr Turner,' she said formally, 'for such an innovative solution. I think it's going to take some time to get our heads around it.'

Matt's eyes must have given away his desperation.

'Why don't we sleep on it?' she said from the darkness.

Arb didn't say another word for the rest of the day, and Matt hardly noticed any of the other presentations. During the remaining explanations of the proposed telecommunications infrastructure, Anna's pet thermal, solar and hydro-electric energy projects, and an update from Rainey regarding the ongoing impact on the marine biology, Matt spent most of his time unnecessarily re-sorting his notes or staring at them vacantly.

Neither Arb nor Matt made it to Jabba's Palace for a drink that evening.

Matt had gone back to the Low Road. He had taken his now immaculately sorted notes and thrown them across the room. He had had every intention of completely rewriting his presentation so that there could be no questions, no complaints, no doubts that it was the best recommendation possible.

He had had every intention. But he took one look at the amount of data and analysis before him, and immediately felt like sleeping. He threw himself on his bed, using one arm as a pillow and the other as an eye-shade. But he couldn't sleep. He pretended he was thinking about the Grid, but he was just repeating his presentation in his head. The only original thoughts were brutal rebuttals and slandering double entendres that he should have used to counter Mr Slick.

'Well, *excuse* me. I'm sorry you'll have to tell all your friends that they'll have to leave their *fleets of cars* at home.' 'No, I'm sorry Isaac, but I wasn't aware we wanted to make all the same mistakes as the rest of the world.' 'Yes I introduced them. Forgive me for paying attention to the Isaac Blackwell school of how to do business. I must have missed the lesson that says these rules do not apply to people who are not Isaac Blackwell.' 'Did I mention that your BMW friend was a pompous, arrogant jerk? 'Fuck off, Blackwell. Everyone else seems to understand.'

He wished he could have the opportunity again, although he couldn't really think of anything he'd do differently. Perhaps the colours were wrong, or the formatting. Maybe he should have spoken more to Anna before the presentation—asked her how to sell the idea to Isaac, or politely requested that she send him on an errand or something . . . to Argentina, maybe!

There was a knock at the door.

Who? Her? Anna maybe? Some words of consolation? Some personal encouragement?

He flew from the bed to the door then stopped, ensuring a look of disappointment and despondency dominated his face. Then he opened the door.

Anna stood there. It was her! Her understanding smiling countenance an immediate comfort.

'Come in, come in,' he said, having stared a moment longer than he needed to.

He stood aside as she walked into the room. Matt was about to close the door when Tom walked in right behind her, smiling.

'Looks like we're just in time,' Anna said, looking at the scattered pages as Matt tried to recover his composure and cover his disappointment at Tom's arrival. 'He hasn't burnt it yet.'

'You could always put it in a bottle and throw it out the window,' suggested Tom helpfully.

Matt just shook his head, his genuine bewilderment now returning. His face showed them both that he clearly didn't understand what had happened up there, or how he could have stopped it.

'Isaac just didn't get it,' soothed Anna. 'You know, I think it's the first time I've ever seen him misjudge an idea, or dismiss it too quickly.'

Matt's eyes were immediately more hopeful.

'Everyone else thought it was a fantastic presentation, Mattie-boy!'

'And so did Isaac,' added Anna. 'I just spoke to him, and he says on second thoughts, it's a great idea and it will serve as a wonderful example of the New World we are trying to create.'

'He said that?'

'More or less,' Anna said, smiling. 'That's what he meant, though.'

Matt couldn't help but laugh. Tom's hand was already rushing forward to congratulate him. Handshakes and back-pats and a glorious kiss on the cheek followed, then they were gone.

And Matt was alone once again with his thoughts of should-have-dones and should-have-saids . . .

'Fuck you, Blackwell! Everyone else did understand.'

There once was a game designed by an idiot: it had no
    written rules,
no stated objective and an unknown time limit. No one
    knew how to
win, or how to tell. But everyone knew how to lose.

this game's for keeps

DAY 601—NINETY EAST RIDGE

Harry Pont was frantic. His usually gruff exterior was unsuited to looking worried, so when he'd appeared in Anna's doorway in a state of near-apoplexy, she too became concerned.

'What is it?' Anna urged. 'Surely it can't be that bad,' she said, knowing by his face that it must be.

In almost forty years of engineering, Harry had seen them all—waterfront blockades, union violence, corporate blackmail, sabotage of parts and equipment, death threats to workers and their families—and he'd learned how to deal with every one of them. That's why he was the best. There were and always would be thousands of people with comparable, if not superior, engineering skills, but Harry Pont was always able to get things done.

'They've sanctioned us.'

'What this means,' Arb explained to an emergency meeting of the Philo Group, 'is that countries or companies that trade with us will be fined or sanctioned themselves.'

'But why?' Matt asked. 'I don't understand why they would do this.'

'It's all about leverage. They can't impact our finances, so they're attacking our access to re-sources. By controlling our access to food, technology, medicine et al, they are hoping to control us.'

'So what do we do?' asked Saul.

Arb answered: 'We have two options. The first is to find out their demands. The sanctioning document merely states that Ninety East Ridge is an unstable influence on the state of world affairs and injunctions should be placed on us until our political, economic and international stances are clear. Once we know what they want, we can see what we can do to comply.'

'And the second option?' asked Matt.

'We consider how we might survive under such embargoes. There is still a sizeable community of rejected societies around the world—Libya, Iran, Cuba—that may be willing to trade with us. There are also countries that may want to make political statements to the powers that be at the UN, such as India with its nuclear weapons program or Germany who are still silently re-stricted from positions of power, such as on the Security Council.'

There were visible cringes at the thought of siding with an exiled, shadow world order. Doubt-ing, downcast eyes and unconvinced shaking heads assessed the potential of acceptable countries going against the UN sanction.

'I don't think it matters,' said Anna, cutting through the growing air of dejection in the room. 'It's clear now that we have to go to the United Nations and defend our rights.'

The next day, Laikali Rulé arrived to discuss options in the face of the UN embargo. Before they could speak about it, however, another emergency meeting was called.

Arb had received notice that seven investors were suing him personally for fraud and breach of contract.

'But we never signed any contracts,' protested Byron Lybrand.

'They're claiming verbal agreements. They're claiming implied terms,' Arb said.

'Did you, or did they, record any of the sell sessions?' asked the politician in Jay Diaglio.

'No. But that's just how they're trying to prove it. Their contention will be based on a question of common sense and reasonableness: why would anyone be willing to donate between fifty and two hundred million dollars each, with no prospect for financial return?'

'I've often asked myself that same question,' said Matt impishly.

His humour today was not appreciated.

He tried to recover, his voice reaching for seriousness. 'So they're saying that we swindled them?'

'Yes.'

'Well, did we?' asked Matt.

Arb did not answer the question when he spoke. 'For the benefit of everyone here, let me explain what is at stake. The money itself is the least of our worries. We could pay it back with interest and still have no financial difficulties.'

'What if all the other investors follow suit, so to speak?' asked Tom.

'Let me just say it is extremely unlikely that we will have to pay back a cent to anyone.'

Worried faces exchanged looks of puzzlement around the room.

'They are not after the money,' said Arb. 'They are after me.'

Xavier Brown stood alone in the rain on the corner where he'd been reliably informed was the place to stand alone.

The long ugly black Buick pulled in slowly to the curb, its wipers working double time, swatting uselessly at the sheets of rain drenching the windshield.

Brown didn't move.

There was no movement inside the Buick.

The rain pelted down, pitter-pounding the pavement.

Brown, hands in his pockets, deftly fingered his Sig-Sauer semi-automatic pistol.

'It gives them the power to arrest and incarcerate me.'

'To what purpose?'

'For starters, they can use the allegations to discredit me, and therefore Ninety East Ridge. If they've got the balls, they might even try to stake an ownership claim. Lastly, and most importantly, I won't be able to enter the United States with a charge like this hanging over my head without being immediately arrested. So I won't be part of the team that goes to the UN to defend us.'

'With all due respect to you, Isaac,' it was Tom, 'I think we are beyond being reliant on one man. Maybe two or three years ago we were. But not now.'

Laikali Rulé stood up, her imposing frame stilling the room. 'That's right, Tom, but even so, Ninety East Ridge is now reliant on whomever you choose to represent you in front of the United Nations.'

He didn't move. Movement could be misconstrued. Fear. Aggression. Worst of all, confusion.

Six feet of driving rain, and nothing else, between him and the car.

Nowhere to run. The building behind him was red brick and windowless. A warehouse without nooks or crannies in which to hide or take cover.

Nothing to do but stare at his own distorted reflection in the rain-soaked tinted window and wait for . . .

The window began to roll down, black slowly replacing his streaked image. Too dark to see anyone. Or a hand. Or a gun.

He was what Musty called 'high and dry', and he was soaking wet. They could shoot him and there was nothing he could do. The Sig was of small comfort; he could guess where to shoot, but he couldn't be sure. He didn't even know how many were in the car.

Then a package, a hand, an arm in a thick black sleeve came out of the darkness.

Xavier Brown took a slow step forward, took the package, then stepped back again.

The hand receded into darkness as he opened the package. There were other ways it could have been delivered if they had just wanted him to receive it. No, they wanted him to see the contents and then they wanted to talk. If what they showed him was of no interest, then he'd turn and walk away. If he stayed, then this game would continue.

'Now, when you go before the Assembly, they will be expecting the usual greetings and platitudes.'

'Like thanks for giving us the opportunity to make our case here today?' Matt checked. 'And statements like we respect the voice and authority of the United Nations?'

'Very good.'

Matt smiled a showman's self-congratulatory smile. 'It's really not that hard,' he said light-heartedly. 'You just need to watch a few episodes of the nightly news, and you soon get the hang of it.'

Arb gave him a stare that said he did not appreciate Matt's efforts to ease the tension in the room.

'Now the speaker of the house will introduce an appointed delegate to read out the concerns of the Assembly. When he or she is doing this, do not shake your head or look upset or scribble furious notes to pass to Anna—it only shows defensiveness and will work against us with the house members.'

Matt looked at Anna, who was sitting beside Arb with her eyes downcast, listening to his instructions. *There's no way she agrees with this*, Matt thought to himself.

'Well, what will work with them? If we wear knitted waistcoats or alma mater sweaters, maybe?'

'Now wait just a second, Turner—' Arb began, but Matt saw a twinge of a smile on Anna's face so he continued with the bravado.

'No, you wait. When does the messing around end and the serious stuff begin? When can we stop with the high-minded self-important gallantry and protocol, and get down to straight talking?'

'This is ridiculous,' dismissed Arb, throwing up his hands as he pushed away from the table. 'You can't seriously want Gameboy here to state our case?'

He had turned to Anna, but her head was still deliberately downcast. *Perhaps in thought*, thought Matt, who realised he had gone too far to stop now.

'All this positioning, all your clever little moves, when do the games end and reality begin?'

Anna tilted her head, *Was that a shake? Or a realisation? Support? For him or Arb?*, then raised it to face them both: 'We all have roles to play, Matt. And those roles, Zac, should be tailored to suit each of us. We chose Matt to represent the common man—it's important he doesn't consciously play these games, or else he just becomes another politician.'

Matt didn't know what to think. His strategy

would be to have no strategy, his game would be to have no game. There was a minor twinge of disappointment that this recognition of him acting without sophistication, acting naturally, was somehow just part of the plan, but there was a greater part of him that noticed that he should feel victorious . . .

Arb was clearly crestfallen. Anna had spoken: Matt stays! Live with it! And not once, in all his time at the Ridge, had Matt seen Arb try to overrule her—not in her selection of Philo Group members, not in her veto of defence intelligence, not her iconoclastic policies, not her actions with the press. Arb paced the room like a caged lion, his thoughts clearly in conflict as he wrestled with her decision.

Xavier reached into the bulky envelope. There were a number of things inside. There was a photo, not too recent, maybe a year or two judging by the discolouration, of . . .—it was Matthew Turner with his arm around a woman. There was another: the two of them kissing. Another: looking into each other's eyes, loving stares, wide smiles.

There was a card. An invitation. A wedding invitation.

James and Melinda Macarthy
are proud to announce
the wedding of
their daughter,
Wendy Jane Macarthy
to
Matthew John Turner

Well, well, well. So Mr Turner had left a bride at the altar. The wedding date had been set for less than a month after the New World was launched. He tried to hide his smile. Never show you're hurting. And never show you're smiling. It always pays to keep 'em guessing.

There was one more thing in the package. It was an inch-thick document bound in a formal cover, red leather with a fine gold, silver and blue emblem embossed on the front. He opened the front cover awkwardly within the package, protecting it from the rain, to see the title page:

Ninety East Ridge submission to the United Nations declaring sovereignty and proposed relations with other member states.

Apparently, the Philo Group was not the only body preparing manifestos for Ninety East Ridge. No doubt, the presentation of this document at the UN would make all their troubles disappear. But at what price?

Still expressionless, he raised his gaze back to the car, the window back up, his own wet warped reflection again looking back at him. His eyes never left the window as he folded back over the opening of the package to keep its contents safe and dry. He wasn't going anywhere. There certainly was more to talk about.

The car door opened . . .

'I'm not surprised you came here,' Arb said, leaning close to Matt, forcing him to take a step backwards.

'What do you mean?'

'You can't seriously expect us to believe that you found designing games a fulfilling, adult profession.'

'Now, Zac!'

'You came here looking for something meaningful.'

'Zac! I don't think that's relevant, do you?'

Retreating with his guns still blazing, Arb turned to Anna: 'You know what I mean. He's never done anything real. Games aren't real.'

'Games are just games,' shrugged Matt, now trying to calm a situation which might soon get out of control.

Arb turned on Matt, his frustration at breaking point: 'This is just what I mean! Dismissed with a shrug and shake of the head—well, that just won't cut it any more! This is serious, Mr Turner. This is no game. It's a fight! And you must win it! Every man, every woman, every child who's put time and money and their future into this place is now looking to you, and they expect to find more than a shrugging, underachieving, wannabe philosopher. You need to understand, this is business, this is politics, this is the way the world works. If at the end of this they say, 'game over', you can't just shrug and hit a restart button! You can't just set the pieces up again!'

Arb took him firmly by the arm, a gesture made to stress the importance of the advice to come, although Matt could not mistake the personal hostility behind it: 'Forget everything else, we are now relying on you for our very survival . . .'

The words hung in the air, their impact even stronger than Arb had meant them. In a moment, Matt's world had again changed. Almost six hundred days ago, he had traded a life of perfect happiness for one of endless possibilities. Since then, like a wonderful dream, every turn of luck, every twist of fate had gone his way. Until today, the possibilities had only turned rosier and rosier. Until today, when Arb had effectively stripped his potential futures down to two: success or failure.

Arb and Anna seemed to feel it too. As if the silence carried with it a shared awareness that Matt's dream was suddenly over—the adventure across land and sea, the round-the-world road-show, the Grid (and the girl?) had been replaced by real-world responsibility. As if they could already feel the pressure of the UN's critical gaze, the gaze of the whole world in fact, as well as the hopeful fearful gaze of their friends and family on the Ridge.

At the same time, it was also clear that there was little point fighting any longer. The decision—right or wrong—had been made. Their course—for better or worse—had been set. Their destiny, their fate, was in the hands of Anna and Matt, and Arb knew that it was now time to put his faith also in the only man on the planet he truly feared.

Perhaps it was this fear that forced him to make one last attempt at authority.

'No more games, Mr Turner,' Arb said, his earlier aggression now tempered. 'This is for keeps.'

'Good evening, Mr Brown,' said P. Jefferson Ford, leaning forward, hand offered in greeting.

Brown shook it, taking in Ford and the man beside him.

The man next to Ford had big hands, thick forearms and broad shoulders. Just another thug, a less experienced operative may have concluded. But his eyes, Brown noticed, were focused and alert—a window to the brain, Musty used to tell him. This must be Fabian Smiles, he thought.

'Mr Ford. Mr Smiles.'

Brown watched Ford and Smiles both try not to look surprised.

'I think you can tell,' Ford said, smiling, 'that we want to be as helpful as we can to your friends' predicament.'

His hand extended out to Smiles, like a surgeon's seeking a scalpel. Into it Smiles placed another envelope and Ford passed it straight on to Brown.

'Of course, you understand . . .'

Brown opened the packet, tipping it so that its contents shuffled into view, the corners of photographs peeking out of the envelope.

'. . . it's only fair of us to expect something in return.'

Brown flipped through the black and white pictures of Isaac Blackwell emerging from a hotel, his lips locked with those of Mary Minken. He did not need to ask when these were taken. A newsstand was also in shot, no doubt the date on a newspaper could be magnified. The hotel was Isaac's usual in New York—he could cross-check both his and her whereabouts. It didn't really matter, Brown knew, what he found to be true. These photos were just a message to Mr Blackwell that Ford was now getting serious.

Gentlemen's rules had been discarded. The Geneva Convention would not apply here. No holds would be barred. Nothing would be sacrosanct.

Brown slipped the photos into the main package with the wedding invitation and the proposed sovereign declaration. He said nothing to Ford or Smiles. He only nodded to show he understood.

Then he stepped out of the car, into the rain, then into the darkness.

Like Ancient Greece, America is a great republic,
But a poor democracy.

what might have been . . .
a true democracy

DAY 3000 (Year 6)—NINETY EAST RIDGE

    The Sanjay Rajiv Mathur Cricket Stadium, like the five other main arenas, was located on the netherdecks, about eight hundred metres below sea level. One hundred thousand people were now all leaving at once. The queues for the Grid were long but moving. Tom Mills let the current take him as the river of slow-stepping people swept towards the western exits. Ten minutes later, he climbed into a mote and told it to take him home.

    The information screen in the mote reminded him that the People's Executive had been called upon to vote by ten o'clock tonight. It also offered him the option of making his vote right now as he made his way home.

    It still made Tom shake his head in amazement. He had grown up with politics; seen it change—over the dinner table, as it were—from adversarial bull-headed idealism to centrist economics-driven spin doctoring. Before his father had become Governor, he had been an international ambassador and thus exposed Tom to other forms of government: religious, dictatorial, socialist. But there was nothing on earth that compared to how they did things here. Even the fact that he had watched Jay Diaglio present it to the Philo Group some seven years ago did little to diminish his wonder. Every time the People's Executive was called upon, Jay's words still rang in his ears.

'For the first time in history, we have the technology to effect true democracy, and damned if we're not going to try!'

The mote zoomed past the deep-sea hydro-electric falls that powered this part of the city.

Tom recalled how hard it had been for Anna to convince Jay and the economist, Saul Obermann, to break the mould for designing the Ridge's systems. He also remembered the day they came around: the day that Matt Turner's winning Grid presentation had shown them that their proposals did not have to be consistent in any way with the rest of the world's.

'As an anthropologist, you'd appreciate that it's never easy to break away from one's history,' Saul had said to Tom, by way of explaining their initial reluctance. 'You can only move forward with the skills and knowledge that you possess. And all of those skills and knowledge come from your history.'

Despite their stated attitudinal change, there was not a single member of the Philo Group, Tom thought, who had not been absolutely stunned by the working outlines Obermann and Diaglio soon presented of their recommended economic and political programs.

Saul: 'No money. No wealth.'

Jay: 'No political parties. No partisan politics.'

'No trade, no stockmarket, no private land, no retirement funds or pension plans.'

'No government grants, no taxation—no money to pay either.'

'No such thing as bankruptcy.'

'No democracy like it on earth.'

Tom shielded his eyes from the sudden daylight as the mote zoomed above the Top Deck. It usually took a moment to readjust. In addition to his optical senses, he often lost his sense of time down in the netherdecks where the sunshine was so limited.

It had taken a long time for people to get used to the moneyless economy, Tom reflected. But they had taken to the new 'true democracy'—as Jay had described it—much more quickly.

*

Diaglio summarised his concept of true inclusive participative democracy:

'Our conclusion is to recommend a democratic system of government, but one with significant differences from the prevailing democracies of the world today.

'We will have a three-way division of power, much like our main contemporaries: a legislative, an executive and a judicial branch. Our legislature, which we refer to as "the Forum" will be a unicameral parliament consisting of both short-term and long-term representatives. Short-term representatives will be elected for four-year terms by geographic districts, similar to the election method of the House of Representatives in the US or the House of Commons in the UK. Long-term reps will be elected to ten-year terms by a national one person–one vote election.

'Note three things. Firstly, no parties are allowed. Representatives will be individuals and are always required to vote according to conscience . . . at least in theory. Secondly, because the houses of legislation and review, which sit separately in many countries, will sit together, the actual procedure of law-making will be strikingly different. This is only possible because of the non-partisan nature of the house. We envisage the for and against cases for new laws often being presented by knowledgeable external interests as well as government-appointed committees. Lastly, the role of Chief Executive—the equivalent of President, Prime Minister, Chief Minister, Chancellor . . . call him, or her, what you will—will not exist. Until our city opens, Anna Spires and Isaac Blackwell share separable veto powers. But on the day we become a nation, the nation itself will assume that role. Where required—for example, on particularly important constitutional matters or in cases of deadlock—the nation will be required to exercise its executive power through an electronic voting system. For the first time in history, we have the technology to effect true democracy, and damned if we're not going to try!'

Tom called up on the info screen today's executive issue:
'That Ninety East Ridge should engage in the Central African Conflict.'

It was a tricky one, Tom knew—no wonder the Forum was deadlocked. There were many issues involved: the role of the military, the role of the Ridge in regional matters, not to mention the Ridge's own large African communities, from both sides of the conflict. Plus, Tom considered, it might also be a precursor to debates about conscription or mandatory national service, practised in other small countries like Singapore and Switzerland.

The info screen gave him options to review the committee presentations and Forum debate records. He could look up the views of specific representatives whom he respected. He could also look at his own voting history if it helped his decision-making.

The response had been unequivocal.

'You can't be serious!'

'But you can't expect the average Joe to make decisions of state like that.'

'Normal people aren't qualified for that level of responsibility.'

Unequivocal, but not unusual. Like Matt Turner and Saul Obermann, Jay had had to stand firm against Old World axioms before he convinced the Philo Group that what he was actually proposing was democracy truly of the people, by the people and for the people. People, he argued, with the right education, will respond to the responsibility and the privilege of living in 'a true democracy, one without the partisan compromises of money and non-representation which dog so many other so-called democracies'.

Not surprisingly, there had been teething problems. But gradually, Ridgits were coming to terms with the process. Tom credited a great deal of that success to the voluntarist economy that was also developing. It gave people more time to consider the society around them. Now that money was not a prerequisite for survival, people were able to think about longer-term issues, such as education, the environment and scientific research.

The academic in Tom was pleased with the values he saw developing around him; the anthropologist in him was fascinated at the spread of those values around the region; the former Philo Group member in him felt the growing regional responsibility; while the man whose vote was an equal share in the country's Executive branch was proud.

He made his vote as the mote pulled up outside his apartment block.

Proud as hell.

He knew more about how this machine worked than anyone.
Her New World made some parts of the machine
redundant;
Oil and money, for example—him as well, perhaps.

master of the machine

'Tell me more about Ford. I still don't understand how one man, completely unknown to the outside world, could wield so much power.'

The two of them were sitting on the edge of the Great Glass Wall as they might have sat on the edge of the Grand Canyon. An ocean instead of a desert behind them, their feet hung over the edge of a seven-kilometre hole in the landscape.

'Think of the world as a machine,' said Laikali to Anna, 'the most complex design imaginable; billions of components, every one of them unique, so many moving parts, each piece somehow connected to another, somehow synchronised on a mind-bogglingly phenomenal scale. A biological example of this extraordinary machine is how we humans breathe in oxygen and breathe out carbon dioxide which trees absorb to help themselves grow. In turn, they break down the CO_2, keep the carbon and release oxygen back into the atmosphere.'

'So you're talking about a circle of life thing?'

'No, more than that. This synchronicity, what more mystical people than myself might call harmony, also exists on physical, economic, even social levels.'

'You mean a butterfly flaps its wings in Sydney and it rains in San Francisco, that sort of thing?'

'Yes, but I sense that you're not quite getting how elaborate and yet tangled this web of connections can be. These seemingly different levels are all part of the one machine.' She groped for a better example to illustrate her point. 'Take the Aswan Dam, a magnificent engineering achievement not unlike this one. The Dam was built to even out the seasonal flooding which, while necessary for Egyptian agriculture, was too changeable, too unpredictable to guarantee crops and therefore market prices. It was also designed to redistribute water and provide perennial irrigation to a largely arid country, not to mention generate substantial amounts of energy. All good ideas—but then this is where the mechanics of the machine kick in. The government needed money to build it. Russia came to the party, but not because of the idea's merits or even its profit potential. Their motive was political. On a social level, millions of people were displaced. On a natural level, silt deprivation and salinization, caused by the Dam, are eroding the Nile Delta, killing off coral and bacteria, and the fish which feed there.'

'I understand,' said Anna. 'Nightmares about the unintended consequences of Ninety East Ridge have kept me up at night too many times to count.

But how does Ford fit into this?'

'Put simply, Ford knows more about how this machine works than any person on the planet. He knows the links, the interconnections of all things. Take Glory's presence in New York and on network television for Isaac's dismissal. First, he fakes a phone call from one of Isaac's secretaries telling Glory to get to Wall Street pronto and that Isaac has made a special arrangement with network news. He then leans on the network, perhaps via one of their major sponsors, to let her present. How did he pressure the sponsor? Any number of ways, really. Perhaps he threatened a government contract or offered the CEO's son an Ivy League scholarship. It's all about leverage. Carrots or sticks.'

'And he's anonymous all this time?'

'It's a craft,' said Laikali, perhaps even admiringly. 'In a way, no one would believe that one person could have their fingers in so many pies. Besides, he uses go-betweens, people like Ridder, to do any public business.'

'But couldn't they reveal him?'

'I suppose so, if he kept them around long enough. Some would see themselves as just doing another job for some senior bureaucrat. It's the ones who've heard of him or recognise the extent of his power that I worry about.'

'I'm not convinced that he's as evil as you make him out to be. He seemed—I'm not quite sure how to describe it—too intelligent, maybe, to be evil.'

'Evil. Dedicated. Call him what you like. The fact is he will do whatever it takes to get whatever he wants. No doubt he's done some good things. I suppose we have him to thank for the defeat of communism, the growth of technology. But the price was high, dearie. Too high for me.'

Anna watched Laikali's eyes glaze over momentarily with what she supposed were visions of her pre-radioactive home.

'Why do you think he wants to kill us?' Anna asked.

'He's too involved now,' said Laikali. 'Too much of what he has done is dependent on particular components of the machine. Your New World is making some of those parts redundant—oil and money, for example—and changing the purpose of other parts, such as science.'

'What do you think is the point of the machine?'

'The point? Of the world, you mean? The meaning of life? I don't know. No one does, dear. Billions of parts, all performing their little functions in the machine, but not one of them knows why. To keep it turning, maybe?'

'Do you think Ford knows?'

Laikali dismissed the thought with a laugh. 'Not a chance,' she said. 'And I don't think he cares either. If it does cross his mind, I suspect it's only because he sees being in control as the best insurance, just in case somebody works it out.'

'Ford's why you wanted Matt on the UN team, isn't he?'

'I merely recommended him. You wanted him.'

Anna ignored Laikali's semantics and pressed on. 'But that's why you recommended him. Ahead of seemingly more qualified people like Jay Diaglio and Saul Obermann.'

Laikali nodded. 'Ford would eat Jay or Saul alive. He would know what they were going to say before it even entered their heads. They're products of the system, of the machine. In a sense, Ford created them.'

'But isn't Matt just the same? Aren't we all?'

'Some parts, I'm happy to say, just don't seem to fit. You didn't fit. I sure as hell don't fit. And when Mr Turner found himself drawn across land and sea to be part of this . . .' She gazed out over the canyon of cranes and concrete taking shape before her. '. . . I think it proved that he too was a reject of the machine.'

Secrets are simply justified lies . . .
But we all have our reasons.

secrets and her smile

He had been surprised when they had selected him in the first place.

Why him, then? Especially if recently exiled 'alleged' embezzler Mr Big Shot disapproved.

Why not Obermann or Diaglio? Surely they would carry more academic and professional weight in such a public forum.

The more he thought about it, the more certain he was that there could only be one answer. And that answer—why Anna would have insisted on his involvement in the face of such certain opposition and such obvious alternatives—both perplexed and excited him tremendously.

They had less than two months before the UN hearing.

Matt waited for Anna in front of the Foundation Building. With the five-hundred metre (or fifteen hundred if you counted the space beneath the Top Deck) tall Crystal Tower-in-progress on one side and the relatively modest in comparison thirty-storey Building One on the other, the two-storey Foundation Building looked ridiculously anachronistic in a city so new that it was not even 'open' yet.

He himself felt like an ant staring up from the base of a quarry. All around him and in the distance he could make out other ants, scurrying up and down concrete mesas and flat-topped mounds of glass and steel. All around him, construction was rapidly progressing. The ocean, the two-thousand-kilometre-thick circle of it that separated the Ridge from land, was forgotten within this madly sprouting concrete jungle.

'Matthew Turner!' she called from behind him. She was standing at an entrance to the 'base' of the Crystal Tower waving for him to join her. 'Follow me,' she said without pleasantries when he reached her, turning and disappearing through the doorway.

'Harry Pont installed these elevators when they were initially filling the first pipewall with cement,' she was saying as Matt stumbled behind, trying to keep up. The corridor was only minimally lit, with single exposed light bulbs hanging from electrical cords loosely strung along the low ceiling. 'We've kept them secret for reasons you'll understand soon enough.'

'I'm not sure why it's a secret,' Matt said as they stepped into a simple, unadorned, steel elevator cabin. 'I don't think anyone imagined going up and down the Crystal Tower without them.'

'That will be a different elevator shaft,' Anna replied as she hit an unlabelled button, then she turned to him with a conspiratorial smirk. 'You see, Matthew Turner, we're not going up.'

The lift plunged for a full fifteen minutes, during which time Anna explained the secrecy, and why Matt was now being included in it.

'If you're going to represent us, you need to understand everything. We won't necessarily reveal all of it to the General Assembly. But if something happens to Isaac or myself, people are going to look to you for leadership. So you need to know everything.'

As they both stood in that most common of Old World stances, just staring at the elevator door the way they'd gaze at the horizon, Matt wondered what could have been kept secret for almost two years in such a confined fall-over-each-other community. What sort of secret was it? Secrets are merely justified lies, but lies can be told or deceived by omission. What was the lie—another agenda for the Ridge?

He laughed self-consciously, playing down his fears with uncertain sarcasm, 'What is it? A secret laboratory or something? You're not an evil villain who wants to blow up the world, are you? Like a James Bond bad guy? Building nuclear warheads or something? Or drilling into the earth's magma?'

She cocked an eyebrow at him—it was like a wink, only more sinister. For a second, he wondered if she really was evil.

'You're so close, Mr Turner. Give the man a cigar! But seriously, this shaft is neither a nuclear torpedo tube nor a Jules Verne drilling machine.'

Then, with a jolt and a loud clang of metal, the cabin stopped. Matt was expecting to get out when

Anna instructed, 'Brace yourself against the back wall.'

He hesitated in confusion. He turned to her, about to ask her why, when he noticed that she was already leaning against the back wall. As with most moments of realisation, it happened just a moment too late.

Matt found himself thrown against the back wall as the lift began to move *horizontally*. It wasn't exactly at bullet or train speed, but the surprise motion had pushed him off balance, and he quickly found himself on his backside, finally leaning against the back wall.

'That's probably the best place,' Anna laughed. 'If anybody ever cleaned this lift, that is.'

Matt suddenly noticed the dust and dirt all over his hands and trousers.

'Don't worry about that now,' Anna said. 'We have one more bump.'

This time, Matt didn't doubt, he just pressed against the back wall.

They travelled forward for a few minutes before, again, there was a jolt and a clang. Then, a moment later, he felt the G-forces pushing him into the floor. They were going back up.

They ascended in silence, Matt's gaze firmly fixed from his place on the floor at the join of the elevator doors as he waited for the inevitable shocking revelation.

What could require such an elaborate ruse? This was something big—it had to be! Surely he couldn't have misjudged her so much? He felt like a loner who had been driving down a deserted highway and picked up by an alien shuttle. He was now on his way to the mother ship with only innocence, fear and an uncontrollable fever of curiosity.

Then, without a jolt, the cabin stopped, and without a bing, the elevator doors opened.

'You've probably guessed what's down here then?' she said casually, as if normal conversation was appropriate here. She led Matt down another dimly lit tunnel.

'I've got a pretty good idea.' *No bloody idea*, he thought, trying to focus, trying in his mind to jump ahead down the twisting, dark tunnel to guess what was down there.

'It's not why we made the place,' Anna emphasised. 'It just seemed like a good idea once we started.'

'Why keep it so secret?' he said, he thought, convincingly.

She shrugged without stopping or turning around. 'Isaac thought that people might get the wrong idea about why we're building the Ridge in the first place. He said the concept of a New World was easier to sell without scientific agendas confusing the issue.'

'Well, he'd know.'

Then she stopped. He almost ran into her. In the half-light he could make out a daring wry smile. Her searing beautiful eyes stared right at him.

'What's that supposed to mean?' she said without malice.

He wondered if he was supposed to apologise

or kiss her. He suddenly noticed the heat down here, noticed he was sweating profusely. He decided to stutter, 'Well, um . . . nothing . . . he just . . . well, what's his agenda? A New World? A New Deal maybe? Or are we supposed to believe that the love of his life wants a new house, seven kays across, a mile deep, in the middle of the ocean, so he builds her one?'

She had her hands provocatively placed on her hips now, and he could see her teeth gently biting at her lower lip in thought, as if she was considering whether his was a good answer. She was sweating also, beads of perspiration on her face, her clothes clinging to the shape of her body. As soon as he'd uttered it, Matt wished he could have his answer back. What had been a cynical aside about His Financial Highness had become a testament about a husband literally giving his wife the world.

'The point is,' she said, getting back to it, 'science and knowledge are still the basis of human progress. Medical research, power generation, communication, exploration—these are the pursuits without which mankind would not advance. One of the key tenets of the New World, from the very beginning, has been that the Old World has lost sight of that, replaced it—some would say, hijacked it—with an economic argument about capital allocation and the market deciding the important issues.'

By now Matt had given up trying to look knowledgeable. All he could do was listen haplessly as Anna's explanation became a tirade.

'In the Old World, pharmaceutical companies withhold drugs from poorer countries because they can't afford them. In the Old World, technological advancements are held back from the market so that old tech can maximise its commercial gain. In the Old World, scientific exploration is no longer a noble endeavour, it's a race, a ruthless corporate profit-driven race. Well, to use an old football expression, Mr Turner, they can't run without legs.'

When she turned to look at him, perhaps for acknowledgement, she realised that he had no idea what she was talking about. Her tirade faded as it became clear to her that he needed to be shown.

'There are around ten thousand scientists who drive the research that drives the world, two thousand of whom now live at the Ridge,' she said, reaching for a button on the wall. A hidden door slid open as she concluded, 'and one hundred of whom now work down here.'

It *was* an evil super-villain's lair.

She led him through a maze of state-of-the-art laboratories, past rec rooms where white-coated men and women played table tennis and watched television, through a shining steel industrial kitchen and out past a large refectory.

'Their accommodations are a little further around,' she was saying, 'although we intend to move them up to the Crystal Tower when it's operational. I've already booked them the very top floors.'

'Where are we now?' Matt asked. 'We are still inside the pipewalls, aren't we?'

Again she smiled a secret smile, as if his question was right on cue. Through one more door, she led him, and there was the most amazing sight Matt had ever seen.

There, bathed in a fading vignette of light from the surface, was Ninety East Ridge.

It was enormous.

The Hoover Dam times seven! The Empire State Building times four! And more than twenty times wider than either! Matt suddenly realised that Harry Pont's comparisons, or his plans on paper, or even the view from inside, didn't do justice to the scale of it.

The Great Glass Wall curved away into the fading distance both to the left and to the right. Through the wall he could make out the frosted, indistinct shapes of the city in progress—the granulated movement of a crane, the silhouetted skeletons of skyscrapers, the ant-sized smudges that may or may not have been human movement. Above him, like blimp-shadows floating in the sky, were the undersides of ships and square anchored oil platforms.

'Where are we?' he repeated, somewhat un-necessarily.

'We call it "the Tree House", as in the place you go to get away from the parents. We're about fifty metres east of the outer pipewall, on a relatively thin mesa of ridge that rises about nine hundred metres from the ocean floor—or more precisely, to about six hundred metres below sea level.'

'How can we see, being so deep?

'Usually you wouldn't be able to. But the light down here has been greatly enhanced by that big highball glass of a window we've inserted into the ocean. Now, even at night, if the sea is perfectly calm, the vision is generally good enough to see the stars in the sky.'

'So this is built on another part of the ridge?'

'Actually, this is built *into* another part of the ridge. One of the researchers, someone you know in fact, was telling me—this is years ago—that deep-sea flora and fish research has made some remarkable contributions to medicine. So when we were testing the terrain for suitable sites, and we found this one, I asked Harry if something like this might be possible.'

'And here it is.'

'Asking Harry if anything is possible is like daring him to say he's incapable. And as you can see, there's not much that our Harry isn't capable of.'

Matt continued to stare at the walled-off Atlantis that towered before him, when he double-took on something Anna had said.

'Someone I know? I think I could count the number of scientific researchers I've met on one hand—if you clenched it into a tight fist, that is.'

There it was again: that I-know-something-you-don't-know smile.

'Oh, I think you do.' Something over his shoulder caught her eye. 'As a matter of fact, here he is now.'

Matt turned to see a smiling, bespectacled,

white-coated Indian man waving hello as he walked towards them.

It was Sanjay Mathur.

'Didn't you know, Mr Turner,' his singsong voice said, 'that all novelists once had real jobs?'

Sanjay, Matt soon discovered, was managing the Tree House and its one hundred new residents. His 'resignation' had been staged only after its completion.

'Yes, I was once a scientist,' Sanjay explained, 'but until this place I found more joy in fiction and superstition. If I wrote about some of the things people are working on down here, you would not believe me. Deep-sea farming, marine-based medicinal cures, thermal power from the earth's mantle, using deep ocean currents to air condition the entire Ridge . . . no scientist, not even a lapsed dormant has-been such as myself, could have resisted such an offer.'

As they descended, shuttled and ascended in the multi-directional elevator about an hour later, Anna outlined what else Matt needed to see.

They emerged from the base of the Crystal Tower and jumped into one of the golf buggies that were being used to run back and forth along the Top Deck until Matt's Grid became operational. Anna wanted to show Matt the emergency escape pods which were built into the Great Glass Wall where it met the Top Deck.

Ninety East Ridge, the geographical landform, not the city, Anna explained, was a meridional ridge that had been created by volcanic magma flows—eruptions—over the past billion or so years. Though the specific site that they had chosen was ninety-nine point nine nine nine per cent certain of stability, the fact remained that most mid-ocean ridges, Ninety East Ridge included, are seismically active.

'You mean, we built our New World on a volcano?'

'No,' said Anna with rehearsed evenness. 'We built it on a dormant volcano. Bear in mind that the whole world is, geographically speaking, a volcano, and that every landmass on the planet was once spewed out of the earth as molten lava which became igneous rock which became—'

Matt held up his hand. 'You've made your point.'

'The point is that we have a number of disaster contingency plans that you need to be aware of. Firstly, in case of a breach, we have a series of floodgates—like locks on a dam or the Panama Canal—which Harry has designed into the nether regions of the city using the third and second pipewalls. Theoretically—let's hope we never have to test it—we could pour Sydney Harbour into the city and still be dry and fully functional on the Top Deck. Or at least close to fully functional, as the idea, once we start to fill the Top Deck, is to move all power generation to the netherdecks.'

As they made their way through the construction chaos of cranes and workers, trucks and raw materials, Anna instinctively lowered her voice. 'You need to know these things in case they do. Nobody wants you freezing in front of the Assembly when they tell you that Ninety East Ridge could erupt at any moment. We need everyone there—that's you and me—to nail any attempt like that to derail us.'

As they drew near the outer pipewall, Matt noticed an endless series of hatches, each spaced about five metres apart, spreading around the wall in both directions.

'These safety pods are actually the last resort. They're simple to us. Come on, I'll show you. You'll see that they're automatically programmed to ascend to the surface and avoid bumping into any other pods or boats or barges or rigs on the way.'

Anna led him inside one after fingering the controls set into the hatchways.

'They are actually a lot more sophisticated than they look,' she said as he looked at the interior. It was oval shaped, with controls at the bow—or at least the end furthest from the entrance—despite Anna's automatic programming claims. Waist to ceiling windows curved up to what appeared to be a steel roof which supported a number of pipes and grills. Around the rim of the pod and through the centre were the bench seats of this submarine life raft. He guessed it could seat maybe twenty, and accommodate a dozen more standing if required.

'Well, they serve a pretty simple task when you get down to it, don't they?'

Anna nodded—with that smile again! 'Which is why, following my own over-pragmatic brand of waste-not-want-not engineering, we have made them multipurpose.'

She pointed at the floor and Matt noticed, though only after a second look, the etching of another hatchway. Anna flipped up a cover then pulled on a hydraulic lever, opening the hatch with a decompressing hiss. She lay on the floor, inviting Matt to do the same from the other side. Together they leaned their heads into the hatch.

'It's a mini-sub,' she explained as Matt looked at the more complicated controls that were squeezed into the long, shallow cabin. 'It's so small that you have to lie forward to fit inside it. The idea is that we can use them to more completely explore the ocean floor around here. There are already a number of them operating out of the Tree House, only they are, understandably, slightly bigger—like the ones you might see exploring the wreckage of the Titanic. As a matter of fact, it occurs to me that if I'd shown you this first, and how to steer one, we could have taken a couple of these instead of the elevator to show you the Tree House properly.'

Matt lifted his head out of the hatchway. 'I think I've had enough new experiences for one day,' he said honestly.

When they rejoined the rest of the Philo Group that evening, Matt couldn't help but feel different. The New World, which challenged the norms of civilisation on so many obvious levels, continued to reveal to him more complicated dimensions and considerations. As did his relationship with Anna.

He felt special and privileged, yet he also realised the weight of responsibility he now bore. It made him nervous, questioned his confidence and, in a manner he felt most acutely, made his position of privilege feel lonely.

Perhaps it was his first sensation of leadership, but as he wandered the site alone, as he passed fellow 'Ridgits' and said hello, he could not help but notice that his relationships with people had also changed. He could sense their feelings of fear and doubt. He could see them assessing, guessing, reckoning whether Matt Turner had what it would take to save them.

He took a deep breath. Sometimes, you have to start something not knowing how it will end. Besides, it was too late to go back now.

Money-based capitalism is like boxing. Tough. Exciting.
A searching test of character. Barbaric. And
    counterproductive.

what might have been . . .
a job well done

Day 4652 (Year 10)—WMHB TELEVISION
    Glory O'Shay stared seriously at the viewers.
    'The moneyless state. A world without trade. A
labour market without pay. A consumer market without
cash, without prices.'
    Switch to Camera Two. Glory effortlessly shifted her
gaze.
    'The press labelled it Freekanomics almost a decade
ago. The academics called it Modern Voluntarism. Both
of them said it would never work, both of them said that
it was not a sustainable economic model.'
    Back to Camera One. A smug yet empathetic smile.
    'Well, both of them were wrong, and my guest
tonight is someone who must be very proud to have
proved them so.'
    A new camera. A familiar face.
    'Anna Spires. Welcome to Old Glory.'
    'Thanks, Glory. As always, a pleasure.'

'An alien concept to the mass consumer markets of the Americas and Europe. But a concept that's spreading like wildfire throughout the developing worlds of East Africa and South Asia. Just yesterday, a spokesman for the Afro-Indian Trade Free Association announced that talks had begun with the Indonesian government. Anna, tell us, ten years ago, when this all began, did you ever imagine it could be this successful?'

Anna shook her head disbelievingly.

'Well, it certainly was not easy, I can tell you that. We had a supply crisis twice a year every year, a number of trading scandals which you yourself would remember, and hundreds of attempts to create underground markets. But I'm proud to say we've seen through all those trials. The acceptance of our economic system by our Indian Ocean neighbours is another validation of our system which I'm also very proud of.'

'For those people watching who have yet to gain a grasp of exactly what voluntarist economics is, can you give us a brief explanation?'

Anna nodded humbly. Ten years in the spotlight had improved her televisual capabilities, especially for empathetic explanations.

'I'd be delighted, Glory. After all, it's not as alien a concept as people might think.' She looked at the camera in a practised unpractised way. 'Look at the way your family or any volunteer organisation where people do what they do, not because they get paid. I don't think anyone out there in TV land would be surprised at how many of our greatest achievements have been made by people who didn't earn a cent for what they did.'

'You're talking about mothers and fathers and people who work soup kitchens . . .'

'Yes, but also mothers and fathers who drive their children to school or help them build a science project. On a grander scale, I'm talking about volunteers who fought in wars or cured diseases in third world countries. I'm talking about Olympic athletes pre-professionalism and adventurers who sailed around the world simply because they put their minds to it. And I'm talking about people who give freely of their time in schools, hospitals and sports carnivals.'

'That's all very well, but I can hear our viewers asking: what about those unwanted jobs like garbage collection and street cleaning? Who is going to do those jobs if they are not paid?'

Again, Anna expressed understanding, but then her head popped up, the answer reassuringly clear.

'My father used to tell me: never underestimate the satisfaction of a job well done.'

Now Glory was nodding. It was important to show that she understood what Anna was saying before she actually finished saying it.

'What he meant,' Anna continued, 'was that people actually like to contribute. You can take away all the money, all the perks, all the prestige of this job or that title. There is no moment finer, he used to say, no moment when a man feels more like a man than when he can stand back and look at a job well done.'

Cut to host. More nodding. Back to guest.

'They also like to be an appreciated part of a team. The problem with garbage collection or street cleaning in money-based economies is not the job, it's the fact that the appreciation is so low.'

'You mean the pay?'

'Sadly, that's how a money-based society measures appreciation.'

'But it's hardly rocket science, is it?'

'No, but you and I both know, Glory, that New York would grind to a halt a lot more quickly if the garbage collectors went on strike than if rocket scientists did.'

'Or the bankers on Wall Street, for that matter,' added Glory cleverly, sharing a laugh with both Anna and her viewing audience. 'But to be fair,' her voice suddenly serious again, as if responding to something that Anna, and not herself, had said, 'bankers finance our power stations, construction work, hospitals, et cetera, et cetera—which raises the question, how do you maintain or build things that require specialists and not volunteers?'

'It's a good question, Glory, and one we struggled with for a long time. But finally, we realised, there is no reason to treat them any differently. We all work hard. And we all have different skills. As long as we contribute—or at least try to contribute—there is no reason to discriminate about one's quality of life.'

'But, for example, do people in Ninety East Ridge who work one hundred and twenty hours a week earn more than, say, a schoolteacher?'

'No.'

'No?'

'No.'

Glory seemed to be shaking cobwebs from her head. 'No? Then why would anyone work so hard?'

'Why indeed?' agreed Anna.

For a glorious moment, Glory O'Shay, Old Glory, 'the face a nation turns to', was lost for words or a suitable televisual expression.

Anna came to her rescue.

'People do it because they want to, Glory. One thing we have discovered is that when you take money out of the mix, people do not seem to suffer in the jobs the way they did, or do, in traditional economies. And another thing we discovered is that if someone likes their job—and by that I mean that they feel they contribute, and that they feel appreciated—if someone really likes their job, then they do it ten times better.'

'And you find people who actually enjoy collecting trash?'

'Well, trash is a bad example because we have a largely automated waste disposal system—but yes, we find people who like street cleaning or waiting tables or stocking supermarket shelves or, yes, negotiating multimillion tonne steel supply contracts. Glory, not everyone wants to rule the world. Most people simply want to be part of a team.'

'But how do you create structure without pay or accountability? I mean, how do you ensure that the riveter on one of your mile-high buildings does his job if there is no threat of lost pay or being fired?'

'Oh, you can be fired, all right. Supervision and accountability don't change just because there's no money. You do your job well because there are other people who rely on you. You'd be surprised how universal that motivation is.'

'Oh no,' said Glory, shaking her head in her wisest, most understanding way. 'I know that's why I get up in the morning. My kids need me to.'

'But if food was free, if the electricity was paid for, if clothes and furniture and education were paid for, you'd still get up in the morning. People need pride, Glory, *and they also take pride in what they do each day, be it raising children, cleaning streets, making furniture, doing medical research, or providing informative and entertaining television.'*

'You can still run your own business on Ninety East Ridge?'

'Absolutely. It works just the same as here, but people do it because they want to, not because it does or does not make a profit. And businesses succeed or fail on their abilities to convince suppliers, employees and customers that their product is a good idea. In fact, Glory, let me tell you a secret: a capitalist economy actually operates better without money. And that's what Ninety East Ridge is: a super-advanced moneyless capitalist economy.'

'Anna, I've known you a long time, but even you must admit how odd that must sound to our viewers.'

'You don't misfit a bolt because of how much you are paid—or at least you shouldn't. It's the same with any business. At the Ridge, because money and therefore profits are not an option, we have different priorities to the average Western business. But higher levels of job satisfaction more than match any motivation pay packets have. Better quality infrastructure across the country, not just where an elite group of individuals can afford it, means improved standards of living and working. We have less societal tension at the Ridge simply because there is no income disparity—there are no haves and have nots. Property ownership is rotated. Trading property is banned and trading or bartering of other goods is very very strictly controlled.'

She paused a moment, aware that her tirade was becoming too detailed for early evening current affairs television. She dumbed her conclusion down.

'*You fit the bolt properly so that when it's all done,
you can look at the Crystal Tower or a clean street or an
unloading supply ship, and say: I helped make that.*'

'*Anna Spires,*' *said Glory O'Shay, wrapping it up,
'as always, thank you so much for your time . . .' and
turning back to Camera One, '. . . and as always, thanks
for yours. I look forward to seeing you tomorrow night
when we have best-selling author and blockbuster movie
director, Matthew Reilly, joining us for an intimate chat
with Old Glory. Take care out there, and good night.*'

*The lights dimmed as the credits rolled and viewers
saw the face a nation turns to reach across the desk to
shake her guest's hand.*

Greatness requires adversity,
The will to cope with it, the courage to challenge it
And the luck to survive it.

nuclear croissants

Fear of failure, Matt concluded, is the most destructive force in the universe.

Yes, there are bombs. Yes, there is sabotage. On a more psychological level, there is jealousy. There's hate. And vengeance.

But even if hateful bombs and jealous sabotage destroyed every structure ever built, the statistics would still show that fear of failure had devastated ten times more buildings, ten times more bridges, and a million times more dreams and visions before they even got off the ground.

Where once they would have been laughed at and overcome, now, with the spectre of the UN's threat to take everything away, every minor setback became a debilitating catastrophe. As if fostered by the fear of failure, a litany of disasters ensued. Power outages, food shortages, mystery flus, rats— 'Rats! Where the hell did they come from?' asked Anna—strikes by workers, strikes by supervisors . . . The UN sanctions meant that every bolt, every girder, every litre of cement, had to be scrounged for, fought for and paid double or triple for.

The whole mood of the construction site went bad, and then from bad to worse. Debates often became unconstructive, but the last thing either Anna or Isaac wanted to do was restrict anyone's freedom of speech. Tempers were fraying as conditions varied between acceptable and not so. Frustration, finger-pointing and the ever-constant heat were beginning to obscure the vision of a New World. Doubts were raised about everything from the economic and political blueprints to the structural integrity of the Great Glass Wall. Both buyers and suppliers, at least those not scared off by the UN threat—after all, this was the biggest customer in history—came to meetings prepared for disagreements and disappointments. Anna could feel people's perceptions changing about just how important this all was; people who would once have claimed to walk over hot coals for the New World now questioned whether all this was worth it.

Tom Mills, in historian mode, tried to be reassuring.

'The way I see it, greatness requires adversity,' he said. 'Every state or nation faces crucial moments of truth, cusps in their history, where they determine by their actions whether they live or die. Like when Elizabeth the First rallied England to stand firm against France—a different choice, a different action, and England, its empire, its industrialisation and the development of the whole world might have been changed.

'Similarly, when Japan first defeated the English in World War Two battles, and every Asian colony suddenly realised that a European power could be defeated. Within a decade, India and Malaya were lost. Within half a century, no European colonialists existed in Asia at all.'

'Of course,' said Mary, who seemed to have developed a knack for turning up at the most inopportune moments, 'let's not forget those cusps which did not turn out so well. Let's remind ourselves that Prussia no longer exists. That Troy and Carthage disappeared from the face of the earth.'

It was now Day 625 on the thousand-day timetable, but most people were now more concerned with a different countdown. The UN showdown was a month away, a date set by a compromise of political strategy and how long Laikali could hold them off.

The session itself, in front of the General Assembly, was expected to last only a few hours, a day at the most, but Laikali stressed that they would need every last minute of the remaining thirty days to prepare. They had to know every last detail about Ninety East Ridge: its environmental impact, its planned systems of government, health, energy, labour, education, justice, trade . . . the list of details seemed endless. They had to know about how this new nation intended to interact with the rest of the world, how it would continue to support itself, the standard of living that its residents might expect—they needed time to prepare every answer to every possible question.

But most of all, they needed the time to prepare themselves.

Anna and Matt were nervous enough already about Arb's repeated reminders that this was no game. But now, as the tension on the Ridge rose daily, every ounce of pressure felt by anyone was somehow doubled so that it could be added to the burden that Anna and Matt already bore.

Surprisingly, it was Anna who cracked first. 'Maybe we should get Jay or Saul to do this?' she said hopefully to Laikali, who was taking her and Matt through the agendas of each General Assembly member likely to ask them questions. 'I don't know if I've got the energy to keep this up another month.'

'My dear, we all feel that way from time to time, whether we're defending a New World or doing our homework.'

'Yes, but—'

'No buts, my dear. You just do what you have to do to get through this.'

'But that's just it. There's nothing I can do. It's all out of my control.'

Matt wanted to speak, wanted to tell her how inspirational she had been, how inspirational she still was—and forever would be to him—but Laikali, the edge off her voice, spoke first: 'My dear, my husband Augusto, dead some thirty years now, helps me every day—to get up in the morning, to eat right, to treat good people well and to castrate my enemies properly. When he died, I was devastated. He was a god to me, my guiding light, my lover, my inspiration. I was still a young woman, just starting out a political career with high ambitions, ambitions which he encouraged.

I couldn't go on without him, I couldn't do it alone. I decided to resign. The world was too tough to fight—and beat—single-handedly. And then, one night, I had a vision.'

Anna nodded, knowing, 'Augusto.'

'No.'

'No?'

'No. It was a croissant.'

'A croissant?'

'Yes. Oh, and a bodyguard.' Anna and Matt didn't really know what to say. Laikali continued, 'Nothing sexual, nothing like that—although I might say I have had, I mean employed some very sexy bodyguards in my time. But that's another story—stories!' she said saucily. 'Anyway, in my dream the bodyguard was asked by his employer to try some food which may have been poisoned. Doing his duty, the bodyguard did, and he died. And when I woke up, I remembered what I'd gone into politics for.'

Anna nodded, remembering a spirited, younger Laikali talking to her at uni. Matt, however, just shook his head, not having the faintest idea what she was talking about.

'I went into politics to give the South Pacific a voice in the world. I wanted to ensure that the rest of the world realised that we, too, are beautiful people, as precious and important as anyone anywhere else. We may not have skyscrapers or highways, but that does not make us inferior or subservient.'

Matt was still shaking his head.

'France was telling us to try its food because it might not be safe.'

Ah, the penny dropped. The bodyguard, island atolls, nuclear croissants.

'You wanted to make sure no one ever tested nuclear weapons in the South Pacific again,' Matt said, unnecessarily.

'Inspiration is a fortune, Anna. I must be one of the luckiest women alive, because I have had two in my lifetime: my Augusto and my cause.'

'But what if you think that your cause cannot win?'

'Well, you can stop any time you like, dearie. You can throw it all in and get a nice, comfortable job drawing structural engineering plans for new football stadiums or government offices. You'd probably be a marquee employee.'

'I wouldn't stop for that. But if I can't win?'

'Then it'll end up that way anyway.' She looked at Anna solemnly, her wide heavy frame suddenly soft and maternal. 'It takes courage to go into the unknown: be it a valley of sin, a new venture, or the future. Inspiration may be a fortune, but courage is a choice. You either take up the fight or walk away. There is nothing wrong with walking away, it's just another option. But there's one thing you can never get around: you have to choose.'

They were spending every day together, being briefed or grilled or both by a revolving army of advisors and experts.

Anna's confidence, or at least the appearance of it, had been restored. After Laikali's tale of nuclear croissants, Matt had added just one thing which had resonated in her head ever since.

'Remember, Anna, it's your vision, your dream.'

She couldn't help but think about it, repeat it over and over in her mind. She had had the vision, the dream. She often forgot that, and sometimes even doubted it—but after he had reminded her, she could see herself everywhere she looked. She knew every inch of this place, every detail from the ocean floor to the still bare tip of the planned Crystal Tower. She knew the status of everything— the state of the hospital, the state of the drainage, the rubbish, the children, the transportation. Flashes of memory raced randomly through her mind—of an ocean, a first straw, then a second, and a third—of plans becoming scaffolded skeletons, becoming structures of glass and steel—of her, at the beginning, of her now . . . how was she different now?

'. . . it's your vision, your dream.'

It made her reassess. In the beginning, she had deferred to Isaac and his confidence. But he hadn't been the right person; he was a doer, an enabler, an implementer, a creator of finance, not a New World. Then she had put her trust in the Philo Group, put her vision at the risk of death by committee. She had let it out there, but luckily she had never let it go, she had never fully let them run away with it, for better or worse. She and Isaac had held them back, or rather held on to the vision whenever they threatened to progress it in a way she didn't desire.

Still, something had changed. She didn't need anyone else's confidence any more. And she knew why. Isaac was her husband, and she respected the

Philo Group—but it wasn't until Matt arrived on the scene that she had found someone whom she could truly trust with her vision. Her vision of the Ridge. And her vision of herself.

Circumstance is the most common basis for friendship. Best friends in school invariably sit next to each other before they become best friends. It is a fateful truism that time, geography, external conditions, are all prerequisites before personalities can connect and friendships be formed. By acting that very moment he saw her, by conquering the geography between them, by good fortune becoming part of her inner circle, Matt had now formed a friendship with the woman whose eyes had so entranced him almost two years ago.

Or perhaps, he hoped, it was more than that.

They talked all the time. Even when the briefings and training sessions were over, they would wax philosophical, talking about anything, from the world to Tom and Mary. Anna told him her life story: about where she'd been and what she'd built, about how she'd met her husband, about her father—although nothing about her mother. Matt, in turn, told her about how an ambitious idealist became a commercial, albeit highly successful, games designer—although nothing of Wendy. They were still a step short of revealing such secrets.

One afternoon, ten days before the UN hearing, as they sat on the third pipewall watching the waves, they were talking about why the world is as it is.

'In many ways, it makes sense, you know,' Matt was saying. 'I mean, it's all very well for us to believe that what we're doing is ultimately a better way. But that's what Hitler thought, that's what Ridder thinks. They may seem to do what they do through sheer short-sightedness, but somehow, somewhere in their heads, they must actually think they're doing the right thing.'

He watched her running the theory through her head, testing it against all the arguments and theses she'd developed over the years. He liked watching her mind work, being able to see the gears ticking over in time with her fingers as they unconsciously tapped the air, seeing the satisfaction or anxiety behind her furrowed brow and, finally, knowing she had a response or a conclusion when her eyes sparked to life.

'No, that's not right. Well, it may be, but not necessarily.' Even when she was unsure, she radiated certainty. 'What you're talking about is momentum. A society thinks it is doing what's right, when really they're just doing what they have to do to survive. Because it's always been done that way. Because that's what the boss said to do. Because they believe in evolution: that the system has been set up, developed, evolved in fact, for the best.' She paused, but Matt did not speak. It was obvious she was building up for a big finish. 'Do they think about what they do? It's possible. Do they honestly think it's the best they could do? It's possible . . .' But she was shaking her head. 'Even if they do, I can't believe it's true. They live in societies racked with violence, poverty, injustice;

402

plagued by money, the media and politics; communities are self-destructing, families are disintegrating, individuals are lost and confused; they can't get a job, they can't afford healthcare or education or to take care of their grandparents; they can't trust their leaders, they can't trust their children . . .' She stopped for breath, then half stated, half implored her conclusion: 'I just don't think it's true, Matthew John Turner, I just don't think it's true.'

'It's not,' said Matt. 'And you're proving it.'

For a minute they said nothing, as if scanning the seas for ideas in the spindrift.

Then Anna spoke: 'I think we should discuss this further. I think it will be an important point in the General Assembly in . . .'

'Ten days,' Matt said with a deep breath.

'Yes, ten days . . . well, as I said, we should discuss this further.' She looked him up and down, as if assessing whether she wanted to say what she was about to say. 'Dinner. Tomorrow. Your place.'

An extra deep breath. 'Okay.'

You judge a diamond by its flaws
But love it for how it sparkles.

what might have been . . . the land of hopeless causes

DAY 10,000 (Year 25)—NINETY EAST RIDGE

The make-shift raft of bamboo and reed had travelled an astonishing three thousand miles. Fleeing political persecution, said the men. Seeking a better life for their children, said the mothers. Looking for food, said the children.

Natasha Spires watched the reports with some consternation. Although she sympathised with their situation, this was the fifth boat this month, and the thirtieth this year. The thirty people squeezed aboard took the total of people who had sought refugee status to over a thousand . . . Surely, Anna had not overcome all that she had just to give it away to beggars, freeloaders and queue-jumpers.

'They're not beggars,' her sister had tried to tell her when the trickle of people had first shown signs of becoming a torrent. 'And technically speaking, we're all freeloaders, now.'

'Well, they're certainly queue-jumpers,' Natasha had

replied. 'There are teachers, doctors, scientists and the like from all corners of the globe waiting their turn, waiting for us to develop a sustainable physical and economic infrastructure capable of supporting them. But these guys, 'cause they turn up hat in hand, expect to go straight to the front of the line. They don't even have skills, not for this place anyway. The last boat was filled with farmers, miners and poorly trained labourers. It's not like we keep cattle or have fields to plough.'

'I'm not sure what they'll do here or what we'll do, how they'll cope or how we'll cope, but I do know that we're not going to tell them to turn their raft around. We'll find a way.'

There it was again, her sister invoking the long-dead hopeless optimism of their father. It was infuriatingly difficult to argue against. It had been when he said it. It still was when she did.

'That's all very well, Anna, but the word has got around. They're coming from everywhere. The press are calling us the Land of Hopeless Causes.'

'The Land of Hopeless Causes?' her sister had repeated, mulling it over for a moment as if trying on the name for size. 'It's probably not far off, come to think of it. We are, after all, the headquarters for a number of charities and non-profit organisations.'

But we're becoming the headquarters for charity cases and non-profit individuals, Taz thought to herself as she walked through Rulé Park. What Anna was failing to realise was that there was genuine resentment growing across the city. And not all of them were racist or elitist, surely. They just wanted to protect what they had helped to build, what they were still building, for God's sake. What was wrong with that?

'But this whole city is a refugee,' her sister had argued in the Forum 'and a voluntary one, at that. It would be hypocritical to reject anyone who had come so far, risked so much to join us.'

But the Forum would not listen to her forever, founder or not.

So wrapped up had she been in her thoughts that Taz did not notice the roar of the Northwest Falls until she set foot on the viewing platform. Seawater surged through the floodgates in a great outward arch before plunging past the platform in a powerful thousand-metre descent that ended in hydroelectric turbines far below. Down there in the abyss was a world unknown to Taz. The deepest netherdecks contained the factories and plants which supported the city: from building materials to mote parts, from desalination to waste processing, from pharmaceutical products to, of course, energy. Apparently, the Northwest Falls generated more electricity than the largest power plant in the world—and there were four such waterfalls and generators spaced around the Great Glass Wall. From what she understood, the Ridge was exporting some twenty times more energy than it used itself.

Though there were always many people on the platform, admiring the spectacle, marvelling at this glimpse of the power of the ocean being held outside, Taz often came here to be alone with her thoughts. A thin mist from the falls always crept across the landing, and the sound, like an endless rumble of thunder, seemed to surround her. She felt cocooned from the outside world. If she needed cheering, she would watch the childlike rainbows playing and hiding within the raging spray.

If she wanted to think, as she did now, she simply stood there and closed her eyes.

It didn't matter whether she agreed with her sister or not about the boat people. That wasn't the issue. It was Anna herself that worried her more. For almost twenty-five years, even after she had ceded all of her executive power to the People's Executive, she had maintained a guiding hand over the Ridge's direction. Her influence had been extraordinary. In moments of crisis, the country had always looked to her for leadership. Her voice was widely regarded as the voice of Ninety East Ridge.

Or at least it had been.

Perhaps she was just out of touch with the populace—she was after all getting older. But less and less did people seem to respect Anna's thoughts. In fact, Taz sensed a certain cynicism creeping into the public mood whenever the founder opened her mouth.

The more she thought about it, the more certain she was that it was probably the Ridge itself that was rejecting Anna. More mature now, its place in the world established, its industry and economy thriving, it was only natural that the city wanted to assert its independence.

It all reminded Taz of watching Anna assert her own independence from their mother. Like here at the Ridge, respect had been the first thing to go. Raised eyebrows, a shake of the head, frustrated sighs, every time her mother dared to speak to her. Some five years after their Dad's death, the distance and tension between them grew too great. And finally their relation-ship snapped.

There had been an argument, she knew that much. Probably about Dad, but she didn't know for sure;

neither her mother nor Anna had ever told her. Her sister had then left the house promising never to return.

'It's not up to me,' her mother had said to Taz when questioned about what she would do. 'Your sister is old enough to make up her own mind. It's my job as a parent to let go.' But she had just been putting up a brave face, Taz could tell. She hadn't really meant it. Sticking to that noble stubbornness had ultimately devastated her mother, left her lost and helpless for so long.

Taz worried that her sister—so much like their mother, though she would not tell her that—was setting herself up for the same heartache with Ninety East Ridge.

'I know. I sense it too,' Anna had confessed when Taz had raised the prospect of the Ridge breaking free. 'It was inevitable really. In many ways, I wish it had happened long ago.'

But Taz was not convinced. It may be inevitable, she thought. But that didn't mean it was a nice feeling when something you so loved and cared for left you behind.

Nothing is more lonely than the hope left behind.

the hope left behind

It's my own fault, she often thought to herself. *I was too this . . . , too that . . . —why couldn't I be different?*

Self-blame, self-doubt, self-loathing—she had been through them all. Occasionally, sanity would prevail and she would realise that there was nothing more, nothing else that she could have done. She was who she was. Better to be left behind to live separately than to coexist on a pretence of love and convention. Better to have a chance of happiness apart than to live together in a frustrated unhappy sham.

Occasionally, sanity would prevail . . .

But mostly, sanity was like the light at the end of a winding tunnel.

She read the note again. For the eleven hundredth time in reality, but every time she read the words, *Dear Zigs*, she was transported back to that day almost twenty-one months ago. She'd walked straight from the front door to the kitchen carrying groceries, and a surprise. She had almost missed it, almost put the big boxed gift directly on top of it. Sometimes, she wondered if she had done just that: put the box on the note, never found it, maybe thrown it away accidentally with the box later, not known where or why he had gone—would she feel better or worse?

After the hundredth time, she had promised herself—forced herself to promise—that she would never read it again. But time and again, she did. A thousand more times she read his scribbled scrawl. A thousand more times she relived that day which began with the continuing assumption that they would spend the rest of their lives together and ended with the wonder if they would ever meet again.

It's my own fault, she often thought to herself.

Dear Zigs, the note began.

The surprise, a present from her parents, lay unopened in the kitchen for a month.

She was alone. He had left to pursue another life, to follow a feeling not even he could explain; *I'm not sure I understand it myself*, the note had said.

It had also said, *I still love you*.

I still love you, as if to sharpen the dagger that gutted her when she read and re-read and re-read it.

I still love you, as if a man who really loved a woman would just decide one day to leave without a second thought, without notice, without discussion; leaving nothing but a note and an empty second-hand life.

And a fading wishful possibility that she clung to with the same cherishing determination with which her hand clung to his note . . .

That maybe, just maybe, her Matthew really did still love her.

How do you console someone
Who has never lost before?

the man who had it all

The phone rang and snapped him out of his introspective stupor. For a moment, he felt oddly removed from what was happening. He wasn't used to either phones ringing or introspection.

'Blackwell,' he said into the receiver.

'I was expecting to have heard from you by now.'

'Ford?'

'I was expecting a reply either way; either one word of reluctant cooperation or two words of proud, independent dismissal.'

This was the first time Arb had spoken to Ford, and the first time in his life he had felt daunted speaking to anyone.

'It's a difficult decision,' he said honestly.

'Yes, I imagine it is.'

A short silence ensued. Arb broke it, trying to take the initiative.

'I understand you're working with my old friend, Rick Ridder?'

'Do all your friends like you so much?'

'Does he still blame me for GJS?'

'Weren't you also doing exactly what you got him fired for?'

'Is that what he says?'

'It's old news, Mr Blackwell,' said Ford, tiring of the digression. 'It doesn't matter to me or you, or the choice now before you.'

'What makes you think it's my choice?'

'Isn't it?'

'It's her world, Ford. Always has been.'

'She's an amazing woman. But it's always been your choice.'

'You think?'

'Mr Blackwell, let me tell you exactly what I think. I think that Ninety East Ridge is the single best idea I ever heard of. I think it's the boldest, most brilliant, most glorious task man's ever undertaken. I think your town planning is incredible, your political plans truly representative, and your economic plans truly inspirational.'

'Then why—'

'I think you know why.'

Another silence. Again, Arb felt compelled to speak.

'I'm not sure,' he said. 'I don't know what she wants to do.'

'That's probably because you haven't asked her.'

Arb tried to control his breathing, tried not to give anything away.

'I've told you what I think, Mr Blackwell,' said Ford, ignoring his minor victory, 'now let me tell you what I know. I know how much you've protected your New World from the real world. I also know that that protection cannot last forever. I also know that agreeing to the manifesto I worked so painstakingly over would be better for all of you than leaving your destiny to the mercy of the General Assembly.'

'I'm expected to believe that you could make the UN go away?'

'You know I could. It's all about pulling the right levers.'

Arb weighed up his options—the devil and the deep blue sea, literally—but he couldn't bring himself to decide. Not yet. Not today.

'I told you,' he said finally. 'I don't know what she wants to do.'

'At this stage of the game, Mr Blackwell,' said Ford, 'you and I both know it doesn't matter what she wants to do. It only matters what she's going to do.'

Arb laughed—a cynical, desperate laugh that must have surprised even Ford.

'I don't know what she's going to do either.'

'You've got nine days to find out,' said Ford, hanging up.

Even less, Arb thought, wondering where she was, pretending that he didn't know. ·

the most amazing, wonderful girl

'If you ask me, I'll answer you,' she said. 'Do you really want to know?'

Yes. No. He didn't know. He didn't know if he wanted to know. He stared at the table, unable to look at her.

But he really, really wanted to know.

He concentrated on the table, then tried to inch his gaze up towards her. But he stopped at her hands, his eyes catching on that evil ring that strangled one of her fingers. His stare retreated back to his own hands, which rubbed and held each other nervously.

Then all of a sudden, he lost control. Just for an instant, something else took over. It was barely a fraction of a second. Something inside him seized his hands, his mind, his heart. It was gone a moment later. But before it departed, it had told his body that this was his one and maybe only chance to do what he had to do. And it had seized his hands and made them reach across the table.

He now held her hand. He thought he could feel her breathing change—he flashed a glance at her eyes for a split second, then looked back at the table. He hoped she was ready for this. And he hoped *he* was.

'You are,' he began, the power inside him gone—he was on his own now, 'the most . . .' He looked up again, as quickly as he could, at her eyes. *What could she be thinking? She must know what I'm trying to say. She could have stopped me by now; given me a signal or just walked away. But she's still here— there must be some tacit agreement in that.*

'Anna,' he began again, his eyes concentrated firmly on her hand held in his, 'you are, without doubt—I mean, you are the most amazing . . .' He stopped to breathe. He could feel his lungs developing a mechanical stiffness, no longer the natural, smooth, reliable set he was born with— suddenly his body felt rented, like a hired television. It wasn't his, so he didn't know how to adjust it, how to operate the remote control, where to kick it to make it work.

He could feel the first drop of perspiration wriggling its way through the pores on his fore- head. Even the muscles in his neck were rebelling, committing mutiny. Refusing to operate, they were threatening to cramp up or collapse in pain. It was a seditious insurrection, masterminded by flesh dissatisfied with the heart's leadership. His mind watched on feebly.

'You are,' he tried again. He wondered if she could see the struggle going on inside him, the confusion, the uncertainty.

And then her hand squeezed his—just the slightest bit of pressure—and he turned his eyes to hers. For the first time since he'd started to speak, he held her gaze. Those eyes, he'd always loved those eyes, those eyes that burnt with passion, conviction and determination. He saw himself reflected in those eyes and he could see that he loved her.

But did those eyes love him? Did she . . .

He had to know. He had to try. He had to stop wondering and put himself on the line. He had to act without knowing what would happen next.

'You are,' he consciously kept his eyes on her, 'the most,' he clasped her hand more tightly, more gently, '—you are the most amazing, wonderful girl that I have ever known, and—'

She let go of his hand, grabbed the back of his head and pulled him to her as she leaned across the table and kissed him. She kissed him. Long and hard—no, soft—so soft, she kissed him.

He forgot about his lungs, the sweat, his neck. With a touch from her lips, the revolt had been crushed.

world without end

[days 650 to ___]

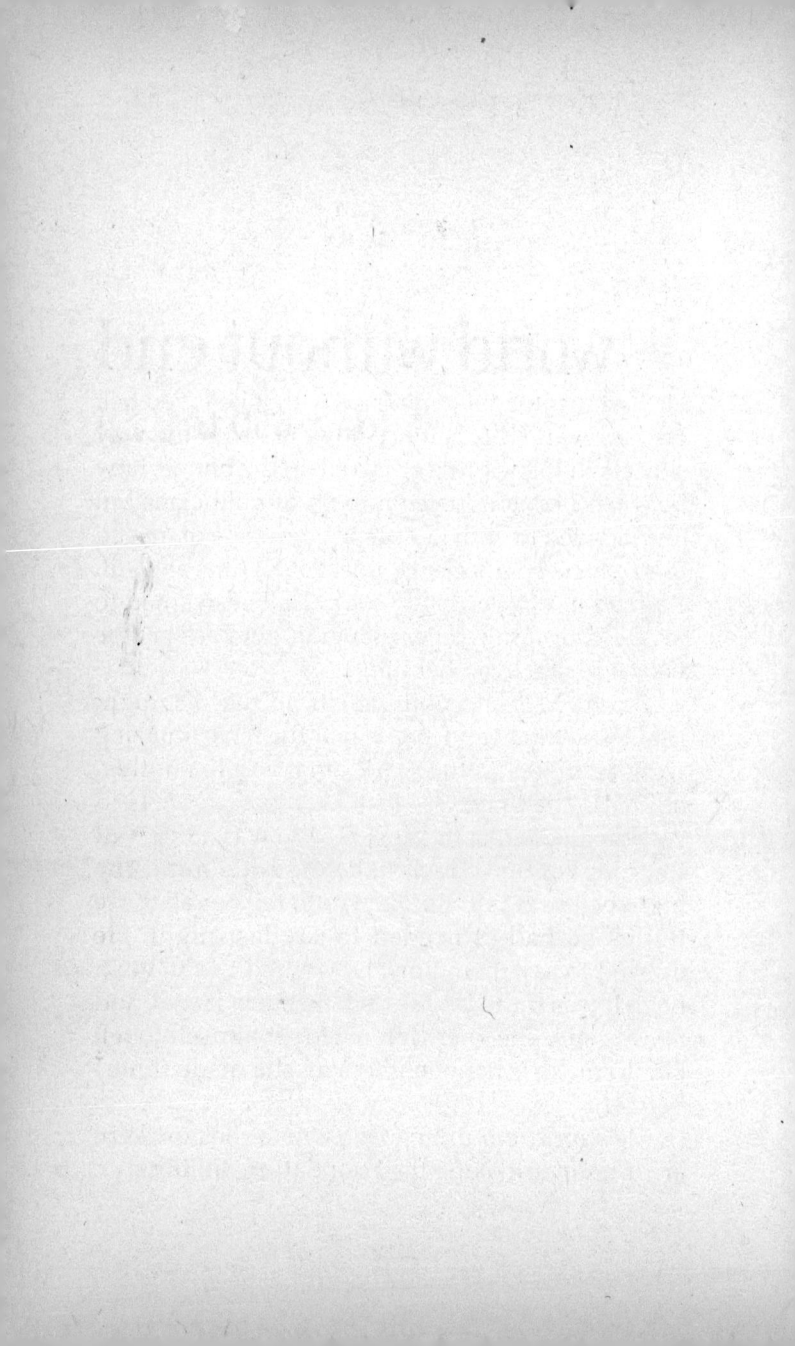

love

He had wanted to say more, say that he loved her. He had wanted to tell her how he loved the way she talked to the press or talked on the phone; how her presence dominated a room of politicians but just blended in with her friends; how she managed the greatest engineering project of all time and still claimed not to be able to cook. He had wanted to say how he admired her thoughts, her passion, the very way she lived her life.

But he had said nothing, afraid that he might ruin everything, and aware that the most amazing wonderful girl in the world, married to another, might do the same.

When he woke the next day he was alone, but the uncertainty which had filled his mind the night before was gone. He would tell her all those things he hadn't needed to say last night. He needed to say them now, he wanted to say them now. It was right, he decided; he knew it was, and he was sure she knew it too. He set himself to tell her, to make it happen, the way she made things happen.

He strode to Building One where she now kept an office overlooking the Foundation Building.

As he rose in the elevator, his eyes staring at the sealed threshold, he breathed deeply, steeling himself. His future lay through those sliding doors. He raised his gaze. *Make it happen.*

When he strode out of the elevators and into Anna's ante-room, Xavier was there talking to the secretary.

'You're looking for Ms Spires, sir?' he asked.

The secretary answered Xavier's question before Matt could.

'I'm sorry, Mr Turner,' she said, 'but Ms Spires has gone home.'

This crazy, crazy world carries on outside my window. Without my permission. Without even consulting me. I feel so powerless . . .

. . . and yet I know that I had my chance.

What else could I have done? An act, a word? I replay those days over and over.

Truth and lies never change, but my memories are almost never the same. How can that be? Do I remember what I want to or what I need to? Or is there some higher power that controls my consciousness as well as my destiny?

If there is, it has a lot to answer for.

Home is where the heart is—a rosy untruth.
Home is where the heart should be.

home

The garden was different. The gate, too. White wooden lattice-work where there was once flaky black iron. The colour of the house had changed— some time ago, it appeared—lemon-yellow peeling paint, specks of white showing through, replacing the once fashionable teal-green of Anna's child- hood. Was the roof different? The guttering maybe? She couldn't tell.

Yet somehow, despite its strangeness and newness, it was the same.

Memories blossomed from corners of the garden—of dancing under hoses over there; there, planting tomatoes; and, was it there? or there? of burying her dearly departed goldfish. Happy screams and laughter ran around the corner and down the side of the house into the back yard. Visions of him striding out the screen door—that, too, had changed—and engulfing both his daughters in his arms. The shadow of her mother watching from the doorway.

The door opened before Anna had closed the gate behind her and she looked up to see that familiar silhouette standing at her post, watching, as if she'd been waiting there for the last seventeen years.

Her mother didn't say a word when she entered. Nor did Anna. What to say after so many years? In fact her mother took a step backwards as she walked in, a deliberate gesture to downplay any threat of forced intimacy.

The foyer, hallway, stairs, all looked the same. Had the carpet changed? It must have. But still the shapes of the place—corners, shadows, doorways and banisters—were immediately familiar. As was the presence of the silent figure that now ghosted her as she moved tenderly around the house, a couple of respectful paces behind.

Into the lounge room: the sunlight through the curtains, pieces of furniture—he used to sit here . . . she placed her hand on the shoulder of his favourite chair. The coffee table was the same, she noticed. The old pendulum clock still on the wall. Even the antique dial telephone had not moved. The television was new. So, too, the heater. And above the heater was a new picture which stopped Anna dead.

Taking pride of place in the room was a photo, enlarged, of herself looking awkwardly over a room full of journalists, presenting her vision of a New World.

A special moment, she thought to herself. She could see it in her own eyes: a moment of pride and achievement, a moment when her dream had truly begun.

There must have been about thirty or forty newspaper photographers and TV crew there that day, but she knew immediately who had taken the photo. She should have known that her sister had always been a double agent.

Other photos, other memories, now caught her eye, each releasing recollections of great days. The static image of her signing her marriage certificate released flashes of her husband, a ring, her sister as maid of honour. A snapshot of her face when the Great Glass Wall was unveiled: Matt fetching her, Harry and his proud grin, the sudden burst of confidence. The whole table, Anna now noticed, the old dining table it was, was filled with photos of her, each rekindling so much more than just the moment: her university graduation, how young she was . . . what was that? No, it couldn't be, but it was: the first bridge she had ever designed and built. Suddenly, the memories were no longer proud and happy.

Suddenly, they felt selfish and bitter.

She could feel her, hovering there behind her. And suddenly she felt so ashamed and small for not sharing those moments. She was so sorry—had been so wrong.

Seventeen years . . . seventeen years of separation. Because of a lie, she had always told herself; because of the disgust she had felt when her father's death had been impugned, because once again her mother had proven herself unworthy.

But for seventeen years, she had only been lying to herself.

She was so sorry—had been so wrong, for so long. Because in that moment when her mother had said that her father may have thrown himself in front of a car on purpose, she had only revealed that she knew him as well as Anna did. And because of that, Anna had walked away—because a wife had known her husband as well as a daughter had.

She was so sorry.

She had been so wrong.

Could her mother forgive? It had been so long.

She hesitated to turn. She wanted to turn. But . . .

Before she could hesitate again, her mother was there. Bridging the gap in an instant. Bridging the space and the years, she was in her arms, protected. Safe. Unconditionally loved.

Home.

Deal or ideal?
Building a better mousetrap is easy,
Selling it to the shareholders is a bitch.

final preparations

'She said to say that she will meet you in New York the day before the hearing,' Xavier had said.

For the next eight days, Matt had suffered alone Arb's final admonitions, the increasingly anxious grillings by Obermann and Diaglio to see that he understood their policies, not to mention the stares of every resident of Ninety East Ridge. He sensed in these looks, once encouraging and ego-boosting, that people were now hedging their bets, distancing themselves, seeing in Matt an excuse, a reason why this pivotal session might cost them everything.

And it could be everything. The numbers, he had been told, were no longer as comforting as they had once been. If the UN decided to cede ownership and control to a US-led administration, as Laikali's information indicated their accusers would recommend, then all of their labour, all of their idealism, 'everything' would have been in vain.

Arb held the red leather manifesto in his hands. Its blue and gold seal presented conflicting

emotions—on one hand, the recognition of identity, the comfort of certainty, the ensured (albeit
compromised) continuing leadership of Anna; on
the other, the loss of all identity.

In his hands, he held an escape route from the
political rout that appeared almost certain. It
wasn't ideal, but at least they would not lose
everything.

*

'They must lose everything,' Ridder said. 'In the
interests of national security. In the interests of
democracy and the free market. I don't understand
why you'd allow a compromise.'

Ford was growing tired of the rabid dog routine.
He didn't even look up from the Federal Budget
draft he was reviewing.

'Have you forgotten why we started this? Have
you forgotten wh—'

'Why don't you tell me, Mr Ridder,' Ford said
softly, still not looking up.

Ridder hadn't been ready for such an opportunity, and his raving suddenly lost its momentum.
He choked on a few deep breaths and opening
words before finally calming down enough to
speak evenly. 'You called me. You called me because
you needed me to slow down, subvert, sabotage
every effort that Blackwell and his hussy made to
build their little hole in the ocean.'

'But why, Mr Ridder?'

'Because it was not in America's best interests.
Or the world's best interests! Environmentally,
economically, politically . . . need I go on?'

427

'Yes, I think you should, Mr Ridder. Because I do not think you understand at all.'

Laikali tallied her numbers again. They were now behind. Well behind. Although it was not a lost cause.

The more recent allegations of misappropriation or misleading fundraising had been a near-fatal blow. Any favours, past or potential, that a delegate might have owed Isaac Blackwell now counted double, but against instead of for him.

To understand which way they would cast their ballot, Laikali had to weigh up the agendas of the country, its leadership, even of the individual ambassadors. She was well aware that few directly related issues would decide the day, even if most anti-Ridge votes were likely to cite as their major rationale the whole issue of international waters: who had claim to it, some had told her over the phone; what limits existed on activities or construction that could be practised there, some had said over a breakfast meeting; whether it was an abusive use of international common ground even though the letter of the Law of the Sea said it was not.

Their strategy needed to be subtle, aggressively taking away the post-vote political and media justification, yet discreetly addressing behind-the-scenes pressures.

She needed to talk to Anna: to brief her again, finalise their strategy and tailor her approach for this final chance at gaining political approval.

But Anna was nowhere to be found.

Matt knew nothing but the sound of the Philo Group's constant coaching in the days leading up to the hearing. Like Laikali, he had been told that Anna was at her mother's house. Like Laikali, he had been unable to get a response on the phone.

But unlike Laikali, his mind could barely concentrate on the debate ahead.

As he flew into New York, he found himself wishing that the plane would raise its nose and head for outer space. But it continued to lose altitude, and Matt was forced to watch as the ground, which he knew waited only to swallow him whole, rose to meet it.

What would he say when he saw her? What could he say?

What would she say?

She'd reject it, that was certain. At least she would if he could contact her.

It would not have mattered how reasonable the document was, and Arb knew, in his business heart, that Ford's proposed constitution was not all that unreasonable.

A 'special territory', not unlike the American protectorate in Guam. Military security as required. Political and economic assistance as required. There were a number of ominous references to the 'unpredictability' of Ninety East Ridge's neighbouring nation-states, partnered by some unnerving assurances that the US would be committed to defending against any such states who may 'seek advantage' by invading Ninety East Ridge's new sovereignty. This assistance, of course, would be requited by the technological advancements made by Ninety East Ridge's steadily growing army of scientists.

Ford was clearly concerned about the sheer number of scientists that Ninety East Ridge had been able to attract in such a short time. What had been a medical cadre of researchers at first, soon broadened into the fields of telecommunications, power and energy, as well as food and biotechnology (even without any agricultural landscape). Ford's proposal would support their work and channel it back into American military and industry.

His proposal was reasonable.

It would save what they had built.

Yes, there would still be Old World markets, motivations, inefficiencies and compromises.

But their hole in the ocean would remain.

Arb weighed Ford's document in one hand, Anna's beautiful world in the other. Deal or ideal? He had a choice to make. For while it had always been her world, it had always been his choice.

'*I* don't understand? *I* don't understand? Listen, while you were playing your little psychological dancing games with the lady engineer, I was out doing the work. I know exactly how whacked out this New World is, how crazy its society is going to be. A communist moneyless state with an ill-qualified, idealistic dictator. You think *I* don't understand?'

'No, Mr Ridder, clearly you do not. Can't you see? Isaac Blackwell, for all his hard-nosed business tactics, is not evil. And Anna Spires, for all her alternative motivations, is not a communist. We are destroying them for one reason: to kill them before they kill us.'

'Kill us? Kill *us*?' Ridder shook his head at the preposterousness of even the thought.

'It's a better mousetrap, Mr Ridder. It's email to our snail mail. It's what solar power would be to oil if we hadn't made it uneconomical by commandeering the patents.'

Ridder was flabbergasted. 'You think that kibbutzian freak show would outshine the land of the free?' He laughed unnaturally at the thought.

'I don't think it. I know it. If it ever got the chance, it would slowly but surely convert every country on this planet to a saner, richer and freer life.'

'Richer? Without money? You've lost it, Ford.' He shook his head with contempt. 'You've lost it. And it's clear that I'm going to have to finish this without you.'

He slammed the door disgustedly behind him.

'Much richer,' mused Paul Jefferson Ford to the empty chair in front of him.

The night before the hearing, Laikali could sense it again. As distinctive as the fresh fragrance in the wind that foretells a storm, she could smell the hunger for blood in the whispers sweeping the corridors.

Arb called the number.

Ford's voice, on the other end, was as always courteous and sincere. It didn't reveal any disappointment or surprise when he delivered his response to the offer.

Matthew Turner, the personality of the day, lay on his hotel bed staring at the ceiling. He had taken the phone off the hook. It had not stopped ringing since he'd arrived: the press, radio, television, all looking for an exclusive insight into the same story, and since neither the Greatest American Hero nor his wife was to be found, he was now the centre of attention.

He had memorised everything he could ever memorise. He had rehearsed every line until he could say them backwards standing on his head. He had practised facial expressions, seating postures, walking postures—nothing could surprise him tomorrow, he thought to himself as he flicked off the lights and closed his eyes. Nothing!

And then someone started pounding on the door.

Laikali watched it on the raised TV in the corner of the delegates' common room.

*

Blackwell turned it on just in time, following a call from Byron Lybrand.

As Matt warily opened the door, Tom Mills burst by to turn on the TV as the President's face appeared on-screen.

They watched in disbelief . . .

432

. . . that it had come to this.

Meanwhile, elsewhere, a pair of eyes, determined and proud but somehow less angry than before, watched not the petty bickerings of worlds old and new, but instead basked inside a beautiful dream where she was sitting on the step watching him create.

A jewellery box.
A philosophical theory.
A better world.

Rubber bands. Relays. Very long pieces of string.
Answers made of magic and comfort,
Even if they were not necessarily untrue.

we all walk west

'. . . otherwise, how would the world turn beneath us?'

That was the answer—in the form of a question, of course—an answer only he could give, intended to start, not end, further inquiry.

And that was the way he taught her, floating fanciful views and possibilities that not even he thought were true, but which also he did not know to be untrue.

He questioned the certain knowledge of anything, but he wasn't a sceptic. He was not espousing some Nietzschean views of *uberman* or life beyond good and evil. His scepticism was just his way of tolerating (or not tolerating) the world as it was.

We all walk west, he'd say. And its meaning had a most convenient capacity to change to suit his mood.

Cynical—the earth was a conveyor belt.

Victimised—a mousewheel or grindstone.

And happy: 'We're all part of one big never-ending relay,' he told her, 'where one of us, at all times, is dragging the sun behind us with an invisible piece of string. And when we meet people and say hello and share our lives and happiness, we pass on the piece of string, so that when we go home and rest, the sun keeps moving around the earth.'

'Daddy,' she said, eager to learn, keen to know more. 'How long's the piece of string, Daddy?'

He suppressed another grin. 'Very long,' he said.

Sometimes, it was a rubber band engine. Other times, the earth was a spinning top, or it was magnetically repelled from Apollo's chariot or, when the weather was bad, it was that crazy earth looking to see if it had a tail. Once, it was the earth's way of protecting its babies—us—turning away from the sun so little boys and girls could get enough sleep to play right through the next day.

But that was Anna's father. An unputdownable book of life, where you found something new every time you opened its pages. A constant work-in-progress, it often appeared rewritten with new fables, new adventures, different words, but always the same voice, always written in the same loving hand. You opened his book to find comfort in a familiar world. And you drew from his words love, inspiration and laughter.

For so long, she had resented her mother for not understanding him. Her exhortations to stop clowning around, that he wasn't helping, that Anna needed to put her head down—her mother had always been so wrong, and Anna had always been going to prove that by her success, by making her father's childish dreams change the world, by showing the wisdom of his eccentricities and the mistake her mother had made betraying them.

Somehow, this day, her head on her mother's shoulder, it all made sense.

'But you don't know everything.' Words said in *thoughtless anger.*

But she did know.

'You don't know that he did it on purpose, do you?' Unforgivable words of so long ago.

She had always known.

'One day, my gorgeous Grub, you're going to have to fly on your own.' Last words. Desperate words.

She wanted to beg forgiveness. But held in arms that felt no bitterness, kept no score, begged no vengeance, she realised that sorrow or gratitude was not necessary here.

'And you're going to be just fine. You're not going to let reality beat you down the way I did. You're not going to start with compromise like I did. You're not going to die wishing . . .' A father's final farewell.

Her mother would never have betrayed him. She never lied to her either.

That day, for the first time, she realised that her mother loved and despised her father for all the same reasons she did.

They spent the week preceding the hearing living together; not speaking much, but in their own way getting to know each other again.

When they did speak, Anna always spoke about the Ridge.

'. . . and then the first wave of families moved

436

into Ninety East Ridge some six months ago. A second wave three months back. A third wave is just about to begin. It's amazing to watch: already, they're gradually settling into a new way of life.'

She found herself rambling, talking fast and often at random, as if trying to fit seventeen years of learning into their time together. Her mother usually just listened. Perhaps she was trying to fill a seventeen-year chasm that had not echoed with her elder daughter's voice.

'Dad would be so pleased—' Anna said at one stage, stopping to check if she had erred. But her mother just smiled—an odd, knowing smirk that said he would have been—and so she rambled on. '. . . the most amazing things are the signs of a new society in the making. A country with no history, and we already have myths and battles and heroes and ideals.'

She explained to her mother how the mix of Western, Indian and African cultures had revitalised ancient myths and how new gods of the sea and fantastic creatures of the deep now delighted and frightened children whose bedroom windows looked out under the Indian Ocean. New myths had formed—'The one I like,' she related excitedly like a schoolgirl, 'is about a god called Tecton of the Underworld who rules *beneath* the sea, a sort of Poseidon or Neptune but more of a monster than a ruler of hell or keeper of lost souls. Tecton can breathe fire underwater and part the seas by raising mountains and islands. The story goes that he created the great Indian subcontinent, right on the site where Ninety East Ridge now stands, and that in a fit of uncontrollable rage, he threw it at the Asian continent—I wish I knew where this all started; Dad would have loved this—and as the new Indian landmass flew across the ocean, it trailed great chunks, relative crumbs, behind, creating a ridge of land to show its path. Not enough to break the surface, this was how the meridional ridge on the 90th parallel was formed—how Ninety East Ridge was created. And—here's the best part—such was the force with which India collided with the Asian continent that the land buckled and thus the Himalayas rose into the sky.'

They went on this way for almost the whole week, Anna talking about a decade and a half that her mother had been forced to share through photographs. She talked about the exhilaration she had felt when Isaac swept her away from those weddings, the excitement of their jetsetting secret romance, the disbelief with which she had listened to him suggest that they make her New World dream come true, and the certain efficiency with which he, a supreme master of his craft, had subsequently made it happen.

And all the while, Anna felt that her mother could tell that there was something—someone— that was left unsaid.

The day before she was due to leave for New York, she stopped rambling just long enough to ask her mother a question.

'When Dad was alive, did you ever . . . you know, did you ever . . .'

'Did I ever love another man?'

'No, ah, I didn't mean love—kiss, yes kiss, did you ever kiss another man?'

'Does it matter?' her mother replied.

Not exactly the response Anna was looking for. She felt herself snap—this was so like her mother, and she said so: 'God damn it, Mum! Does it matter? Why worry? You can't change it anyway?'

'But you can't.'

'We're not talking about my ears!'

'Aren't we? They're all just part of you. Would you prefer it if I said you can change your heart? Because you can't.'

Anna felt lost for words. She could argue theology with the Pope, socioeconomics with Obermann and structural dynamics with Harry, but with her mother . . . she had never been able to contend with her mother's stubborn stoic logic.

Years ago, she would have stormed out in contempt and disgust. *Irrelevant!* she would have thought. *So non sequitur! Ridiculous, always ridiculous!*

But this day, she did not walk away. Age tends to soften the dramatic value of childish tempers. And time often creates the distance to improve one's perspective.

The truth was that her mother's insights had always been too powerful for her to contend with. Not because she knew more about the subject, or because experience had taught her things that Anna would only learn with age—no, Anna's mother always played the man, or in this case Anna, not the ball. And admit it or not—and for as

439

long as she could remember, Anna had not—her mother had usually been right.

'Dad used to say,' reflected Anna, a tear in her eye, 'love your sister, because she's the only one you've got, and while you can change your friends, you can't change your family.'

'He was always a softie,' said her mother, as if it were a criticism.

Anna found herself wanting to cry again, found herself wanting her mother's shoulder. And like magic, it was there again, absorbing her tears.

'What he meant,' continued Josephine Spires, stroking her daughter's hair, 'was that you can't change who you are. And no matter what you do . . .' Anna thought she heard her mother's voice cracking, although she could not be sure because of her own muffled sobs, 'that he would be so proud of you.'

We all stand alone. Together.

us against the world

The message had been that Anna would meet him in the lobby, and from there they would make their way to the Assembly. Of course, it would not just be the two of them. Tom Mills, Saul, Jay, Byron and an entourage of support staff would be with them the whole day, at hand to pass Matt or Anna any information they might require. As he descended alone in the elevator, he suddenly felt a desire for it to break down; for him to be stuck in there all day; for him to avoid having to deal with the United Bloody Nations, the President and his warships, and of course—most of all—her.

But the elevator did not stop until it reached the lobby, and when it did, the doors opened to absolute mayhem.

'He's here!' 'Over here!' 'Mr Turner!' 'Mr Turner!'

Lights, microphones, shouts, faces assaulted him.

'Mr Turner, what did you think of the President's address last night?''Do you agree with the President's—' 'Does the decision to send warships—' 'What will you—' 'Is Ninety East Ridge a clear and present danger to the US?'

He shielded his eyes while they adjusted. Tried to keep moving forward. The buffeting scrum of reporters and cameramen lurched with him.

'Is it true—' 'Do you believe—' '—that Ninety East Ridge has stolen half of America's scientific community?' 'What do you think—'

'I think,' Matt said, raising his voice, instantly hushing the awkwardly moving rabble, 'that you can make up your own minds about a President who sends warships to surround an unarmed country.'

A blast of counter-questioning overwhelmed him. Matt didn't even know which way he was walking now. He was relieved when Byron Lybrand squeezed his way through the media phalanx and took his arm. He steered Matt, and the attached swarm of journalists, into the street.

'Mr Turner! Mr Turner!' 'Will you respect the decision of the General Assembly?' 'What will you do if—' 'What will you say to—'

The bubble of people surrounding Matt and Byron pressed and then spread itself against the waiting car. Byron pushed forward and reached for the door.

'What if—' 'Can you comment on—' 'Anna Spires! Anna Spires!'

There she was, in the open car doorway, waving him to get in, get in. Her face, like an angel's, appeared so calm, despite the fury of the storm surrounding it. With a surge of determined forcefulness, he shot through the space and into the limousine, Byron slamming the door behind him.

As he sat up opposite her, Matt noticed that *he* was here also. The uncontrollable smile that had appeared when she did evaporated instantly.

'Sorry to surprise you like this,' said Isaac Blackwell. 'But, arrest warrant or not, I had to be here, especially after what that puppet said yesterday.'

Matt's first thought was whether he'd been bumped off the team. A second thought quickly followed, questioning whether he wanted to be or not.

Perhaps reading his thoughts, Anna spoke: 'You're still representing us.'

'Yes, yes,' Arb assured him. 'There are just some things I'd like to say when the opportunity arises, that's all.'

'About what the President said?'

'No. The clear and present danger part was just an excuse to send the warships. The warships themselves are just a powerplay, to try to influence the Assembly, and to scare their scientists into leaving.'

'Why? Do they want to? Would they?'

'Oh no,' nodded Arb proudly. 'You don't send warships to endear yourself to scientists whom you want to come home. You send them to muscle through a constitution or manifesto you want a new country to adopt.'

'But what will they do?' Matt asked. 'The warships, I mean.'

Arb shook his head. 'I don't think they'll do anything. They would never torpedo or bomb us, especially with their most elite scientists there.'

'It's a mistake,' said Anna, also shaking her head. 'In fact, I can't believe that Ford took it this far. He'll look stupid if they lose, and a tyrant if they win.'

'I don't think he cares what he'll look like if they win,' said Isaac.

But Anna's head was still shaking. No . . . no, something wasn't right here.

They stood alone, just the three of them, in the deserted foyer, a limbo that stood between the manic throng of the media outside and the profound uncertainty of the UN inside.

The door to the main chamber was heavy and ornate. Their future, and the future of Ninety East Ridge, lay beyond it. Vision, Matt had once told Anna, was what had made her successful, the vision to look through doors such as this one, and open them without fully knowing what lay on the other side.

He saw Arb pause at the door and look back at each of them. Deep breaths. Sweat on his brow—it was the first time Matt had ever seen him nervous. He watched him smile widely, attempting to draw their attention away from the handkerchief patting his forehead.

Anna stood next to him, her eyes focused like a prize fighter—like a champion prize fighter. She had no doubts, no fear, and no intention of messing around. Her eyes were staring at but not seeing the door before her; they were envisioning a third-round knockout. She was not here to showpony, she was here to get the job done.

And then there was Matt himself, uncomfortable in his new suit and slicked-back hair, unrecognisable from the boat person who had hitchhiked six thousand kilometres to a hole in the ocean. Today he was Matthew John Turner, Ninety East Ridge's official expert in scenario management and unofficial representative of the 'common man'.

It was likely that he would be the only common man in the chamber, Laikali had told him. 'So don't overdo it. They might not appreciate it. Though most of them will know instantly by the way you wear your suit.'

The suit bothered him. Laikali's comments bothered him. What did she mean, the way he wore his suit? He watched Arb out the corner of his eye, adjusting his cufflinks without looking. He fumbled at his own cufflinks, cursing in his mind those people who were too rich for buttons. As he looked down, he noticed his shoes were scuffed—*shit!*—he must have done it getting out of the car.

'You okay, Turner? You missing something?' It was Arb, calming his own nerves by being aggressive.

'What? No. No, I'm fine,' assured Matt, realising that his head had turned to glance back at the way they had come in, as if he could unscuff his shoes by re-entering the building.

'All right, then. We ready?'

Anna didn't say a word, her eyes still forward, her mind so focused.

Matt nodded and took the deepest breath of his life.

The heavy doors opened slowly before them. For a moment, indiscriminate noise. Then silence.

Lights. Eyes. Space. Eyes. Mahogany. Faces. Fascinated stares. Intimidating. A sea of enemies and strangers. The enormous chamber was jam-packed. And every eye, every face was turned to the three small figures now entering the hall.

Matt must have hesitated. He hadn't meant to. But he must have. All of a sudden, he was under the scrutiny of the most powerful people in the world—he must have, because Anna was now stopped beside him.

'Come on, Matthew Turner,' she whispered. 'It's time to change the world.'

She took his hand. He saw that she also took Arb's. And together, eyes forward, eyes focused, hearts, souls and minds determined, they strode to the front of the chamber.

Perhaps the best way to describe the Matt that she had fallen in love with was that his suit always looked borrowed. But not today. From half a world away, Wendy watched the television through tears of loss and desire and pride as the man that now strode into battle, eyes fixed for a fight, was—yes, he was—everything that that man had aspired to be.

They took their places at the front of the auditorium. The Special Committee sat facing them, facing the entire Assembly. The Chairman of the Special Committee read out the purpose of the hearing:

'To determine the sovereign status of the development known as Ninety East Ridge.'

Then, following a pause to allow the translators

446

to catch up, 'The Chair recognises the Special Representative for the United States.'

'Thank you, Mr Chairman,' said Aldrich Ridder.

Laikali looked on with concern from her usual seat in the gallery. She had breathed a sigh of relief as the purpose was read out—it had taken a great deal of last-minute politicking to avoid the Americans' preferred phrasing of 'legal status'—but the devil's right hand himself now had the floor . . .

'As most of the members would be aware, the President of the United States last night stated the position of my country as follows: that the development known as Ninety East Ridge, previously known as the New World Project, misappropriated over four point four trillion dollars for its construction, and furthermore, in so constructing concentric concrete shafts across an area the size of Manhattan in the middle of the Indian Ocean, caused irreversible damage to the marine ecology of not just that vicinity but the entire Indian Ocean basin.

'Therefore, on the basis of its questionable financing and its outrageous disregard for the environment and its neighbours, the United States urges the United Nations not to recognise Ninety East Ridge as a sovereign state, and in order to ensure a proper and legal return for all investors, that the United Nations assume administrative control of the development—immediately, and by force if necessary—to guard against what our intelligence believes is an "if we can't have it, no one can", win-at-all costs attitude held by the self-appointed leadership of the development.'

My God! If only she'd known . . . if only she'd known what their real intentions were. What had started as just petty acts of bitter jealousy—a little inside information here, a little industrial espionage there—would never have become so traitorous. Mary watched the camera zoom in on the Utopian Three, as the TV commentators insisted on calling them, her husband clear in the background. How must Tom feel about her now . . . how could he have loved her for so long knowing, as he must have always known, that her heart had never fully belonged to him. And would he ever take her back if he found out how much she had told Ridder about the Philo Group, or how she had set up the compromising photo of Isaac.

'As an opening remark, if I may,' Anna was saying, 'I would like to add to Mr Ridder's summary of the President's remarks last night. The President also declared Ninety East Ridge to be, and I quote, "a clear and present danger to the scientific and technological advancement that the United States requires if it is to remain a global leader in the vital industries of information technology, telecommunications, health and pharmaceuticals, and defence".'

She paused for a moment, letting the weight of the President's words rest on the ears of every global competitor, before she went on: 'I would also like to remark that this session here today is to recognise our status as a sovereign state.'

'Ms Spires, if I may—'

'No, you may not—'

'Yes, I must,' Ridder insisted, raising his voice. 'You are here—'

'Mr Chairman, I must object.'

'—because Ninety East Ridge illegally acquired universal ocean territory and committed crimes against the global ecology.'

'Mr Ridder, you will desist,' said the Chairman forcefully. 'Our protocols will not tolerate further interruptions.'

'You're so smart, little Anna, aren't you? First you make every other country on earth realise that a vote for your Ridge is a competitive blow against the US. Then you make Ridder look like the child he is.'

Maybe she can win, Ford thought, shaking his head.

As the protocols of professional politics quickened the pace, the proceedings began to rush by Matt Turner like a dream in which time and physics bent and collapsed. A succession of images quickly blurred into memory . . .

Anna saying, 'Our claim to sovereignty satisfies every accepted criteria' . . . 'has been freely self-determined' . . . those eyes . . . 'we are self-sufficient, financially and politically' . . . 'already geographically and ideologically independent' . . . those deep, determined eyes . . . 'no reason why any of our plans or policies should be dictated to us by a foreign power' . . .

Arb on his feet, 'Let me make absolutely clear' . . . the arrogance in his voice . . . 'We broke no laws' . . . almost challenging the most powerful people in the world . . . 'no financial laws' . . . 'no environmental laws' . . . 'nor any laws of the sea' . . . challenging them to defy him . . . 'Now you can choose to close that loophole' . . . 'but you can't close the greatest feat of engineering the world has ever seen' . . . 'and you can't take credit for it' . . . and looking right at Ridder, 'and you can't take control of it' . . .

And Matt himself, like a third party in his own swooping kaleidoscopic dream, 'I am no doctor of economics' . . . 'have no experience as a mayor or town planner' . . . so many people watching . . . 'in fact, I've spent most of my life trying to escape reality' . . . staring at him . . . 'but reality eventually caught me, in the most unlikely place' . . . some smiling, some hating, some curious . . . 'in an idea that belongs in science fiction' . . . and the rest with indecipherable faces of stone . . . 'in a seven-kilometre wide straw that now stands on end, drained in the centre of the Indian Ocean' . . . and amongst those faces, his friends: Tom, Miles, even Jay and Saul, and Laikali in the gallery . . . 'where the way of life will be different' . . . 'where the goals of life will be different' . . . and Anna beside him, smiling in proud agreement up at him . . . 'where the measure of a man or a woman will be different' . . . up at him, this 'everyman' . . . 'where I would be the luckiest man in the world to live' . . .

I see the way he looks at her, for support, for understanding . . . for love? Still, I'm so proud of him.

And then Matt's already otherworldly dream tipped crazily on its head . . .

Debate opening up to the floor . . . Ridder accusing, 'irresponsible neglect of our planet' . . . 'ecological devastation' . . . 'damage that can never be repaired!' . . . Ridder despairing, 'May not be against the laws of the sea' . . . 'but surely a crime against the laws of nature' . . .

Impassioned defences, Arb and Anna both, 'The site was deliberately chosen' . . . 'was a barren, underwater wasteland' . . . 'more care' . . . 'more research' . . . 'than all the oil operations in the world combined' . . .

Paper waving . . . Finger pointing . . . Civilised debate degenerating . . .

'Whole whale and fish migration patterns affected' . . .

'How can you say that when already half of the world's leading biologists live at the Ridge' . . .

Shaking heads . . . Pens tossed in frustration . . .

'No natural resources, they reject global financial norms' . . .

'Deliberately original policies, developed by experts in their fields' . . .

'How long, how long, I ask you, until the global community will be called upon for food and financial aid?'

'Never—the whole point is a viable alternative economy' . . .

Hands in the air, as if appealing for divine insight, 'Here we are again, as if childish utopian idealism is a real argument!' . . .

You're winning, Laikali thought. You're winning— and you're right: an unusual concurrence in the world of political debate. Just don't lose your cool. Stay on the subject. Ridder knows he's losing and he's trying to make your idealism sound foolish and irresponsible.

'Not Utopia—just different, certainly no worse' . . .

'Some people might find your idealism moving, Ms Spires. But I find it naive and offensive' . . .

'Feel free not to visit. Rest assured, Mr Ridder, that not everyone is inspired by your ideals' . . .

'My ideals? Like democracy perhaps?'

'Oh, *we* will have democracy, Mr Ridder . . .' said Anna.

—*Be careful, little Anna. That sharp, sarcastic tongue may cause you ulcers.*

—*Where are you going with this, my dear?*

The whirl of words and images whipping past Matt slowed to focus on her.

'. . . but a fair, inclusive, participative democracy, where money, military or old school ties have no value.'

—*Well played, little Anna.*

—*She almost sent me and my heart to join Augusto.*

'This is exactly the sort of impractical, unrealistic idealism which the United States does not believe the world should have to bail out when it inevitably fails. No political parties? No money, Ms Spires? No wealth? No pensions? No stockmarket? No trade?'

'No compromise, Mr Ridder.'

'No future, Ms Spires.'

'No future, Mr Ridder, where fundraising buys presidents and policies. No future where investments tie us to an energy source which is systematically destroying the planet. No future where wealth determined by a baseless number on a board determines your standard of living.'

'Cynicism has no place in the real world,' said Ridder patronisingly.

'No, it doesn't,' agreed Anna surprisingly. 'Unless you can back it up with a real alternative.'

And you can, thought Tom.

Yeah baby, thought Miles.

We're going to win, thought Byron.

We're going to win, thought Jay.

We're going to win, thought Saul.

Thank God! They're going to win, thought Mary.

Matt took what felt like his first breath of the day. The unreal flurry of real images slowed again as he focused on Anna summing up:

'That's all we're offering, Mr Chairman. An alternative. A real, idealistic alternative. Yes, it's idealistic—we want to start with the ideals and make them real, rather than work from a base with limitations. And let me make the base that we have used clear: Ninety East Ridge broke no laws to be here today—no financial laws, no environmental laws, no sovereign laws. We swindled no one. We bullied no one. We invaded no one. The truth is that no one stopped us because no one believed what we've achieved was possible. Well, let me tell you again: it *is* possible, it is *all* possible—a hole in the ocean, a city from nothing, a New World, and a better one.'

Enjoy. Fight on. Keep on moving forward.

every day you can

They broke for a short recess, and the foyer outside the heavy mahogany doors filled with people.

Arb, Matt and Anna let themselves be carried with the flow. Tom, Byron, Saul, Jay and Miles fell in around them, enthusing about how well they thought it had gone so far. Arb wouldn't be drawn to comment, except to say that Ridder was a 'power-mad patsy to Ford who will commit suicide one day when he realises just how insignificant he really is'.

They had only just stepped onto the foyer's marble floor when she saw him. For just a moment, passing like a ghost through a door at the end of the room. It was Ford. He was here. She looked around for Matt or Isaac, but a wedge of people had driven Matt towards the doors and she could see Isaac retreating to a far corner with Saul and Jay to discuss strategy. She looked back for Ford, but he was gone.

She broke into a half-run, trying not to draw attention to herself as she rushed and sidestepped her way across the crowded marble floor. Brushing and bumping people, important people, people crucial to the survival of the Ridge, she ignored them or mumbled a semi-coherent apology or 'excuse me'. She kept one eye on the door through which Ford had disappeared while the other tried to guide her through the crowded corridor of power.

Then, without thought, without knocking, she burst through the door.

Paul Jefferson Ford stood at the window. For a moment, he reminded her of her father, staring at the future which lies on the horizon. You don't need to be able to see to look in that direction.

'Ms Spires,' he said, still 'looking' out the window. 'You made good time across a very crowded room. This is some enchanted evening.'

She just stood there breathing heavily. Now that she was here, she did not know what to say.

'A lively session, wouldn't you say?' He jerked his head back towards her when she didn't reply, as if checking with his peculiar eyes that she was still there. 'I'm not sure myself. It could still go either way, don't you think?'

He chuckled to himself, as if he knew something she did not, and turned back to the window.

'When did you become so blind?'

'Who said I was blind?' laughed Ford. 'I have an eye condition that is sensitive to bright light. You must have assumed—'

'I wasn't talking about your sight. I wanted to know when you stopped being able to see.'

'You think I've closed my eyes to your vision of the future?'

'I do.'

'You think I do not see how your New World could change the rest of the world?'

'I do.'

He turned again and looked right at her. 'You're wrong, little Anna.'

And she knew she was. Just the way he said her name told her that he understood exactly what Ninety East Ridge meant.

'Then why?'

'It's too late. You don't seem to understand, we could not afford to change—even if we wanted to. It would cost and hurt too much.'

'One drop at a time,' Anna said.

A dismissive snort, Ford's only reply.

'We are going to win today, Paul.'

'You silly girl, don't you see. No matter what happens today, no matter how hard you fight, you can't win. I—we—are too strong.'

'How can you beat someone who won't stop fighting?'

He walked over slowly and stood in front of her. He took hold of her by the shoulders, pulling her close. His cheek brushed hers the way it had on her birthday, and again he whispered gravely in her ear.

'You knock them out, Anna. You shoot them dead.'

Fear rose inside her, but she fought it down and held her nerve.

'They're lining up, Paul. You might beat one, or two, or even fifty or a thousand, but you can't beat them all.'

'We do, Anna, day after day.'

'You can't believe that, Paul. One day you'll fall. Every empire does. Someone always comes along who is stronger, faster or smarter. You've become a gunslinger, slaying any man or idea that dares to challenge you. But you can't be a gunslinger all your life, Paul. No one can.'

'Yes, you can,' he whispered back, his voice almost failing him. 'If you just keep on fighting . . .'

For a moment, she felt scared for him.

'You made this happen, when you think about it. You gave us the education, the access to capital, the ambition and the belief that made this possible.'

He turned on her sharply. 'You're pitying me?' And when she did not reply: 'You've got no idea what I did to make this possible, or what I do every day to protect it.'

'You did what you thought was best. You made your decisions, right or wrong. And you'll make more decisions today and tomorrow and every day until some challenger finally comes and shoots *you* dead.'

'I'm not the one at risk here, little Anna. There's still time, you know. For compromise.'

She shook her head. 'There's still time to change, Paul. Join us.'

'You can't honestly believe I'd join you.'

'You can't honestly believe we'd compromise.'

She made to turn away, to leave him on her terms and not look back.

But she couldn't.

'When it's all said and done,' she said, stopping at the door and eyeballing him over her shoulder, 'when your market-driven society has eliminated

457

the weak and uncompetitive, what will be left?'

'Survival of the fittest, Ms Spires.'

'No, Paul. Because if it continues this way, what survives won't be society, just the winners.'

Late in the afternoon, the chamber was silent. The debate was over. It was time for the committee to deliver its judgement.

'In the very words of Ms Spires herself, the human race has made more progress in science and technology in the last century than in the rest of history combined. This committee would like to think that we could also extend that accolade to the concepts of living standards, justice and humanity. I say we'd *like* to think that—but it's a lot more difficult to prove than advances such as flight and telephone calls and men on the moon. Who's to say that a man who has never seen television is worse off? And despite the homogenising pressure of globalisation, the world, for the better I believe, continues to travel along diverse paths of religion, culture and social priorities. These diverse paths are what makes our world so special. But the Committee wishes to remind everyone in the Assembly that diversity does not need to be historical. History has made mistakes, its path has taken many wrong turns. The Committee believes that the Ninety East Ridge development reminds us that the future is, and will always be, more important than the past. In it, we can carve new paths, and provided these paths do not violate our agreed standards of human rights and international laws, it is not for the United Nations to bar them, lest we look back in another hundred years and be unable to say those same words with which I started the summation.'

We're home, realised Matt suddenly.

Ridder was now on his feet. 'With respect, Mr Chairman, what about the flagrant destruction of sea life and marine ecology? Or the egregious fundraising tactics?'

The Chairman's eyes narrowed when he responded, making clear that there would be no further debate. 'The Committee is completely satisfied that every environmental precaution was adequately undertaken, and that the financing of this development, whilst unusual, was in no way improper.'

We're home!

'The Committee hereby recommends that the Assembly sanction the completion and imminent sovereignty of Ninety East Ridge.'

We did it!

The cheers from the gallery were unrestrained. Hoops and shouts and hollers and hoorays echoed through the once-austere chamber. The entire team was on its feet, waving fists of triumph, shedding tears of joy, hugging each other. Looking up, Matt suddenly felt far away. He wanted to turn and hug . . . he reached across Anna, grabbed Arb by the lapel and wrenched him back across her into an emphatic bear hug. Then Matt reached out with one arm, looped it around her neck and dragged Anna into a three-way embrace.

Minutes of euphoric clapping and cheering passed before the sound of the gavel could be heard.

'That concludes this special hearing,' the Chairman shouted over the celebrations. 'We urge you to make the most of this special privilege you've been afforded. We wish you the best of luck in your endeavours.'

As they pushed their way through the media outside the auditorium, Anna spoke loudly and clearly, so that every ear, tape recorder and microphone could hear her: 'I'd like to thank the Special Committee for handing down what I believe to be a wise decision, a decision that international laws— none of which we have ever broken!—compelled them to make.

'But I'd also like to remind everyone that Ninety East Ridge, this "New World", was inspired for the sole purpose of escaping this old one. *We* created this "special privilege" that the Chairman claimed to grant us. *We* planned and laboured and succeeded on our own, without international assistance or permission. We came here because we respect the purpose of this Assembly, and would like to be recognised as part of the international community. We thank you for your approval but don't pretend we sought it. Don't think we came here looking for any "special privileges". Good day, people. We wish *you* the best of luck in *your* endeavours.'

The crowd was silent—thunderstruck in fact. The teeming scrum stopped and parted for Anna and her entourage like the Red Sea struck dumb.

Arb's face reflected that of every media-hound

in the room. Eyes wide, mouth open, breath held frozen in that part of the lungs controlled by fear and amazement.

Matt, too, gazed at her, but in utter awe and inspiration.

The man sitting in his shadowed mahogany office, listening through a special speaker on his desk, shook his head in exasperated admiration.

'Enjoy this day,' Ford whispered to himself, before he sighed and his voice turned sad. 'Enjoy every day you can, little Anna.'

We did this—
And nothing can take that away.

team victorious

And enjoy the day she did!

They all did!

A thirty-three hour journey later, every news organisation in the world covered the fireworks set off from a hundred barges encircling the city. Cameras zoomed in on their blooming explosions and their splintered reflections off every un- dulation in the waves. Everyone was dancing, singing, kissing and hugging, and no one cared what they looked like, sounded like, danced, sang or kissed like. It was euphoric. It was pandemonic. It was glorious. It didn't matter that the whole world was watching, because all that mattered was that the New World existed!

Anna's mother Jo was there, as was Natasha. Laikali had, without much cajoling, also joined Team Victorious on its triumphant return to the Ridge. Like footballers floating on the feeling of retelling their tale of glory, not Matt nor Tom, not Miles nor Byron, not Saul nor Jay, and certainly not Arb showed any of the effects of the long effort they had immediately made to get home and celebrate.

The day after the hearing, as the team was in the air, the UN had rushed out declarations of international agreements, similar to its space treaties, which were designed to stop all similar sea-based projects without international consensus. Between the loud bright bursts of fireworks, Byron explained the significance of the declaration: 'They've effectively stopped everyone else! Ironically, they've made us the one and only! They've closed the loophole, but it's too late to stop us—we've already gone through.'

'Dearie, you were wonderful!' Laikali almost swallowed Anna in her embrace. 'And if you think I'm impressed, you should hear how Augusto is raving about you! And Isaac Blackwell, my dear,' she said, swapping bodies like teddy bears, 'you are one hard-nosed son of a bitch,' although he didn't look it, pressed like an overloved grandchild to Laikali's chest.

Then she turned to Matt, who instinctively backed away. 'And you! Common man, my big brown Polynesian a—' Matt didn't hear the rest, his ears smothered by Laikali's affectionate bearhug.

He was released only to fall into the arms of more adulators.

'Well, now we're in trouble,' yelled Tom over the music, holding up his beer bottle.

'Why?' cried Matt.

'Because now we actually have to go through with it!' shouted Tom, clinking his bottle with Matt's.

'Excuse me, ladies and gentlemen. Excuse me.' The music stopped. 'Excuse me!' yelled Byron too loudly into a microphone, hushing the buzz that was lost without echo over the ocean. 'Our Commander-in-Chief would like to say a few words!'

A roar greeted Anna as she rose onto a makeshift stage consisting of a chair on a table.

'A toast!' she started, raising a champagne glass, 'to Rick Ridder!'

'Boooooo!'

'No, seriously. Okay, okay, okay,' she soothed. 'To Childish Utopian Idealism! May it never stop. May it never give up trying to create a better world. May it never presume that what we've achieved with this world is ever good enough. And may it always shine bright on Ninety East Ridge.'

'To Childish Utopian Idealism!' yelled Harry Pont from the floor.

'Childish Utopian Idealism!' echoed the crowd.

Matt watched her from a distance as she swept the crowd into the rushing current of her beautiful world. They looked on her with pride. They felt a sense of possession—she was their leader, she was their courage.

But there was no need for jealousy. Matt Turner's mind was made up. His path was certain. He had no doubts. He was sure of the truth. And just as sure of their future.

His confidence, like his certainty, was at an all-time high. The party, the dancing, the fireworks, they might all have been for him. He moved like a debonair movie star, graciously acknowledging pats on the back without slowing, waving with understated style at shouts of congratulation. And never once did he take his eyes off her.

He was maybe ten metres away when he noticed the music change—from a tubthumping technosound to a classic romantic track. *What luck*, he thought.

He was maybe five metres away, about to catch her eye, when someone else caught her eye and her hand, and asked her to make good on a promise she had made a long time ago to a stranger who later became her dreammaker who later became her husband.

Matt turned away, the moment, like his confidence, lost. Not knowing what to do, struggling to convince himself that it didn't matter, pausing before he dared to turn and look again, he saw her head resting lightly on Arb's shoulder, her eyes closed in . . . in tiredness? in relief? in what he could only hope was not true love.

Certain only of uncertainty, he left the party and headed back to his room.

He slammed the door behind him, shutting out the world behind it. Despair is an extreme side-effect of uncertainty, and jealous desperate thoughts that risked it all were racing through his mind.

Two steps inside, he noticed that the light was already on.

Someone was here.

And then he saw it.

The note on the table.

Dear Zigs, it began.

the note

Dear Zigs,
*I don't expect you'll understand this. I'm not sure I
understand it myself. Today, I saw a woman on
television announcing her plans to build a New World
in the Indian Ocean. I don't know how I'll get there. I
don't know what I'll do there. I don't know what it is
that makes me know, but I know I have to go. All I
know is that there's a New World waiting for me
there, waiting for me to help build it, help create it. I
still love you, Wendy (my God, I called you Wendy!)
but please do not wait for me.
All my love,
Matt.*

When he'd finished reading it, he asked the
empty room, 'Are you here?'
Wendy stepped gently into the room, 'Yes.'

So this was it.
This was how it would be resolved.

end games

Matt stormed out of the elevator, continued past the secretary without checking and barged straight into Arb's office.

'How dare you—' he started before he looked up and realised it was actually Anna sitting behind the desk. His face, so dark and angry a moment ago, lit up with hope. As he groped clumsily to shut the door behind him, he made to speak—to explain, or not explain, to say what he would have said last night perhaps—when he saw Arb standing in one corner of the room.

'You were saying?' Arb goaded coolly.

'Good, I'm glad you're here,' said Anna briskly.

'You are?' said Matt.

'Yes,' she said, keeping her tone serious and businesslike, her eyes downcast. 'We need to call a Philo Group meeting immediately.'

'Why? What's going on? I don't want to sound uneager, but don't you think that after last night, maybe they should get the day off?'

'For God's sake, Gizmo!' said Arb behind him,

directing with a glance Matt's attention to a monitor on the desk.

'The warships are still here?' cried Matt in disbelief, looking at the three US gunships on the screen.

'That's the view from a camera on Platform Three,' Arb said. 'There are eight in total surrounding us.'

'We need to get Jay in here to interpret,' Anna was saying.

'The media,' Arb continued, 'says they're just waiting for instructions about where to go next.'

'Did the US accept the UN judgement?'

Anna pointed a remote control at the monitor. 'Let Mr Ridder answer your question,' she said, starting a videotape. 'This was recorded as he left the UN building.'

The screen showed Aldrich Ridder emerging through the doors. The image lurched and bounced as the media dashed to engulf him in a way Matt was now only too familiar with. The first question was exactly Matt's.

'Of course the United States will accept the Special Committee's recommendation regarding sovereignty and international rights. My own feelings are that this is a mistake—and that the world will find out sooner rather than later that this whole development has been flawed, not just in its political and economic naivety but in every facet, from conception to design to financing to construction.'

A question about whether the US would consider unilateral action rose above the scramble for Ridder's attention.

'As I said, the United States will abide in every way with the UN's recommendations. The issue of American scientists, however, and the danger that national security is being jeopardised by this mass emigration, is not a United Nations matter—we will, as we are entitled to, draw our own conclusions. Thank you very much.'

Voices clambered for one last question, but Ridder was already nodding and smiling politely as if they had just had him over for dinner.

'There you have it,' said Anna, switching it back to the observation of the silent naval warships. 'What brought you in here anyway?'

'I, ah,' Matt leaned across the table, lowering his voice, 'have to talk to you.'

'Then why did you come in here?' she asked. It was, after all, Isaac's office.

'Yes, um, well, I wanted to have a few words with your husband here who . . .' He let his voice trail off, hoping that Anna would take the hint not to ask.

'Yes?' she said.

'He thought I might like to be surprised by the woman I left to come here two years ago.'

'You what?' reacted Anna angrily to Arb.

'I thought he'd be pleased,' Arb opined. 'After all, she's his fiancée.'

'She's what?' This time to Matt.

Matt snapped back at Arb, 'You know damn well that's no longer the case!'

'How would I know that?'

'How did you find out about her in the first place?' Matt demanded.

'I don't have to explain myself to you!' Arb declared, taking a step towards him.

'I think you do!' retorted Matt, also stepping forward.

'That's enough!' shouted Anna. 'This has gone just far enough. As you can see, we have far more pressing concerns just—'

The phone startled them all.

'Not now!' she roared into it. 'I said, not—my God, you're here?'

'Who?' Arb inquired, but she waved him away, listening intently for almost a minute as Arb and Matt stood awkwardly in what were supposed to be aggressive defiant postures.

When she hung up, she ran for the door. 'I have to go,' she said.

'But Anna!' Arb cried after her.

'You two figure it out!' she yelled back as she ran for the elevators.

They both took a moment to try to absorb what had just happened. Simultaneously, they both seemed to realise that they were now alone. Arb shut the door slowly, gently, deliberately.

'So, how's your fiancée?'

Matt tried to control the rage bubbling inside him.

'I imagine you must have a lot to talk about.'

'Not really,' said Matt, thinking it best to keep words to a minimum.

'Come, come. Nothing's happened in the six hundred and sixty-five days since you left without a word?'

'You know damn well—'

'Not the forgiving type, hey?'

'Wendy's more giving, more generous than anybody could ever dream of.'

'I don't know,' mused Arb. 'Have you met my wife?'

Matt didn't know what to say. He hadn't known what to say last night to Wendy either.

They had stared at each other for what seemed like hours, before trading harmless inquiries about each other's health.

'You look well,' he had said.

'You're unrecognisable,' she had replied.

He had looked down at himself, examining his body as if it was new. 'I've been busy, I guess.' And they had shared an awkward laugh.

'They told me that you wanted me to come, but . . .' He had looked up to see her finishing the sentence slowly, shaking her head, aware now that it wasn't true.

She had looked so sad. But there was nothing Matt could do.

'I'm sorry,' he had said.

'No, I'm sorry,' she had said, edging closer.

He hadn't known what she wanted—a kiss? a hug? just to touch?—but he had instinctively pulled away.

'I should have known,' she had said, looking around the spartan room but seeing the entire project. 'I always knew,' she had corrected, 'that you'd live out your dreams one day.'

He had found it hard to look at her. He had

wanted to cry and yet so desperately not to. Shrugging his shoulders, he had tried to find the lighter side, 'At least it happened before we were married.'

It had then been Wendy's turn to hold back tears. Her head down shielding her eyes, her hand tenderly brushing his shoulder as she walked past him, she had turned back to face him only when she was halfway out the door.

'For the record,' she had said, her voice faintly cracking, 'I never took "for better or worse" as something that would only start on our wedding day . . .'

She had looked like she wanted to say more, but then her voice had failed her. He had felt like there was something he should say, but he had said nothing. They had stared at each other, as if having one last look, for what seemed like hours before she had turned and walked away.

'Can't you just take a hint?' said Arb, snapping Matt back to the present. 'You've played the game. You've had your moment in the spotlight. Your girl's here to pick you up—your own girl!—so how about you accept that you got a pretty good deal out of this, and go home.'

Matt was angry now. Thoughts of last night's awkward reunion made him seethe with disgust. He scoffed at Arb's 'pretty good deal': 'It's always a deal with you, isn't it? Always the arbitrageur. I can't tell you how much I hate people like you.'

'I suspect you're going to.'

'You're leeches. You're parasites who suck

money like blood from something someone else has built. You don't make anything yourself. You don't *do* anything except prey on other people's misfortune or lack of knowledge.'

Arb lifted his eyes to the ceiling as if he'd heard all this before. 'Don't pretend what I do is any different to building cars or selling soap. All I do is spot gaps in the market and fill them. That's all I do.'

'Bullshit it is. How can you compare building something with taking shares in an idea that you added nothing except money to.'

'You just don't get it, do you, schmuck? We make the world go round, whether you like it or not. We make it efficient. We make it easy. When you buy a pack of cigarettes, it doesn't just arrive because someone rolled up some leaves in some paper. It arrives because we fund it, because we make it happen, from the plantations to the factory, from the paper to the label with the surgeon general's warning. There wouldn't be any businesses without us. People wouldn't get paid without us. People wouldn't eat.'

'Gee, surprise, surprise! I'm so impressed. Maybe that's why there's no place for you in the New World. Oh dear, there's no money.'

'Not on the inside maybe, but this New World needs us to do a damn good job internationally if we're going to survive.'

'Oh, I don't deny we need you now. But I also know when we become self-sufficient, I will personally write you a letter wishing you good luck finding a real job that contributes to society.'

'You're still living in your dream world, Turner. You really believe that what I do would have no value in a moneyless economy.'

'Controlling the world and contributing to it are very different things.'

They were edging closer and closer again. Arb's contempt was palpable, as was Matt's disdain and jealousy.

'You know it's easy to talk the talk,' said Arb provocatively. 'But it's not me who sits on the sidelines watching the game instead of playing it, is it? It's not me who prefers escapism to the real thing. I make the world go round. You do nothing but watch and create fancy sandcastles.'

'You're so deluded. You make the world go round? The egotism! You think people would notice if Isaac "the Iceman" Blackwell died? There'd be another ten arbitrageurs lining up within ten minutes to take your place and nobody—but nobody!—would notice. When a great artist or musician or novelist dies, the queue goes out the cathedral and round the block. How long do you think the procession will be when money dies?'

'You stupid fuck! Money has always made the world go round. Do you think da Vinci would have done squat without a patron? Or Mozart, or Shakespeare? Don't get all high and mighty with me. It's been this way since civilisation began. You can bet your life that Plato, Socrates and Ari-fuckin'-stotle didn't get by on their high-minded wit. They needed financial support to buy food to eat and a place to sleep, and they needed whoever it was that was financing the aqueducts, the fishermen, the builders, to have food to buy a water to drink and houses to live in. You know, I give you credit: for someone who's supposed to be so common, you don't disappoint.'

By the time he was done, Arb was making each point by pressing his finger into Matt's chest. But Matt was not going to back down either. He smacked Arb's hand away and jabbed his chest with his own points.

'Don't you see, Blackwell? You're infrastructure! You're no great leader! For all your playboy games and riches, the only inspiring thing about you is your wallet.'

Arb backed off a step, but only to make room to brush Matt's arm away.

'Don't give me that money crap—I've heard it all before. You people just don't get it, so pay attention. I made this possible!'

'Bullshit you made this poss—'

'You'd still be ordering pizza over the computer in your garage if it wasn't for me!'

'And you'd be delivering it to me if you hadn't been born rich!'

The argument lulled for a moment, as if they'd exhausted not just their insults but themselves. They stared at each other as their minds recharged to deliver another volley.

But there was nothing more to say. They both knew how they felt about each other. And they both knew how this was going to end.

'This isn't about me,' said Arb finally.

Matt stood with his arms by his side. 'No, it isn't,' he agreed.

'Well, what should we do about it?' said Arb, already walking past Matt to the rack by the closed door.

Matt continued to face forward as he spoke to Arb, who was now behind him, 'I don't know.'

'I think you do.'

Matt wheeled around to see Arb, his coat now on the rack, his hands now undoing that fucking windsor knot.

'You're kidding,' said Matt. 'That won't solve anything.'

Arb shrugged. 'Maybe. Maybe not.'

So this was it. This was how it would be resolved. After all the posturing, all the talk, all the love, they would end it like this. Like animals. Like children. Proving one's rights by beating the enemy into submission.

Fine.

How can you beat someone who won't stop fighting?
You knock them out. You shoot them dead.

hammer blow

Anna burst out the doors of Building One and immediately broke into a run towards the Found-ation Building. The fifty-metre wide Foundation Spoke was still serving as both promenade and street until the Grid removed the need for wheel-based vehicles. Dodging and weaving her way between golf buggies carrying people and tip-tray trucks carrying building materials, she was now hastily drawing nearer the Foundation Building.

People—builders, admin, scientists, parents and children—crisscrossed before her in crowded, anonymous patterns. She didn't know where to look. Her head bounced from left to right. She craned her neck and stood on her tiptoes. She tried to be systematic in scanning the area in front of her, but found herself too panicked, too unnerved.

Breathless, flustered and frightened, she finally arrived at the steps of the Foundation Building.

And there he was, patiently waiting for her.

Paul Jefferson Ford.

Matt ripped his jacket off and threw it to a corner as Arb moved in an arc around him back to the centre of the room.

They began to circle, sizing each other up. Arb's stance, like everything else he did, looked trained, his left raised, his right cocked. Matt just crouched, balling up his body with his fists, as if he might explode.

The posturing, it seemed, was not over. Arb feinted one way, then dipped his shoulder the other; Matt made to kick, made to punch, but did neither. They both fell back into their circular dance. It was almost as if each one expected the other to give in before they started. Again, Arb faked an attack, but closer this time. Matt, thinking it real . . .

Threw himself forward!

His fists flew without control. Arms swinging like wild windmills. His head burrowing forward, driving Arb backwards. Hitting a shoulder, a forearm, a jaw?—he couldn't tell, his eyes were closed as he swung furiously. He felt a blow to the side of his head, another to the ribs, his own arms still swinging. Then Arb's arm wrapped around his neck. Eyes open now, bent over in Arb's headlock, Matt drove him into the wall. He felt the air oomph out of Arb's lungs, then Arb's knee rise into his own chest. The world tilted as they both fell to the floor, Arb's bodyweight landing fully on Matt's ribs.

Matt's head, held like a football, was now trapped and exposed, and Arb started pounding at his defenceless face. Matt's arms and legs reached and kicked, his body bucking crazily to escape. Arb shifted his weight, trying to secure his position. Matt tried to roll, and suddenly Arb fell backwards, his head against the floor, his body bent, feet hanging in the air, and Matt's free hand hammering his face and chest.

Now Arb had no leverage and his body reared and shuddered in a desperate attempt to break away. Matt was able to unload a dozen blows before Arb was finally able to roll clear, pushing them apart.

'I'm sorry,' Ford said. 'There was nothing I could do.'

'I know,' she said.

'How do you know?' he quipped. 'I've done nothing but sabotage and subvert you since the beginning.'

'That may be so,' she said, 'but I knew you were convinced when you danced with me on my birthday. You just distracted me with that barb about my mother.'

He bowed his head and replied softly, sadly, 'How can you not hate me?'

She lifted his chin and looked him in the eye— that basic act still held truth and seriousness for her, even if he could hardly see her. 'In a way, you remind me of my father—clever, handsome, inspiring, insecure. You just want a better world and you're doing whatever you can to make it so.'

'Your father would be very proud of his daughter.'

She smiled sombrely—it meant a lot to her.

'Your mother is too, I understand.'

'I should thank you for that actually. In the end, you made me realise that my grievance—with her and with you—is about the future, not the past.'

'I'm so sorry,' he repeated.

And though his doomed expression told her that her worst nightmares were about to come true, she could not help but marvel at the man before her.

'Thank you for coming,' she said, her hand on his shoulder.

Matt's body crashed into Arb's, but Arb spun them as they careered into the wall. There was no more posturing—only fighting to win.

His cheek was swelling, his nose was throbbing and his back was bursting with pain, but there was no way Matt was going to give in. He reached back, grabbing Arb by the hair, then pivoted, slamming his head into the wall.

What was that?

As Arb's head had thumped the wall, there had been another sound, lower, far away . . . Arb lashed out with his right hand, catching Matt on the ear. Tightening his grip on Arb's hair, Matt again rammed Arb's head into the wall.

Arb grunted and his whole body rebounded off the wall. Using the momentum, he threw his shoulder into Matt, raising his elbow into Matt's chin as he fell away. Matt staggered backwards.

There it was again, Matt thought. *A rumbling sound that shook the floor.*

But Arb didn't seem to notice, grabbing Matt by the collar and planting another roundhouse right on his chin. Matt staggered back, off balance, fighting on instincts long forgotten, landing two punches of his own as Arb moved in again. The ocean maybe? Only it wasn't the ocean, the feeling was different. A jab to Matt's cheek, then another, and another. Matt backed away, straining to return the punches. He held his hands up trying to protect his face, and then he felt Arb's fist plunging deep into his stomach.

At first, Arb seemed to be backing away, then Matt felt the hard floor break his fall. Then Arb was suddenly rushing closer, diving on top of him to finish him off.

'You give?' Arb growled as he bombed away. 'Give!' It wasn't a question. 'I don't want—' left 'to see you—' right 'anywhere—' left-right 'near here—' right-left 'or Anna any more.' A pause. 'Had enough?'

He finished by saying, 'But you'd better hurry. You don't have much time.'

He turned to walk away. From nowhere, Fabian Smiles was at his side to guide him.

'Paul,' called Anna after him. He paused tilting his head back to her. 'You are a great man, Paul. We couldn't have come this far without you.'

He turned, waving his arm in a wide arc at everything. 'You seemed to have done quite well on your own.'

'I wasn't talking about Ninety East Ridge.'

He took two steps towards her. 'Don't you see, Anna? *I* was wrong. For all these years I have been instrumental in creating and shaping a world that has accelerated the human race, and crippled it at the same time. And all this time, I was sure I was doing the right thing . . .'

'Well, you did the right thing today.'

'Too little, too late, I'm afraid,' he said gravely, irritatedly wiping what could have been a tear leaking from his near-useless eyes as another rumble, the most obvious so far, shook the Top Deck. 'Hurry, Anna. It's begun.'

Matt tried to speak clearly when he responded: 'I . . . don't . . . think so!'

Summoning all the strength he had left, every last ounce of energy, of emotion, of pain, of love for Anna, true love for Anna, he convinced himself he would never yield. From flat on his back he wrenched his right arm free and struck Arb in the cheek. Arb tried to grab the arm, but Matt landed another two strikes first. Even when Arb got hold of his wrist, Matt kept pumping and, although not as effectively, hit Arb repeatedly.

Unable to stop the blows, Arb resorted to throwing his own, releasing his hold and punching Matt in the chest and the kidneys. But Matt's body knew no more pain. If Arb was to win this fight, he would have to beat the resolve and determination that Matt wore in his face, in his eyes, in his gritted teeth.

Matt was now sitting up, now kneeling, now standing, raining blows at will. Arb began to stagger back, his counterpunches now weakening, his face, his eyes, his open mouth, all showing his increasing desperation. He was going to fall, Matt could feel it, he was going to fall. Matt wound up for the finishing blow when suddenly, with what seemed like all the strength his opponent had left, Arb threw his arms around Matt's head, then launched their bodies forward, sending them crashing headlong into the full-length window. They hit the window together, the heavy glass shaking with their weight.

But the glass did not stop shaking. The rumbling Matt had heard before re-entered his consciousness. He had no idea how long it had been going, so absorbed had he been in the battle. But now, their faces pressed against the glass by the other's desperate hands, they could see it was more than the glass that was shaking.

The Foundation Building was collapsing.

Not just the Foundation Building. Pieces were falling from other buildings, finished or in progress. Tiles and bricks rained down from the would-be Crystal Tower. People ran in terror through the streets.

'My God,' said Arb, his face looking down on the quaking city.

'Tecton,' whispered Matt.

Grabbing Matt by the collar, Arb wrenched him to his feet.

'You find Anna,' he said, looking Matt in the eye. 'You get her out of here. I'll get her mother and sister.'

And for the first time—I could see it in his eyes—I could see that he truly loved her too.

Fists, fire, floods and all other physical disasters
Pale next to what we ourselves are capable of.

tecton of the underworld

Images of panic and destruction . . . racing through the crumbling city . . . telling myself everything would be okay . . . provided the pipewalls held . . . the street shook, buildings and half-finished motor tubes rocked, and the walls rumbled ominously . . .

I know what I should have expected to find, but for some reason, probably to do with egotism and machismo, I was surprised at the state in which I found her.

'Leave it!' she was yelling. 'Leave it all! You won't be able to replace your life! Now move!'

I stopped where I was, some ten metres away, as much out of uncertainty about what to say as to stay out of the way of the procession of people she was herding towards the escape vessels.

'Matt!' she yelled, spotting me across the stream of people between us. 'What are you doing here? You've got an emergency vessel waiting for you at Lock Seven.' She wasn't even looking at me now, her head jerking back and forth, shouting out orders, directing traffic, marshalling stragglers, yet

still able to order me to: 'Get the hell out of here!'
'I . . . no . . . I . . .'

So much for my hero's rescue. It was obvious that the last thing she needed was my help.

'Well if you're not going to leave, don't just stand there! Help me!' And for a second, a fraction of a second, she turned her eyes to me and a smile flickered across her general's face, a smile that said thank you for coming, that she was glad I was here, that she was glad we were here together. 'Hey, where the hell do you think you're going, Missy?' she screamed at a thirteen year old straying from the bustling exodus.

Even as I started directing human traffic, fetching wandering children like lost sheep, helping the small or frail clamber over fallen rubble, I thought of Arb.

I'd always known he loved her. At least, I should have known . . . time and again he defended her and supported her, denying the exclusive club he came from, rejecting the oil industry, rejecting politics, even forsaking money. All these things went against everything he had ever believed: about success, about progress—every concession he made for her diminished his own life's accomplishments. But time and again he compromised his principles for her, changed them, not as a martyring patron as I had made myself believe, but as a devoted follower, a man in love. He had made this possible, even if he had never understood. Arb, just like me, was captured by those eyes and absolutely convinced that everything in the world was

485

secondary to Anna and her dream, even if he didn't understand, even if he never would.

To this day, I don't know if he realised just how great Ninety East Ridge was. Both before and after it was destroyed.

A procession of people was now being shepherded to safety, a snaking path dodging and weaving between falling bricks, tiles and scattered debris. Rubble showered down on them, bouncing off overhangs or falling straight between the Foundation Spokes into the one-kilometre drop below. Every crash of stone or glass was echoed by panicked screams and tearful cries. Mothers shielded their children. Fathers shielded mothers. Hands were held tight. Shoulders were hunched as they hurried through the shaking city.

Driving them all, her presence everywhere, one minute at the head of the procession giving directions, the next halfway back roaring at a fallen man or woman to 'Get up! Get up! None of us are leaving without you!' Desperate evacuees clung to her as she passed, trying to absorb some of her strength. So determined was her stare that young children held their nerve, too afraid to show fear before her.

I covered the rear, ensuring no one was left behind. I could see her sweep in and out of view far in front of me, exhorting, yelling, commanding every weary foot to stride on, every hand to help the person beside them, every mind not to panic, not to be afraid and never ever to give up.

'You heard her,' I said to a woman down on one

knee, convinced that she couldn't go on. 'We're not leaving without you!' She had no choice but to get up, to go on, and she tried in vain to lift herself before four people descended on her and rose again with her in their arms. When an old man fell in front of her, she squirmed out of her human sedan to resume walking on her own two feet, even struggling to help the old man rise and take her place.

As Anna drove them forward, like a dog driving cattle, the herd grew, sucking stragglers into their exodus. The awesome Great Glass Wall rose before us, and spread across it, the endless row of holes, each marking an escape to safety. Anna dashed from door to door ensuring that each of the pods was filled—'Twenty to a pod!' she yelled—the lock properly secured and the pod then released.

I did the same, urging people to hurry. I could feel the third pipewall shaking. The Wall and the floor—the entire Top Deck—felt like they might give at any moment. It didn't matter which went first. We all had to be in those pods before it happened.

In a surprising moment of clarity, I suddenly reflected that Anna looked like Noah driving all the animals, two by two, into lifeboats. Amid the pandemonium, the thought then struck me: how odd it was to consider the possibility of evacuating Noah's sinking ark.

Though the odds of an earthquake were a million to one, I suddenly became aware of our helplessness, suddenly aware of our lack of power over the ocean, over time and luck, over God or Tecton. Mankind can claim to have conquered the oceans, the mountains, the sky, even the moon. But our boats and pipewalls, ropes, planes and spaceships are really just loopholes—loopholes we can be very proud of, but merely loopholes nonetheless, allowing us to survive in a universe so large and complex that it still defies not only our control, but our comprehension.

'Come on!' I yelled to her as the last of the thousands disappeared through the locks in the wall.

'I'm going back,' she shouted, beginning to run back down the spoke. 'To see if there is anyone else.'

'No,' I cried uselessly. But she was already disappearing back into the city.

The floor, the Wall, the buildings between which Anna had disappeared were quaking like cardboard. The pod to safety was two metres away.

I had no choice.

I ran after her.

Far ahead of me I saw her, ducking in and out of alleys and side streets—anywhere that a scared little child or scared little adult might hide—her hand cupped around her mouth like a mini-megaphone.

'Anna!' I screamed.

She didn't hear me—or didn't show it—continuing to race through the ruins of the city, dodging debris like a running back.

I chased after her, not half as confident about hurdling rubble.

Somehow I caught up with her.

'Get back to the pods, you idiot!' she screamed at me.

'Not without you,' I replied, trying to sound equally forceful.

She just arched her eyebrows at me with a 'no time for arguing' look, and continued to dart from building to building, alley to alley.

I grabbed her by the arm. She struggled free and ran on towards the centre of the city, as much to get away from me as to look for lost souls.

We hurtled onwards, deserted half-buildings and streets rushing past us—horizontally and vertically—half an eye looking for survivors, half an eye on each other.

'We have to get out of here!' I shouted.

'Then get out of here!' she growled, not letting me close.

Finally, I tackled her. Lying on top of her, holding her wrists, I pinned her to the ground.

'Get off me!' she shrieked, bucking and kicking. 'Let me go!'

'Anna! We have to leave! You can't save any more!'

'Yes, I can! I can!'

'No, you can't!'

'I have to!' she screamed. 'I have to try! I can't stop—'

She stopped.

I heard it too.

Crying. A child crying. I let her go.

'Over there,' I said.

'No, over here!' She was already running. I followed close behind.

A wall, semi-shattered, leaned against the cracked remains of a building. Without fear or hesitation, Anna ran under the wall. A small boy sat huddled in the shadows, crying. Beside him, legs—his father's maybe—the rest of the body under the heavy debris.

She grabbed the boy by the shoulders, almost throwing him back at me, before she began to wrench brick after brick off the fallen man.

I held the boy close to me. He was crying hysterically, no idea where he was or what to do. I patted his head as I assured him that the man—his father?—was 'going to be okay'. I felt so helpless.

'He's dead,' she said flatly, easing herself out from behind the leaning wall. 'Take the boy back to the pod and get yourselves to safety.'

'Not without you!' I said back.

At that moment, the Foundation Spoke we stood on groaned like a great beast about to die. We could feel it cracking beneath our feet.

'Anna, please!'

She grabbed me by the hair, pulled me close and kissed me. I knew what she was going to say.

'No.'

I ran through the rubble, half carrying, half bouncing the boy on his feet as we flew back towards the Great Glass Wall.

The road in front of us bowed and buckled like

a rope bridge. The fifty metres of steel and cement cracked and flexed at random angles, shooting up instant hurdles or randomly making us change our path so as not to fall twenty metres—or a thousand.

The ground beneath our feet rumbled and quaked—Tecton indeed had awoken—roaring his anger, bellowing his decision to destroy our world.

The Wall drew near up ahead and I dragged the boy towards one of the remaining escape hatches. I had just thrown him inside when behind me I heard a sound so frightening that I froze where I stood.

The deafening crack didn't stop. It was like a long explosion. The Wall, somewhere, had broken, was collapsing, and another sound, even louder than the first, was rising behind it.

The thunderous roar of the ocean reclaiming its space should have made me dive into the pod straight away.

But I couldn't. Not without her.

I closed the boy inside the pod and released it using the controls on my side. The pod and the boy shot to safety.

I took two steps back towards the city, then stopped dead. There was nowhere to go. The Foundation Spoke had shifted, and would surely fall at any moment. A section some fifty metres away had buckled, carving a ten-metre cliff I could not possibly climb. On either side, entire buildings were now tumbling. Between them, I could see the ocean tearing apart the far wall.

'Please Anna,' I breathed, petrified. Helpless. 'Come back to me.'

And then there she was.

First her hands, then her face appeared at the top of the cement-steel cliff. Instantly I was running towards her, hurtling over the uneven ground, mindless of the toppling buildings and the roaring flood flowing in above and rising up from below.

She swung her body around and swiftly lowered herself over the cliff. I hurdled a girder and ducked a falling mote, charging towards her.

She hung from the cliff by her fingertips, summoning up the courage to make the three-storey plunge.

'Wait!' I yelled, half tripping. 'Wait!'

She let go.

I threw myself under her, breaking her fall—and probably my back, but I didn't feel a thing.

Within seconds, we were both up and careering through the ever-increasing carnage around us.

'There!' I yelled, steering us towards the last pod-hatch.

I looked behind me as if Tecton himself were chasing us. I could now see the water rising. We'd only just make it.

Anna dived into the pod, I threw myself in behind her.

'Hit the switch!' she yelled, pointing to the internal controls beside me.

The hydraulic door sucked closed, Tecton's roar was muted, and the titanic sounds of Ninety East Ridge's destruction were suddenly gone.

We sat there in silence as the pod pushed away from the wall, automatically making its way to the surface. Like twins in the womb, the ocean all around us, a vacuum protecting us from the world outside—we were suddenly alone. For a few moments there was no history, no Ninety East Ridge, no husbands or fiancées; all that existed was the world inside that pod. For a few moments, we contemplated each other with the complete artlessness of unborn babies. And in those few moments, as the pod drifted up towards the light, towards rebirth, a life of love together flashed before our eyes.

Life is choices.
Your own and those about you.

choices

After Tecton, after the chaos, after the raging pandemonium of noise and destruction, it was so calm . . .

Randomly spaced pods bobbed on the now-friendly sea, the now-flat, holeless, friendly sea. They drifted in synchronised formation towards Platform Seven and the warships in the distance.

I watched Anna take in the destruction of her New World, her vision, the last two years—no, five? fifteen? a lifetime maybe?—I didn't know what to say.

'I'm sure Isaac saved Natasha and your mother,' I said finally.

Life is choices.

Even though Ninety East Ridge was completely swallowed by the Indian Ocean, it would be wrong to say that Tecton completely destroyed Anna's dream. Anna's dream was about more than glass walls, crystal towers and tubular transport grids. It was about more than holes in the ocean and New Worlds.

It was about change. It was about her father.

In life, her father created for his daughter a beautiful world that was turned by rubber band engines, people walking west and planets chasing their tails. So full of possibilities and opportunities and love, surely love.

In death, her father—so cherished, so missed—destroyed that beautiful world he'd worked so hard to create for her. His death, which could not be changed, created in Anna an unchangeable belief that this world—so compromised, so flawed—could in fact not change in its current form, and must therefore be started again.

The birth of Ninety East Ridge brought back her father's beautiful world, not even for a thousand days, but long enough. What remained when it was destroyed was the awareness—in me, Arb, her mother, everyone who knew her, even Paul Jefferson Ford—of what was possible. What is possible. That anything is possible with enough nights spent dreaming and enough days spent doing.

The death of Ninety East Ridge reminded Anna of the flaw in her father's beautiful world. The future cannot be created in a vacuum. It is inextricably connected to history, and always at the mercy of the present. Death, the world, the ocean, the rest of nature or human nature can reach up at any time and pull it back into the sea.

'They were with Sanjay,' she said, staring at our entwined hands. 'Having blood tests,' she added, 'to see what their chances in the future are.'

I nodded. There was nothing else to say.

We stared at the ocean, gently undulating into the distance as if nothing had happened since one woman with a bucket began bailing a hole in it almost two years ago. Construction platforms were scattered across the horizon as if in virgin waters, as if about to begin. A fleet of ships, somewhat different to the supply ships, were strategically deployed around those waters.

Random words of Laikali Rulé wandered into my thoughts: 'Inspiration is a fortune . . . I know you have something to offer this place . . . and that Ninety East Ridge has something to offer you . . . but there's one thing you can never get around . . .

'You have to choose.'

Life is choices.

US warships were already picking up the bobbing safety pods. We floated slowly but surely across the ocean towards them.

Maybe we weren't ready for Ninety East Ridge? Maybe it was a bad idea? Or was a great dream destroyed by small-minded people—or perhaps even a higher power—who felt it more important to protect a familiar Old World than to live with the uncertainty of a brave new one?

Was it Tecton? Was it an earthquake? Was it a structural weakness? Were there spies amongst the faithful? Did the warships fire torpedoes into the Ridge to simulate a seismic quake as some maintain? Ford told Anna just before it started that saboteurs—undercover commandos—had been

496

planting bombs for weeks, and that Ridder—not he—had given unchangeable detonation orders.

Believe what you want, I can't change what happened, whatever it was. And when all's said and done, I can't change what you believe. I don't think it matters. The New World is gone but the one that remains is not the old one that existed before.

A newer world, one that now lives with only the memory of Ninety East Ridge, exists in its place. Ninety East Ridge may have been destroyed that day, but nothing, not even Tecton, could touch her truly great achievements. She once spoke about the pipewalls and mote-tubes and the great Crystal Tower as being merely the paper on which we would write the Ridge's story. I wonder if she realises how many of us now look back on our own stories written on six hundred and sixty-six of a thousand blank pages, and are grateful just for a moment of knowing her and her dreams.

I hope she does. I hope she also knows that while the Ridge could not survive in isolation, the world cannot now continue without the influence of Ninety East Ridge. Or Anna Spires.

Life is choices.

Her eyes. They looked at me. And I could tell she was thinking my thoughts, pondering the same possibilities. But plus one.

The media, as always, focused on scandal first and impact last. Reporters raced each other in a game of speculative scapegoating, finger-pointing and after-the-event, behind-the-back blame attribution.

'*So ends perhaps the century's most foolish folly. The millennium's, maybe?*' Glory would say, pausing for poignancy. '*When will we learn that even the greatest of man's achievements can be destroyed with but a flick of God's hand, a rumble of his displeasure.*'

'Thank God,' she would say to her cameraman when he gave her the thumbs-up. 'I'm sick of all the sun and salt water—it's killing my complexion.'

She is now one of the world's foremost journalists.

Of course, I'm disappointed. But glory soon fades. I have to believe that greatness lingers.

Life is choices.

Together, our eyes turned to the mini-sub hatch that lay etched in the floor. Together, we now considered all the options. But alone, I knew, she had to choose.

If you look carefully, you can see that not all of Anna's new beautiful world was destroyed that day. Even as the bricks and mortar were swallowed by the sea, there was Paul Jefferson Ford, the staunch resolute symbol of the Old World warning her, changing because of her, believing at least in saving those who had dared to create such a different world from his. And those he saved—some ten thousand survivors—were scattered to the four winds like pollen, spreading through the world the possibility of an ideal, the very real possibility of a beautiful world.

I understand Paul Ford now spends his days on a beach in Palwali, playing games—of chess instead of politics—with that Polynesian country's most renowned retired statesperson, Laikali Rulé.

Not long after the Ridge was destroyed, Aldrich Ridder was arrested in Moscow for suspected espionage. Despite ranting protestations of drugged kidnappings and conspiracy set-ups, he was convicted with surprisingly little American protest and is presently serving a twenty-five year sentence in a Siberian prison.

Life is choices.

US warships were already picking up the bobbing safety pods. We floated towards them.

Her eyes. They looked at me. And I could tell she was thinking my thoughts, pondering the same possibilities. But plus one.

Together, our eyes turned to the mini-sub hatch that lay etched in the floor.

I turned my back.

Life is choices.

But not all life's choices can be our own.

For the rest of her life . . .

the stars of history

After siren sounds and holes in the ocean, after
swearing at Presidents and dancing with devils,
after Old Worlds, New Worlds and worlds torn
asunder, after notes and letters and mother-
daughter reconciliations, after standing side by side
against the world, after fist-fight resolutions, after
Tecton, after choices, it was so calm . . .

I stood with my back to the mini-sub hatch.

And the siren sound was lost.

*I stand now near the window, red wine in my hand. A
lifetime recalled in a moment.*

*I still believe in long life and beautiful dreams. I still
believe that some people get to live those dreams . . . I
find it harder to believe that I might again be one of those
people.*

*'Ha!' I shout, trying to throw myself out of my
misery. I think about throwing the wine glass out the
window, but it strikes me as a weak, shallow act.*

Anna chose Arb.

Oh, she never said it out loud, there was just the

hydraulic hiss of the hatch behind me.

Strangely, I think, that day on the ocean, that day when Tecton destroyed all our dreams, that day she left me, I understood. Only later was I devastated. Only later did I try to resent him, and his money, his looks, his fame, his everything. It took me many years to re-realise what I'd known that day: that despite everything that he had given away for her, despite his power and despite his sacrifice, he too had been powerless to affect her choice. She had made that choice on her own.

At the time, I understood. Only later, still alone, did I try to convince myself that she might have gone back just to make sure he was okay, but that when she saw him, she could not bring herself to leave. I tried to convince myself that she went back because of some outdated, misplaced sense of integrity that constrained her from breaking her lifelong vows. I've tried to convince myself, I've tried, I've tried . . . but I can't. When she disappeared into the sea, the same sea that engulfed her New World, swallowed it whole, she made it clear that he was the most important thing in the world to her.

You see, you can love two people. But you can't love two people the same. You always love someone more.

Rejection is the hardest thing in the world. It's always personal.

The stars of history watch over us, following our tales of love and loss, of passion and glory. They shine and sparkle in elation and distress, they dim and fade in bitterness and disappointment. But they cannot interfere—no matter how much they want to, they can never interfere.

I stand staring back at those stars, my wife and kids playing happily in the next room. I remind myself that I am a lucky man—I am, I was, and I always will be if I work hard enough.

She lives now, with Arb, at the bottom of the sea. Their Tree House has apparently expanded along the ridge, a series of tunnels connecting scattered pockets of life. A handful of scientists remain—and only a handful of people know about it.

No doubt, the world's great governments are also aware of their ongoing existence. They won't attack though, not again. You see, Ninety East Ridge is not a threat any more. The public doesn't know. The legal loopholes surrounding international waters no longer exist. If anything, Anna and her world are allowed to continue as some sort of liable-less experiment. Can civilisation prosper under the sea? they ask. What great discoveries can they make?

I want to go and join them. Join her. But I can't. That was, and remains, not for me to decide.

The sounds of the street pass beneath my window. But all I can think of is her. The red wine tastes like her. The firelight's corona makes me imagine crystal towers. I look at the stars and I can feel her presence. I close my eyes and there she is—her eyes, her small ears, her smile, asymmetric and pure, and her touch reaching out to me . . . I open my eyes and she's gone.

'Ha,' I cry again. This time I do throw my glass—it flies across the room, a red wine catherine wheel, smashing into the hearth. It smashes loudly, and then the sound is lost. The bright red flames lick the dark red globules from the walls of the fireplace.

I'm staring up at the stars again when Wendy rushes into the room. I'm okay. She's seen it before. Somehow, she understands. She says nothing and simply puts her arms around me. That's what love is. The kids stand silently at the door. They must wonder sometimes what's wrong with their father, but they soon come and put their arms around me too.

Yes, Wendy stands beside me once again. She always has. Accepting me for who I am, and for who I may have wanted to be. Don't think for a minute that she's a compromise! And don't believe that just because I think about Anna every day, that I don't love her. Life's not like that. Every instant that passes will never be repeated—our lives are the memories we make of those instants. Anna taught me not to waste a moment; Wendy taught me that not a moment is wasted, past, present or future.

They hold me as I stare at the stars and I know that today the world is as it should be. It's up to me to tip, turn it, change it, so that it can be what it should be tomorrow.

I make myself believe that Anna, too, stands at the window, staring at the stars shimmering through the now calm, clear waters. She stands there wondering if I'm wondering about her. Arb and their own kids make an effort to talk normally in the next room. She smiles at me, then turns and walks back to her family.

The stars of history watch over us but they cannot interfere.

For the rest of her life, I am a star.

The End

acknowledgements

To Mum and Dad, who always allowed me to be/think/do whatever I wanted to be/think/do.

To my brother, Matt, whose ruthless critical eye was invaluable and whose encouragement and support was unconditional.

To David Gill, (for his long friendship, but also) for his intelligent, thoughtful and thorough editing of multiple drafts (simultaneously!).

To Melinda and James Goodsell, Emma Chellew, Allison Elliott, Andrew McGarry, Sue Buchanan and, of course, Helen and Mick, for reviewing drafts and telling me what they really thought.

To Paul Roach (and his Uncle Steve), for his ideas regarding leasing the naming rights for the national flag.

To Nikki Christer, Chris Mattey and Chrissa Favaloro at Pan Macmillan, for seeing me through this whole business.

Most of all, special thanks to my wife, Rebecca, who inspires me, supports me and loves me (she should know better).